SOME BATTLES BLEED so much, and for so long, that the earth never truly forgets their dead. Some battles are born of oppression, some of greed, and some simply because it was written in the stars. Some battles begin with a name, a single breath of air, cutting through the night like the sound of dark wings rising.

Annals of Sigon Book IV

One

Hamquist and Crakes

A S THEY EMERGED from the gloom, Crakes thought what a dark, dreadful place this was—and how fitting for their purpose, from the isolated road, to the murky river, to the lines of tall, sickly trees that cast tenebrous shadows in the fading light.

"Athene," Hamquist said from behind him.

"What about her?" Crakes replied.

"That's not her real name. The women called her something different."

The *women*. The word filled him with ice. Crakes didn't often experience sensations; he didn't like this one. "It stinks here," he said.

"It's just the Mist," Hamquist replied. "It always makes that smell."

Crakes remained uneasy. "The sooner we can get this over with and go home, the better," he said.

"Yes, of course. Athene, then home."

Crakes shifted uncomfortably. When Hamquist said "home" his voice lacked conviction. What if this was only the beginning, rather than the end? Crakes didn't understand this world, or its rules, or his place in it. At home, to think of somewhere was to be there. Here, if it wasn't for the Mist, they would be stranded.

Hamquist pointed to the riverbank. "That's where we'll wait for her."

As they walked, Crakes noticed Hamquist's usually fluid movements were laboured, as though dragging a weight far greater than the sword that hung from his waist.

"What did she do, anyway?" Crakes asked.

"We weren't told."

"I don't like it."

"That's not for you to say."

"I suppose it makes no difference." Crakes jabbed at the air with the one fist he had left.

"She won't go without a fight," Hamquist said, an edge to his voice.

Did he mean that if the "women" feared her, so should they? Surely not. Whatever else, this Athene was just a mortal.

"I think I can handle her." He jabbed again, this time making a smacking sound as he landed the imaginary punch.

"She is dangerous, and is more than she seems."

"Then why send us? What have we to do with it? Why not summon filthy minions from the deep, or whatever they usually do?"

Hamquist pulled back his cloak revealing his huge two-handed sword, the steel glinting naked and blue against his woollen breeches. "Have we ever needed more than this?" Hamquist replied. "Ever?"

That's not what Crakes had meant, but he played along. "What a big sword you have."

Hamquist grinned, then suddenly swung around and grabbed Crakes's throat.

"W-what are you do-ing," Crakes choked.

"Tonight you reek of carelessness, throwing punches around like some carnival puppet. Fussing about *the stink* as though we're on a . . . a *sniffing* expedition." He added in falsetto, "*It's so smelly here! Oh, where did I put my pomander?"*

"I-I . . ." Crakes couldn't breathe.

Hamquist let go, and Crakes doubled over choking. "Remember the last time you got careless?"

He tried to nod; speaking was impossible. Humiliated, Crakes studied the ground, but failing to fix on anything, inspected a small clump of mud on the tip of his boot. He picked up a stick and poked at it.

"You lost your hand and that's why you wave that ugly stump around." Hamquist pointed at a nearby tree stump. "Oh! Look at that!" he said with sudden alacrity. "Twins!" He laughed manically and slapped Crakes on the back. Crakes found himself laughing too. The joke wasn't funny, but it broke the tension, a distraction from their real purpose, which they both knew was rotten to the core. Holding his sides, Hamquist was about to make another crack, when suddenly his eyes narrowed and his face became serious as stone.

"Athene," he said, sweeping his nose back and forth. "She is coming."

Headlights appeared around the corner.

"That's curious," Hamquist said.

"What?"

"She knows we're here."

"Does it make a difference?"

"No."

Then it was time.

Crakes dropped his cloak, proud of his six-foot-three frame of muscle and sinew, of the scars that covered his chest. He had put some effort into his wardrobe: concentric circles of mustard-coloured leather armour ran up and down his legs in scallops, and at his crotch was a fine codpiece. Crakes adjusted a twisted buckle and then fastened a large iron thimble over his stump. He calculated the distance, speed, and velocity of the car and stepped into the road.

She slammed on the brakes and the smell of burning

rubber filled the air. He watched with disappointment as the car skidded to a halt just in front of him. He'd planned to stop the car by smashing his fist into its hot metal grill, crumpling the hood, impressing the woman. Instead he was caught like a startled deer, his codpiece glowing in the halogen.

The woman killed the engine and turned off the lights. The tiny insect motes disappeared and silence filled the night. The door opened and she stepped out of the car. She wore a neat blue coat.

"Well?" she said. The voice was calm but the hands trembled.

"We have come for you," he replied.

"I see that."

"Any last words?"

She considered. "Nice pants."

He feinted one way and swung the other, connecting cleanly with her temple. The haunting green eyes stared at him for a second, then she slumped to the asphalt, unconscious.

Easy, he thought. *Was it too easy?*

In a blink, Hamquist was beside him, blade out.

"No!" Crakes shouted. "They told us to take her alive! Remember?"

Hamquist shuddered, battling the almost overwhelming urge to separate her head from her neck.

"Please!" Crakes implored.

Hamquist dropped the sword and grabbed Crakes's shoulders to steady himself. The bones ground together and Crakes bit his tongue. Slowly Hamquist's eyes turned from crimson to black and the danger passed. Together, they stared at the woman.

"She's beautiful," Crakes said.

"For a mortal." Hamquist picked her up and slung her over his shoulder.

Crakes pushed the car off the road and into the ditch. Hamquist spoke a command to the air and the Mist descended, wrapping around their legs. The next moment, they were gone.

Two

Charlemagne

CHARLEMAGNE WOKE WITH a start, her head bouncing on the back of her seat. She had drifted off and had another nightmare about her mother. Unable to sleep at night, dreams came to her in the daytime instead. Had she called out? No. Neither of her sisters were staring at her. Furtively, she wiped a bead of sweat from her brow.

"Afternoon," Penny said glancing up from her book and smiling. Charlemagne's little sister looked tired and it wasn't just the journey. None of them slept well these days.

"Is it past twelve yet?" Charlemagne asked.

"Just."

"What have I missed?"

"Nothing," Cairo replied, "just grey sky and green fields followed by more grey sky and more fields. Sometimes there's a cow, sometimes not."

"That much?"

Cairo shrugged. "I still don't know why we had to come here. It's not fair."

Cairo hadn't wanted to come to England, she'd wanted to stay in America and spend the summer with friends, but what any of them wanted didn't seem to count for much anymore.

Charlemagne could have screamed with frustration, she was so angry with her father. She knew why he had sent them away—it was so he could fall apart in splendid isolation, without the check of his daughters, so he could grieve for their mother alone. It was selfish of him, and now it was Charlemagne, not he, who was responsible for her sisters.

"Do you know, Charlie," Penny said, glancing up from her book, "that 'being sent to Coventry' means that nobody will speak to you."

Cairo turned from the window, and looked quizzically at Charlemagne.

"I'm sure it doesn't apply to our grandparents," Charlemagne said.

Cairo sighed, and resumed her vigil of the fields. It had been a long trip: a taxi to the airport, the "red-eye" flight and then the "Tube," travelling on which had turned Charlemagne's tissue black when she blew her nose. Finally, they'd caught the train and emerged from London on a damp, grey, drizzly Saturday. It was the beginning of summer, and judging by the skirts and tank tops of some of the girls in the carriage, it was considered a hot day in England.

A voice broke over the speaker. "The next station is Coventry. The next station is Coventry. Change here for . . ."

Charlemagne had met her grandparents before, but she didn't remember them. The family had moved to America when she was four and Cairo was just a baby. That was thirteen years ago. There had been some sort of irreconcilable breach, but her parents refused to speak about it.

Charlemagne and Penny once asked their other, American grandparents, what happened—Granny Hickory was a notorious gossip after all. Grandpa would often joke, "I haven't spoken to my wife in years . . . I don't want to interrupt her." But on this subject, and even after too much sherry, Granny would say little.

"Best leave it alone, dears. Too much pain there."

Poor Granny Hickory died last summer, and Grandpa followed shortly after with a broken heart. The girls had no other family in America, but it was still a shock when their father announced they would spend the summer in England without him, especially after all that had happened. The train slowed, pulling into the station.

"Come on, Cairo," Charlemagne said, "we're going to be getting out in a minute."

Cairo turned from the window, blinking. "I can't wait."

"I wonder what they'll look like," Penny said. "I hope we'll recognise them."

"Of course we will," Charlemagne said, trying to sound cheerful. "They'll look like Dad."

As it turned out, they didn't have to recognise anybody. As they made their way through the barrier at the end of the platform, a small, slightly rounded man with a huge white beard and white curly hair called out to them waving. "Ladies! Ladies of the Americas!"

Twenty heads turned to stare at him.

"Please, no . . ." Cairo shrank into her jacket.

Despite his short stature, the man's head bobbed above the crowd and for a moment it looked as though he were somehow levitating in mid-air. Then Charlemagne realised he was standing on top of a large plant pot so he could see over everyone. He grinned a huge grin and hopped from one foot to the next.

"Our grandfather is a hobbit," Cairo said.

"Shh!"

In one hand he held an umbrella, straight above his head like some sort of tour guide. With the other he casually flicked a coin up and down, catching it on his wrist.

"Yes, that's right, over here, ladies," he called again, motioning with the umbrella. He must have accidentally pressed something because the umbrella suddenly opened, engulfing his entire body. Charlemagne heard a muffled, 'oh dear, oh dear,' as he wrestled to pull it down, but instead he lost his balance and fell off the pot with a crash. He landed on his back, the umbrella beneath him, feet flailing in the air. Behind them, people were laughing. The three sisters hurried towards him.

"Are you okay?" Charlemagne asked, helping him to his feet.

"Of course, of course, just err . . . a costume malfunction." He brushed himself down.

"But are you hurt?" Penny said, picking up his coin and handing it to him.

"Grrr . . . no. Just my pride, my dear."

As if to dispel any doubts, he laughed and then, with a flourish, tossed the coin high in the air and caught it on the back of his wrist.

"How did you know it was us when we came through?" Penny said.

"Oh, that was easy," he said. "One, I could smell that you were from across the great sea. Two, you were the only girls who looked the part, with your fair, dark, and red hair. And three—and the most important, I find—I made a lucky guess." He looked at the coin, grimaced slightly, and slipped it into his pocket.

Cairo stared at him as though he was completely mad.

"Anyway, come over here and give your grandfather a hug! Grrr!"

Stepping forward, he enveloped Penny in his outstretched arms. Although Penny was only thirteen, and not tall for her age, the two were about the same size.

Cairo leant over and whispered into Charlemagne's ear, "Did he just growl?"

"Shh!"

"He did!" Cairo continued. "He just *growled!*"

Their grandfather buried his head in Penny's hair and seemed to sniff her. "Beautiful black hair, little hands, smaller than your sisters," he said releasing her. He pulled out a worn piece of paper and unfolded it. "Let me see, let me see . . ." He glanced at some notes. "Yes, here we are . . . hair of the obsidian, likes books and . . . and a penchant for pickles, but don't even think about custard. You must be Penny!"

"Pardon?" Penny said.

"You must be Penny."

"Yes, but what's that?"

"What's what?" He thrust his hand and the paper behind his back, blinked at her and smiled, then turned his attention to Charlemagne and Cairo. "Now for . . ." He flicked his head back and forth between the two of them. "Now for, now for . . ." He trailed off and squinted towards the sky. When Penny looked up, he pulled out the paper again and quickly glanced at it.

"Yes, Charlemagne of the golden tresses, the eldest. We meet again! You haven't changed a bit you know. Grrr!"

Charlemagne felt a little awkward as he took her in his arms. She was seven or eight inches taller than him—a very self-conscious height for hugging—but he didn't seem to mind. He held her tight and she could feel his warmth pass through her. It felt good to be held.

Finally he turned his attention to Cairo. He looked at her intently for a moment, obviously trying to think what to say, and then, glancing sheepishly at Penny, read from the paper. "Cairo: red and charming as the night is long, fiery as a mandrake."

"What?" Cairo snapped.

Their grandfather said nothing further, but pushed the paper into his pocket and stepped forward to give her a hug. Cairo stepped backwards as if to say *no hugging allowed*.

He sniffed. "Yes . . . Cairo, of course." He gave her a stiff little bow instead. Then, in one swift movement, he flicked up the umbrella, closed it, and threw it to Penny, who fumbled a little but managed to catch it.

"Very good," he said, grinning. "Come on then." He picked up Penny's and Charlemagne's suitcases and headed towards the glass doors leading to the parking lot. The bags were heavy, but by the way he carried them they seemed filled with air. Cairo was left to struggle with her own. Charlemagne put out a hand to help, but Cairo shook her head. They hurried to catch up with him.

"What was that paper?" Penny asked as soon as they were level.

"Oh . . . just some notes from the Ogg, so I'd know who's who and wouldn't make a gaff."

"The Ogg?"

"Come to think of it though, she did tell me to memorise it." Turning to them every couple of steps, he rambled on. "Yes, I'm afraid your dear grandmother couldn't be here. She's preparing for the wake this evening. A very important lady, your grandmother."

"Wake?" Charlemagne felt suddenly nauseous. Surely not for their mother? She was missing, but not declared dead. Not yet.

Their grandfather stared at her quizzically. "Yes, for the poor Drakefield boy. Family friend you know. You'll have to come. She won't hear otherwise. I thought you probably wouldn't want to, it being a bit close to the bone and . . . Well, anyway, she said, 'Now don't be a silly Gaffer, they'll love it. Some wine, some singing, some local lads. It's just what those poor girls need.' And she's right you know. She *always* is. When I was your age, I loved a good wake."

"There's no way I'm going," Cairo said in an angry whisper to Charlemagne, and then louder, "I'm a little tired. I was hoping to stay in tonight."

"You'll get bored."

"I could watch TV."

"TV?"

"Yes."

"We don't have one of those."

Cairo looked incredulous. "What?"

Their grandfather didn't reply, as though he hadn't heard.

"Maybe I'll just go to bed early," Cairo said.

But their grandfather didn't seem to hear that either but walked faster across the asphalt towards a beaten-up Volvo that stood nearby. He pressed a button on his keychain but nothing happened. "Damn boot," he muttered, banging his fist on the hood. The trunk sprung open. Inside, junk filled every corner. There were pieces of pipe, a length of rope, four or five long metal rods, a couple of bricks, sacks of sand and sacks of something else Charlemagne couldn't identify.

"How are we going to fit our bags in there?" Cairo asked.

"Easy," he said, and with incredible speed began hauling everything out. He then picked up all the cases and squashed them in.

"Are you allowed to do that?" Cairo said.

"Allowed to do what?"

"Leave things dumped in the parking lot."

"Umm . . ." He paused and stared up at the sky. "Yes!" He flashed a smile, took the umbrella from Penny, tossed it on top of the cases and slammed the "boot" shut.

"Really?" Cairo said.

"Someone will pick them up. Find them useful, too."

"I doubt it."

Charlemagne tensed. This was just like Cairo. Either she was moping around, or being breathtakingly charming, or doing this third thing, the not letting go thing, like a dog with a smelly rag.

Their grandfather said nothing.

"I really doubt it," she repeated.

"How do you know?" Their grandfather folded his arms. "Someone could see this stuff and think, well, if that's not just what I need to finish my bathroom! Something to caulk the walls, lay the pipes, I can even prop up the heater with a couple of bricks. Christmas will have come early for them. Yes it will indeed."

"Er . . . okay, Granddad," said Cairo, opening the door to the back seat.

"Don't call me Granddad," he snapped.

They all got in. There was an awkward silence. Their grand-father went to put the key in the ignition, then stopped and sighed. He tapped his fingers on the dashboard and then turned around. "Everyone calls me Gaffer," he said. "Or *the* Gaffer on account of my old job . . . glass, you know. 'Granddad' is too, too . . ." He didn't finish the sentence but instead seemed to drift off. Again there was a pause. "Ah, yes, where were we?" he said suddenly. "The car." He reversed out, manoeuvring around the pile of junk. Charlemagne noticed the car had been in a space reserved for handicapped parking.

Thankfully it was a short ride, and they only drove for about twenty minutes before Gaffer turned left into a secluded entrance that was almost like a hole in the hedgerow. Sweeping poplars and elms lined the drive for about five hundred yards, opening out to a large pond circled with weeping willows. Behind the pond was a pointy, Gothic-looking mansion with high, irregular arches, ornate stone overhangs and flying buttresses. Anyone could see it was in need of repair. Wisteria covered the whole façade, but Charlemagne couldn't tell if it was helping to hold up the house, or pull it down. The paint around the windows was flaking, the roof was missing tiles, and the house seemed to sough under its own weight. The rusticated stone of the walls was weathered and cracked, and missing chunks in certain areas. Mossy, misshapen stone steps led up to the front door.

"Before you say anything," Gaffer said pulling up, "I know, *I know*."

"Know what?" Penny said.

"That this old lady's seen better days."

"The house?" Penny looked around.

"Well I don't mean Ogg, although that may well be true of her too." He chuckled. "I didn't say that, no, no I didn't."

Cairo, who had been curled up with her headphones and music, opened her eyes. She looked at the house, looked at Charlemagne, and slowly shook her head.

"A couple of years ago, it was even worse. The lead peeled off the roof in the heat of '78. Vandals got the rest. The whole place was flooded and mouldy, so I got it for a song."

"A couple of years? Thirty more like," whispered Cairo to Charlemagne.

"What's a 'song'?" asked Penny.

"I thought you'd never ask," Gaffer said, beaming, and spontaneously broke into a ditty about a golden girl who found a golden pearl, all the while tapping his feet so that the car kept shuddering forward and then violently stopping.

Penny stared at him wide-eyed. Cairo arched her eyebrows at Charlemagne, and Charlemagne tried not to giggle. When they were younger, whenever Cairo disapproved of something she would arch her eyebrows and say 'bad cheese.' Cairo always claimed it wasn't her, but her imaginary friend, Song, who came up with the derogatory term. Even though Cairo hadn't said it for years, Charlemagne knew exactly what she was thinking. This house, indeed the prospect of the next nine weeks, was *very* bad cheese indeed.

"Did you get the mould out?" Penny asked when he'd finished.

"The mould? I'm not sure. How do I smell to you?" Gaffer lifted his arm and had a sniff.

Cairo shook her head but Penny was lapping it up. This man, with his strange charm and stranger humour, was winning her over. He whispered something to Penny and they both broke out in peals of laughter.

As the car pulled up in front of the house, the front door opened and two dogs came flying out. They jumped up excitedly as the sisters got out of the car.

"What are they?" asked Penny.

"Brindle lurchers, my dear. The chocolaty one is Cowper, the lighter one is Siam."

"Do they shed?" Penny asked.

"Do they what?"

"You know, do they shed hair and skin and stuff?"

Gaffer frowned. "Change their skin? They're not one of those."

Penny looked puzzled. "No, I mean do they cause allergies?"

"Ah! Don't worry, these two dogs don't know what an allergy is. Come on. Down Cowper! Down Siam! You'll have to excuse them. They're not used to visitors, and I'm not much of a fancier, so they run a bit wild."

Cairo arched her eyebrows again and Charlemagne giggled. She couldn't help it.

"Well," Gaffer said, misinterpreting Charlemagne's mirth, "you try finding time for training wild things when you have a house and land to look after, and . . . and other things, the Ogg for a start." Gaffer looked up and then chuckled nervously. "Grrr, and here she is."

"Come here, my dears, come here! I am your grandmother!" said a woman stepping out of the house to meet them. "But *please* call me Ogg."

Ogg was as huge as Gaffer was tiny. Six foot at least and with the girth to match. She was striking, with deep blue eyes and a gigantic swirl of white hair that made the top of her head look like a softy ice cream. Wearing what seemed to be a purple velvet bath robe she hopped down the steps in two strides. Charlemagne dared not look at Cairo to see what face she was pulling.

Charlemagne was about to put out her hand and say a stiff, "Very pleased to meet you," but Penny beat her to it, throwing her arms around their grandmother and squeezing her tight. At the same time, Cowper and Siam jumped up on Penny, making one happy Penny-doggy-oggy-group-hug.

"Bad cheese," muttered Cairo.

"Ah, my children, it has been too long," Ogg said, still holding Penny but looking over her head at Charlemagne. "The unfortunate loss of your mother has brought us all together."

"Loss!" Cairo said, indignant. "We don't know it's a *loss*."

"And *you* must be *Cairo*," Ogg said with a peculiar smile.

"Why does everyone keep saying that?" Cairo snapped.

"Yes, fiery as a mandrake, charming as the night is long. Of course. Come and give Ogg a hug."

"She is a fire brand," joined in Gaffer, "I didn't need your note to tell me that."

As Ogg stepped towards her, Cairo stepped back in the same way she had with Gaffer, but Ogg was quick and had her arms wrapped around Cairo in the wink of an eye. Cowper and Siam followed, and Gaffer put his hand on her back.

To Charlemagne's relief, Cairo allowed herself to be embraced, even if she did stand a little rigid. Again, Gaffer appeared to sniff Cairo's hair, almost as though he was trying to detect something. Finally Charlemagne too was hugged by "the Ogg" while Cowper and Siam licked her jeans, hands, boots and anything else they could reach.

"We are very much honoured to have you *all*," Ogg said, bowing low. Penny bowed back. Charlemagne nodded her head and Cairo stood awkwardly. "Now let's not dawdle, I've got some hot scones and a nice cup of tea on. Just the thing after a long journey." She smiled and gestured for them to come in.

The sisters moved to collect their bags from the trunk but Gaffer waved them on with an, "I've got those, dears."

The entranceway was a long, narrow corridor with polished wooden floors. The walls were oak-panelled and decorated with starkly framed photographs. At first, the black-and-white pictures seemed to be relatively conventional portraits, but closer inspection revealed that all the poses were slightly off.

Charlemagne paused to study them. There was a boy with

a bow and arrow, just about to let loose the shaft, except that the camera had caught the string breaking; the face was one of pain as the shoulder extended backwards, the resistance suddenly gone. There was another, this one a triptych of three poses of a woman in the act of throwing a pair of strangely shaped dice on a table. In the first frame she was smiling, in the second puzzled, and in the third her expression was one of deep dismay as the objects came to rest. Finally, there was one of an old crone, her confused eyes staring into the lens as she let out a silent scream.

"Come on, come on. Don't dilly-dally!" Ogg called from further down the corridor. "The tea will get cold. I will give you the full tour when you've had a cuppa." She nodded to Gaffer who took the bags upstairs while she led the girls into what she called "the lounge."

The room, plush with gilt cornices, thick velvet curtains, and dark damask wallpaper, seemed to press its opulence in on them. A huge candelabrum sat in the middle of a polished mahogany table. Outside the huge bay windows was a beautiful garden, enclosed in tall evergreens, stretching away from the house for at least an acre.

"Gaffer's pride and joy," said Ogg. "He spends more time with the garden, mowing grass and counting flowers, than he does with me. There are so many things to fix around the house, but he's too busy pottering about outside. He tells people he bought this house because it has character, but really it was for the land. The house could have been falling down for all he cared, and it was."

"It's beautiful," Penny said.

"Is that a forest beyond the garden?" Cairo said.

"Yes, an ancient one. You should go and explore if the weather's nice tomorrow."

Explore? thought Charlemagne. Did she think they were ten? Enid Blyton's adventurous three. But then she checked herself. Their grandmother was only trying to be a good host.

Ogg pulled a big flowery tea cosy off a big flowery teapot that sat on the table. The scent of honey and spices filled the air. To the left of the pot were scones, preserves, and clotted cream, to the right, a stack of cucumber sandwiches. It was all so . . . English.

"Mmm that looks lovely," Penny said.

Cairo wrinkled her nose. "Excuse me, but do you have any coffee?"

Ogg poured the tea into four cups. "Just try this," she said when she was finished. "If you don't like it, I'll make you some coffee. But please try. It's a special home brew."

Cairo let out a silent sigh and Ogg passed around the drinks.

"Help yourselves to scones and jam, won't you?"

Cairo piled three scones onto her plate and a generous helping of cream. She then sniffed the tea and took a small sip. Charlemagne had a scone with just a touch of jam, Penny, a couple of sandwiches. They hadn't eaten anything since breakfast on the plane seven or so hours ago, and no real food since leaving America. Mouths watering, they ate in silence.

Charlemagne noticed how the cups and plates matched the pattern on the pot and tea cosy. It made her feel happy somehow, as though everything was going to be just fine. Ogg smiled warmly at her, as if reading her thoughts, and in that moment Ogg became more radiant somehow, younger than her seventy-something years. Charlemagne returned the smile and leant back on the couch, taking a bite of a second scone and washing it down with the hot tea.

Charlemagne, like Cairo, was not a fan of tea; she found it too bland. But, unlike Cairo, she was too polite to say anything. This tea was a pleasant surprise, however, sweet with honey and something else she couldn't place. The hot liquid passed through her, relaxing and refreshing. Ogg poured some of the tea into a saucer and put it on the floor. Eagerly, Cowper lapped it up.

"This is great!" Penny said.

"Yes," Cairo said. She paused as if searching for the words. "Delectable," she said finally.

Cowper wagged his tail.

"If there is one thing I know how to do well, it is a decent cuppa," Ogg said.

"I'm sure there's more than that," Penny said.

Ogg smiled, but her eyes flashed with irritation, as though Penny had somehow offended her.

"What's in it?" Charlemagne asked hurriedly. "The tea, I mean. What gives it that flavour?"

"Manderlay," Ogg said, "my secret ingredient."

Charlemagne was about to ask what that was, when a loud, low groan reverberated around the house. Again Charlemagne experienced that strange sensation, as though the walls were pressing in, the damask swimming in front of her eyes. Cowper's brown ears pricked up.

Ogg held her teacup suspended and stared out the window. When the noise stopped she put her teacup back on the saucer and smiled at them all again.

"What was that?" Penny asked.

"It's just the house," Ogg said casually. "It moans and groans like an old lady. The ancient wood shifts in the wind, and in the sun, and in the cold. You don't get houses this old in America, do you?"

"How old is it?" Penny said.

"Too old."

Gaffer shouted something from the top of the stairs. It sounded like he was asking which room to put the girls in.

"Useless creature," muttered Ogg finishing her tea in a single gulp. "Please excuse me." She got up and Cowper trotted out after her, wagging his tail.

For the second time Charlemagne admired how quickly Ogg moved for a large woman. Up and out in a flash. No arthritis in those knees. She was incredible for her age. Nothing like Granny Hickory had been, all bent at the waist, moving in pained, stiff steps.

"What a queer noise," Penny said, taking a bite of her third cucumber sandwich.

"What queer inhabitants," replied Cairo, standing up and walking to the window. She turned back to them, her white teeth flashing in a broad grin. "Although I have to say, I feel a lot better for that tea. It picks you up, doesn't it? I feel like going for a walk down the garden right now. Anyone want to come?"

"Actually I feel pretty beat." Penny nestled on the couch. "If we're going out tonight I need to rest first."

"Charlie?" Cairo said, raising her eyebrows.

"You've certainly perked up," replied Charlemagne.

"Don't get excited, I'm sure I'll be back to my miserable self again shortly." She flashed another smile and helped herself to another scone.

That's her fourth, thought Charlemagne, *but at least she's eating.*

"So anyway, what do you think of our crazy grandparents?" Cairo said, her mouth half-full.

"I think they're lovely," Penny said.

"You would," Cairo replied, laughing.

"They're not what I expected," Charlemagne said.

"Better or worse?"

"Neither . . . and both, I guess. I don't know. I expected them to be highly strung somehow, and yet more . . . normal. They just don't seem the type to have not spoken to Dad for almost fifteen years."

The truth was that she didn't know what to make of them. Gaffer was friendly, strangely comforting and familiar, but Ogg . . . There was something about her, something that demanded attention, and something else too, a sort of other-worldliness. It was probably just being with different people in a different place. Perhaps all elderly English couples were this eccentric. Even their names were strange. But that ran in the family.

The three sisters had eventually grown into their names, but Cairo, Pendragon and Charlemagne Agonistes? She often wondered what her parents were thinking. Try to order anything on the phone and it took three hours. Pendragon was the worst, but everyone called her Penny.

"Maybe ask me about them again, after the wake," Charlemagne said.

Cairo tapped on the glass and peered out over the back garden. "Yes. After tonight." She cocked her head and ran a hand through her long auburn hair. "I'm still not going you know," she said, sashaying slightly as she spoke.

Charlemagne smiled. She knew Cairo *was* going to go, and deep down, for whatever reason, she was looking forward to it. Whenever Cairo was happy, she unconsciously danced on the spot—subtly, but enough to notice. She had done it since she was a small child, charming everyone she met.

The three-year-old Cairo had told Granny Hickory matter-of-factly that she was dancing to the song in her head. Granny Hickory then repeated this story to everyone else. But even at the age of five, Charlemagne knew Granny Hickory had it wrong. Cairo meant she was dancing *with Song*, who lived in her head, her imaginary play fellow, with whom she had talked, played, and shared secrets throughout her childhood.

Cairo tapped the window again. "Look at those oak trees in the distance. They're huge. They must be a hundred years old."

"They're much older than that, my child," Ogg said, appearing behind them, Cowper at her heels. She had come into the room so silently no one had heard her. Charlemagne felt herself flush. How long had she been there? And how did a six-foot, two hundred pound lady move so quietly? At least they hadn't said anything awful. Cowper trotted over to Penny and nuzzled her hand. Penny sneezed.

"How old?" Cairo asked.

"A thousand years if a day," Ogg said. "They're even bigger than they look. Farther away, too. There are three fields between the end of our garden and where the forest begins." She looked at their plates. "Now, if you've finished with your tea, I'll clear up." Ogg put the teapot and remaining scones and sandwiches on a tray. The sisters carried over their empties.

"Thank you, dears," she said. "Just so you know, I serve tea at three o'clock sharp every day. It's a tradition. I always make a cuppa for myself and Gaffer, and we always have a sandwich or something small with it. So if you want tea, just come down at three, but never afterwards or you'll spoil your dinner. Call it a house rule."

"Where is Grand— uh, I mean Gaffer, now?" Penny said.

"Oh, he's got his cup of tea upstairs. He's taking care of something," Ogg said dismissively. "Now, while we're on house rules, there are just a couple of others. Firstly, *please* treat the house as if it were your own. When you get up in the morning and want breakfast, help yourselves, don't wait to be asked. If you get cold, turn up the heat. If you want to go out for a walk, just go. I can't stand people who dither, wondering if they can do this or that."

Cowper wagged his tail at the word "walk."

"Number two, I don't care what you youngsters get up to, but while you're here, you need to be home before dark so we don't worry. We lock the doors at night. We've never had anyone break in, but one can't be too careful."

"What time does it get dark?" Cairo asked, scooping up the last scone before the dish was taken away.

"About ten. So let's say be back by then."

Ten o'clock, thought Charlemagne. What did she expect them to do? They were in the middle of the countryside and Penny was only thirteen. She wasn't allowed out alone at home.

"Now, talking of locked doors brings me to rule number three. When I take you around the house, I'll show you the door to a room. It's on the third floor on the left hand side of the staircase. You can't go in and I'd prefer it if you didn't go up there at all."

"Oooh, how very mysterious," gushed Penny.

Ogg smiled thinly. "Actually, it's not safe. The ceiling is coming down. Plaster comes loose all the time and hits the floor with an almighty thump. That's another noise you might hear. I've told Gaffer a hundred times we have to get it fixed, but he insists on doing everything himself. He always has, which is why everything is such a shambles. In and out he goes, inspecting the room, making plans, but the hole in the roof doesn't get any smaller." Ogg shook her head. "Anyway, apart from that, you may do as you please." Cowper and Siam barked and thumped their tails on the carpet.

"Oh yes. The dogs. If you go out, try to take them with you. They'll get in a dreadful sulk otherwise."

"That all sounds very reasonable," Cairo said pleasantly.

"Yes, now if you'll just excuse me, I'll put away the tea things and Gaffer will show you to your room. Get some rest and then tidy yourselves up a little bit. The wake is a rather formal affair, and it's important to me that my grandchildren look the part."

Three

WHEN CHARLEMAGNE AWOKE, it was past five o'clock. She hadn't wanted to sleep, but the journey and the jet lag and a month of sleepless nights had taken their toll. She had lain down to rest her eyes for a moment, conscious of both the musty smell of the pillow and the slight burn in her stomach that sucked her energy, digesting the tea and scones. And as the energy left her body, a weight seemed to press down on her, and down and down until she couldn't have moved even if her life had depended on it.

Next to her, Penny slept curled up and snoring softly. Cairo was nowhere to be seen—perhaps she had gone for that walk. Wherever she was, Charlemagne hoped she would be back soon. Gaffer said they were leaving at six, and it was clear Ogg wanted them to be presentable.

Charlemagne had not protested because she didn't want to give Cairo an excuse, but she couldn't understand why her grandparents wanted them to go to a wake for someone they didn't know, after everything that had happened with their mother, and on the very same day that they had arrived. It was grotesque, or at the very least insensitive. However, Charlemagne didn't want to argue. She had the sense that once her grandmother made up her mind, that was it.

Charlemagne stroked Penny's hair and whispered, "Wake up." Her sister stirred and opened her eyes. For a moment she looked bewildered, until she saw Charlemagne's face.

"I had the strangest dream, Charlie," she said, yawning.

"We've had a strange couple of days."

"No, but I dreamt of a stormy black sea, and—"

"Not now," Charlemagne snapped, cutting her off.

Penny loved to talk about her dreams and go over all the possible meanings. When she was younger, interpretations ranged from "and this means I will get a puppy for my birthday," to "this means I will not live past my sixteenth year." Until recently, Charlemagne had liked to hear about them. They made her laugh, even the sad ones. But the last dream concerned their mother: Penny described how she saw her taken in the night, imprisoned in a wooden cage, and tortured. They were both crying by the end. It wouldn't have been so awful if Charlemagne wasn't having nightmares of her own.

Their mother, Athene Agonistes, was legally missing, not declared dead for another four months as the law defined it, but gone all the same. Charlemagne had read a statistic somewhere about missing people and abandoned cars. If the person was not found within seventy-two hours, the chance of being found alive was less than five percent. It had been six weeks. In that time, all the police had uncovered was a half-full bottle of anti-depressants in the glove compartment. It was strange. Charlemagne had thought her mother was happy. Neither her father nor her sisters had known she was on medication, but for the police it seemed to add up: the car at the side of the road, no body, a fast moving river. The police played along, but their attitude suggested the case was closed.

She noticed Penny staring at her, probably hurt by her abrupt reply.

"Tell me about your dream later," Charlemagne said gently. "We have to get ready for tonight."

"Did you try Dad again?" Penny asked, gesturing to their

shared cell phone.

"Not yet. I left a message though. When he checks it, he'll know we arrived safely."

Penny pulled herself up, trying not to wake Siam who had curled around her ankles at the foot of the bed. "You know, Charlie," she said, stretching, "I was so tired, but Ogg said we'd feel refreshed after a nap and some of her special tea, and I do. I wonder what that Manderlay stuff is."

"A type of Ginseng maybe?"

"You think?" Penny picked up her towel and wash bag. "I better have a shower," she said. She opened the bedroom door, then paused. "Don't you think its cosy, us all being in here?" She smiled at Charlemagne, and instead of waiting for a reply, disappeared down the long second-floor landing.

Cosy was one word for it. The house had plenty of bedrooms, but for some reason Gaffer put them all in one room, like little children. Penny suggested this was to save on air conditioning, but Charlemagne reminded her that they were in England, and so there was no air conditioning, not even the box-in-the-window type, but there was rarely any sun either, so it balanced itself out.

The room was spacious and overlooked the tree-lined drive and pond. There was a bunk bed and a single bed, a couch, a dressing table and a desk. Charlemagne liked it. Yes, it was musty, but that only reminded her of the lake house they used to go to with their parents when they were younger. This room had none of the opulence of the living room. The furniture didn't match, and peeling posters covered the walls: Ché Guevara and Lenin, a Celtic cross, Hearn the Hunter, and other pagan figures. And band posters: The Cure, Siouxsie and the Banshees, the Sisters of Mercy, and other ancient black eye-liner groups Charlemagne didn't recognise. It was a room she imagined belonging to someone who wore dark, full-length trench coats and reeked of petunia oil—the type of person she tried to stay clear of at school. And yet Ogg had said it belonged to her father.

Her father. She remembered his parting words to her: "Take care of your sisters, especially Cairo. She's older than Penny but in many ways needs the most looking after."

Then why did he have to send us away? And to a place where they knew nobody.

Her father had given no explanation beyond, "You will be safe with them. They are all the family we've got now."

As far as Charlemagne knew, her father had not spoken to his parents since they fell out many years ago, and the details of the visit had been hurriedly decided over a single, fraught phone call. He wouldn't have thought of them at all, except that when their mother disappeared Ogg had contacted him out of the blue, wanting to reconcile. She'd heard something about what happened from a friend of a friend, or maybe that friend had seen something online. Her father was hazy about the details. Charlemagne had been furious. How dare he send them away? They were hurting too. But he didn't seem to notice. He had always been brooding, distant and sometimes too hard on them, but in the last few weeks he had become more withdrawn than ever. She worried about him.

About four days after their mother disappeared, he left the house and didn't come back all night, or the next night. Charlemagne lied to Cairo and Penny, telling them he'd phoned to say he had to go away for work. But he didn't call, and he didn't leave a note, he just didn't come home.

Charlemagne was left wondering if, in the space of seven days, they were to become orphans. He did finally turn up, mid-morning of the third day. Her sisters were at school, but she had called in sick, feigning illness in order to wait. She remembered it vividly.

When she first heard the car she was relieved and then furious in quick succession. She ran outside just in time to see the old Toyota skid and crash into the side of the garage. Her father was a careful driver. Her fury turned to worry.

"Dad?"

His suit was muddied and torn. His cheek was cut, his face sickly white.

"My dear girl," he said.

"Dad, where have you been?"

He tottered towards her, unsteady on his feet. If she didn't know him better she would have said he was drunk. His eyes swooned out of focus and he fainted in the middle of the drive. She felt sick to her stomach. Thank goodness Penny and Cairo weren't there. Charlemagne removed her sweater and propped up his head with it. She then gently shook him until he came around.

"Dad?" she said.

"Sh-she's gone, Charlie," he stuttered. "She's gone for good."

"We don't know that."

"I do. I do now." His eyes were fevered and blood-shot.

"What do you mean?"

"She's been taken from us," he said, to himself as much as to his daughter. "She's been taken!"

That was all he would say, and shortly afterwards he'd arranged to send them away.

Siam stirred and wagged her tail gently. Her ears pricked back listening to the sound of someone running down the corridor. The door pushed open and Penny came in dripping wet, her long dark hair washed and mussed.

"That bathroom's *freezing*," she said, shivering, "I thought I was going to die when I got out."

"I'm glad you made it back alive," Charlemagne said, smiling. She thought how grown up Penny had become lately. At thirteen, she was beginning to look like a real teenager and not a kid anymore, and her piercing brown eyes seemed wise beyond their years. Penny was the cleverest of the sisters. Too clever, Charlemagne sometimes worried. It distanced her from people her own age and she didn't have many friends to begin with. There was a girl from her Taekwondo class she sometimes hung out with, but that was it.

Having dried herself and wrapped a towel around her hair, Penny began to pull out her make-up. She had only recently begun wearing it—one of the few secrets she kept from their father. Unselfconscious in front of Charlemagne, she dabbed some powder on her forehead, her nose, her chin and last of all on her cheek to cover the small, slightly raised birthmark. Without powder it looked like a pink fingernail; with powder it could have been a large mole. Although she never spoke of it, Charlemagne knew it upset her. Recently a boy at school found out she liked him and promptly told his friends he would never go out with Blob-face. A tearful Penny confided in Charlemagne, who in turn tried to impart some sisterly wisdom:

"Boys at that age—they're all just trying to prove how tough they are. It doesn't mean anything. He probably really likes you but is too afraid to say anything."

Her mother would have known how to handle it, what to say, but Charlemagne's words didn't help and Penny was inconsolable for days. The makeup came out shortly after that.

Charlemagne watched Penny apply a touch of mascara, and then lipstick, smacking her lips together and dabbing them on a tissue. "You look pretty," she said.

"Thanks," Penny replied, snapping her compact closed. "Where's Cairo?"

"I don't know, but she better be back soon."

As if on cue, they heard the back door slam, a muffled "Sorry!" and then feet running up the stairs. Cairo burst into the room. Though the girl had travelled through the night, had hardly any sleep, and was still wearing yesterday's clothes, she looked radiant.

"Hi," she said, beaming at both of them.

"Cairo, you've been happy for a couple of hours now. You're scaring me. I'm beginning to think I'm getting my sister back," Charlemagne said.

"I went for a walk down the fields. It's incredible down there. This place backs onto a forest, or 'spinney,' as the locals call it. But it goes on forever."

"The locals?"

"I met . . ." She paused. "I met someone out with a dog."

"Who?" Penny said.

"Someone. Anyway, I just saw Gran downstairs and—"

"You mean Ogg," cut in Penny.

"Yeah, right, because I'm really going to call her *Ogg*." Cairo shook her head. "She said we need to get a move on because it's almost time to go. They told me not to hurry, but they're already downstairs fussing around." She giggled. "Just wait until you see them. You have no idea."

"What do you mean?" Charlemagne asked.

"Just wait."

Charlemagne took a quick shower. Cairo stepped in after her and was in and out in a flash. Back in the bedroom, Charlemagne flipped open her suitcase, threw on a dress, and suggested Cairo do the same. "It is a wake," she added.

Normally her sister hated to be told what to wear, but she was actually humming as she slipped on her skirt. Something had definitely changed. Cairo had moped around for weeks, and now suddenly, in the most unlikely of circumstances, she had become her old charming self. Charlemagne felt happier just being near her.

They were ready in eight minutes flat, which Charlemagne supposed was pretty good for girls. Most teenage boys took longer, with their gel and things. For the sisters, this speed was a result of living in a house that had four women and only one bathroom. Charlemagne rapidly applied some lipstick and eyeliner. Cairo didn't bother; she never did. Her red and cream complexion needed no augmentation.

"We're ready!" Cairo said, skipping down the stairs.

Penny glanced at Charlemagne, who shrugged.

Gaffer and Ogg stood in the hallway. Their attire was

startling. Gaffer had changed from his puffy jeans and baggy, patterned cardigan to full evening regalia. He wore a long, charcoal-grey jacket with red satin lining that came to a semi-circle at his rump. His bottom half consisted of flared trousers, also charcoal grey, with red satin turn-ups. The trousers had probably fitted perfectly well in the seventies, but were now a little, well, snug. His shirt was white with a slight lilac wash, and heavily ruffled. A long lacquer pipe protruded from his mouth. His beard was oiled and curled, no longer the bird's nest it had been earlier.

Cairo turned to her sisters with a wicked grin and whispered, "If there are any female hobbits at the party, I hope they can control themselves." Penny stifled a giggle.

Ogg, on the other hand, wore a shimmering gold-and-fuchsia ball gown. Long swathes of silk cascaded down her figure and hung in artistic folds. Tiny gold scales were sewn into the fabric. Surprisingly, the cut flattered her curves, and the strange mix of colour worked somehow, bringing out her exotic eye-shadow. Charlemagne noticed she wore flat shoes, presumably to stop her towering a full foot and a half over Gaffer. She was larger than life, almost stifling. Charlemagne was transfixed.

"Ah, there you are, girls," said Gaffer, sucking on his unlit pipe.

"Don't they all look *lovely*," said Ogg. "We were just saying, we should have a hot toddy before we go, to get into the swing of things."

"I . . . don't really drink," Penny said.

"Not at all, not at all," Gaffer said, dismissing her. He disappeared into the kitchen and returned with a bottle. Ogg took five fluted glasses out of a cupboard and Gaffer filled them with a pale, slightly bubbly liquid.

"Champagne. Champagne for everyone," Ogg said, extending out her arms in that way she had.

"Vintage," said Gaffer. "A hundred years old, this stuff. The last of the manderlay."

"We really don't drink," Charlemagne said, wondering at the name of the unfamiliar spice again.

"Child, one glass won't hurt, and a touch of this will pick up your spirits."

"Aye, Ogg, aye," said Gaffer, handing around the glasses.

"I'm in," said Cairo. She took a glass from Gaffer. Penny gave Charlemagne a brief, questioning look, then shrugged and did the same. Charlemagne also took a glass and sighed inwardly. She wondered if this was what her father meant by looking after her sisters.

"Chin-chin then," said Gaffer, and he drained his glass in one quick draught.

"Chin-chin," repeated Ogg and did the same.

Charlemagne watched Penny sip the champagne tentatively and, probably concluding that she wasn't going to like it, downed it like a shot of medicine. Charlemagne took a sip. It was not like any champagne she had tasted before, but to be fair, the only champagne she had drunk was of this century and very bubbly. This drink was flatter, sweeter and slightly cloying, but it also had a compelling aroma that made it bearable. However, she thought it best to follow Penny's example and swallowed the rest in a single mouthful.

She felt the liquid work its way down into her. It was a strange, hot sensation. She had drunk alcohol with friends at parties—in fact, before her mother went missing, she'd even had a social life—but she had never experienced anything like this. She felt a weight lift from her, taking with it the anxiety and sorrow of the past few months.

Ogg stared at her intently, making her feel slightly uncomfortable.

"Good, good. All done?" Gaffer said. "Let's be having us then, we don't want to be late for Drakefield."

As they walked out, Charlemagne glanced at the photos again. When her eyes passed over them, they seemed to move.

It was incredible how they caught the motion—the act of the string breaking with the boy and the bow, the triptych of despair from the gambler, and the old lady's silent scream. Charlemagne's breath caught in her throat. She could swear she saw the old lady's eyes flicker, but surely it was a trick of the light, or of the sweet wine they had drunk.

Getting into the car was a bit of a squeeze. Gaffer had loaded the back with boxes of wine and a crate of some sort of strange smelling fruit, all of which they were bringing with them. In addition, Cowper and Siam were curled up on the floor, Siam in the front, Cowper in the back. As a result, Cairo, Penny and Charlemagne were almost sitting on top of each other.

"How did you know Drakefield?" Penny asked Ogg.

"He was a young boy. The child of some good friends of ours. Very sad," Ogg said turning around.

"A young boy?" Penny said wide-eyed. "How did he die?"

"He passed on," Ogg replied, frowning.

"Yes, but what did he pass on . . . of?" Penny asked in a smaller voice.

Gaffer growled quietly and Ogg stared forward, saying nothing. There was an awkward silence until Siam suddenly gave a yelp from the front as though her tail had been stepped on.

"Oh Siam, oh Siam, you naughty Siam," Ogg said in a sing-song way. "Are you the Queen of Siam?"

"Ye-S I-AM!" roared Gaffer and they both dissolved into well-worn chuckles.

Charlemagne sighed. She wanted to ask what type of church the ceremony would take place in, but thought that was inappropriate somehow. Charlemagne's own parents hadn't practiced any kind of religion, and she had no idea about Gaffer and Ogg.

They drove for about ten minutes before the car took a turn down a wooded road and pulled into a makeshift lot in the middle of a country park. Cairo caught her eye, smiled and mouthed, "Hippies."

Cars were parking in neat rows, and all around them families were getting out, unloading various provisions and making their way up a hill. Everyone was dressed in eccentric clothing and a festive atmosphere prevailed. Parents walked with laughing toddlers on their shoulders. Young men and women strolled arm-in-arm, enjoying the warm evening. Even the elderly had a spring in their step, almost trotting up the hill to wherever everyone was going.

"Insane," Cairo whispered as they got out.

"This is *England*," Charlemagne whispered back.

"I know, but look," she said, "there's even a wizard over there." She nodded towards a man getting out of a battered old van. He had a huge white beard, an extravagant purple cloak, and boots that curled up at the toe.

"Look at those shoes."

"Shh . . ."

"He's got a bird on his shoulder!"

"No he hasn't," Charlemagne said.

"Yes, he has!"

Charlemagne turned and was startled to see a falcon perched on the man's shoulder. How could she have missed that? It must have hopped out of the old man's van before he shut the door.

Each of the girls carried an armful of the spiky, smelly fruit while Gaffer brought the wine, somehow balancing four boxes across his stubby arms. Ogg took nothing, and without waiting for them, set off up the hill, resplendent in her golden dress.

"A bit rude," muttered Cairo.

No, Charlemagne thought, *that is as it should be.*

Their grandmother was too distinguished to have to carry anything.

When they reached the top of the hill, Charlemagne sucked in her breath. The scene was not what she had expected: there wasn't a church or even a funeral home, but marquees with tables on which were laid out all manner of food and drink. This wasn't going to be any kind of ceremony she was familiar with.

"Look at those," Cairo said, pointing at two huge tents set against the edge of a great body of water, one raised with golden curtains draped over its front, the second, larger one draped in purple.

"Do you think this is legal?" Penny asked matter-of-factly.

"Who cares?" Cairo replied.

With everyone in their fantastic ball gowns and billowing cloaks, the wake had a grandeur worthy of the most extravagant wedding. In the centre of one of the marquees were two huge pigs on spits over a fire, the fat sizzling.

Penny screwed up her nose. "Meat," she said disdainfully.

Waiting staff relieved them of their fruit and brought it to the huge serving tables. Winking, Gaffer handed over the wine, saying something about the "old stuff." Then they joined Ogg, who stood at the entrance of the main marquee. Gaffer began to greet the arriving guests, almost as though he and Ogg were hosts of the whole affair.

"All right, my dears," Ogg said in between greetings, "go and mingle with the young-uns and try not to get into trouble." She gestured with her head in no particular direction, as though she expected the girls to seek them out.

"Young-uns, where are you?" Cairo whispered, but she needed no second invitation and immediately made for the fire and the group of teenagers standing around it. Charlemagne hung back with Penny.

"Hello, Mikecroft!" roared Gaffer, slapping Cairo's "wizard" on the back. The bird hopped with the blow, ruffled its feathers, and got comfortable again. Mikecroft turned around and, with a huge grin, embraced Gaffer.

"Still sucking on that thing?" he asked, gesturing to Gaffer's empty pipe. "Mine lost the taste long ago."

"I can't taste it, but sometimes I can smell it and I thought tonight, well, you know . . ."

"You and your smells," Mikecroft said and gave Gaffer another hug.

He then bowed deferentially to Ogg, but oddly did not actually greet her; instead, he turned his attention back to Gaffer, who was making comments on the size of the pigs, and how many pounds they probably weighed when they were alive. Charlemagne noticed the bird took an occasional peck at Gaffer's hair. Perhaps it was looking for a new nest. Siam played at Mikecroft's feet, licking his hand and wagging her tail in admiration.

A very thin, very tall man in a sleek black suit approached Ogg. Charlemagne could have sworn she heard her grandmother greet him as "Manciple," or rather *the* Manciple, but that wasn't a name, was it? He wore a thick sable cloak around his shoulders that seemed far too heavy for the relatively warm summer evening. The pale yellow hue of his slicked-back hair and tight ponytail was the only hint of colour on him. Ogg said something and glanced towards the fire, or possibly at Cairo who walked around it. The man cracked a thin smile that didn't reach his eyes. He fingered the greased, forked beard on his chin and muttered something in return, something that sounded like "the Alsatians." He must have meant the dogs, which was strange, because Cowper and Siam were brindle lurchers.

As he spoke to her, Ogg's expression changed and her eyes seemed to radiate pleasure. What was he saying? She put out her hand, and he kissed it in an intimate but deferential gesture. If Charlemagne didn't know better, despite their disparity in age, she might have thought this man was Ogg's husband, and Gaffer just another subject.

Subject?

Where had that thought come from? Although that was how Ogg and this *Manciple* seemed to regard everyone around them. Everyone stopped to talk to Gaffer before entering the marquee, shaking his hand or, more often, giving him a hearty bear-hug. In contrast, Ogg stood where the ground was slightly elevated, removed from the entrance. Most of the older ones gave her a quick bow, like Mikecroft had, before they stepped inside. The Manciple studied them all, never leaving Ogg's side. He did not smile again.

What am I watching them for? Charlemagne thought. *They'll catch me staring in a moment.* But she couldn't help herself. She was transfixed by Ogg, by how she had suddenly become a *presence* somehow larger and more radiant than her physical self.

"Champagne?" a waiter said, offering Charlemagne a glass from his tray.

"Thank you," Charlemagne replied, taking it because she wanted something to hold onto, rather than because she wanted a drink. Her hands had felt awkward at her sides, but now, holding the glass and not drinking, also made her feel self-conscious. She took a sip. It was similar in taste to the drink Gaffer had given them back at the house, except it was even flatter and had an oaky aroma—more like wine than champagne. The affect was the same. It warmed her as she drank, blurring the edges.

She noticed Cairo was now on the other side of the pigs and had attracted a boy. He was offering her a cigarette, or perhaps not even a cigarette, because it looked hand-rolled.

"We seem to be a little under-dressed," Penny murmured, brushing down the front of her plain black outfit.

"I wouldn't worry about it. We didn't know we'd be going to a *ball*, and anyway, these are the best clothes we have."

"Still, it's a little intimidating."

"Yes, it is." Charlemagne took another sip of her drink.

"Cairo looks pretty though."

"Yes, she does." The two sisters exchanged a knowing smile.

Another waiter appeared balancing a tray of drinks. Charlemagne held up her half-full glass and said, "I'm fine, thanks," but the waiter misunderstood and handed her another one. *Well,* she thought, *eighteen is the legal age in England, so why not?* She was only a couple of months away. Two glasses wouldn't kill her. The waiter paused and Charlemagne flushed, thinking he was waiting for a tip before she realised with relief that he was waiting for Penny to take a glass.

"Do you have any soda?" Penny asked.

"Any what?"

"Soda. You know, soft drinks."

"No. Just this," the waiter said.

"Oh. Does anyone have any?"

"Oh yes, I think so, but I haven't seen him in a while. I'd have one of these. It's not strong."

Penny shrugged, took one, and the waiter weaved away.

"Penny!" Charlemagne whispered.

"Don't worry, Charlie, I won't have it all. And anyway, as Ogg said, we need to get into the spirit of the thing."

"Cairo already has." She nodded in their sister's direction. Cairo seemed completely at ease, laughing with her new friend. At least a dozen other heads were turned towards them, her merriment drawing them in.

"The usual order has been restored," Penny muttered.

They each took a sip of their drinks. The hum of the crowd grew.

"Don't the waiters look deathly pale with their white tuxedos? It's as though they were chosen especially to offset the colour of all these lords and ladies," Charlemagne said.

"Lords and ladies?"

"I-I mean guests."

Cairo appeared by their side with the boy she had been talking to. She clutched a glass of champagne in one hand, a braised pork roll in the other. It was like a hot dog except the pork was cut in wedges and the bun was coarse, homemade bread. Penny frowned. Cairo claimed she was a vegetarian, except when it came to eating something that looked particularly tasty. The boy excused himself for a moment and weaved off after one of the champagne trays.

"Who's that?" Penny said.

"Eryn," Cairo replied, staring proudly after him. "We're old friends now."

"What?" Charlemagne said, confused.

"You mean, he was the person you met on your walk? The one with the dog?" Penny asked.

"That's right." Cairo beamed.

"And now he's here," Penny said.

"Right again. I found him on his own, hanging out by the pigs, so I thought I'd bring him over." She took a bite of the roll and smiled. Eryn reappeared, glass refreshed, and put his hand around Cairo's waist. She didn't brush him off. "He makes a great . . . what did you call it?"

"Ham butty," he said, smiling.

With her mouth half-full she added, "And he knows our crazy grandparents."

Eryn was the only poorly dressed person at the wake. He looked like he had been savaged by a ferret, with his shabby suit, scuffed shoes and moth-eaten shirt. He didn't even wear a tie. His face was pale and he had dark, hollow circles underneath his eyes. Despite this, his aquiline features were handsome, and when he smiled, there was something strangely captivating about him. She thought he was probably in his late teens, or possibly early twenties, it was difficult to tell. Charlemagne hoped he wasn't that old. He looked like he lived rough, and his eyes had that unsettling quality of having seen too much for their years. He smoked an awful-smelling concoction, and it was through a cloud of greyish smoke that he reached out to shake her hand.

"Charmed," he said, his hair falling across his cheek in dirty red ringlets. When he took Penny's hand, his expression faltered, his good humour disappearing—replaced by a look of loathing that was only present for an instant, then gone. It was so peculiar. Had Charlemagne imagined it? No, judging by Penny's face, her sister saw it too.

"Pleased to meet you," he said, forcing a smile.

"So you know Gaffer and . . . our grandmother?" Charlemagne said. She couldn't bring herself to say "Ogg" publicly.

"How could I not know your folks? Especially the lady," he said. "My people have known them for years."

"You mean your parents?" Charlemagne asked.

"If you like," Erin replied and took a drag on his cigarette, but the smoke must have gone down the wrong way because he fell into a fit of coughing.

Where did Cairo find these guys?

"Eryn has been to one of these before. Tell them," Cairo said.

"Oh yes . . . a long time ago. It was set up just like this, but larger, of course. I remember thinking, why is everyone so happy? But they have great *faith*, these people, they believe in the old times, the old ways." He sounded bitter.

"Who was it? The person at the other. . . wake," Penny asked.

"He was an important man, head of an old family from Castagna."

Castagna? thought Charlemagne. *Must be somewhere in England.*

"And what happened?" she asked.

"They took him to an ancient lake like this one." He gestured across the water with a sweeping motion.

"You mean reservoir," Penny said.

"If that's what *you* see," he said, narrowing his eyes and baring his teeth slightly.

He's crazy, thought Charlemagne, but the funny thing was, the reservoir did now look like a lake, surrounded by tall, ancient oaks and low hanging willows. A thick mist rose from its surface. How could she have missed that before?

And the people, too, strange characters that she noticed for the first time: someone in a harlequin outfit juggled wooden skittles; a troop of bald-headed monks passed through the crowd ringing what looked like small cowbells; a piper and someone playing goblet drums; a tall, grave man on a white horse rode slowly towards the front. Charlemagne blinked, trying to clear her head, but no, they were all still there, and as the horseman came closer, she recognised him as the Manciple and shivered visibly. As he shifted in his saddle, she noticed something hanging from his side—a sword?

Beside her, Penny squinted at the water but said nothing. Cairo grinned widely, seemingly having the time of her life. Charlemagne studied the glass of the strangely spiced, almost bubble-less champagne. Was there something in it? Something other than alcohol?

She noticed Eryn staring at her. He looked different now, somehow less shabby, his long red hair framing his slender jaw. Like the reservoir, he too had somehow transformed.

"Yes," Eryn continued in a dreamy, almost hypnotic voice, "I remember the wake well. I stood on the edge of a precipice, watching them all. The banks teemed with the people of the city, and the flags of the great houses lolled and creased in the wind. There were blazing fires all along the littoral, a mark of respect, and pine smoke filled the air like incense. I remember the ceremony, five thousand heads bowed in prayer, the stories of his valour, and finally the Manciple plucking a ripe, young girl from the crowd."

"Ripe?" said Penny.

"They are a burning people," Eryn continued, ignoring her, "and when the old Lord died, they built a pyre on one of their long, narrow boats. It lit up the river when they set it on fire, the night sky alive with colour and flame, and with the burning Lord lay the girl, to warm the his pillow in the next world."

"That's ridiculous." Penny hated fictions of any kind.

Charlemagne shuddered. There was something about his

voice—he couldn't be telling the truth, and yet . . . the grain of his voice had the ring of truth about it. Cairo laughed as though it was all one big joke.

"Why ridiculous?" Eryn said, shrugging. "The girl's family was poor and was well compensated. The girl didn't feel anything, she was drugged or dead before they put her into the flames."

"Eryn," Cairo said, still grinning from ear to ear, "you're frightening my baby sister."

"Of course he's not," Penny snapped, "because I don't believe a word of it."

But Charlemagne felt very hot all of a sudden. Somehow she knew it had happened, perhaps long ago, perhaps far from here, but it was *real.*

"Your sister believes it," Eryn said, fixing his perfect green eyes on Charlemagne. As he did so, Charlemagne heard him say, *Manderlay flows through your veins. You better watch yourself.* But that was impossible, because his lips remained closed. Her head swam, and with an effort she pulled her gaze away from him.

"Are you okay?" Penny put her hand on Charlemagne's shoulder.

"P-pardon?"

"Your eyes just glazed over. You looked like you were going to faint."

"Did I?"

"It's the champagne!" Cairo giggled. "Big sis can't take it!"

"I'm fine, really."

But she was not. The world was coming in at the edges. The monks chanted in some language she didn't understand; the children held hands and walked around the fire as if performing some ancient ritual. Her own stomach seemed to burn with the flames, either in anticipation or fright, because she knew that this evening they would set alight the body of this boy, out there on the river, and when they did, they would take someone with him, a young girl, sacrificed to warm his bed in the underworld.

A gong sounded, two quick peals. For the first time Charlemagne saw the family of the deceased, all of whom were dressed in identical mourning cloaks. Slowly, they made their way to the front to sit before the raised dais and the two tents, one purple and one gold, that lined the river bank.

Servants made their way through the crowd and said in hushed tones, "Please take your seats now . . . please take your seats . . . thank you." They bobbed up and down in their white suits, leading the guests to their places. Mikecroft, who continued to feed strips of ham to his falcon, had to be asked three times to sit down. He finally did so, but not before taking a fistful of meat from one of the buffet plates.

"This is so much fun!" said Cairo. "I wish I'd met this Drakefield!"

"Sir," said a white-coated attendant to Eryn and pointed towards the back.

"Get away from me," Eryn snapped.

Three more attendants appeared. "Sir, you really must," repeated the first attendant, his voice polite, but firm. Eryn held their gaze, not moving. For a moment, he seemed to tower above them, outshining them, despite his size and shabby appearance, the atmosphere suddenly electric. Then he looked at Cairo and seemed to make a decision. "Another time," he muttered.

"What is it?" Cairo asked him, concern in her voice.

"Nothing," Eryn replied. "Ladies, it has been a pleasure to meet you, but I must now take my leave." In a low voice, he added to Charlemagne with a wink, "Just stand near the back, eh? Don't let the Manciple notice you." He nodded. "Gentlemen," he said to the attendants, and turned on his heel.

"Why's he speaking so fancy all of a sudden?" Penny said.

"Because he's got style," Cairo said.

"That's one way to describe it," Charlemagne said.

Gaffer appeared at their side. "Come on, children, come on! Don't dilly-dally here, time to find our seats." He ushered them to wooden chairs about ten rows from the front. "And maybe after, I'll introduce you to Mikecroft. Very interesting man, Mikecroft, he'd like to meet you."

"What about Eryn? Do you know him?" Penny asked.

"Who?"

"Him," Penny said pointing to Eryn, who was now well beyond the back row and being escorted out.

Gaffer squinted. "Eryn, did he say? Grrr. *Eryn* indeed."

"What?" Cairo laughed.

"I'd stay away from that one, dear," he said to her. "The Ogg wouldn't like you bringing him round to tea. No, she wouldn't."

Ogg, Charlemagne thought. Where was she? Charlemagne couldn't see Ogg anywhere in the marquee, and she . . . wanted to.

"Why? He said he knew you," Penny asked.

"Knows us? Oh, he knows us, more's the pity."

"But—"

"No more talking now. It's about to begin," Gaffer said.

Nearly everyone was seated now, staring at the purple tent at the front, and beyond it, the river. As they slid into their row, Charlemagne realised her head was spinning. She held onto a chair to steady herself before sitting down. Turning, she said quietly to Penny, "What do you see? Are we at a reservoir or . . . or a river?"

"Don't be ridiculous!"

"Just tell me!"

"We're at a place called Dreycote Reservoir. It said so as we drove in. Apparently they're available for weddings and funerals, although how that is possible, I have absolutely no idea. They would never allow this in America."

Charlemagne tried to focus on the scene before her. She saw a lake, she saw oaks, she saw sweeping willows and poplars, and she saw great folk all around her. She felt dizzy.

Penny gave her a concerned look. "But I suppose it looks a bit like a river in this light."

The gong sounded again, this time a single sombre note, and silence fell over the crowd.

Out of the purple tent stepped the Manciple. "My dear friends," he said, but the word seem to be said with scorn, as though he had no time for friends. Charlemagne felt another shiver down her spine. For some reason, he frightened her. He had no microphone, but his crisp, cold voice carried easily. "We are gathered here to celebrate the life of one who walked among us as David Field."

To her horror, Charlemagne saw Cairo stifle a laugh into her champagne glass. Fortunately nobody else seemed to notice.

"David was a promising young man who passed on in the prime of life, just twenty-three years old. Today we will celebrate his journey in the traditional way. But first a few words from the family."

A blonde lady from the front row stood up, her eyes red and bloodshot. She talked about David, her son. How he had excelled at school and taken an apprenticeship at some place Charlemagne had never heard of. The speech ended with an emotional, *to you, David.* The crowd raised their glasses, and those with any drink left finished it in the toast.

She noticed the serving staff, having put down the gongs, were passing out drinks again, albeit in a more covert manner. Gaffer gestured with two fingers and received two glasses. It was like at a baseball match when the innings changed. More of the family stood up. This time it was a brother and an uncle, but their speeches were short and largely unintelligible. They slurred their words and seemed to be a little worse for wear. They kept talking emotionally about David's choices or something like that.

When they were finished, the Manciple cupped his hands together, smiled and surveyed the audience. "Now we come together, as is our *duty*, to ask, as our Lady taught us . . ."

To the left of the Manciple, the thick curtains of the golden marquee parted and, sitting on a chair on a raised platform, was a lady in a golden robe. She sat perfectly still, her eyes closed, hands clenched, her face carrying the expression of someone meditating, at one with the life around her.

"Ogg!" Charlemagne exclaimed under her breath. All around them, heads bowed and Charlemagne experienced a rush of awe. Her common sense told her Ogg was some sort of ceremonial dignitary, but Charlemagne felt something else. With three hundred people bowing, it was easy to feel . . . reverence.

The Manciple repeated, "Ask, as *our Lady* taught us, who will accompany young David on his journey?" His eyes bored into the crowd.

"What did he say?" Penny said.

"The dead boy needs a companion," Cairo said.

"Shh," Charlemagne whispered, horrified.

"That's what he said!"

A girl two rows from the front shouted, "I will!" She stood up. "I," she shouted again, turning in her place and looking at everyone behind her. She was slender, with long blonde hair and a flowery dress. She flushed a deep pink. She swayed a little, as though having drunk too much champagne, but if anything, her parents on either side seemed to approve. She looked about thirteen. There was a smattering of uncertain applause. The girl smiled nervously.

The Manciple said nothing.

Another girl stood up, this time a few rows behind where they were sitting, and shouted, "I will go with David Field!" In unison, the congregation turned in their seats. This girl was a little older and dressed in white muslin. She, too, had cascading blonde hair covered by a headdress of flowers. She looked the part, a perfect waif, a child bride.

The applause was louder this time. One portly bearded man

right at the front shouted, "Aye! That one!" It was the brother who had given the speech. A ripple of laughter passed through the crowd.

Charlemagne didn't join in. She couldn't shake the sense of trepidation. These girls, whether they knew it or not, were in danger.

The Manciple glared and said nothing.

A few more stood up in turn, all girls, all young, all blonde or fair. Each time the cry was different, more elaborate and ornamented. "I will do the final homage to David," cried one. "I will take the ship to the other side," shouted another. "I will ride on my liege Lord's last journey," piped a third. It was getting ridiculous, but still, the first girl was probably kicking herself over her simple "I."

After each announced her intention there was cheering and applause but none louder than for the second girl. A woman in her twenties stood up, ancient compared to the children who went before her. Her figure was voluptuous and she wore a golden ball gown. Charlemagne thought she was beautiful but clearly out of place, like those adults who wear princess dresses when they go to Disney World. She, too, received the shouts and claps, but as with the others, she didn't seem to command the general acclamation of the second girl. The bearded man even booed, but the family members quickly shushed him.

Six girls and one woman were now standing. There was a long pause. Charlemagne reckoned the waif would clinch it, clearly the crowd favourite. Still the Manciple said nothing, and his eyes continued to pierce the congregation like a bird of prey.

How many more does he need?

The sun had gone down and dusk descended. All around torches were lit by the white seneschals.

Seneschal, thought Charlemagne, *where did that word come from?* She could sense the crowd becoming restless, uncomfortable. Some of the girls began looking at the floor or their hands, their faces tired from their fixed smiles.

Suddenly, Charlemagne sensed a movement to the side of her and someone else stood up. With an infectious, cascading laugh, the girl cried, "I will go the winding way with Lord Drakefield!"

This time there was absolute silence.

Charlemagne froze.

Cairo.

Her first thought was horror. All the concern and trepidation came flooding back. Her second thought, only slightly less powerful, was mortification as absolute silence reigned across the rows. Cairo had said the wrong thing or done the wrong thing. *Drakefield.* Nobody had said Drakefield. Only their crazy grandparents called him that.

Somebody coughed and the sound seemed to echo across the rows. Still nobody spoke or clapped. Even the bearded man was silent. Gaffer looked aghast.

Cairo just stood beaming at everyone. At that moment, Charlemagne saw her sister through the eyes of the congregation: her red hair, swept across her face, shimmering like a river of jewels; her entrancing red smile that sat perfectly on her milky-brown complexion; and her eyes, those mysterious and indescribably rare green eyes that sucked people in and twisted their souls. She was breathtakingly beautiful and radiated charm. The crowd was entranced. Of course they were, how could they not be? Since she was little, Cairo was the one everyone fell in love with. The silence was the result of three hundred people witnessing infinite beauty for the first time.

Finally someone cheered, then someone whistled, and in the front row, Charlemagne could hear someone saying, "This one? This one?" A patter of applause broke out, uncertainly at first and then overtaking the whole crowd. The bald-headed man gave a faint smile, but his eyes narrowed. He then raised his hands to quiet the crowd, but the applause went on and on.

Was he actually going to choose her?

Charlemagne had to do something. Later, she liked to think she did it to protect her little sister. Cairo was in danger and she promised her father that she would look after her. She had no choice. It was a desperate measure born of a desperate situation. A darker voice, a voice she pretended not to have, told her she did it for a different reason, a baser reason, a truer reason:

She did it because she was jealous.

Charlemagne stood up and said, "I will cross the oceans of time with the Lord of Marches."

Cairo looked across and beamed at her. "Isn't this fun!" she whispered.

Gaffer smiled and said, "Yes, yes."

Penny gaped.

From the dais, Charlemagne thought she saw Ogg nod.

Her heart thumped so loudly she could hear the blood in her ears. What was she thinking? She wouldn't even save Cairo. Charlemagne had nothing on her sister. The rest of the girls had ceased to exist as the crowd fixed its attention on Charlemagne and Cairo, cheering for the platinum and the red, the house of York and Lancaster, as their father used to call them. They would choose Cairo and then . . . and then what?

The Manciple shouted, "Enough!" and the crowd immediately fell silent. In a quieter voice, he said, "Enough, good *friends*. The *Lady* has spoken to me, and the yonder golden child it *shall* be." He raised his hand and pointed a bony finger directly at Charlemagne's heart.

Charlemagne's breath stuck in her throat. The family got to their feet. Gaffer held her arm and whispered in her ear, "Go up to the front, love, quickly. You have to embrace the family before entering."

Cairo sat down with a flourish and folded her arms. Charlemagne hesitated, standing but not moving.

"Go on, girl!" urged Gaffer.

"Charlie?" Penny said.

"It will be all right," Charlemagne replied, shivering in the suddenly cold night air. Feeling utterly exposed, she made her way to the front of the congregation. The large bearded brother came out and embraced her, then the mother with the puffy red eyes, then the rest of the family, hugging her one by one like she was some long-lost friend. Finally she was in front of the Manciple. He put a hand on her shoulder. It felt as cold as ice.

"Welcome this child," he said to the congregation, then turned to her. "Bow to the *Lady*." She bowed, and as she did so, she felt his steely hand across her shoulder blades, pushing her lower. Ogg smiled in return, but it was hard to think of her as their grandmother, so intensely was she playing the part. It was almost as if there was someone else behind those eyes, staring down at her.

"Now come inside," the Manciple said, and held open the flap of the purple tent. But Charlemagne did not move, felt frozen to the spot. "Sisters," he hissed.

Two women in red cassocks appeared at the tent's opening and walked down to her. They each took an arm and half-led, half-dragged Charlemagne inside. The flaps closed behind her.

No turning back.

Inside a fire was burning, the smoke going up through a flue attached to the back. Heavily patterned oriental drapes hung from the walls. On the ground were thick shag carpets and furs. Incense burned in brass thuribles and directly in front of her was an open casket—in the casket, a dead man.

Charlemagne let out a silent scream. She had never seen a corpse before. It was so clay-like, so waxen, so yellow and cold. His face was like a papier-mâché lantern with the light extinguished. He was young, she could see that, and must have been very handsome when he was alive.

Charlemagne edged forward, not able to stop herself, fascinated. His hair was golden and curly and greased with a balm. Was everyone in England so fair? Back at home, with her blue eyes and blonde hair and skin that went pink at the first sign of sun, she was in the minority, but here it seemed everyone had her colouring. He wore a dark flannel cowl embroidered with a coat of arms, a bird flying over an empty landscape.

She suddenly became conscious of the Manciple. With his sharp face and hungry eyes, he looked like a bird of prey.

"The Drake and Field. The family emblem," he said, his face creasing into a slight smile to reveal sharp, white teeth. "An ancient family. They honour us all," he said.

One of the Sisters appeared behind her. "Drink this," she said, pushing a goblet of something under her chin.

"I think I've had enough . . ."

"Drink," she said. "It's part of the ceremony." The woman's powdered white face was about three inches from her own, invading her space. "Drink," she repeated.

Charlemagne tipped back the liquid. It scalded her throat and a curious sensation of heat passed through her, hot tendrils that reached every extremity of her body.

"Relax, child," said the other woman smiling. "Lie down."

She motioned to a makeshift bed, a gurney with a blanket draped over it. Charlemagne looked into her eyes for reassurance. This Sister looked friendlier than the other. Charlemagne's limbs suddenly felt heavy, and only by leaning on the red-cassocked woman for support could she lower herself.

The other Sister appeared at Charlemagne's side and began tying a silk handkerchief around her neck. She then pushed it gently into Charlemagne's mouth; she could not speak, she could not cry out. She felt the world close in around her. She wanted to lift her arms but they felt so tired. Her legs now seemed weighted down with a hundred thousand stones. The Manciple had disappeared.

The Sisters began slipping off her clothes until she lay in just her underwear and bra. Listening, she heard a faint *mm-mm-www* sound. It took a moment to realise it was coming from her own throat. Her eyes opened wide in a gesture of appeal. The Sisters continued their rites. They rubbed ointment into her skin. She detected the odour of chamomile and something else.

The first said, "This will help you on your travels." The second incanted, "Henbane, belladonna, damiana, datura . . ."

The Sisters pressed the creamy, tingling lotion into her skin. Another ointment was prepared and the chanting continued. The scent of mint filled the air. "Sweet mint, marjoram, thyme and patchouli," the Sisters chanted in unison. Her skin drank in the oil. It became part of her. At the same time, she felt like she was floating, high, yet not elated, coming out of herself, and yet trapped.

The first Sister whispered, "Now this won't hurt at all, but it may feel a wee bit strange." She pulled out what looked like a piece of charcoal and to Charlemagne's alarm began to write on her skin.

"Your sigils and signs," the second Sister said.

Charlemagne could not make out what they were writing. She found it difficult to see and even more difficult to concentrate. There was a triangle on her thigh and something else, an eye on her shoulder, a strangely shaped star across her breast.

Helping Charlemagne up, the Sisters wrapped a cloak around her body, but making sure to leave the symbols visible. They were like tattoos. The Manciple appeared again and stood behind the open casket. A feeling of cold creeping panic overtook her.

Each Sister took an arm and led her to the tent's entrance. As the flap opened, the sound of music, the smell of smoke and the roar of laughter greeted her ears. The crowd danced and drank in groups around the fire. A motley array of musicians played fiddles, flutes and hand drums. Champagne flowed freely and the crowd seemed a whirling, swirling mass of people. She could make out Cairo somewhere in the middle near the fires, sweeping her hair back and forth and moving her hips in time to the music. She was surrounded by three or four admirers. Penny stood to the side, wide-eyed and worried. Gaffer was hopping back and forth in time to a drum. The *Lady* still sat on the plinth, eyes closed, her face a mask. Charlemagne found it more difficult than ever to remember that this lady was her grandmother, Ogg.

The Manciple stepped from the tent and the music stopped. Charlemagne noticed that in the silence that followed, Cairo still lilted back and forth, still dancing to her own tune, smiling at her sister.

"I present the loyal Mistress of the Marches!" the Manciple cried.

"The Mistress of the Marches!" the crowd roared back.

Charlemagne's head spun. The smell of the ointment and the effect of the drink disoriented her. The sisters removed her cloak, revealing her underwear and the impromptu tattoos that covered her body. Mesmerised, the crowd stared at her. The Sisters turned her slowly, displaying her like a human waxwork. Charlemagne was unsteady on her feet but the Sisters held her tight. The crowd applauded, the cloak was replaced, and she was pulled back into the tent. The flaps closed behind her.

Perhaps for the last time, she thought.

The Sisters sat her on a high-backed oak chair about a foot away from Drakefield's body. In the flickering candlelight the dead man's features seemed to come alive. She tried to look away but could not.

One of the Sisters pushed her wrists against the elaborately carved arms of the chair, palms upwards, and tied a silk bandage around each. The other Sister secured her ankles to the legs of the chair. She did not use silk, but something coarser. Charlemagne wanted to protest, but her head felt so heavy now, the most she could do was let out a small groan. When finished, they stepped back to inspect their handiwork. Satisfied, each kissed Charlemagne on the forehead and left the tent. The ice-cold touch of their lips lingered on her skin.

The Manciple stepped out from the shadows, pulling the short sword from the scabbard that hung at his waist.

"Nnnn . . ." Charlemagne said.

"A blade from our people," he said. "A silver seax—a spirit dagger."

He smiled, unsheathing it slowly. Gently he touched the blade against his palm and a line of blood appeared. He then placed the cold edge on her arm and drew it along her skin. She did not flinch. The ointment had numbed her, and only the plume of blood told her she should feel pain.

The Manciple smiled thinly and took a small urn and held it under her arm. He caught her blood as it fell. *Drop, drop, drop, drop*, she counted. *Five, six, seven* . . .

Charlemagne felt like she was floating above herself and over the body, over the boy, over *her* Lord. She felt like she was going to pass out and then . . . suddenly she was with him.

Four

"Y LADY," HE said and took her hand.

"My lord," Charlemagne replied.

She was in a huge townhouse that dominated the city square. She knew by instinct it was *theirs*, a wedding gift from her husband's family. She also knew this couldn't be happening, that she was dreaming or dead, but as she looked into her Lord's eyes, that feeling passed and in just a few moments more she remembered nothing of her old self. With the last flicker of consciousness, a voice inside her asked, *So is this the after-life?* It was barely more than an echo.

Her name was Charlemagne of the House of Serendip and her Lord, betrothed in a match arranged by her father, was her love and her life. She smiled at him and they embraced, a long, warm embrace. They had been married just six months.

"What will you do while I'm gone?" he asked.

"Wait here and think of you," she replied.

"I'll miss you."

"I know."

He gave her one last kiss and turned to leave. She thought how handsome he looked in his golden epaulettes and officer's uniform, and she felt a pang, knowing that one day they would grow old, that he would never be as young, vibrant and handsome as he was now.

She supposed it was a strange thought, but *time* haunted her, played tricks on her. She had a sense of something wrong in their future, something on the horizon, cloudy and grey. Perhaps with the great uncertainty of her life settled, she was left to dwell on imagined uncertainties. But it was peculiar how her mind kept returning to that cloud, a dark miasma that caused her veins to fill with ice.

A gong sounded and a servant appeared with her early evening drink. Like all the members of their household he wore a plain suit and golden cravat around the neck, the traditional mark of service. A peculiar looking man, he was short, a little grizzled and pointy. Dumas had been the family servant since he was a little boy. His uneven eyes made her uncomfortable; one was brown and one was blue. It was considered unlucky. Her husband told her to give him time.

"Dumas looks odd and he doesn't talk much, but he is loyal."

She took the manderlay wine from the tray, thanked Dumas, and sat down. She stared out over the vista of the square and at the statues, and beyond to the entire western portion of the city. Dumas regarded her from the corner of the room.

Her life had been one of privileged existence, she knew, and now she was married to a fine lord, she would try to take the part of the lady.

Married and in my nineteenth year—how grand and grown up that sounds.

Unconsciously but inevitably, her thoughts turned to her childhood love. It seemed only yesterday that she was running wild by the great river, Loki at her side.

When she'd reached her eleventh name day, her parents removed her from the local Ecole and commissioned a governess, a deathly woman from Khare who made Charlemagne's life miserable, to teach her the chronicles, classical balance, possibility, Parley and the lore of races.

If Charlemagne couldn't remember the date of the battle of Sigon, *rap!* the ruler descended on her knuckles. If she fell off the beam while holding two bowls of water, *rap! rap!* on the back of her legs.

"A lady must have balance," the governess would snap. "What characterises the race of Serendip? What's that? Golden hair and complexion fair?"—*rap! rap! rap!*—"And don't forget our Lady!" *Rap!*

There was no respite. Even in summer, when the fragrance of freshly cut grass and the sounds of children playing would come through the window, Charlemagne would be puzzling over the properties of onyx, amber and quicksilver. She couldn't stand it. She had to get away.

"My father says I'm to learn the harpsichord."

Her governess coloured. "But I don't teach—"

"He has already found a master."

"Oh." She paused. "And when will these lessons take place?"

"In the afternoon."

"Which afternoon?"

"All of them."

Her governess never thought to ask her father about the lessons; unable to teach music herself, she was embarrassed by the deficiency. Charlemagne's father, having left his daughter's education in the hands of the governess, saw no need to take an interest himself.

During her first week of freedom, Charlemagne played in the city square with other Serendips her own age but soon realised this was a mistake. There were too many people her parents knew passing through the square each day. If just one of them made a chance remark that they had seen her, she would be caught. But where could she go instead? Somewhere she wouldn't be recognised; somewhere no Serendip was likely to be. She would go to Castagna's southern villages, down to the river where the commonfolk lived.

The next day, she was standing at the river's edge skimming stones when a rock whistled past her head and plunged into the water. She spun around and saw three children not a hundred yards away.

"What do you want?" she asked, her stomach tingling uncomfortably.

Their answer was another volley of missiles. The rocks missed her, but only just. They seemed to change trajectory in mid-air, veering away at the last moment.

Panicking, she began to run, but then a sharp pain exploded in her stomach and she doubled over in agony. A rock must have hit her after all.

"Get the sower!" one of the boys yelled and together they charged. Each, gripping sticks for weapons, looked at least two years older than she. Suddenly she was very afraid. The boys she knew did not attack girls—not with sticks, not three on one, not at all. But it wasn't just that. What scared her most was that her insides felt like she had swallowed a flaming coal. She was burning from the inside out. Surely a rock couldn't have done that?

The boys were almost upon her. In her palm she still clutched a smooth round stone. She weighed it for a moment, pulled back her arm and hurled it at the tallest boy. As she released it, the burning in her stomach became even more intense, and only then did she realise that she was experiencing the *Hafram Dura*.

The stone caught the boy square in the nose, but it was she who buckled over, consumed by pain.

The *Hafram Dura* was a rite of passage that first came on at the cusp of womanhood. Some of her kind did not possess the gift; most had a penchant for lucky outcomes, but a few—maybe one in a hundred—could feel the flames. In those few the gift was strong, and in time they could control not only the pain, but also fate itself. The rocks that had changed flight in mid-air were the workings of this gift, the power of the Lady, goddess of the Serendips.

"The birthright of our kind is the Golden Lady," her governess had said. "Every event, every outcome is influenced by Her. When fate is set in motion, so the Lady's face is set in motion, spinning in the flames. If she smiles, fate flows in your favour, if she frowns, fate is adverse, and if she grimaces, that is when we go to our grave."

The tall boy clutched his face. "She broke my nose!" he howled. "The sower broke my nose!"

The others hesitated for a moment and then rushed forward. The first boy swung his stick but it arced just wide. The second tackled Charlemagne around the waist and wrestled her to the ground. She tried to fight but he was much stronger and pinned her down. He knelt on her stomach, digging in his knees.

"Now then, beast," he said, breathing heavily, "what are you?"

She knew she could end it in an instant by telling them who she was. Commonfolk would never dare attack a Serendip, but despite the pain and despite being afraid, she said nothing. It had been her choice to come to the river. She clenched her teeth and struggled.

"Now then, beast, I said!" the boy yelled and pushed down harder on her chest.

She could hardly breathe. Blood pounded in her ears.

"What do you think we should do with her?" he said to the others.

Charlemagne noticed his eyes were red and bloodshot. He had been chewing tanis root. The curse of the commonfolk: euphoria, aggression and release all rolled into one herb. Chew it for enough years, and you would eventually forget everything, even who you were.

The tall boy with the broken nose lumbered towards them, his hands cupped over his face, blood dripping through his fingers. "We should flay her," he said, spitting blood. "She looks like meat-sower scum to me."

"Are you sowing scum?" rasped the boy on top of her.

Still Charlemagne said nothing.

"Are you sowing scum?" he shouted.

His face was so close to hers she could see the tanis stains on his teeth. Charlemagne felt like she was going to black out.

"Let's break *her* nose!" the tall boy said.

From the corner of her eye she saw a stick come down and for a moment she thought it would take her head off. She closed her eyes and waited for the impact, but instead it crashed down on the boy on top of her. He became suddenly limp and Charlemagne pushed him off.

Expecting another blow, she braced herself but again nothing came. Looking up, she saw the stick slice sideways into the broken nosed boy who was now staring wide-eyed at his turncoat companion. He tried to move out of the way, but was caught in the ribs. Another blow to the back and he collapsed to the ground, moaning.

The boy with the stick turned to her and smiled a crooked smile.

"Come on," he said. "Before they get up."

He helped her to her feet and they ran, not stopping until they were at least half a mile down the river, almost to the southern forests. She stood gasping for air, but at least the pain in her stomach had subsided. The skinny boy was barely winded at all.

"Why did you attack me?" Charlemagne wheezed.

"The ostlers have begun a stone war," he said as if that explained everything.

"What?"

"Ostlers, saddlers and farriers have begun a stone war."

"Why?"

"They say it's the natural order of things don't they?"

"But why attack me?"

"Thought you were a meat-sower didn't they? Wanted to thump you a bit."

"Doesn't anyone stop it? Their folks?"

"Their folks?" the boy said cocking his head. "Stop it?"

"Yes, someone could get hurt or even killed!"

"It was their folks' idea. Puts the others in their place and makes the ostlers feel like the Serendips of the southern villages."

Oppression and violence makes them feel like Serendips, she thought, and flushed. If the boy noticed, he said nothing.

"And you? You're with them?" She cocked her head in the same way the boy had.

"Nah," he said and stared at his naked feet.

"You are! You attacked me!"

"No, I just run with 'em sometimes," he said quietly. "I'm not one of 'em."

Charlemagne looked at him closely for the first time. His clothes were rags and he was covered in cuts and bruises. His long dark hair was unkempt and he looked half-starved. No, he was not one of them, he was an orphan, and his dark features marked him as one of the *Forgotten* races, set upon by all sides and in return setting upon all. It was always the way, whether the wars were fought with sticks and stones or blades and alembic powder.

"So why did you help me?" Charlemagne said.

The boy kicked at the earth and said nothing.

"Race you to the mudflats," she said.

He looked at her, grinned that crooked grin, and they took off.

And so, together, Loki and Charlemagne terrorised the southern villages, waging the war of stones against ostlers and farriers. The meat-sowers were their allies, mostly, but nobody was ever allowed into their gang of two—Charlemagne, the high born daughter of the city dwelling Serendips, and Loki, a foundling at the gates of Castagna when he was five, taken in only because an innkeeper needed a pair of hands to carry the slops.

If her parents ever found out, she would have been sent to the northern territories where her cousins lived in the stone-cold city of Khare, the last Serendip outpost before the haunting crystal lands of Acraphea. But she was never found out. No one ever considered something as absurd as a Serendip consorting with commonfolk. Besides, she was lucky; the Lady always seemed to smile.

The years passed until they were no longer children and their games had changed. She went to the southern villages in the evenings, if she went at all. Loki became a merchant's sword and was gone for weeks at a time. When they were together they would lose themselves in the hubbub of the taverns, mingling with the commonfolk, playing knucklebones or seven tiles for coppers. Charlemagne, with her probability-altering gift, always won the pot and the orphans in the street no longer went in rags. But by then, when Loki took her hands, it had become suddenly awkward. Awkward because Charlemagne wanted Loki to take her in his arms, and awkward because she knew he never could.

When she was eighteen, Charlemagne became a debutant in Serendip high society. She had already refused two proposals. It would not be long before her father insisted she accept one. But she could never do that while there was Loki. And it wasn't only that. Coming to the villages no longer seemed right. For the first time she felt her difference, that she was somehow betraying her people, but even more importantly, betraying the friends she'd made by the river and betraying *him*. The week after her eighteenth name day, Charlemagne told Loki she couldn't see him anymore.

"But why?" he said.

"I just can't."

How tall he looked then, and how handsome with his dark hair and dark eyes.

"Is it because you are ashamed of me?"

The words cut deep, but his expression cut deeper. She had

seen him beaten. She had seen him half-starved. She had seen him lashed in the street accused of stealing a bracelet made from cockatrice shells. She had never seen tears well in his eyes until this moment.

"Because of my duty," she said, knowing the words were empty.

"Duty? Duty to what?" he spat.

She could not reply, had no reply.

"The Serendip's duty is to oppress the commonfolk!" He turned away from her. She pulled him back. She wouldn't let it end like this.

"I'm sorry," she said and kissed him on the cheek.

He turned and kissed her full on the mouth, holding her there. He looked like death when he eventually pulled away, and he was trembling. It was their first kiss. The next day he left with a merchant's party and didn't come back.

Her thoughts returned to the present. Dumas, the grey-haired servant, had appeared at her side to take her empty glass.

"Would you like another, my Lady?"

"Please."

He had the colourless liquid already poured, chilled to the perfect temperature. They said anticipation was the rarest and most valuable trait in the serving classes, and he had been in service all his life. A second glass would make her a little dizzy, she knew, but she was in the mood to drink.

The sun was setting as she looked out over the city, and from where she sat she could almost make out the southern villages and the river. The fires would begin soon. She felt melancholy somehow, and her thoughts turned to her husband.

He was handsome and her father had chosen well. Long golden ringlets bordered his heart-shaped face, a gentle, boyish face. He was a lord and an officer. Although never hardened in real battle, her husband's arrows could break a hawk in two at a hundred feet. His sword was dented with training and he wore with pride the gilded Drake and Field arms of his people.

She, too, would now wear those glittering colours; her old formalwear, with its emblem of ancient oaks, would remain packed in its chest keeping company with another keepsake, a beautiful bracelet made from cockatrice shells.

The first six months of their marriage had passed pleasantly. In the evenings they drank wine and played achromatic chess and Demons to Dust. She let him win, or at least she let him win most of the time so it wasn't obvious. It made him happy.

Lord Drakefield captained a regiment of Thegn bannermen and was responsible for keeping watch on the northern road. The Serendips had not been at war for a generation, but they still liked to keep the *Forgotten* away from their borders.

Since the war of Sigon, only two races rivalled their power: the House of Acraphea in the west and the House of Gildas in the south. The lands of Seraphina had been at peace for longer than almost anyone could remember.

Charlemagne took another sip of the manderlay wine, the grey servant standing obediently by her side.

She blinked.

Charlemagne sat and watched her children play and thought how quickly time passes. It seemed only yesterday she was a newlywed, and now it was already the third name day of their third daughter.

She was rounder than ten years ago but was happy and told herself that her husband was a good man. He sat on the council now, an honour for one so young, and he commanded an entire regiment of Thegns.

He would come home after drinking with his men, boasting about skirmishes on the eastern road with Forgotten, and how his regiment cut down the ragtag horde of barbarians. "Great sport! Great sport!"

She only partially listened. They never *really* talked anymore, and the Demons to Dust board gathered dust of its own. He was too busy, out until late fulfilling the duties of his post. She heard whispers about her husband and "night kites," too many to be without substance, but she chose to ignore them as any true lady must. Besides, she was not a hypocrite; their union had not been perfect.

Charlemagne had also fallen once while her husband was away; one drop of romance in a lifetime of duty. It was her greatest shame and her happiest moment. The rest she bore as penance. And besides, there were her children to think about. They were her pride, her joy, her comfort. She loved them more than life, especially the youngest, Saffron. Saffron drew her like a moth to a flame. There was something about her, something Charlemagne could not place, as though one day she was destined for great things.

Charlemagne stared out the window to the south. She had memorised the view by now, the tall angular buildings of the square, opulent and foreboding; the columns in each corner; the Golden Lady's faces smiling for an eternity on their summit.

Half a mile from the square were the humbler accommodations of the Thegns, and beyond that, the forest and the holdfasts, and then the villages, the river, and the shroud of smoke from the fires for warmth, for cooking, for light.

By her side, the old grey-haired Dumas still waited in his corner, watching over them, anticipating her needs. In all these years Charlemagne had never asked him which village he was from. A silent blush crossed her face.

She blinked.

It was winter and Charlemagne was getting old. She felt the cold when she went outside and the mirror reflected a woman with greying hair. Her lord said his little wife was being vain, but she knew. Her eldest girls were already married. They were too young, but her lord had insisted; they were advantageous matches.

Her lord. He led raiding parties almost continually now. Sometimes he was gone for a month or more. It was said that the Forgotten had begun to gather on the great plains of Corocupina. They attacked villages and pressed on the civilised cities of the Western Pangaea. The commonfolk whispered that a great leader had emerged, uniting the scattered tribes together. Ancient quarrels were set aside and the Forgotten, expelled from their lands after the great war of Sigon more than fifty years ago, had come together with one blade, one hammer, one spear.

Their alliance was futile, her husband said, and this great leader would be crushed. Even in numbers they could not stand against his men. The Forgotten barbarians fought iron against steel, throwing spears against a rain of arrows. If they ever made it to Castagna, a hundred would be slain for every Thegn, a thousand for every Serendip. He swore it.

However, battles had been lost and the rumours persisted. The old crone of Carabrienne, the perfumed fortune-teller of the docks, pronounced war was coming: "A red rage to scourge the selfish race of the Golden Lady." She would have been flogged, if anyone took her seriously. Even so, the few of Forgotten descent who lived in Castagna were expelled from the city gates.

As Charlemagne sat in the drawing room her youngest, now eleven, asked her, "Is it true the barbarians consort with witches?"

"Why do you say that?"

"I heard the barleyman talking to Rhonda in the kitchens."

"Witches aren't real. They're just something to give a *boo* to Granny Drake's stories." Charlemagne made a note to talk to Dumas about Rhonda.

Saffron looked at her with those haunting brown eyes, so unusual for their kind. "And basilisks and manticores and prehensile arachnids?"

"Yes, child. All part of the boo."

As gloomy as the world was outside their walls, Charlemagne could not be sad, not while she had Saffron happy at her side.

Her daughter could be a witch herself so much did she enchant and spellbind those around her. Even the legendary impartiality of Dumas wasn't immune. He called her his little spice—a spice whose hair was blacker than the night, an anomaly in their society of golden-haired children. Poor Dumas. He was getting very old now. These days Charlemagne heard him wheeze when he went up the main stairs, and the yellow cravat of service seemed heavy around his neck.

Her dear child's face only ever clouded when Charlemagne said she couldn't go down to the great river to play. It was not safe. The children were rough and the commonfolk were not the same as in her day. They seethed with discontent as though the Serendips themselves had caused this unholy winter. They even fought strangers with sticks and stones.

She blinked.

Charlemagne stood by her favourite spot near the window and looked out across the City. She could see herself reflected faintly in the glass. In recognition of the holiday, she wore her finest dress, a light purple silk gown and matching surcoat lined with ermine. The grand attire could not hide what she knew to be true—that the lustre of her youth had now faded. Time seemed to pass more quickly than ever; another three years had gone in a blink of an eye. At least the fighting with the Forgotten was all but over, or so her husband said. She sighed and told herself, *Tonight I* will *be happy*.

It was the Feast of Enninmyra, a day when no Serendip crossed the threshold; the night when the Golden Lady was said to walk among them, her face always smiling. They ate, they drank, they gave thanks to their goddess of fate, secure in the comfort of a well-protected city. They shared gifts, they shared stories and they celebrated their good fortune by welcoming the dawn as one people.

After dinner, Charlemagne sat back in her chair, closed her eyes and let the warmth of her daughter wash over her.

It was just her and Saffron. Her lord was drinking with his men. Dumas was there, of course, frail and grey but insistent on waiting on them on this, their holiest of days.

The tranquil evening was filled with the song of lyrebirds and Charlemagne could hear the Blue-Black Sea breaking beyond the hills. Soon it would be midnight.

"Can we go outside, Mother? I can hear the celebrations."

"It is late and we have to be up before the dawn."

"Please, I have never seen the fireworks before," Saffron implored.

"No," Charlemagne said but she lacked conviction and on the third plea, gave in. She could never refuse Saffron anything.

Hundreds of neighbours, friends and relatives thronged the square. Piled high on tables were more viands and vittles than the commonfolk saw in a month. And above them all, on each of the ancient columns, a golden bust of the Lady smiled with approval.

When had the Serendips become so self-satisfied?

Across the cobbled square her second daughter, Aries, roared loudly with her in-laws, slopping ale over the side of her tankard. She was red-faced and unsteady on her feet. The union with that family was a mistake. They were wealthy, arrogant and uncultured.

As the clock struck midnight, the captains and officers rode up through the streets to join the festivities. Raised high on his golden courser, her lord saluted the revellers, swaying in his saddle.

The people danced and sang and soon there would be fireworks. This year's feast had been the wildest she had ever known. In prior years she would have danced with them, but she was tired now and felt her age. Her lord was drunk on manderlay wine, as were the rest of his men—seemingly *all* the men. The city of Castagna was one big festival of light and merriment right down to the river and southern villages.

Saffron was at her side, yawning and tired. She was fourteen but sometimes seemed much younger.

"Come on," said Charlemagne, taking her by the arm.

"But the fireworks are just beginning," she said, pointing to a shooting red light just over the eastern wall.

That's strange, why would they light the fireworks over there? Charlemagne's thoughts lingered for a moment before the eastern gate exploded into splinters. Around her, only a few looked up. Manderlay wine had dulled their senses and most thought the explosion was somehow the beginning of the display. Smoke and ashes rose where the gate once stood. Charlemagne's head reeled.

It didn't make sense; only Acrapheans had alembic powder. Nothing else could breach the wall. The blast of a horn filled the air and then knights on destriers rode through the clouds of dust. Their armour was black, their hair as dark as a moonless night.

It was the Fyrd! The knights of Acraphea. They had not been seen here for half a century. The Serendips were the unrivalled masters of the west, the Acrapheans the east, and the Gildas, the south. The three great races on whom, since the war of Sigon, Seraphina's peace depended. In the watchtower, a sentry rang the bell furiously. He was picked off by an arrow and fell to his death.

If the Lady bestowed on the Serendips the latent ability to influence fate, then the Acraphean's faith gave them an uncanny foresight. No Serendip ever thought an attack from the east was even possible. A single bridge crossed the great river, linking the perimeter of the city with the town.

Against barbarians, the gate to the bridge could be defended for days by a dozen men in sentry towers. Against Fyrd knights and no gate, and with the entire city half drunk on manderlay, the defences fell apart. The garrison of Thegns was shot down even as they ran to the ramparts. The destriers charged the bridge four abreast.

Charlemagne's lord roused himself. He was in a daze,

only just beginning to understand what was happening. Carabrienne's "red war" had come.

She blinked.

All around her people were dying. Blood and death flowed in the gutters of Castagna and the city of the Lady lay broken in pieces. At first the Serendips tried to rally; they outnumbered the Fyrd ten to one, but before they could repel them, the second wave broke. Hordes of Forgotten joined the battle, pouring through the breach in the eastern gate. The barbarians rode bareback on giant prehensile arachnids and they had with them a basilisk in chains, a huge cockatrice whose eyes froze the hearts of men.

The Serendips were slaughtered in their thousands, men, women and children. Only commonfolk and vassals were left untouched.

The question of why died bloody and unanswered, to linger on the carrion air.

Charlemagne's lord was dead, as were her two eldest daughters, cut down by the arcing skeggox axes and deadly arrows of the Fyrd. They had been trapped in the square, corralled like cattle. For herself she felt no fear, no panic and almost impossibly, no surprise. Her mind was clear, focused on a higher purpose: Saffron. Only her daughter mattered now.

Knights bore down fast upon them, but the arrows whistled past and the axes fell short. Charlemagne's stomach burned like the city itself. It was the sensation of the Lady, her face spinning, altering probability around her.

At one point Saffron slipped, and fell into the path of an oncoming horse. But as the axe descended, a figure in grey dashed from the shadows. Scooping her up, he took the blow in her stead. Mortally wounded and armed only with a cane, the man swung around and caught the knight square in the chest, causing him to buckle and fall from his horse. The knight hit the ground, his bloodshot eyes wide with surprise. With another blow, the figure in grey knocked him unconscious before he himself slumped over. It was Dumas, their ancient servant and his last act of service. He had not surrendered with the others and had paid the iron price.

"Is my spice safe?" he wheezed.

Saffron lay on the ground, in shock but unhurt.

"Yes," Charlemagne whispered, crying.

"Then go!" His chest rattled, then stopped moving altogether. She gently closed his eyes, took Saffron by the hand and ran.

Charlemagne dodged from one secluded alleyway to the next, dragging Saffron behind her. All of the main roads from the city's centre were sealed. Her plan was to try and make it down to the river. It was their only chance to escape. From her days with the commonfolk, she knew where boats could be found unattended. Once they were beyond the walls of the city, they could make their way to the Thegn farmlands and from there hire a wagon to one of the other Serendip cities—Khare or Sandor or one of the smaller towns. Or, if they too were destroyed, to Gildas or even the Plains.

"I'm frightened," Saffron said, panting.

"So am I."

"They are all dead, aren't they?"

"Yes."

Charlemagne made her way to a little-known trail called the Night Kite's Way. It was less than a person wide and ran from behind the council buildings all the way to the Thegn's city dwellings.

Charlemagne had used it herself as a child—the one path she could be sure of not meeting anyone she knew, frequented as it was by disreputable women. If there were soldiers guarding it, at least they would only be able to come one at a time. They ducked down the passageway, the high walls of the council building shielding their flight.

For twenty minutes they ran, Charlemagne expecting to see sentries at every junction, but they made it, her stomach burning. She guided them through a maze of Thegn houses and on another mile to the small forest that continued almost up to the river's edge. They were both breathing heavily, Saffron dragging like a ton weight. Charlemagne turned to implore her daughter to pick up her feet, but then she saw that Saffron was trembling with exhaustion. Instead she said gently, "Not far now." Behind them, all was in flames.

If they moved quickly, they could make it to the water in a matter of minutes. No one knew this stretch of forest as well as her. It was the city's natural border between the commonfolk, the Thegns and the Serendips, and not many crossed it. Still holding hands, they picked their way through trees and thickets of bracken. They were almost through. Then Charlemagne felt the familiar sensation. Probability shifting, the Lady's face spinning . . . but for once, not smiling.

With a dull thud, a throwing axe sliced through her thigh. She cried in pain and her leg buckled under her. Saffron turned, wide-eyed and white.

"Mother!" she cried.

Saffron.

Charlemagne tried to stand, but her leg screamed in pain and gave way again. "We can still make it," she said, but knew she could not.

Four men emerged from a clearing in front of them, weapons drawn. They looked like Forgotten, except they wore the dark colours of Acraphea.

Adrenalin and fear coursed through her veins. With a reserve of strength Charlemagne didn't know she possessed, she pulled the axe from her thigh and threw it at the first man. Her stomach burned and the axe swerved into the soldier's forehead, felling him to the ground. Blood from the wound in her thigh flowed thick and fast.

The second barbarian looked at his fallen companion and then back at her. "You will die painfully for that," he growled.

"What are you? Butchers?" Charlemagne cried.

"What have your kind been to us?" he said and walked towards her, raising his sword.

"Run!" Charlemagne shouted at Saffron.

"But Mother—"

"*Run!*"

Saffron turned and ran. Two soldiers came at Charlemagne, the third went after her daughter. Charlemagne knew it was a mere gesture, but she swung her fist at the first, hoping to catch him by surprise, to go down fighting. The years in the villages had taught her how to punch; she caught him in the face, but as she did so, his sword thrust under her arm and into her. She shuddered as he pulled it out and then raised it to her head. She closed her eyes and waited for the blow to come. Her last thought, a desperate hope that Saffron would somehow get away.

"No," someone said from behind her. The tone was ice-cold. It was a voice she had heard somewhere before, and the voice of a leader.

The ground crashed towards her and she realised she had collapsed. There was no time to put out her arms. She smelled the pine needles, dead leaves, and musty earth. She didn't know if her eyes were open or closed and except for a growing coldness. All feeling had gone; her wounds were dull aches but nothing more. She could hear what seemed to be the sea in her ears.

"Charlemagne," the voice said. Her head was propped and the man with the voice held her hand.

"You," she whispered, her breath failing.

"I," he said.

"You are the wildling king the commonfolk spoke of?"

He nodded.

Loki.

After the war of Sigon, the defeated races were dispersed and scattered to become the Forgotten barbarians of the Great Planes. The tribes eked out an existence, poaching on farmlands, harrying merchant wagons and fighting among themselves. Then the wildling king unified them all and, joining with the great House of Acraphea, had brought red war to the Serendips. How, she did not know. Loki must have hated them all this time, hated her. She could not dwell on that now. She was dying.

"I have a daughter," she whispered.

"My men have her."

"Look after her," she said, so quietly she couldn't even hear herself. "Swear it."

"I swear it."

"She is . . . yours."

The last remnants of energy left her. A tear dropped on her cheek. Whether it was hers or Loki's she could not tell, but it was the last thing she ever felt.

Five

HARLEMAGNE DROWNED IN the darkness, in the void, until her head snapped back and she gulped for air. Then she heard a voice. A man stood before her, his eyes fixed on hers, a cruel curl to his lip. Images and people flooded into her mind: Penny, Cairo, the wake. She blinked and felt herself return to one life, one world. The vestiges of Castagna faded into the background. In a few moments, the here and now would overtake her and she would be almost convinced that Castagna was just an elaborate dream. Almost.

"Saffron," she said weakly.

The experience had been so immense, so strange, and yet it felt like it had all happened before. Charlemagne sat dazed as reality, if that's what it was, washed over her. She was seventeen and in the tent again, still afraid of this raptor of a man. But she was no longer the same person. She had been a Lady, had lived a life—not her own life, but that of . . . whom?

Working quickly the man, the Manciple, cut the bindings on her arms and legs. Strength returned to her limbs. He pulled her up out of the chair, removed her gag, and rubbed a white, chalky ointment on the small cut on her arm, immediately stanching the light flow of blood. He wrapped the wound with a swath of fabric cut from the tunic of the dead man. He then took the urn that was filled with drops of her blood—and placed it in the corpse's hands. Incongruously, she wondered if this was her lord, the person she married all those years ago? No, he was some poor boy-corpse, whereas her lord had been a man. They were nothing alike.

"Kiss him," the Manciple said quietly.

"Wh-what? No."

"To complete the ceremony, to send him on his journey to the Lady, you must kiss him," he said, his tone flat.

"I can't."

His eye squinted slightly, then he grabbed her neck and pulled her over to the casket. He pushed her head down until her lips brushed those of the dead man. They were colder than anything she had ever felt. He pulled her back up, his grip like steel.

"Do not disrespect the old ways," he said in her ear.

She wanted to scream. How dare he handle her like that? But another part of her felt the power of his words. Who was she to question the ways of the Lady? Instead, she said, "I-I'm sorry."

The Manciple smiled. "That's better." He released his grip.

"H-how long was I gone?"

"No more than five minutes. I brought you back."

"You didn't, I . . ." He hadn't brought her back, she had died, fallen into the void.

The Manciple regarded her with interest for a moment, then clapped his hands. "Sisters!" he called. The two women appeared. "Help our young mistress with her clothes." Hurriedly they collected her clothes from where they hung neatly in the corner and helped her dress.

"Can I leave now?" Her voice sounded *so young* in her ears.

"No. Your body is with him and must stay with him until it has burned. You can watch from here, from the rear of the tent. It is important the congregation does not see you until it is over." To the sisters, he said, "The casket."

The women pulled down the heavy lid and fastened it, draping a large embroidered blanket over the top. She noticed the coat of arms—the bird and the field. She could smell the paraffin on the cloth. She thought of her blood gripped in the boy's hands and shuddered.

Using a gurney, the two women pushed the casket through the rear of the tent, bowing to the Manciple as they did so. He watched them go, and strode back out to the crowd. Charlemagne hesitated, then followed the two women.

The air outside was damp and chilly. It must be late now. A full moon was out and its likeness played on the water. A small, flat boat sat at the water's edge. It was bigger than a rowboat, but not by much. The prow and stern both came up in a curved loop. It had a mast and a sail which, like the blanket, carried the emblem of a bird flying over a field. The boat was wooden, but the base was some sort of metal. In the cavity where people usually sat, kindling and wood was piled high. With some effort, the Sisters slid the casket onto the boat. They untethered the ropes, and then one of the Sisters took out a match, struck it, and flicked it onto the blanket. The flame flickered for a moment and then caught. The fire spread quickly. With one shove she pushed it off the launch and into the water. The flames lifted higher and higher. Again Charlemagne thought of her blood trapped inside the urn, soon to be boiled and consumed. The boat steered towards where the moonlight hit the water's surface. A slight breeze picked up the sail, until that, too, began to burn.

Behind Charlemagne, the music ceased and silence descended with just the occasional "oooh" and "ahhh" as the boat crackled and burned.

She heard the Manciple's voice from the front of the tent. Even though she could not make out all the words, the tone seemed to convey some dark, implicit threat about those who might wander from the one true path. The congregation chanted in return, and she imagined his eyes boring into the crowd, his bird-of-prey face searching for potential transgressors. She shook away the image and concentrated on the boat. Even as it began to come apart, it plotted a steady course out into the centre of the reservoir—because of course it *was* a reservoir. Turning, Charlemagne was surprised to see one of the Sisters with a radio control device in her hands.

"Keeps the boat on course," she said. "Everything else burns except the tin bottom and the motor. And even that gives out when the thing sinks."

"This outfit gets awfully clingy," said the other Sister, pulling off her cassock. Underneath she wore jeans and a t-shirt. Without the hood, she looked younger and a lot less intimidating. She had short, fashionably cropped platinum hair and must have been in her early twenties, if that.

Complexion fair and golden hair; the House of Serendip.

"Fancy a brew, Sand?" she said, pulling out a small cooler from under the velvet curtain.

"Please," the other Sister said, catching the bottle of beer with one hand and removing its screw-top while simultaneously steering the boat with the other. "Ta, Rachel."

"Want one?"

Charlemagne shook her head, astonished at their transformation.

"Are you sure? Don't worry, he won't be coming back." She didn't need to say who. "That chant you heard, that was the parting prayer. Now they all bow to the old lady, and then it's off and into the night."

Old Lady! Charlemagne felt a slight, irrational flare of anger. "N-no thank you," she said.

"Suit yourself." Rachel took a gulp. "Sandy and I have to clear everything away, but we always have a couple of brews first."

"Yeh, and what a pain it is. First we have to pull the tin-bottomed boat out of the water with this metal cord. Then it's folding up the tent, packing away the props and driving it all the way back to the warehouse."

"Three hundred quid though."

"True, and we shouldn't complain. The old folks like it."

"Don't you believe in . . . in it?" Charlemagne asked, without really knowing what she was asking.

"Believe? I don't believe in anything. Do you, Sand?"

"Nothing except Father Christmas."

They both laughed. The boat veered slightly as Sandy took her hand off the control. The blazing yellow inferno headed west.

"Don't get us wrong, the old ones believe in it." Sandy gestured to the front of the tent with her thumb.

"Or pretend to," Rachel muttered.

"And the man who brought you in, he's a flippin' fanatic. Don't know if half the stuff he does is legal even."

"Sand!" Rachel said sharply.

"He's gone."

"All the same, watch what you say. You *know* he has a way of hearing about things, finding out things."

Sandy didn't reply, and Charlemagne realised that for all their sudden levity, they were afraid of him too. For a moment the three stood in silence, watching the boat, Sandy and Rachel swigging their beer.

"Well anyway," Sandy said finally, "I don't know anyone in our generation who takes any of this seriously." When she said "this" she gestured around her, as if to take in the water, the tent, and the ceremony.

"Me neither," Rachel said quietly, "not a single one."

"It's good for the grieving family, I suppose. Gives them a sense of community." Sandy took another draught of beer and smiled. "You were a great sport, by the way. Gave them just what they wanted. Oh, here we go. The boat's a goner."

"Woo-hoo," Rachel said dryly.

Charlemagne looked across the water. There were just a few flickers of flame left now; half the boat had already gone under.

"Give it a couple more minutes and you can go back to your folks. Everyone dashes for the car once it begins to sink."

"It's etiquette," said Sandy, "the family likes to be left alone with the final glow."

The last of the flames flickered and died leaving only a few embers on the surface. "Better pop off then," Rachel said. Charlemagne hugged them both, even Rachel who had been rather unpleasant during the ceremony, and left.

It was silent in front of the tent. As Sandy had said, only the mother and the rest of the family were still standing, looking out across the water, tears in their eyes. Even the raucous, bearded brother seemed to be crying now, his broad shoulders heaving uncontrollably. Charlemagne crept past.

Stragglers made their way down the hill, some stumbling from too much drink. A couple of people glanced at her sideways but ignored her, the show over. Charlemagne thought she could just make out a horse and rider on the horizon, galloping off into the distance. Was she imagining it? The last images of the other world, superimposed on this one? When she blinked, it had gone.

Gaffer and Ogg waited for her by the car.

"Well, I bet you didn't expect that," Ogg said, her eyes twinkling.

"No," replied Charlemagne. She almost added, "my Lady," but instead she said, "It was an experience."

"An experience, yes. That and more." Ogg looked more radiant than ever.

"You did very well," Gaffer said, but his smile seemed uneasy.

"Thank you," Charlemagne replied a little bashfully.

Penny hovered by her arm. "What happened?"

Charlemagne looked at the small, carefully tied bandage and the round blot of blood. "I'll tell you later," she said and climbed into the back seat.

"You really reek. Stale eggs or something," said Cairo,

curling up her nose.

"Great."

Gaffer turned around to them. "So what did you think of the funeral, girls?"

"Funeral?" said Cairo. "That wasn't a funeral. That was the best party I've ever been to. When I die, that's how it's gotta be!"

Six

Crakes

HE SPARK HAS caught, it flickers into a flame, but she wonders, the red one, the black one, or . . . both," Hamquist said, staring at Crakes through cloudy, bloodshot eyes.

"What?"

"The red one, the black one, or both?" Hamquist repeated, and took a gulp of sour beer from his rusty tankard. Crakes shook his head. Back home their libation of choice was ambrosia sipped from rare cockatrice shells. They were served by gilded eunuchs who sang as they poured, their golden robes swishing gently back and forth. But here? Crakes didn't even know where *here* was.

"Well?" Hamquist said.

"No idea," Crakes said finally.

"Guess."

"No."

"*Guess*," Hamquist said again, this time through gritted teeth.

Crakes sighed. Sometimes it was better to humour him. Safer. "Both," he said.

Hamquist shuffled his cards and said nothing. A minute

passed, maybe two. He smacked his lips and took another draught of beer. Crakes couldn't tell if Hamquist was *trying* to annoy him. Either way, it was working.

"Well?" Crakes was curious now, despite himself.

"Well what?"

"What's the answer?"

"To what?"

"To the question!"

"How should I know?"

"But you asked me!"

"It doesn't mean I know the answer."

Crakes smashed his stump onto the table. The cards flew everywhere and their pebbles clattered to the ground. Hamquist lunged for his earthbound tankard, plucking it from the air with a flick of his wrist.

"But what does the question even mean?" Crakes asked, trying to control his voice.

"I don't know that either."

Crakes cast his eyes to the ceiling and concentrated on taking deep breaths.

One, two, three . . .

As he stared at the plaster he noticed how dirty it was, how the paint peeled and how the fungus covered extensive patches. It was rank. He could actually see the mould moving and breathing, could feel its existence. He clicked his tongue in disgust. He had never even seen the stuff before coming to this world, to this hole. The mould irritated him. Only yesterday they had been in a golden age of chariots and worship, meting out divine justice to all. Perhaps it wasn't actually yesterday, but metaphorically yesterday. He couldn't tell exactly *when* yesterday was. When you existed forever, time was difficult to judge. There were events that punctuated existence, of course—memorable events like great wars that transcended the day-to-day of mopping up after one god or another—but there had never been anything like this; they were displaced, enslaved, caught up in a mania over which they had no control. Not that Crakes could mention any of this to Hamquist; to even think it was dangerous.

At the back of his mind he felt a small *ping!*

Now that *was* interesting. The mould had sensed his presence. It stared down at him with a thousand tiny green eyes, curious. The mould hadn't seen anything like him in eons of existence, yet it had been here before almost anything else, adapting to survive through countless millennia. Perhaps that's why it irritated him so much.

He screamed at it with his mind: *You insignificant spore! You immaterial plague! We are the ones who are supposed to be immune to change! Immutable and inevitable as the elements. But now look at us. Look at us! We are not what we were.*

They had begun to fade. This world, their actions in it, had diminished them. It began with the Erinyes, who sent them here with the Wandering Mist to apprehend the lady with green eyes. That was supposed to be the end of it, but after delivering her to the witches, the Mist brought them back here, stranding them on the doorstep of this very house. Hamquist said they were to stay here, to wait for orders. Crakes had demanded to know, since when did they take orders from witches? Hamquist gave no answer but, for the insubordination, nearly separated Crakes's head from his shoulders. He hadn't asked again.

However, the unnatural act of dealing with those foul women unbalanced Hamquist. He began to fall apart. First he could not sit still, but was up and agitated the whole time, flicking things, pinching things, stroking things, poking things. One day he spent nine hours chopping vegetables into smaller and smaller pieces with his sword. They were practically gluons by the time he had finished. How Crakes got through that period without going crazy himself, he didn't know. Then, just as it couldn't get any worse, something unexpected happened: a boon in the night, as unanticipated as it was peculiar.

Hamquist was smashing chunks out of the wall in the

kitchen after a dispute with a pickle jar when there was a knock on the front door. Crakes ignored it, hoping whoever it was would go away. They were supposed to keep a low profile, so doing nothing was usually the best course of action. The knock came again, more urgent this time.

"Aye?" he said warily.

"Can you open up?" a girl's voice said. She didn't sound pleased.

"What do you want?"

"Open the door."

"Why?"

"I can't stand out here all night. Open up."

He sighed and pulled the door open a crack. A small figure stared up at him, five foot nothing and maybe a hundred pounds. Her hair was short, black and spiky, her expression fierce and her bottom lip jutted like she was trying to be tough. She wore sweat pants, a loosely fitting tee-shirt with some meaningless name on it, and a soft woolly zip-up top. Under her eyes were dark circles; the eyes themselves, framed by round, black spectacles, were fierce, even angry. She pushed the door open a couple of feet. Crakes didn't resist; he rather liked her pluck.

"I've been trying to decide whether to come round or not."

"Oh aye."

"Yes. For the last couple of hours in fact."

"Oh."

"I finally cracked and came over."

"I see."

The girl ran her hand through her hair, as though unsure how to proceed. "I live next door, in the house attached to yours." She paused and then sucked her teeth, making a high-pitched sucking noise. Most people probably couldn't hear it, but Crakes could.

"And we can't sleep. I can't sleep, my baby sister can't sleep. Mum can sleep because of the pills, but we can't. We're wide awake, all bright eyed and bushy tailed."

Crakes had a quick peek around her back. *No tail.* He had caught her in a lie. Not a good sign. She could be a spy, though for whom, he wasn't sure.

"It. Is. Almost. Two. In. The. Morning!" she suddenly burst out, emphasising each word with a slap on the door frame. "My. Sister. Is. Five!" *Slap, slap, slap, slap*! And then in a quieter voice, and without slapping, "I have to get her to school tomorrow."

"Oh," he said. "I'll keep my, er . . . dog under control."

She peered into the room. "Dog?" she muttered.

*Touch*é, he thought.

Her eyes widened at the state of the place. Crakes hadn't put much effort into the cleaning side of things. There were piles of food, empty bottles, tins and broken furniture everywhere. They weren't used to life on their own. Back home the eunuchs tidied away everything before you could say 'chop-chop!' He couldn't explain all that though; all the girl saw was the carnage. Her nose wrinkled. Crakes quite liked the expression. He quickly tried it himself while she wasn't looking.

"Look, just keep it down, okay?" she said, staring at his nose. "I don't want to sound like a granny, but it's late, you know?" She kicked the ground with the toe of her left shoe.

"Aye," he replied. Crakes was just about to close the door when he suddenly sensed Hamquist behind him, sword at the ready; he wanted her head. Crakes cursed under his breath. Why had he let her speak? Why hadn't he slammed the door in her face straight away? Or better still, not answered it at all. She had told him to *keep it down*. It was more of a request than a command, but the words had drawn Hamquist out anyway. By confronting a god on his hearth, she had violated their honour, and to Hamquist that meant death.

Crakes was filled with a strange sensation. Was it regret? They were huge and nasty-looking, in a nasty-looking house, in a nasty world, yet this girl was not afraid. If it were up to him, he would let it go.

But it wasn't up to him.

Take the wench now! Hamquist commanded.

Crakes balled his fist and then . . . nothing. He turned around, puzzled. There was something strange about Hamquist's command. It lacked the usual . . . what was it? Compulsion. Crakes heard the command in his mind, the same as always, but for the first time he had a choice whether to obey.

Was this part of Hamquist's fading?

Instead of striking her, knocking her into the oblivion of unconsciousness that would allow Hamquist to take her head, he said, "We'll do our best to keep it down."

"Thank you," she replied with a tired smile. "I'm Mia, by the way." She put out her hand and Crakes looked at it suspended in the air. He had been here long enough to know what the gesture meant, what he was supposed to do in return, but he left her hand alone, hovering, untouched.

Her gaze inevitably fell to his right arm, and for the first time she noticed the angry wreck of tissue. He expected her to scream, or at least grimace. Even the eunuchs pulled a queer face when they thought he wasn't looking. But she betrayed nothing. She sucked her teeth again. Crakes liked the sound. Mia reached across, picked up his left hand and shook it with her right, twisting her wrist so their palms met.

"Pleased to meet you," she said.

Crakes said nothing, unable to speak, unable to think of what to say.

"This is where you are supposed to reply, I'm pleased to meet you too, my name is . . ." She looked at him expectantly.

"Chanticleer?" he said.

She wrinkled her nose. "Good night then," she said shortly, dropping his hand. Turning on her heel, she stalked off to the end of the drive, turned left, walked up her own drive and into the semi-detached house. Crakes watched her all the way.

As soon as she had gone, Hamquist raged over his *disloyalty*, but Crakes noticed that while he raged, he kept the noise down. He even stopped hitting chunks out of the kitchen wall. The mortal encounter had been good for him too.

To their surprise, Mia came around the next afternoon to say thank you and apologise that she had been "a bit uptight last night" and that really, as far as she was concerned, she welcomed them to the neighbourhood, as they added some much needed diversity.

At first Hamquist pointed his finger at her and said, "*Leave now, wench!*" but she just laughed.

"You're funny!" she said. "Wow, this place."

"What about it?" Crakes said.

"You've completely trashed it."

"What's trashed?"

And that was when their relationship began.

In the land of the Seraph sun, they considered themselves all knowing—not omnipotent, exactly, but not too far off. In the land of the solar sun, they were like fish out of water, floundering in their own ignorance. They needed their little Mia to explain how this world worked, tell them when to put out the rubbish bins and how to play Snap.

For her part, she claimed she liked their company; they were interesting and she had no other friends because "only idiots went to her school and she spent most of her time looking after her little sister anyway."

Crakes reflected that Mia was only their second mortal encounter that hadn't ended in death. The lady with green eyes was the first. Of course there were a few awkward moments, such as when she asked, "What exactly do you two do all day?"

Neither of them stuck to the agreed story. They were supposed to be two old hoteliers, Fred and Chanticleer, who, having travelled the world, had retired to this quiet English street of semi-detached houses. If the questions continued, they were to state calmly but firmly that they were very particular about their privacy. If curiosity persisted, Hamquist said they were instructed to end it, ". . . but make sure the body can't be found." Divine instruction at its most vernacular.

They weren't prepared for Mia, though. Someone who listened to them, someone they could unburden themselves to.

" . . . Over the years we've put ten thousand souls to the sword. I knock them unconscious and he takes their heads," Crakes said.

"What? Every one of them?"

He nodded. "We cannot rest until the justice of the gods is served. Until we have taken them beyond the vale. Until their consciousness passes on."

Crakes avoided Hamquist's name. He couldn't remember who was supposed to be whom, so to play safe he referred to Hamquist as *he*. Mia was as sharp as a skeggox, though. Nothing got past her.

"What are your names again?"

"Chanticleer and Fred."

"And which one did you say you were?"

"Pardon?"

"What's your name?"

He paused. "Fred."

"I see." Her eyebrows arched above her spectacles. "And why is it that way around?"

"I . . . I've always been Fred," Crakes said looking at Hamquist.

"Of course you have. I meant why do you . . . knock out and Chanticleer over there takes the head?"

"Because that's just the way it is. It is the natural order of things. I cannot take a life and Ham— I mean *Chanticleer* cannot *not* take a life. It is what death does—" He stopped suddenly. "I mean, it is *like* what death does." *Good save.*

"I see," she said again, eyebrows still arched. "Ten thousand sounds an awful lot."

"What are you writing down?" Crakes said.

"Nothing," she said. "Just a note to remind myself to pick up washing detergent."

"Quite a long note."

"And some bleach," she said, smiling.

"It may seem like a lot," Crakes continued, "but over a millennium, it is not so many. Only when the crime warrants the justice of the gods are we summoned."

No reaction except more scribbles.

"I can remember the name, circumstances and transgression for each and every conscience brought to justice. It is like remembering your own self. When you touch someone's mind, it seeps into you, forever."

His own mind unconsciously reached back and picked at the ever-present sore:

I can still feel the lady with green eyes.
Alive, but tormented by Erinyes.
In great pain, she reaches out to me and
Pulls me in, an entire world away.

"You sound autistic to me," she said and scribbled something else. That was typical Mia. She was always labelling them as this or that.

Maybe she only half-believed what they told her, but she didn't run away. She came to see them every day, always with her notepad, always ready to teach them something new and ask questions herself. And that itself was a puzzle.

Crakes knew enough about this world to know that a young girl who spent time with two middle-aged men, one of whom had a sword slid through his belt, was not quite right. Perhaps she was a spy after all. Or perhaps she had found in them what they found in her: a reassuring bond, a connection in this otherwise senseless place.

Mia was the reason Crakes was on edge this evening, why they were playing cards, and why he felt particularly pensive.

He stared at the mould. It had stopped listening long ago; it just blinked and moved and changed without changing.

"Come on," Hamquist said, rousing Crakes from his reverie. "What are you doing? Collecting wool?"

"It's gathering wool, *actually*."

"It's wool-gathering, *actually*," Hamquist replied, tapping his nose and winking.

"Another new mannerism," Crakes said.

The truth was they were forgetting who they were, becoming more like this world despite not belonging.

"Come on," Hamquist repeated.

Crakes sighed. The game was not going well. What did the Serendips say? The Lady's face was not smiling. He began to turn over his card, which was not easy with a stump. He had to slide out the card with his thumb and then walk the card up over his hand, turning it over and over from one finger to the next,—index, middle, ring, pinkie. Holding the card between ring finger and pinkie, he flipped it onto the pile. *Not bad for one hand*.

Crakes saw it, but too late; Hamquist was quicker. He always had been. Quicker, more graceful, calmer, more *quistful*.

"Snap!" Hamquist roared, thrusting his hand on top of the pile, palm flat.

Crakes' stump was there also, but laid on top of Hamquist's knuckles, a laggard lump of meat.

"*I'll* take those," Hamquist said, scooping up the cards and chuckling to himself. Crakes cursed, there were only a few cards left and the chance of having another go to win the pile was as slim as his codpiece was fat.

That was the problem with Snap. There wasn't always a *last chance*. He fingered his stump. He didn't want to lose this one. The stakes were too high. Flustered, he took a sip from his tankard to calm his nerves. The cherryade tasted very sweet, but very good, one of the better things about this world. He turned over the first card of the new pile with his good hand and the ritual began again.

"I forgot to tell you, we're up," Hamquist said, pausing

before adding his card to the pile.

"What?"

"We can go home."

Crakes nearly fell off his chair. "And you didn't say anything until now because—?"

Hamquist shrugged and added a card to the pile. *No snap.*

"What are we waiting for then?" Crakes said through his teeth. "Where's the Mist? Let's go."

Hamquist stared at the cards. "We have to do something first."

Crakes didn't like his tone. "What?"

"See for yourself."

Hamquist closed his eyes and Crakes prepared to receive the divine instruction. Until the lady with green eyes, the command had always been a multi-layered vision—a person, a name, a place, a time—all wrapped in a single moment, the mortal's transgression crystal-clear.

With the lady with green eyes, there had been no crime, but a stuttered, broken utterance:

G-go to the Erinyes . . . acc-accept their gift . . . and do wh-whatever they ask.

And Hamquist had been compelled to obey. He could not ignore a call for the gods' justice, but how was this justice? The Erinyes bestowed the Wandering Mist and they had travelled across worlds for the lady with green eyes. Nothing had been the same since.

The new command filled his mind. This one was just a face and a name, and an echo:

Death, yes, but the red one, the black one, or both?

Crakes' jaw almost hit the table. Hamquist's question and all that stuff about the flickering flame had not come from Hamquist at all, but was the entrails of a deity's musings—a non-sequitur with a sting in its tail. Hamquist and Crakes had been together for millennia, and in all that time there had never been anything like this. Divinity, as a rule, was not unsure. The voice was stronger this time, more powerful, more like a deity's actual bidding. But at the same time, Crakes couldn't shake the feeling that somehow they were being tricked, that somehow this wasn't justice at all. Why the question? By definition deities were supposed to be all-knowing.

"The rules here are different," Hamquist said, answering the unspoken thought. "The command is all we need to know, and then we can go home."

Home, Crakes thought and experienced a pang. At least they were back to taking lives, rather than delivering unconscious bodies to witches.

"I went to see her," Hamquist said, and Crakes noticed again how bloodshot his eyes seemed.

"Who?"

"The face."

The face of the girl they had to kill. "Why?"

Hamquist shrugged; as Mia would say, *no big deal*. Except that Hamquist had never gone anywhere without him before. Crakes began to speak but Hamquist shook his head. No more questions.

"Just play your card," he said.

Shaking slightly, Crakes tried to turn his attention to the game. Finger, finger, finger and flip. No snap. Another round gone, and then another, and another. No snap. Just five cards left.

"There is something else," Hamquist said slowly, his long grey hair flopping over the front of his face, covering one eye. It was his dark and brooding look, reserved for unsavoury tasks.

"Oh yes?" Crakes said.

"You have to . . . look, I don't know how to say this."

"What?"

"Can I write it down?"

"Just say it."

"I can write it on a piece of paper just as easily."

"For goodness sake, man!"

"I'm not a man, I'm a demigod of the first order—"

"Say it!"

"All right, all right!" he said, and then more quietly, "all right." Hamquist took a deep breath. "You have to get rid of those mustard yellow leather stockings, and absolutely *no* codpieces."

Crakes choked, spraying cherryade all over the table. "What?"

"It, er . . . it lowers the tone."

Crakes smashed his stump onto the table again. Pebbles and cards fell earthward. Again, Hamquist plucked his tankard from the air just before it hit the ground.

"The tone! The tone! It was for the tone that I did it! The cloaks were too . . . We needed something!"

"Maybe back at home but not here."

"Why?"

"I got the impression it isn't the correct . . . etiquette."

"Well, what was the *tone* of the command?" Crakes said.

"Displeased."

"I'm displeased myself."

"Oh aye."

"Yes, and . . . I'm going to ask Mia her opinion."

"I wouldn't," Hamquist said and prised another can of Special Brew from one of the round plastic holes encasing it. He seemed suddenly fascinated by the plastic, the way it bent, the way it felt. "You, er, haven't got them on now, have you?"

"You know I haven't."

"They could be on . . . you know, underneath."

"They're not."

Crakes was in the woollen breeches he used for everyday wear. The leather was for best, not for around the house. He was thankful for this small mercy. Having to remove them in front of Hamquist didn't bear thinking about.

"I will ask Mia, you know."

"Your turn to discard," Hamquist said, gathering the cards

and pebbles from the floor. He stuffed the cards into Crakes' hand and dropped the pebbles back into their original places, exact counts on each pile. The whole thing took less than a second. Crakes knew he couldn't move like that on his best day and Hamquist was now on his fourteenth tin of that brown stuff.

Thumb, finger, finger, finger, finger, draw!

"Snap," Hamquist said, his hand flat on the pack.

"You cheated!"

"Prove it."

Crakes gave a weak, slightly high-pitched giggle.

"You have three cards left," Hamquist said.

"Hiya, tramps!" Mia said, suddenly appearing at the front door, grinning. She didn't bother to knock anymore. She pulled up a chair. "What's up?" Neither of them spoke. She was so bubbly she almost bounced off the seat. "Shall I put on the kettle?"

"Not so fast, little one," Hamquist said. "Three more cards and the game is over."

"It's rude to keep playing now company is here," Crakes muttered.

"Play."

Mia watched transfixed as Crakes played his card. No snap. The second card. No snap. If Crakes could sweat, he'd be sweating now. The third card . . . no snap. The game was over.

"Ha!" shouted Hamquist, "I win. I win!"

Crakes said nothing. Sometimes he hated Hamquist.

"Don't be sad, Crakes," Mia said.

They had given up using their fake names long ago. They couldn't keep them straight, and Mia said she knew they were lying anyway. She said that the make-believe names were "all part of their narrative fantasy," whatever that meant.

"It's only a game, you know." Her bright eyes twinkled at him.

"Aye," Crakes replied, rubbing his temple. That's what you think.

"I have a new question for you today," she said.

Always a new question. "Go on."

"You say you've put ten thousand souls to the sword."

Not this again. "Aye."

"But what compels you to act?"

Recently, anything the Divine commands. Crakes looked uneasily at Hamquist.

"Well?" Mia said.

Crakes hesitated. "We . . . we enforce the natural law that binds our world together, avenging crimes against the gods, crimes committed without conscience, without remorse."

"Until they look up and see us, that is," Hamquist added.

"By which time it's too late," Crakes added.

"And does everyone believe in you?" Mia said.

"Some only believe when Hamquist's blade severs their head from their neck."

"And some, not even then."

"By which time it's too late," Crakes said.

"Aye."

"Jeez, change the record," Mia said. She thought for a moment and then added flippantly, "You two are going to Hell."

Crakes was tempted to add, *Been there actually, Mia. Not nice.* However, he knew when to keep quiet. Unlike Hamquist.

"Hell?" Hamquist asked, all interested.

"Where God sends you when you're bad."

"That's not right," Hamquist said, shaking his head.

"Yes it is, everyone knows that."

"No," Hamquist said, pouting a little and folding his gigantic arms.

"Where does God send you then?"

"Here."

For the second time that day, Crakes sprayed the table with cherryade. They all stared at the tiny red bubbles.

"Ew," said Mia.

"We can't go to Hell," Crakes said, trying to change the subject before they got hit by a bolt of lightning. "What we do is divine justice. I am the Will and Hamquist is the Way. Some call us the *Kalasians.*"

"So what exactly are you doing *here* then?"

"The Will," says Hamquist.

"A job," Crakes said, trying to use the correct vernacular for this world.

"Oh."

"Yes, we have come to enforce a god's justice," Crakes said, knowing even as he spoke the words that this was no longer true. The rules had changed. The lady with green eyes had done nothing, and yet they had taken her. And it had altered them, altered everything. They weren't meddlers, they didn't meddle, they dealt in absolutes: life and death, divine justice.

"I think I understand. Your delusion is based on an old myth. I looked it up. You think you're the Furies."

"The what?" Crakes said.

"The Furies, usually depicted as three old women, avenging the abuse of natural law. Some call them the Erinyes."

"What did you say?" Crakes asked, serious as stone.

"What?" Mia replied, her cheeks flushing.

"That word. Erinyes. It exists where we come from."

At that moment, Crakes sensed a change in Mia. She saw something new in their endless eyes, in their gravity, in their truth. She pulled away, her cheeks fading to a deathly white, the blood instinctively retreating deep into her body, ready for fight or flight. There would be no banter today. No cup of tea and plate of biscuits. No skateboarding lessons. Mia got up from the table and slowly backed away. Crakes noticed she'd dropped her precious pad of notes on the floor. Definitely flight.

"Who exactly is it that you have to . . . kill?"

"A girl."

"Oh." She took another two steps backwards before turning

and running for the door. Hamquist nodded to Crakes.

Stop her!

In less than a blink, Crakes caught up with her, blocking the exit. Mia turned and bolted in the other direction, through the back door and into the garden. In two strides he had her, clasped firmly but gently around the shoulders. She didn't try to struggle; she knew there was no point.

"Mia." Crakes could hear her heart thumping.

"Don't," she said.

"Don't what?"

"Don't kill me."

"I can't kill you. I am just a herald of death, Hamquist is the one who—"

"I know, I know," she said, frantic. "I mean, you and Hamquist, both, *don't*."

He understood then. Mia thought *she* was the girl.

"We're not going to do anything to you," Crakes said quietly.

"Then why are you holding me?"

"Because you ran away."

"But your eyes. Your voices. They were suddenly different. Real. You're actually real!"

"As mustard," he said, using one of Mia's own expressions.

For a moment she looked as though she was about to correct him, but then shook her head. Instead she said, "Who?"

"Who what?"

"Who's the girl, if it's not me?"

"It's not important."

"But—"

Crakes cut her off. "You need to listen, not ask questions all the time." She folded her hands and pulled a Mia face, but said nothing. Crakes took a deep breath. "You have to leave today and not cross our threshold again. We cannot consort with mortals and your presence will eventually be sensed by the divine. It is inevitable. Hamquist feels it. And *if* the order comes, we will not be able to stop ourselves. On the merest whim, the merest breath of a thought, your life will be forfeit. Do you understand? You are not supposed to be here. We've told you too much. Let you in too far. That wasn't supposed to happen." It was the longest speech Crakes had ever made.

"Do you know what I think?" Mia said.

"What?"

"I think you're losing faith in your gods."

His fist flew at her temple. Quicker than thought, Hamquist was beside him. His hand shot out and caught the fist less than an inch from her face.

"I would have pulled back," Crakes said.

"Perhaps," Hamquist replied, and disappeared back into the house.

"Whoa," Mia whispered, her voice shaking.

"You need to be careful. Some things are . . . instinctive."

"Right," she replied.

Crakes suddenly felt sadder than he had ever felt. He would never see her again, never hear her heartbeat, or watch her nose wrinkle, or smell her sweet breath.

Mia looked up at him, eyes red. "Why are you the one telling me?" she asked.

"I lost," he said simply. She looked puzzled. "The game of snap."

"Oh." For a moment she seemed lost in thought, until she said quietly, "I'm glad it was you." She looped her arms up around his neck, pulled him towards her and gave him the lightest, softest kiss on the cheek.

Crakes had lived for well over a thousand years and, outside of battle, had been touched maybe half a dozen times. One of those times was when Mia shook his hand. When she finally let go, he could feel the unnatural sensation of water filling his eyes. His throat went dry and he couldn't speak.

"You are so cold," she said.

"We are," he managed, half-choking on his words.

"I need to go."

"Yes."

"Shall I say goodbye to Hamquist?"

"He said he'd watch you from the window. He's not good at goodbyes."

Neither can he touch a mortal with anything but a blade. It pains him, he thought, but did not say.

Mia sniffed. She turned to leave, but then hesitated. Crakes knew she had a question. With Mia there was always *one last question*. It made him smile.

She wrinkled her nose. "What law did the girl break?" Crakes shook his head. "Just the name then."

"Why?"

"It would help me leave you . . . in peace."

Crakes glanced a little uneasily at the window. Hamquist could hear his thoughts if he was listening, which he was, and the divine could hear Hamquist's. Instead of replying, Crakes said, "I have a question for you first."

"And then mine?" she said.

"And then yours."

"Deal," she said.

"What do you think of codpieces?"

She laughed and asked why. He explained. Her face told him all he needed to know, but she shared her opinion anyway, giggling hysterically. There *was* a tone issue; perhaps the Divine was all-knowing after all.

"Now will you tell me her name?"

"I will tell you, but then you must not look at me. You must turn and go and never look back."

"I will."

He drew a deep breath. "Her name is Cairo Agonistes."

Seven

Penny

ENNY SAT ON the end of her bed in a state of agitation. There was something important she had to tell them, but she couldn't remember what it was. Her sisters were up already, Cairo clattering around the bedroom looking for socks, Charlemagne at the dresser, brushing her hair and staring into space. Her eldest sister looked tired and pale, as though she was coming down with something. Over the last few days she had become increasingly listless.

Penny leant over to the side table and picked up her cell phone; no messages. They had been in England a whole week now, and they had heard from their father only once. Feeling homesick, Penny had left a message two days earlier asking him to call, but so far nothing. She dialled the number and again it went straight to voicemail. Why did he have a cell phone if it was never on? Frustrated, she hung up.

"He'll call back, Pen, don't worry," Cairo said.

"But I don't understand it, he must have heard my message by now. What if something's happened?"

"Like what?" Cairo said.

"I don't know. What do you think, Charlie?" Charlemagne didn't reply, but continued to stare into the mirror. "Charlie!"

"What?" Charlemagne said, coming out of her daze.

"Do you think something's happened to Dad?"

"I'm sure he's fine. I'm sure he'll call us today."

Why were her sisters not concerned? Or were they just trying to make her feel better? They did that sometimes and Penny didn't like it. She usually saw more of what was going on than they did.

She saw more!

Suddenly, what she was trying to remember came to her in a flash. How could she have forgotten?

"There was somebody in our room last night!" she said.

Cairo looked up. "There can't have been."

"I'm telling you there was!"

"Are you sure?" Charlemagne said.

"Yes!"

"How come you didn't say anything then?" Cairo said, giving up on the socks and going straight for the tennis shoes.

"When?" They had only woken up five minutes ago.

"When whoever it was came in the room. You didn't yell out or anything."

"I couldn't."

"Why?"

Penny glared at Cairo and then pulled a chair over from the vanity and placed it just inside the door. She climbed onto the chair and pushed her arms towards the ceiling to make herself taller. "Look," she said, "they were just here. And I was over there." Penny pointed to her bed. "I was lying down and I couldn't move. It was as though I was paralysed. It wasn't fear exactly, although I *was* afraid and . . ." Penny knew how this next part would sound but she had to tell them. ". . . and I wanted to call out but I couldn't. As though whoever it was wouldn't let me."

Cairo laughed. "You were dreaming. Another one of your crazy dreams."

"It was not a dream," replied Penny through clenched teeth.

She stepped off the chair.

"Was it Gaffer or Ogg? Checking on us?" Charlemagne asked, rubbing her temples.

"No!" Penny knew that Charlemagne was trying to be supportive, but if it had been her grandparents, she would have said so. "Is Gaffer that tall? Is Ogg? And it was a man, anyway. Six foot five at least!"

"And what were we doing all this time while this phantom was upon us?" Cairo tied her laces. Lately she was always in a hurry to be somewhere. It couldn't be much past eight o'clock.

"Snoring," Penny said.

"I don't snore!"

"How do you know?"

"I don't, do I, Charlie?"

"I was asleep," Charlemagne said drily.

Of course Cairo didn't snore. She didn't do anything *un-attractive*. But that was beside the point. Her sisters did not believe her. Penny felt her cheeks flush red.

"So if we were quietly asleep, or at least if Charlie was quiet and I was snoring like an elephant, what did this thing do?" Cairo asked.

"It wasn't a *thing*, it was a person. He just stood there looking at us and . . . and you in particular."

"Me particularly? I don't like the sound of that! He didn't like my snoring! Then what?"

"He . . . he sniffed the air and this sort of mist filled the room. Then he disappeared."

"How spooky! No, *of course* it wasn't a dream!" Cairo said with exaggerated gravity.

Charlemagne put a hand on Penny's shoulder. "And you still couldn't move when they left?"

"I . . . I fell asleep." Just before the figure left, she'd felt a weight press down upon her. She tried to fight it, but the heaviness dragged her under. The next thing she knew it was morning and her sisters were already up and getting ready for the day. For Penny, a fitful sleeper by nature, dreamless sleep was unnatural. On waking, it had left her dazed and unrefreshed.

"Sniffing the air, you say?" Cairo arched her eyebrows.

"Yes!"

"I hope nobody had done a blow-off!" Cairo laughed, using their childhood phrase for breaking wind. Charlemagne smiled and Penny also felt a wave of happiness wash over her, but she ignored it.

"Very funny, thanks for listening." She picked up her wash bag and stormed off to the shower. When she returned, her hair dripping, a towel wrapped around her torso, both sisters were gone. In their place was Siam, who lay on Charlemagne's tidy comforter, regarding with an air of disgust Cairo's bed, which of course looked like a bomb had hit it.

"Hey girl," said Penny kneeling down to rub her back. "Do you know who it was?" Siam just thumped her tail.

Penny checked her phone again, then noticed Charlemagne had left her schoolwork on the dresser. They'd all missed some school when their mother disappeared, and all three of them had assignments to complete over the summer, though Penny had already done hers. There was her file of notes and textbooks—history, English, science. Charlemagne was supposed to be catching up on all the work from last semester. To that end, all week she had locked herself in the room Gaffer called the library. In reality it was just a large room with a desk and books stacked in chaotic piles all over the floor.

She opened the file.

The first page was blank.

The second page was blank.

The third page was blank.

The whole file was blank.

Wait! No, not quite.

In the middle of the binder, several of the pages were covered in sketches. There were figures in strange clothes, knights on horses, a cityscape covered in snow and ice, and then the same cityscape on fire. At first she thought it was a rather creative history assignment until she looked more closely. There was a girl, drawn lovingly in different poses and at different ages, her face captured against a variety of fantastic backgrounds. There was an old servant with uneven eyes holding a tray. In another sketch a handsome man stood rugged against a horse and wagon, proudly brandishing a sword and smiling. Next to that drawing, the same man crouched over a dying woman, holding her hand. Tears were in his eyes.

Some of the sketches could almost accompany the photographs downstairs: the stricken gambler, the unlucky archer and the crone. The most impressive sketch was of a lady, awesome in aspect, shimmering above her people, her expression mercurial, but with the hint of a smile. She looked like Ogg. Penny felt gooseflesh on her arms. She knew her sister's artistic capacity—or lack thereof—from the homemade birthday cards she insisted on making: the best she could do was stick figures. Where had she learned to draw like this?

"What are you doing?"

Charlemagne stood in the doorway. Her voice was flat.

Penny flushed. "Just . . . looking." Charlemagne regarded her for a moment. "I forgot my books," she said, and walked over to the vanity.

Charlemagne stopped, her eyes resting on the sketches. A sort of shadow passed over her face and in that moment Penny's sister, who was not yet eighteen, looked suddenly old. Charlemagne shook her head slightly and the shadow disappeared. She reached down and snapped the binder shut.

"Charlie, I—"

"It's all right, Penny, really," she said gathering her things.

"What are—?" Penny began, but Charlemagne had already left the room.

Penny wondered again if Charlemagne was sick. She said she was fine, but over the last few days she had become distant. Only when Ogg was around did her sister seem to revive, like a flower in the sunlight. They would sit for hours together, drinking that spiced tea. While Ogg was with her, nobody else seemed to exist. What was going on? Penny knew it sounded ridiculous, but she was convinced Charlemagne was avoiding her, avoiding them all actually, to spend time with Ogg.

She wished she could talk to Cairo about it but Cairo was, well, flighty, and had also changed since coming here, though for the better. The light that burned inside her, almost extinguished by the loss of their mother, was now brighter and more powerful than ever before. Just being near Cairo made Penny feel warmer, happier and more vibrant. Penny had to check herself when that happened, hold her emotions back. When Cairo's sun dimmed, the shade felt much colder for it, and after the last few weeks, Penny was afraid of the cold.

When their mother disappeared, Penny thought she would almost go mad with the grief and the not knowing. It felt as though her world had cracked and that a fragment of her heart was missing. Ever since she could remember, Penny had a tremendous fear of *loss*, as though the pieces that made up her being were already fragile, as if she had already suffered some great trauma. And now there was no word from her father. She shivered as she wondered if he too had somehow vanished. With an effort she shook away the thought.

What would she do today?

Perhaps she could help Gaffer in the garden again. Perhaps try *the forbidden room*. She had checked on it every day; she felt compelled to. It was always locked. She knew it was against the house rules, but she was drawn to it and besides, surely her grandparents wouldn't *really* mind. She was just curious.

Ogg said the roof had fallen in, that it was unsafe, but when Penny asked Gaffer why they didn't fix it, he became flustered and rubbed his beard as though trying to remember what the correct answer was. And there was another thing: from the outside, the roof looked perfectly intact—a bit battered, like the rest of the house, but structurally sound. She had decided that the room hid something; she knew it. Something to do with her father, from when he was younger, that Ogg didn't want them to see. But what?

No, she decided, she would not check the room today. It would only be locked, just like every other day. She would try and tag along with Cairo. For the last week her sister had breezed out of the house shortly after breakfast saying she was going for a walk. She returned later and later each day, never once explaining where she had been or asking anyone else if they wanted to come. Well, today Penny would ask to go. She fancied a walk, even though it was a bit rainy.

"Come on, girl," she said to Siam and went downstairs.

Cairo was still in the kitchen and, judging by the chaos surrounding her, had been making sandwiches. She was now in the process of wrapping them in foil. Despite her old, patched-up shorts and t-shirt, she looked stunning. It was her lush red hair, its slight curls, her huge green eyes, her flawless complexion, body, and poise. Her perfection was enough to give Penny a complex.

"Hey," she said.

Cairo spun round. "Oh . . . hi."

"Going somewhere?"

"Yes . . . it's such a nice day I thought I'd take myself off for a walk, you know, get out of the house."

"It's raining," said Penny, nodding at the shorts.

"Only drizzle, and it's going to stop."

Cairo was hardly dressed for rain, but then again she didn't seem to mind the elements. Cairo never got colds in the winter, or complained of being cold. She never sunburned in summer, or complained of being hot. Cairo put it down to good circulation; Penny just thought it was another Cairo-ism. There were many, ranging from her being the only teenager never to have a breakout—or even a single pimple—to being able to charm anything from anyone. Their father was the only person who ever refused Cairo anything, like not letting her stay in

America when he wanted them to come to England.

The kitchen door swung open and Gaffer crashed in, Cowper barking behind him.

"Morning, fiddlers!" he said. In one hand he held a huge mug of tea, in the other his car keys, and dangling from his mouth was the pipe he never actually smoked.

"Morning," the girls replied. The sisters exchanged the now customary glance that said *look what he's wearing,* which today happened to be a large, round, orange hat, his bird-nest hair poking out of the front.

"Gaffer, no dawdling now!" Ogg called from the hallway.

Gaffer grinned at them. "Where's the other fiddler?" For some reason Gaffer had taken to calling them the "fiddlers" or "fiddlers three" when they were together instead of using their names. He said it was easier for him to remember.

"She's in the library," Penny said.

Gaffer raised his eyebrows and his orange hat bobbed. "What? Again? All work and no play will make a very dull tune," he said, then added in a whisper, "Maybe you should take her out of there, get some fresh air."

"Gaffer!" Ogg called.

"Coming, dear!" he shouted back. To the girls he said, "We're just off to do a bit of shopping. Stock up a bit. Anything you'd especially like?" Cowper thumped his tail on the floor, and Siam, copying him, did the same. "Now, now . . . you can't come with us, they won't let you in." Gaffer waved his finger at the dogs. They began to whine. "Remember the last time. We were chased out after you two skidded into a stack of baked bean tins and knock them all flying. We didn't even get the dog biscuits in the end." In a quieter voice he added, "Which is all we really went in for." The dogs continued to whine pathetically and their big eyes drooped. They were such hams.

"Oh dear," Gaffer said. "Look, stay with the fiddlers and I'll bring you both a tin of heavy and maybe even a sheep brain."

The dogs stopped whining and broke out into low barks

of delight. Having listened to her grandfather's vernacular for a while, Penny knew that a "tin of heavy" meant a disgusting brown beer that he was always bribing the dogs with. The sheep brain was new, however, and the thought of it, even in a dog bowl, made Penny feel sick. It was a wonder they looked so healthy. Back home there was probably a law against serving alcohol to household pets.

"Gaffer!" Ogg boomed.

"Aye! Aye! Coming!" he yelled, cupping his hand as if it was a makeshift megaphone. Then in a whisper he said again to the girls, "Sure there's nothing you'd like?" They shook their heads. "Are you sure now?" He eyed them strangely. "Is there nothing you'd like me to do for you?"

"No, sir," said Penny automatically and then regretted it immediately. The "sir" had just slipped out.

"What's that?" said Gaffer, bobbing up and down. "It's the hat isn't it?"

"Gaffer!" The walls seemed to vibrate with Ogg's yell.

"Yes, sir!" he shouted back and winked at Penny. "Better be off. Cheerio then, fiddlers. Siam, Cowper, be good now." He put his mug by the sink and left.

As the kitchen door closed, Penny whispered, "Did he seem normal to you?"

"Normal!" Cairo laughed. "How can anyone with a hat shaped like a pumpkin seem normal!"

"No, I mean normal for him."

"Given that normal for him is certifiably insane, then yes. You know sometimes I don't think he can possibly exist. Why do you ask?"

"I don't know. He seemed on edge to me."

"If I had the gargantuan yelling at me, I'd be agitated too."

Cairo was always calling Ogg something derogatory, though not when her grandparents or Charlemagne were around.

"No, that's not it. Something else. He was acting peculiar, as though he wanted to tell us something. In fact I'm sure of it."

"Oh fiddler," said Cairo, eyes twinkling, "first a phantom drifts into our room, paralysing you with his cold stare before disappearing in a puff of smoke, and now our pathologically weird grandfather is acting *all weird*. Shocker. I wonder what's next. Charlemagne replaced by a body snatcher? Have you checked her fingerprints lately? She is looking a bit peaky."

"I'm being serious!" said Penny.

"Oh, I know." Cairo beamed.

Penny was annoyed with the phantom reference, but Cairo's charm was infectious and she couldn't help smiling back.

Cairo quickly cleared up the mess around her, or at least "tidied" it. She then stuffed the sandwiches into a knapsack along with some cold meat, chips, some fruit, a pork pie and a thermos of coffee.

"That's a lot of food," Penny said.

"I'm hungry."

"A-are you going by yourself?"

"Planning on it."

Penny leant back on the kitchen cabinet, saying nothing, and Cairo turned to the leave. She took two steps towards the door, stopped and sighed. "Oh, come on then, Pen, but hurry up and bring something to eat. You're not having any of mine."

Penny felt Siam nudge her hand. "Can we take the dogs?"

"Why not? The more the merrier," Cairo replied in a tone that sounded like she meant the opposite. She slung the knapsack over her shoulders and walked outside, not bothering to wait. Pulling on her coat, Penny opened the door for the dogs, grabbed an apple from the bowl and ran into the garden after her sister.

Even in drizzle, the garden was beautiful. She had spent the last three days helping Gaffer to bed the roses, weed the petunia beds, and even spread manure. Sucking on his imaginary tobacco, he explained to Penny how the garden was where he worked out his problems, how he liked to count the plants every night, and how he didn't feel quite right until he had "staked out his little place in the world." His eyes were sort of misty when he said it. Then, coughing something back, he took her on the grand tour, teaching her the names of everything. Apart from the roses and petunias, there were violets and white hyacinth, baby's breath and lilac hydrangea, pockets of clustering honeysuckle, lavender verbenas and geraniums.

When Penny remarked on all the shades of purple, Gaffer muttered, "Reminds me of home," adding, "the colour of royalty, you know."

The immaculate lawn was bordered by huge, healthy conifer trees that stretched southwards in a large, verdant rectangle for over an acre. The grass was very soft, not at all like the hard, yellow-green grass they had at home which hurt to walk on in bare feet. Penny supposed it was all the rain, which had stopped, probably temporarily judging by the clouds lurking in the pale blue sky.

Cowper and Siam chased each other down the garden path and then sprinted back to Penny and Cairo, and then down to the gate, and back to the girls again in the roundabout trajectory that only makes sense to dogs. They were on their second lap and just in front of the fence when a man stepped out from behind one of the evergreens and stopped them in their tracks. He was about thirty feet away from the girls.

"Who's that?" Penny whispered.

"Don't worry," Cairo replied nonchalantly.

"Hey!" the man shouted. He was tall and thin and wore a brown suit and yellow cravat. He pointed at Cairo, but his small watery eyes were fixed on Penny.

"I know this one," he said. "This one's been past here every day this week. But I don't know this one." He moved his outstretched arm in a long sweeping arc and pointed at Penny. "Who are you?"

"I beg your pardon?" said Penny, bristling.

"Hard of hearing, are you?"

"No," Penny replied, "just—"

"Yes?" he interrupted. "Well, I'll repeat myself then." He raised his voice. "This one,"—he pointed at Cairo again—"this one, I say yes!" He then swung his arm and pointed at Penny. "This one, I say no! Who is it? What is it? *Why* is it?"

"And what business is it of yours?" Penny said.

"Mine?" His eyes bulged. "I watch when the mistress is away." He jerked his thumb towards the house.

"They're not away," said Penny.

"Liar! I saw them leave."

"They only went to the shops!" said Penny, making deliberate use of her newly acquired British English. The "shop" at home was where you took your car when it needed as service. Here the word covered everything from a tiny bodega selling newspapers to an entire department store.

"Then they are away, which makes *me* the ward."

The man was clearly deranged. "How did you get in here?" Penny asked.

"I crossed the threshold."

"What?"

"He hopped over the fence," Cairo whispered.

"But—"

"I ask the questions!" he snapped. "Who are you? What are you? Why are you?" He rubbed his forehead manically as though he had a headache.

"Fr-eak," muttered Cairo in a quiet voice. Then she said, smiling, "We are guests, you already know that."

"If you are staying *here,* then why are you going *there*?" He pointed towards the trees.

"For a walk," Cairo said.

"Well . . . well stay on the path," the man said and abruptly disappeared back through the trees to the fence. They heard a scrambling sound, and an "oof!" as he hit the ground on the other side.

"Who was that guy?"

"I don't really know, but he always comes out just as you

reach the bottom of the garden. He's like the troll under the bridge, always asking the same questions. But he's harmless really. I asked Gaffer and he said the poor man's obsessed with Neighbourhood Watch. Told me to tell him we're guests. It's like the magic word that sends the troll away. Gaffer said something about him never getting over the war."

"Which war?"

"He didn't say."

"And what if you're not a guest?"

"Who knows? He looks pretty harmless to me."

At the bottom of the garden was an ornate grey wall with a gate in the middle and a rockery on each side. Catsfoot, forget-me-nots and foxgloves were planted in pretty clusters and water ran over the granite into a pool before being pumped back to the top by a small electric motor. Two newts flicked in and out of view as the breeze played on the water's surface. The placement of the stones and the small clusters of flowers were geometrically perfect. *Gaffer must have a* lot *of problems to work out*, Penny thought.

"Come on," Cairo said, holding the gate. To their left, golden corn came up past Penny's waist and to the right was a trail about half a foot wide. The trail served as the border between the field and the perimeter of hedgerows that made up the loose row of houses that were their grandparent's neighbours. Each section was about a hundred feet long.

As they moved from one house's periphery to the next, Penny could sense the presence of the different families. One garden belonged to a family who played sport together and ran up and down their back yard, even the mother. Penny could feel their feet breaking the grass as they hit a shuttlecock back and forth, playing bowls, soccer, volleyball. They were athletic and gifted, especially the mother, who at one time could have played badminton in the Olympics but for the hole in her heart. Her family worried about her, and in the quiet corners of the night she worried herself, but never let it show.

The next garden was rarely used. The family stayed indoors with the curtains shut as though they were hiding something— or at least that was the assumption. The two teenage boys had few friends because they were painfully shy and awkward and preferred books to people. The two parents were of a nervous disposition and kept to themselves. In the evening they enjoyed tea and lamb sandwiches by the fire. The mother had been in a bad car crash and didn't like loud noises or bright lights. A rumour circulated that the father was once convicted for abuse. It began mysteriously at about the same time he called the local shopkeeper to account for the odd ten pence or so that was always forgotten in the change. The parents did not know about the rumours. They were avoided and could not understand why. The children knew, taunted as they were at school, but could not bring themselves to say anything. They were an oddly English family. Penny wanted to weep.

"You're very quiet," Cairo said as they walked.

"I'm just thinking."

"What about?"

"Nothing."

Penny never talked about her insights to anyone, not even to her mother. For as long as she could remember she had been aware of a strange intuition lingering at the borders of her consciousness. She had always been a creative child. She loved to pretend, and at first she believed this was a by-product of her already wild imagination. But in recent months these intuitions were becoming clearer and stronger, the flashes of perception as frequent as they were impossible. Sometimes, when events unfolded around her, she could anticipate what was coming next. She got a chill just thinking about it. It wasn't natural.

The sisters continued to walk along the circumference of the fields, turning south away from the residential area towards the forest.

"Where exactly are we going?" Penny asked.

"You'll see."

Entering the forest, Penny and Cairo picked their way through the undergrowth until they came upon a clearing. It was a little oasis, a few hundred square feet of grass covered in buttercups, daisies and red clover. Two storks floated on the surface of a pond. A canopy of oak leaves shaded them overhead. It was silent except for the sound of their steps and the buzzing neurosis of insects.

A figure sat at the table, looking out over the water, his back to them.

Eryn! The boy with the crooked teeth and dangerous eyes. So this was who Cairo had been sneaking off to meet every day. To his left was a tarpaulin held up by three branches tied together in a makeshift fly tent. No wonder he looked a little rough at the wake.

"Hi," Cairo called out so as not to startle him.

His head remained fixed on the pond, his shoulders tensed. "You've brought someone," he replied coldly.

"Er . . . yes, my sister."

"I told you not to tell *anyone*," he snapped. He did not turn around.

Penny tensed. At least at the wake he had shown a little courtesy.

"I know . . . but . . . I thought it would be all right," Cairo said, flustered.

"Did you bring the food?"

Cairo handed him her backpack and he tore open the flap. For the next five minutes they stood in an uncomfortable triangle of silence. Penny did not like the way Cairo looked at him. It was as though she was hypnotised, as though this man was doing to her what Cairo unconsciously did to just about everyone else. Eryn ignored both of them while he devoured the food. First the sandwiches, then the cold meat, then the chips and then the fruit. He barely paused for breath.

His hair was red. Not the golden red of Cairo's, but a kind

of dusky dark red that hung to his shoulders. His eyes were green, like pebbles of jade placed in ice-cold water, and the corners slanted ever so slightly upwards suggesting an Asiatic heritage. His face was thin and chiselled with a long aquiline nose, and he had the reddest lips she had ever seen on a man. If he wasn't so dishevelled and unfriendly, he would be beautiful.

Penny checked herself. *What am I thinking?*

It was incredible, though, how much better he looked than he had at the wake. Was all he needed some food? She wondered at his age. At the wake she would have guessed mid-twenties, but now? He had the face of a youth, maybe eighteen—Charlemagne's age—but the air of a much more mature man. His face was no longer that painful, dusky yellow but a creamy, flawless pearl, offset by a dark cloak, not at all appropriate for the summer. Underneath the cloak were more warm layers: a hairy black sweater, dirty black jeans and boots that looked like they had seen better days. Clearly the shabby suit he wore at the wake was for best.

Eryn finished eating and then washed it all down with steaming coffee from Cairo's Thermos.

"I have an apple too, if you want it," Penny said, trying to make friends but then worrying she might sound sarcastic.

Eryn regarded the apple hungrily. His gaze then shifted to Penny; he looked through her rather than at her, as though trying to avoid her eyes. His head twitched a couple of times and then he smiled suddenly. "Thank you. That's *very* kind but"—his voice was soft, almost honeyed—"how about I *trade* you something for it?"

"There's no need, you can have it."

"Oh but there is," he said, still smiling. Penny threw him the apple so as not to get too close. "Thank you." Four or five bites and it was gone. He wiped his mouth with the back of his hand and threw the empty knapsack back to Cairo. "Thank you," he said again, and after a pause added, "both of you." He drew a silver hip flask from his pocket.

"Why are you living here?" asked Penny, her curiosity getting the better of her.

"She didn't tell you?" He flicked his eyes to Cairo.

"No."

"And you don't know?"

"How could I?"

"I thought you knew *everything*," he said.

"I don't," said Penny, casting an angry glance at Cairo, wondering what her sister had been saying about her. Cairo shook her head, but whether at her or Eryn she couldn't tell.

"Then perhaps it's better left unsaid." Eryn took a long pull on the flask, wincing at the taste. He then coughed and took another swig. He wiped his lips with the back of his hand and peered into the flask's mouth, as though contemplating more. Penny couldn't help staring, her eyes drawn to his captivating face.

"Don't look at me like that, girl. I don't answer to you," he rasped without moving his head.

Penny said nothing, afraid to anger him further. Eryn was clearly not stable and Penny could sense the stress cascading from Cairo in waves; the air was thick with it. Whatever reaction Cairo had expected from her new friend, it was not this. Penny almost regretted coming, but then she would never have seen what her sister was up to. And despite the hostility, there was something about him. She couldn't quite put her finger on it, but her intuition was burning; there was definitely more to him than met the eye.

Suddenly the dogs skidded between them, barking playfully. Cowper ran back and forth and then began to lick Penny's hand. Siam jumped up at Cairo and then, failing to get a reaction, jumped up at Eryn instead. Their clamour dispelled the tension and Siam seemed to have taken it upon herself to lick Eryn into good humour. At any rate, he began to laugh until finally he murmured, "Down girl, that's enough now."

Siam turned over and Eryn tickled her on the belly, her legs twitching with pleasure.

"I have a dog," Eryn said gently.

"Yes," said Cairo, her tone artificially bright, "where is he?"

"Hunting," replied Eryn. "He'll be back at nightfall with a rabbit or deer something."

"Dogs don't hunt deer," Penny blurted.

"This one does," he snapped, but then suddenly laughed and shook his head, his red curls bouncing from side to side. "You must excuse me, ladies, I am not the paragon of charm I once was. You could say I've fallen on bad times." He looked up and for the first time met Penny's eyes. With an apparent effort he said, "I . . . I am glad you've come." He turned his attention back Siam, scratching her belly as she licked his hand.

"You seem so different from a week ago," Penny said.

"What?" The streak of venom was suddenly back in his voice before he checked himself again. "Well, if I am different, it's thanks to the care of your lovely sister."

Cairo blushed and looked at her feet. "It's nothing," she said.

"Nothing? Food, whisky, your company, that's not nothing!" Eryn broke into an uncontrollable, lung-wrenching cough.

"Oh!" Cairo reached out to him, placing her hand on his back. "Your poor cough!"

"Don't worry, that really *is* nothing. It's getting better. *I'm* getting better. If it wasn't for this infernal damp weather they have." He gestured with his arm, as if to take in the whole country.

"I thought you said you were from around here," Penny said.

"I said I knew your grandparents. Not the same thing. Are you from here?"

"Well, no, but . . . we're from America."

"Of course you are," he said, almost sarcastically. "You know, I think it's time you were going. I have things I need to attend to."

"So soon?" The hurt was embarrassingly clear in Cairo's voice, her face drained of all colour. Penny had never seen her in awe of anyone.

"Come back tomorrow." He took Cairo's hands. "Tomorrow will be a special day." He smiled, and just like that his mood had swung again, his voice rich, his aspect charming. "And to you, Penny," he said, again looking slightly beyond her, "you thought I'd forgotten, didn't you? Forgotten, but too polite to say anything. Well, I have something." Eryn rummaged around in his pocket. "Ah, here it is."

His fingerless glove pulled out a small, grubby-looking glass ball. It reminded Penny of the small crystals that hung on the chandeliers in the curry restaurant they sometimes went to back home. "Believe it or not, this is a family heirloom, but let's see what your glyph eyes make of it."

Glyph?

He tossed it to her. Penny flapped at it but missed and it rolled into the bracken. The throw was good but catching things had never been Penny's forte.

"Whoops!" Eryn chuckled, but not unkindly.

"Sorry," she said, stooping to pick it up, reaching between the vegetation. Suddenly Cowper was at her side also trying to forage for it, growling softly. "Easy boy," said Penny, picking it out. For some reason the crystal disturbed the dog. It was probably the strange light it refracted. He was still snapping around her ankles when Penny put it in her pocket.

"Thank you," she said.

"It's nothing. Just a little something in exchange for your apple. One symbol of knowledge for another."

Penny didn't know what to say, so she said "thanks" again.

"Don't thank me yet," he replied, eyes twinkling.

Instinctively the dogs sensed they were about to leave and came to take their slobbery goodbye of the stranger. Eryn knelt down and the dogs licked his face, and then suddenly impatient, they barked and ran out of the clearing. Eryn gave a slight bow to both of the girls and then without another word he, too, set off with a limping gait in the other direction. Cairo stared after him.

"He's never given me anything," she said quietly. Only when he was completely out of sight did she turn to go. At first they walked in silence. The dogs followed at their heels, occasionally yapping, occasionally tumbling, but with less gusto than before. It was as though the energy had gone out of the day. Cairo picked up a stick of willow and swished at the corn as they walked home in silence.

When they reached the garden Penny saw someone's head flash out from behind one of the spruces, but it was only for an instant. "Who was that?"

"Where?"

"Someone behind the trees, watching us."

"I didn't see anything. The troll probably."

"It didn't look like him. He was tall. "

"It was him," Cairo said indifferently.

Outside the house, Cairo mumbled something about taking a nap and disappeared inside.

Cairo never napped; she was annoyed with Penny. Cairo hadn't actually said anything and she was trying not to show it but Penny could feel it. Cairo had clearly been expecting to spend most of the day with Eryn, but he'd cut it short and Cairo blamed her sister. Penny sat on the bench outside the back door, her hand gently petting Siam.

Well, that was all very awkward.

Eryn reeked of trouble. The grandparents did not like him and he was given a wide berth at the wake. He lived rough, scrounged food, and he was using Cairo dreadfully. Stealing whisky from their grandparents? Worse than all of that, though, was the affect he had on her. Flighty, lackadaisical, laid back Cairo seemed suddenly and unconditionally devoted. To *him*.

Unconsciously, Penny's thoughts drifted back to her lost mother. If only she was here, she would know what to do, what to say to Cairo. But her mother was gone. She shivered as an image of her mother filled her mind, not from life, but from her recurring nightmare. The dream was always the same: a cold, moonless night with a storm rolling in over a vast and alien blue-black sea. Two huge figures stepped out of the night. One carried a woman slung over his shoulder, her feet and hands bound. Three cloaked women waited for them. As the two figures approached, the women clapped and cawed. They were very beautiful, as fair as anyone Penny had ever seen, except that she knew their terrible secret. She could see their insides. They were black and seething and their dark thoughts threatened to consume everything around them. It was like staring into a pit of serpents. The unconscious woman was laid ceremoniously at their feet. The victim's face cast up to the sky, her expression frozen in anguish and pain. It was her mother.

Penny had awoken screaming, her skin wet with the rain of the storm but later she told herself it was sweat. What else could it have been? The dream did not fade like the others but became more vivid, imprinting itself on her consciousness until she was convinced it was real, until she was afraid to close her eyes again.

Her train of thought was broken by something cutting into the top of her thigh.

The crystal.

She didn't know why Eryn had given it to her. It was so random. Perhaps he did not want to be beholden to her, even for something as small as an apple. Perhaps this was all he had. The glass was tight against her jeans and she had to pull it out with two fingers. It was indeed like something that had fallen off a chandelier—a miniature disco ball.

A family heirloom, he had said. His? Then why give it to her? The glass caught the light and refracted it onto the back of her hand in a rainbow. For some reason Penny began to count the colours, trying to separate out the seven hues, and as she did so, everything around her changed.

Eight

THE LONE MERCHANT'S wagon made its way across the great plains. It was a cold clear morning, not yet dawn, the stars still in the sky. The only sound was the soft clump of horses' hooves and the occasional chink of a bridle.

Penny gasped.

What was happening?

One moment she was sitting on a bench, the next, she was here. Thoughts not her own flooded her mind. She was returning from the Thessaly fair, weary but in high spirits. The journey had been worthwhile. A village worth of gold had been won through trade, gambling, and yes, if truth be told, a little cheating.

Penny pushed the thoughts away. *This is not real*, she told herself. *It can't be real. Focus on what you can see. Grasp onto something solid.*

She concentrated on the view through the flap in the front. The sky looked familiar, the stars, the smell of the place, the tang of sea salt in the air, but at the same time her surroundings were completely alien. Yet somehow she knew that to the south were the fertile lands of the Gildas, to the north were the westerly Acraphean cities of Montoch and Cyrodil, and to the north-west, Sandor, the second largest Serendip city, and her home.

How did she know this? She had never been here.

Three other travellers, sitting on the stoop, had not yet noticed her. There was a grizzled man shaped like an enormous barrel. He turned to the others to share a joke and let out a low, full-bellied laugh. To his left was a boy who was about Penny's age and who looked a little uncomfortable. The old man slapped him on the back and the boy gave a reluctant grin. Next to him was a young woman, not much older than twenty. She was laughing, enjoying the joke.

"Hello?" Penny said tentatively, not wanting to startle them. Nobody turned around. "Hello," she repeated, louder this time. No reaction at all. Somehow, they must not have heard her.

Panicking, she made her way to the front, stepping between the large casks of wine. She felt dizzy, almost as if she could float away.

Her travelling companions had blonde hair and pale complexions and their voices sang with an unusual lilt. Penny tried to make out what they were saying but heard more in her mind than from their words.

The boy was nearest. She took a deep breath and tapped him on the shoulder. Her hand passed right through him, but she felt . . . everything; his consciousness became part of her, overwhelming her, sweeping her own identity away. She had to hang on. She tried to push against his thoughts but instead found herself looking out through alien eyes. She felt strange, physically different. It was the boy. She was inside the body of the boy!

"The Golden Lady obliged us, eh?" said the old man, turning and looking straight at her, at *Offa*. She was fading rapidly now, rising above herself. With a final effort, she called out, but there was no sound. Penny was no more. Her name was Offa.

"Yes, Uncle," he replied.

Offa felt snug under the woollen blanket; it had kept his legs warm during the chill of the night. Sitting side by side, they took it in turns to take the reins and lead the horses. They changed over at every passing farm, which in this part of the world meant at least five or six miles.

His uncle Beortrich set an unhurried pace, slowing often to light his pipeweed and take a draw from his wineskin. In contrast, Offa liked to take the horses at a clip. They had to get home before the dawn and besides, the sooner his shift was over, the sooner he could thrust his hands back underneath the blanket. It was his turn now and he could not feel his fingers. His uncle kept telling him to stop the horses breaking into a trot to prevent them from tiring, but Offa's eyes were always straining forward, looking for the next Tanist post that marked out the land in the Thegn-Weld. Finally he saw it. The signpost showed a kite, an ox and a golden ball and underneath in golden letters, the name of the landowner, *Tanist Eodred.*

"Cynne," he said, passing the reigns.

"Thank you, coz," she said, taking them eagerly in her mittens. His cousin, Cynneforth, liked to keep the reins as long as possible and would often try to hold onto them well after her turn. Offa felt bad about this, as though somehow he wasn't doing his share.

"I have no gloves," he mumbled to point out that he had forgotten them in the rush to leave.

"Aye, pumpkin, we know your hands are delicate-like." Beortrich laughed. His uncle never wore gloves, but then he had his pipeweed and wineskin to warm him.

"It's what comes of being a born on high," joined in Cynne.

"Then thank the Lady we're from the wrong side of the family," said the man, still chuckling. "Don't know what I'd do if I was from the pumpkin patch."

Although Offa knew they were only joking, their words upset him. His cousin and uncle didn't know how inadequate he felt. His family was one of the most important in Sandor, and yet he was in awe of his less highborn uncle and cousin. In truth, he idolised them; his uncle although an old man, had been a hero in the war of Sigon, more than fifty years ago, and Cynneforth had graduated first in her class at the Ecole. She was destined to be a great Hale, a healer of wounds.

"You all right, Offa?" the man said, slapping him heartily on the back.

"Yes, yes, Uncle, I'm fine," Offa said, trying to smile.

"What an adventure, eh?" his uncle said.

"Yes, sir."

"No need to call me sir. I'm not a Sir, as you know."

"Yes, Uncle."

The man raised his eyebrows and grinned at the girl. She gave a small chuckle in return and pulled on the reins. Offa fidgeted. They were going too slowly; they would never make it back in time. It seemed like such a good idea yesterday, but now it was almost dawn and Sandor was still two leagues away. His uncle gave him another sideways glance. "The great Thegn Fair! We're rich now, eh?"

"Yes," replied Offa.

"Offa's already rich uncle."

"Yes, but nothing like having your own ill-gotten gains, eh? Grr . . . Ha-ha! What are you going to do with your share, Cynne? A new robe to charm all those young suitors that snap at your heels? Eh? I know, I know."

Cynne coloured. "I was thinking of getting a new sword," she said abruptly.

"Ha-ha! That's right! Poke 'em away! Begone, foul suitors! Plenty of time for that."

So their uncle hadn't heard. Offa knew Cynne already had a suitor, someone she had been walking out with for months. And he was high in Serendip society, as high as Offa's parents. Was she too embarrassed to tell Beortrich? And what would her suitor think of Cynne being away, tonight of all nights?

"And what about you, Offa?" Beortrich asked.

Offa didn't reply. He was distracted by a new thought. His uncle had said they would be back in time for the Feast. He'd promised, but they were not even close. They had left at dawn the day before and journeyed all morning to where the Thegn-Weld met the border of Serendip lands. It was midday before they'd set up their stall. The market was the largest gathering of Thegns and commonfolk Offa had ever seen. Even Castagna didn't have a market this big. They came from all corners of Enninmyra's hinterlands and continued to arrive all afternoon.

As darkness descended, they lit torches and began feasting, drinking and making merry. As the night wore on, Offa's uncle seemed to lose all interest in getting back to Sandor. Instead, they played the bones with Thegns and commonfolk into the early hours. They accumulated more copper and bronze coins than Offa thought possible, but as it got late he became anxious.

What would his parents think?

He had never done anything like this. Cynne was bound to get in trouble too. They said her father had a vicious temper after a night on the sour beer and she had no mother to restrain him. Offa felt bad for her.

"Offa?" Cynne said.

"Huh?"

"Got wax in your ears, lad?" Beortrich said.

"Lost in dreams again," added Cynne.

"I wasn't."

"What were you thinking about then?" Cynne asked.

"Oh . . . nothing. Do you really think my father won't mind us being late?"

"Oh, he might," said the old man with a chuckle.

"But you said last night that he wouldn't!"

"Aye."

Offa threw up his arms in frustration. The horses trotted slowly on. Offa thought about pulling the reigns away from his cousin to try to spur them forward, but knew it would do no good. Even if they galloped the rest of the way, the Feast of Enninmyra would be over with first light and dawn was already breaking. Offa bit his nails.

"What time did you tell my father we would be back?"

"Time?" Beortrich replied, cupping his hand and lighting his old catlinite pipe. "I didn't tell him any time."

That was peculiar. His father was very particular. He would have wanted to know. "Didn't he ask?"

Beortrich puffed on his pipe. "No."

"Don't worry, Offa," Cynne said. "We'll just blame it *all* on Uncle."

The old man chuckled again and blew a smoke ring.

"But it is the Feast!" Offa said. "We are honour-bound to spend it with our kind, within the threshold. It is an insult to the Lady and our kin not to."

"Exactly," Cynne said. "How else do you think we could get into the Thessaly Fair unrecognised? Your golden curls alone would have made them wary, but everyone knows that *no* Serendip walks abroad on the day of the Feast, so nobody even suspected. The poor Thegns didn't know what hit them. Do you think they would have come to our table if they did?"

"Maybe," said Beortrich, "but we would have a got a crack on the head when we pulled out the bones! Grr-ha-ha!"

"At the very least." Cynne laughed.

"Then you, my dear, would have had to fix our wounds— my little Hale-in-waiting," Beortrich said.

"We haven't done heads yet, Uncle. Infestations, achromatic fevers and broken limbs I can do, but the head and any part of the chest below the sternum and you're out of luck."

"What does that mean?" asked Offa.

"It means we'd be better off keeping in one piece if we can manage it," replied his uncle, taking another puff on his pipe.

They had passed themselves off as simple Thegns. An old knight and his grandchildren trying to make a living on the road by trading in home-brewed ale and running a knuck-lebones table on the side. The table itself was painted with an effigy of the Golden Lady to bestow luck on the players. Beortrich wore an old chain-mail hauberk and carried a sword with a rusted hilt. He didn't even bother wearing a belt, so instead of being held in tight to his body, the chainmail draped comically around his legs, completing the image of the sad old warrior. The sword's blade was engraved with the Lady's smiling face but, as it was never drawn, the flaw in the disguise didn't matter.

There were many other gaming stalls, but Beortrich offered the best odds: double the pot plus a bronze for beating the house. They had to lose occasionally to ward off suspicious eyes, and at losing Beortrich was a master. He would effortless-ly slip shaved bones into the game—a heavily weighted pair to produce a poor score for him, and another pair to produce a high score for his customers. When his throw was a bad one, he would shout out loudly in disgust, cursing his fortune, cursing the Lady of Serendip herself.

For the next few throws there would be no room at the stall, the commonfolk believing that to take the Lady's name in vain would surely lead to a bad run. Beortrich would lose a few more times, just to whet the appetite, and then on his next turn he'd slip the normal bones back in and take the pot throw after throw. The players would eventually thin out and Beortrich would begin the pantomime all over again.

On the journey there, Offa had asked, "But why do you need shaved bones? Surely if you are trying to lose and want your opponents to win, you can? Why doesn't the Lady help you herself? You have the gift."

His uncle had chuckled. "Always straight to the heart of it, my boy, always *straight* to the heart. The Lady is a fickle wench, our blessing *and* our curse."

Offa cringed. He was used to his uncle's irreverence, but words like these were dangerous. At the least they would invoke an obscenity charge from the authorities, worthy of a whipping.

Beortrich continued, his tone sombre, "The Lady twists fate through the smile on her face, and every time she smiles, fortune is cheated. But understand this: she only spins in a single direction, never the other. You cannot one day aim a shaft at an enemy and want it to hit, and the next day miss. It's called the Prime Motive, a cultural pattern, if you will, and the Lady runs in that groove, never wavering, strong with those who have her running in their veins, weak with those who do not. Understand?"

"No," said Offa at the same time Cynne said, "Yes."

Offa had been tutored on Possibility at the Ecole, but this kind of interpretation was curiously omitted. Offa could have sworn that the power of the Lady was only ever a blessing, the gift to her chosen people. He tried to explain this to his uncle.

Beortrich shifted in his seat. "Do they teach you nothing? You are too old to be such a baby. The Lady's path is straight, fortune impacted positively for her subject even when her subject does not wish it. If you are born with a strong sense of her within you, and very few are, the only way to stop her is to try and cheat her, to deceive the face spinning in the flames."

Offa gulped and even Cynne sucked in her breath. In a quiet voice she asked, "How do you do that, Uncle?"

"You'll see. One day. You're too young yet," was all he replied, suddenly morose as they pulled up to the perimeter of tents and banners that marked the entrance to the Fair.

Once inside, the heavy mood was soon forgotten, and by the end of the Fair they had amassed about a hundred golden ladies from the bones table and about twelve bronze lions from the wine. They still had four of their seven casks left but, if anything, Beortrich seemed pleased about that.

Dawn broke over the horizon marking the end of the Feast of Enninmyra. Beortrich took a long pull on his wineskin and passed it to Cynne. Offa just stared ahead, anxiety gnawing at him. They had missed the feast on Enninmyra. He would never be allowed out again.

"Well," Beortrich said and squeezed Offa's shoulder, "what's it all about, anyway? Is it to *honour* the Lady? Really? No, the Feast is about being with your closest kin and I have been fortunate enough to be with mine. The Lady be damned. To my favourite nephew and niece, may you always do the right thing."

"Aww," said Cynne, taking a draft, "here's to that." Cynne's tone was light, but Offa could see the welling in her eyes. He felt it too. He loved his uncle and cousin. Their friendship meant everything to him. Cynne quickly wiped her eyes with the back of her hand and passed the wineskin to Offa. He regarded it for a moment as the sweet aroma of manderlay filled his nostrils, and then took a swig. Beortrich relit his pipeweed. He was smiling.

"Do you think we'll be denounced by the Manciple?" Offa asked.

Beortrich took a deep puff on his pipe. He looked up at the sky for a moment and then blew out the smoke. "I'd like to see him try," he replied.

Offa's uncle was already out of favour with the holy order—and possibly the gods themselves—but his brother had married into high Serendip blood, or a "pumpkin" as Beortrich called them. Offa supposed their crowns of office did rather look like pumpkins—orange, puffy, and divided into segments that ran from the top of the crown to its base. Offa used to think they were quite regal before his uncle compared them to a vegetable.

Either way, it would take a brave Manciple to castigate him openly. Half a century ago, Beortrich had fought in the final years of the war of Sigon—the "bloody end" it was called—when all sides lost faith in the possibility of peace. It was said that Beortrich was terrible to behold in battle. Offa knew the scrolls by heart, every battle, every race, every great deed. Of course Beortrich was old now and some said too fond of the wineskin and pipeweed. The lines of blood and fighting had become smoothed by the stoutness of his face. Some even said the scrolls flattered his uncle, but Offa refused to believe it.

The wagon rolled slowly on. A fence post with a sign showing a yellow crescent moon on a blue background with the words "Tanist Eadbald" announced the border of a new farm. Beortrich put down his pipe and rubbed his hands. For the first time in their journey Offa thought his uncle looked tired. He was over eighty now, although that was not *so* old. Offa had another uncle who was a hundred and seventeen, but admittedly he largely stayed indoors these days.

"Let me carry on, Uncle," Cynne said, the reins cradled in her padded mittens. "Please."

Beortrich hesitated for a moment. "All right, child, thank you."

They were now close enough that they would soon be able to see the city gates on the horizon. Sandor was the third largest city in West Seraphina, rivalled only by the capital, Castagna, and Khare way up in the North. Cyrodil, an ebony city of stone and smoke just to the east, was also bigger, but that was a colony of the House of Acraphea—the other victors of Sigon—a dark, powerful race, with the gift of foresight.

Cyrodil was ceded to the Acrapheans as part of the treaty of Sigon. Before then the far North was the exclusive domain of the stone-wielding Visigottes, now long gone, scattered to become Forgotten.

Putting the wineskin aside, Beortrich said, "Ah, that's better, that hit the—" He broke off. His face became suddenly grey and his eyes took on a peculiar aspect.

"Uncle," Cynne said, "what is it?"

Beortrich sniffed the air.

"Uncle?" Offa said.

"Something's wrong."

"What?"

"Cities are burning," Beortrich said.

"Not Sandor!" Cynne cried.

Offa could smell it too, a faint but distinct tang of smoke mixed with something else, a sweet smell. On the horizon, the orange and red that Offa had assumed was the sun refracted through cloud now looked like something else.

Fire! But that was impossible, surely?

"Hold the horses still a moment," Beortrich said to Cynne in a strained voice, then he disappeared into the back of the wagon.

"What's going on?" Offa asked in a whisper.

"I have no idea, but he can't mean Sandor." Cynne didn't sound sure, but perhaps she was right. Thegns often had fires at this time of year to purge the farmland. The smell could be coming from outside the city. And the great towers of Cyrodil were always burning things. But then the smoke wouldn't drift this far south.

In the distance, Offa could just make out what his uncle had already spied: four horses galloping towards them at a break-neck pace, eating up the ground in huge strides. They were not the farm horses of this land; they were huge coursers, built and bred for war, dressed in the dark armour of Acraphea. They were mounted Fyrd warriors, the knights of the east.

"The Fyrd? Here?" Cynne whispered with a gasp.

Offa was excited. To see the Fyrd in the flesh was like seeing a story step out of the scrolls. He had only seen one Fyrd knight before, and that was at a carnival so it didn't really count. But why were they here? Cyrodil was thirty leagues away.

Beortrich appeared at the front of the wagon wearing the old hauberk and sword, this time with the thick leather belt to hold the armour in place over his thighs and trunk. Offa thought it looked less amusing now than when he was pretending to be a knight.

"Give me the reins." He pulled the wagon hard and left, off the dirt track and onto a wooded path running alongside one of Eadbald's fields. To the oncoming horses they would look like farmers returning home from the market.

"Uncle, what is it?" Cynne said.

"Maybe nothing, but I've a bad feeling in my bones."

"But can't we hail them? They are guests in our land," said Offa. His uncle said nothing but carried on alongside the field's perimeter. Their horses were almost cantering but somehow Beortrich made them look unhurried. It was an old talent.

The knights were almost upon them, and now that they were closer Offa could see the magnificent weapons hanging from their backs—skeggox battle-axes for close quarters, and long, lethal composite bows for distance.

"Their formation!" Offa said, looking over his shoulder in awe.

"Yes, they are riding in a diamond, the war footing. The question is why?" Beortrich reverted unconsciously to high speech.

"I still think we should hail them," said Offa.

Beortrich turned. "If they pass us, chalk it up to my war wound itching. If they stop, do not hesitate to try and work the art in our favour—I know you both have it, I can feel it in you. And whatever you do, do *not* tell them we are Serendips."

"Why?" asked Offa.

"No questions now," Beortrich replied, his expression grim.

The wagon was now about four hundred feet from the highway. The knights galloped past. Beortrich breathed a sigh of relief, though his face was still etched with concern. Offa noticed that even Cynne had perspiration on her brow despite the chill of the morning. They continued away from the road and down the path. After a moment, all that could be seen of the coursers was a faint trail of dust.

Offa relaxed. "Shall we turn back now?"

"Wait," snapped Beortrich, not letting up on the reins.

Offa huffed and dangled his arm out of the wagon trying to catch an ear of corn. He wondered if his uncle thought too much of the old times. The Fyrd were vassals and knights to the House of Acraphea in the same way that the Thegns were vassals to the Serendips. They were charged with *keeping* the peace, and there had been no hostility between the lands of Enninmyra and Acraphea for fifty years. Even then, attacking an unarmed wagon was unheard of; it was against the disciplines of war. Offa sighed, it would have been something to see them up close. But perhaps his uncle was right. The wagon rolled on.

"Uncle," said Cynne in a quiet voice, "they've turned around."

Offa pivoted in his seat. It was true. The knights were galloping back towards them, veering off the highway and cutting across the fields, heading straight for their wagon.

"By our Lady, here we go," muttered Beortrich.

"Ho there!" hailed the point of the diamond as they rode up. The three others fell in behind him.

"Whoa!" Beortrich said, reining in the horses.

The lead knight tipped his head slightly. "Greetings from Lord DelaStrang of the House of the Fyrd."

Offa marvelled at his strange appearance. He wore a black plate that matched the armour of the horses, but no visor. His breastplate comprised discs inlaid with ivory, the pattern of which was repeated on his shin and arm guards. He had long, lignite hair, and hair on his upper lip, but no beard. Offa had never seen hair so black. Their skeggox axes were strapped over their left shoulders, their bows and small quivers over the right.

"Hail and well met from Tanist Eadbald of the House of the Thegns," replied Beortrich in the same high speech.

"Where are you going, travellers three?" DelaStrang replied, his accent thick with the east.

"Returning to our farm," replied Beortrich.

Farm? thought Offa. They weren't Thegns; they had no farm. They were returning to Sandor and of the grand House of Serendip. Offa knew his father would be mortified. The etiquette was to hail guests from foreign regions, not lie to them. But Offa knew his uncle was an honourable man; if he was lying, he had his reasons.

Offa glanced at Cynne. She stared blankly into space, her expression inscrutable, almost vacant. Perhaps she thought that's what a farmer's daughter looked like. She fingered something beneath her woollen cloak.

"Returning to your farm," the knight repeated, now in common tongue. "Then why the hauberk, old man?"

"We are returning from the Thessaly Fair. We have travelled through the night to reach home, and these roads can be dangerous."

The rising sun glinted off the ivory in the knight's breast-plate. Beortrich's hand rested on the crystal pommel of his sword.

"Ah yes, the great Thessaly Fair. Even I've heard of it." He stroked his beard. They made no motion to leave. One of the coursers snorted. The silence that followed was heavy, and grew heavier.

"Why the inquisition, DelaStrang of the House of the Fyrd?" Beortrich said.

Offa gulped. For a farmer to challenge a knight was audacious, bordering on disrespectful. True, Thegns and Fyrd were equals under the treaty of Sigon, but they themselves were supposed to be common landsmen, not knights.

"Duty, old sir. There is some business the Fyrd have in these parts." DelaStrang hesitated again, then turned to his men and made the signal to move out.

Offa wanted to say something, to hail the knights in high speech as Beortrich had done, but he dared not. For years he had dreamt of these warriors and those like them and now, because of his uncle's warning, he could not say anything at all. They would only remember him as a little boy in an old man's wagon.

DelaStrang shifted in his seat and turned back towards them. "One last question, travellers three. What are your wares?"

"Just a little ale and wine," replied Beortrich.

"And some knucklebones," piped Offa.

There! He had spoken at last.

Cynne sucked in her breath. What was wrong with her? It was the truth. Anyone could see that their single wagon wasn't big enough to hold enough casks, if that was their only means of trade. The knight would have realised that straight away. Traders of wineskins and sour beer had at least three wagons in a train.

The knight turned to him and smiled. "Knucklebones," he said slowly. "Is that so?"

Offa flushed. "Yes, sir."

"I've heard Thegns are fond of gambling. What's the saying? *One bronze for the pot to warm the stomach, two for the tavern to warm the heart, and three for the Lady to make her smile.* We Fyrd don't have a Lady. Tell me, what's your name?"

Offa was about to reply when he felt the familiar sensation in his stomach, the Lady's face spinning in the flames. He changed his mind. He would lie too.

"Alfred," he said, "son of Gialfred."

"Well, my young Thegn, let's have a game."

"A game?"

"Of knucklebones. I have three silver crescents that say I can beat you."

Offa's heart skipped a beat and for the first time he felt an acute unease about the knights. He looked at Beortrich, whose knuckles were white on his sword's crystal pommel.

"Our bench is not set up, sir," Offer said.

"We need no bench. Here, let me get down and then we can play on the ground . . . like children."

"My son does not gamble, sir, and we are tired," Beortrich said.

"Well then, let's just play for fun. We can use stones. We won't keep you long. Please, I would love to tell my boy that I played the bones with some Thegns. He's about your age."

With a giant stride DelaStrang dismounted. His men followed suit.

"Well," said Beortrich. "We would not want to be inhospitable. Come, Alfred, let's get the knucklebones, and if not a bench, we can at least find a board to play on." Beortrich slipped off the seat, his mail chinking. Offa followed him into the back of the caravan.

"Sorry, Uncle," he whispered, "I didn't mean to say anything, it just slipped out."

His uncle turned to look at him, cocking his head slightly. "Just slipped out, you say?"

"Yes."

"Hmm, that's bad. You may have said your death."

Offa's stomach turned over. "I don't understand. We're at peace with Acraphea. They would not attack an unarmed group of Thegn farmers. It's against the knight's code."

"Do I look unarmed? And are we Thegns? And do you know anything about knights other than what you've read in your scrolls? I have seen knights kill women and their babes in the name of duty. In war there is no code."

"War?"

Beortrich looked more serious than Offa had ever seen him. He put his hand on Offa's shoulder and leant close. "There's something not right here," he whispered. "It's not just the Fyrd. I've felt it for weeks now, as if the Lady herself were talking to me. And believe me, I have a rocky relationship with Her. Something is driving those Fyrd on with their questions. Some other force is working on them. Several times they could have chosen to take their leave, happy with our answers, yet they stay. Why?" He rubbed his beard. "Offa, we can't let them know who we are. It will mean trouble. I say again, I feel it in my bones."

"Maybe it wouldn't be a bad thing to tell them, Uncle. Maybe they know what is going on."

"Four Fyrd knights in full battle array? The only thing we

would learn about is the sharpness of their skeggox. You have lived in a time of peace. It has not always been so."

"Perhaps they are tracking a Forgotten raiding party?"

"Near Cyrodil, perhaps, but we are not near Cyrodil. They would be unlikely to track them this deep into Serendip lands."

A voice came in from outside: "What holds, old man? Come, you are tired, and we grow impatient."

Cynne lifted the flap of the wagon to peer back at them, her eyes wide. "Hurry!" she whispered.

"Coming, sir. One of the bones fell under a cask. I've found it now," Beortrich shouted back. Then he whispered, "Listen. You'll win every hand, you know that, and by doing so they will know you as Serendip. You have to find a way to slip the shaved bones into the game so you can lose but, by our Lady, test the air before doing so. If you are seen, it will mean our lives, I know it. But if you don't try it, well, it could mean the same. You have a strong sense of the Lady. You don't see it yet, but I do. Our good knight will throw badly due to her influence. There's nothing you can do about that but wish him better luck. But you, you have to use the shaved bones for your turn."

Beortrich handed him the altered bones. They were darker and much heavier one side than the normal ones, and they had been chiselled away at the sides. Beortrich had assured him at the Fair that nobody would be able to tell the difference, but to Offa's keen eye and hand they seemed considerably smaller. He guessed that when someone won due to a poor throw by an opponent, it didn't matter whether they were throwing a sheep's bone or the whole sheep. Offa wondered if the Fyrd would be so easy to fool. He raised the canvas flap, clutching the balanced bones, a leather pouch full of pebbles and the makeshift playing board. The shaved bones were stuffed up the sleeve of his smock. He just had to hope he could keep his arm at an angle without anyone noticing or the bones tumbling out.

The knight sat on the ground joking with his men, who still stood, making a small semi-circle around him. Beortrich took his place back on the wagon's stoop next to Cynne.

"Ah, there you are. Come down, Alfred," said DelaStrang good-humouredly.

Offa climbed off the wagon and placed the board on a relatively flat piece of earth in the middle of the knights. He offered DelaStrang the bones to inspect.

"Now what are the correct words?" asked the Fyrd knight.

"The etiquette of the bone?"

"Yes."

"You hold them like this," Offa said, balancing two of the bones on each hand. On the left the bones rested on his knuckles; on the right he held them in his palm. He then performed an elaborate weighing gesture, mimicking the movement of scales, the same Beortrich had taught him. He felt the even weight and smiled. He then handed the bones to DelaStrang. The knight repeated the ritual and although his scales motion was incorrect, Offa said nothing. The knight handed them back.

"If you are happy with the bones, you must now state: *The weight is true, the shape is true, the game is true*," Offa said.

"The weight is true, the shape is true, but I don't know about the game until I've played it!" DelaStrang laughed. His men joined in behind him.

"No, of course, but you have felt the weight and seen the bones. There are no shaved corners, no varied edges. The game is therefore true." DelaStrang smiled but said nothing. Offa continued, "Each of the bones has four sides—concave, convex, smooth and rough. Each side has a value—one bronze, three bronze, four bronze and six bronze. Throw one of each and the call is Venus, and you win the pot. Throw all ones and that's Canis, and you lose the pot. Any other throw and you must add bronze to the pot, depending on the total."

"But we're not playing for bronze lions, Alfred."

"No, of course, but we have pebbles." Offa took out the small cloth pouch. "We use these at large fairs where the site of a pot of lions might be too tempting for the, ah, less honourable."

DelaStrang nodded and stroked his moustache. "You are a very clever boy, Alfred. You remind me of my own son, many miles away."

Offa passed a handful of pebbles to DelaStrang. As he did so, Offa felt the weighted bones fall into his cuff. He wondered how he was going to slip them into the game. They all tended heavily to *one*, so it would always be a losing throw. Perhaps losing once would be enough.

"All right, let's play," said DelaStrang, arranging his dozen pebbles in front of him.

"Two pebbles in," said Offa. They both placed their stones in the centre of the board. "The etiquette states that the visitor must take first throw so as to have the first chance to win the pot."

"Or the first chance to lose it."

"Yes, I suppose so," Offa said nervously.

DelaStrang picked up the bones and then, cupping his hands, blew on them. The other knights laughed.

He threw.

Offa felt the tingle within him as the bones spun in the air. He wanted to scratch his stomach, the sensation was so intense. This was a bad sign. It wasn't even his throw. The bones landed.

"All ones!" said DelaStrang, looking up.

"Canis. The dog's maw," Offa replied.

"Rather an unfortunate beginning, don't you think? Though I suppose the first throw means nothing." DelaStrang raised his eyebrows. He leant forward over the board and said quietly so only Offa could hear, "You haven't been keeping anything from me have you, Alfred? That would not be good." His eyes glinted like black pearls.

Offa said nothing, but shook his head.

DelaStrang held Offa in his gaze, a piercing look that seemed to pass right through him. Then the knight's eye twitched and he sat back again.

"The boy has luck!" he announced to his knights and the wagon. "Let's see if I can be so lucky when the stakes are higher!" He put four of his pebbles into the pot. Offa added four of his own. DelaStrang then picked up the bones, and with a genial smile, handed them to Offa.

"Your turn," he said.

When trying to switch the shaved bones into the game, Beortrich did something that was so simple it shouldn't have worked but almost always did. He would take a casual swig from the wineskin and as he did so he would focus on a point on the wall opposite him or an object someone might be holding. Curious, the players would turn to see what he was looking at and, when they did, he would slip the weighted bones from his cloak sleeve. His success had something to do with his way with the Lady. A half chance that the players would be both curious and yet unsuspicious became a certainty, and they would all turn in unison.

Sitting in the open air, without the hustle and bustle of the Fair, and with four Red Shadows staring at him, the switch would be almost impossible, yet he had to try it. Offa focused on a tree, looking just over and to the right of DelaStrang's head. A burning sensation passed through his stomach. Three knights turned and in that split second Offa could have tried it except that DelaStrang remained fixed on him.

Some other force is working on them, Beortrich had said.

Offa had no choice but to make his throw with the evenly balanced knucklebones. That of course meant the throw was based solely on Serendip luck. The bones felt sweaty in his palms. Out of the corner of his eye he could see Beortrich turn red with concentration. A vein in his forehead rose and throbbed like an angry blue snake. Offa suddenly realised Beortrich was trying to distort the power of the Lady, check her face, willing it not to smile. But how could you change a god's will?

Offa closed his eyes and threw the bones into the air. The fire burned within his stomach and the bones landed in a perfect Venus.

"Well now," said DelaStrang slowly, "look at that. You win again."

"It's a young boy's luck, as you said yourself." Offa could hear the strain in Beortrich's voice.

DelaStrang sighed and put his hand up to his forehead as though pondering the next move in a game of achromatic chess. Slowly he rubbed his palm down over his eyes and face.

"Yes, of course. Luck. Let's play again." His voice drained of its prior animation. DelaStrang pushed the pot towards Offa's pile, and as he did so, Offa saw him gesture to one of the knights behind him. It was the smallest of winks, but it was a sign. Offa's blood ran cold. DelaStrang added his last six pebbles to the pot in the centre of the board and picked up the bones, but instead of throwing, handed them to Offa.

"You throw," he said.

"But it's your turn," Offa said, panicking, the shaved bones still in his sleeve.

DelaStrang nodded to the bones. "Throw."

Offa threw. Again the bones landed as Venus.

The knight behind him began to move but DelaStrang held up his hand. "Not so fast," he said, "we have to be sure." He pushed the bones towards Offa. "Again."

It was hopeless. Offa could do nothing but obey, and when he threw, the outcome was inevitable.

"Venus!" exclaimed DelaStrang. He leapt to his feet, his body rigid. "You are Serendip!" And then more quietly, and as if speaking to the air, "*You are Serendip.*" The three knights behind him tensed.

"And what is that to you?" asked Beortrich.

DelaStrang said nothing, his eyes fixed on Offa. They

seemed sad, like a man with no appetite for his work. "You are supposed to be in Sandor," he said slowly. "It is the morning after the Feast, the holiest of days. No Serendip walks abroad this day."

"And what of it?" Beortrich repeated, his voice harsh.

DelaStrang said nothing but pulled the huge two-handed battle-axe from his back. When handled by an experienced Fyrd knight, the axe could cleave a mounted Thegn in two— horse, Thegn, and anything that fell within its looping arc. DelaStrang's weapon was magnificent, rune bound and crafted with a crystal edge. It was the weapon of a High Lord. His men likewise drew their steel and composite bows, arranging themselves in the diamond formation: two bows, two axes. DelaStrang and the knight behind him would melee while the flanks provided cover through a ranged attack.

Offa's head swam. He saw the knights in front of him, their weapons, and the resolution in their cold eyes. And yet a part of him could still not come to terms with what he saw. Their bloody actions would go against every code of conduct, every breath of honour, everything he had read and believed hitherto.

As if in response to Offa's thoughts, DelaStrang hesitated. His axe remained in front of him, his hands placed firmly on each end of the long shaft. The bows were drawn but not yet trained on any target. The air seemed deathly still as though time itself had stopped. Cynne and Beortrich were statues in their seats, their lips tight, jaws jutted.

DelaStrang roused himself. "Serendips," he said, "you must know, before what comes to you this day, that your people have been judged and found guilty by one higher than us. The verdict is final, the sentence, death. No Serendip survives in Castagna, Khare or Sandor. The plains and smaller citadels are cleared of your kind. I sincerely wish you were simple Thegns, for then you would be spared. But you are of the Golden Lady. Prepare yourselves to meet her."

Even in his terror, Offa thought the knight's decree was

somehow flawed. It was neither in high speech or common tongue—*not scroll material at all.*

Offa shook himself. What was he thinking? He knew he should run but was rooted to the ground, frozen. And in that split second, a thousand memories rushed into his head. Was this *his* life passing before his eyes?

His life.

A highborn boy whose father was ashamed of him. He was too small and too sensitive. At the same time, he showed none of the diplomatic skill or intellect at the Ecole that was taken for granted in his family. He was always running to catch up, and left grasping, but for what? For an eccentric uncle whose overriding quality was being an outcast himself? For Cynne, his cousin, who ploughed her own furrow and refused to do anything she didn't believe in, despite her father's iron rule and cruel hand? With them he had been free to be himself without expectations. With them he had *lived.*

Once they had trekked through the forbidden forests of Enninmyra and saw wild mannequins locking antlers, their cleft hooves tearing the ground, their golden nostrils steaming. It was a magical sight. Another time they journeyed all the way to the towers of Cyrodil, just to look on them, to camp outside the walls for a single night, just to say they'd been there. It was these journeys he loved, sitting up front with Cynne and his uncle, watching the world go by and talking about his uncle's adventures in older times. He did not realise how much he enjoyed it until now, nor how much he would miss it.

They were going to kill him. The Fyrd.

In the name of Acraphea, they had slaughtered his people, because of what? The stars they were born under. How many Serendips had died this night? He thought of his uncle Beortrich, dragging him and his cousin out of bed hours before dawn to go to the Thessaly Fair on their holiest of days. Why? It was forbidden to cross the threshold, but his uncle had pressed so hard that Offa went when he should have said no. And now

Sandor and the other cities were laid waste, his people, dust.

Was it possible?

The Serendips were mighty warriors. Castagna was almost impregnable and its perimeter had never been breached. And Sandor? The high walls were thick and turreted and— Offa gulped. He should have been there to give what fight he had to give. Why had his father let him go? Or had he? Had Beortrich lied?

Dust.

Sandor, his father, his mother, his friends were all dust. Offa was rooted to the ground, paralysed by the weight of seven thousand lives. A part of him would welcome the axe's crystal edge and its sickly sweet bite.

DelaStrang stepped back and in a single fluid movement drew out his battle-axe and raised it high above his head.

He's aiming for my neck, thought Offa. He wants a clean cut.

Time seemed to slow down.

To his left and right, arrows thrummed towards his uncle and cousin. Although the knights were only thirty feet away from their targets, they missed their mark. The Fyrd were expert archers, but the shafts took on an unnatural aspect, changing flight mid-air, drawn off by the power of the Lady. Then, with a roar, and at a speed that belied his age, Beortrich leapt from the wagon, unsheathing his blue-black sword. Only the hilt was rusty; the blade was sharp and oiled.

DelaStrang's axe arced downwards and Offa felt like he was going to vomit with the burning that ripped through his stomach. The spinning face. His knee buckled just as the crystal edge was about to connect, collapsing his body to the left. Missing his neck, the axe sliced across his arm, tearing flesh and fabric. Blood plumed from his shoulder to his elbow and Offa fell to his knees.

Cursing, DelaStrang swung the axe up behind his head, preparing for the killing blow. From out of nowhere, Beortrich lunged forward. Catching DelaStrang mid-swing, he thrust his sword deep under the knight's armpit, piercing between the black plates. Face distorted with rage, Beortrich pushed the blade home. DelaStrang grunted and the magnificent axe fell to the ground; underestimating the old man's speed and strength had cost him his life. As he slumped forward, Offa could have sworn the knight's expression was not one of surprise or even fear, but of relief.

Two more arrows thrummed through the air.

The first was true and pierced Beortrich's hauberk just above the thigh. The second, destined for Cynne, never left the bow. The string snapped and the arrow dropped harmlessly to the ground. Standing high on the wagon's stoop, Cynne drew a long, thin dagger from the recesses of her cloak and threw it at her attacker's unprotected head. He raised a hand but was too late; the spinning blade lodged in his neck and the knight fell.

As Beortrich pulled his sword from DelaStrang's body, the second knight closed in, swinging his skeggox at the old man's head. Again, Beortrich was too quick. He parried the blow before changing the angle of his blade and slashing it across the knight. The sword cleft the plate in two, the edge as sharp as its master.

At the same time, another arrow was released. This time it penetrated deep into Beortrich's chest. Offa's uncle grunted but retained his concentration on the figure before him. The wounded knight swung hard and low, but Beortrich pivoted away and delivered an immense sideways blow. The third of the Fyrd keeled over.

But there was a fourth.

Another dull twang, and another feathered shard protruded from Beortrich's chest.

"Uncle!" cried Offa as Beortrich fell backwards.

The knight pulled his skeggox from his back and in the same fluid movement swung at Beortrich's head. The old warrior raised his blade to parry but this time only just made it.

Offa could see dark patches of blood welling from his uncle's chest and thigh. He wondered how he could possibly stay on his feet. The weapons clashed again and Beortrich fell back a step. Another weak parry, another fatal step. Sensing victory, the oncoming Fyrd swung at Beortrich's chest. With a sickening thud, the axe sliced through the hauberk. Beortrich's eyes bulged and his sword fell limp at his side, but he held on. The knight adjusted his grip and angled the skeggox back towards Beortrich's head.

"No!" Offa cried.

Mid-swing the knight froze and his white face turned a shade paler. The strength left his arms and the skeggox clattered to the ground. He clawed desperately at the small of his back and as he turned, Offa could see the long thin blade of a dragon's tooth sword sticking from his spine, Cynne still gripping the hilt.

With a final effort, Beortrich stepped towards the struggling knight and cleaved his skull in two. Offa vomited. It was like butchering a sick cow. The scrolls had lied. Battle was not noble, but a brutal, bloody mess that fed the worms.

The knight crumpled to the ground, followed by Beortrich.

"Uncle!" cried Cynne running to his side.

He held his chest, blood welling between his fingers. "Leave me," he rasped. Cynne bent over him ripping her cloak to stanch the wound. "For the Love of the lady, leave me! Help your cousin. I will keep."

"I'm fine," Offa said urgently. He was still on his knees, holding his arm. The wound was deep. The crystal blade's bite had been almost gentle as it sliced his skin and tissue, and in the heat of the battle, he had not noticed how much blood he had lost. Now his head swam and his teeth chattered in shock. Even so, Offa knew that his uncle's need was more dire than his own.

Seemingly caught in two minds, Cynne continued to tend her uncle until he rolled away from her, cursing. "No! Your cousin!" She then ran to Offa and went to work on his arm; pulling another dagger from her boot, she cut three even bands of woollen fabric from her cloak.

"How many weapons do you carry exactly?"

"Quiet." Cynne's eyes narrowed with concentration as she wrapped the arm, stopping now and again to apply pressure and pinch the skin tight before completing the compress. Then, with smaller strips, she tied bands every thumb-width or so across the length of the wound.

"I have some gila flesh in my pack that will take away the pain and hurry the clotting," she said.

"Uncle first! Hurry, help me up!"

Cynne pulled him to his feet. His head swam and he almost fainted, but he managed to stay upright and walk gingerly to where Beortrich lay in a pool of crimson, his breath coming in low, long rasps. His hand had fallen away from his chest and Offa could see where the axe had cut through his mail in a purple-red line. Below the line were the fatal arrows. His eyes were closed as though asleep, but Offa knew he must be unconscious. Cynne knelt down and felt his neck, his blood-beat.

"Oh! It's so weak," she said.

"But I'm still here," Beortrich muttered, "an old dog dying."

"No!" Offa cried.

"Aye," he replied.

"I can help. I have herbs in my pack that will help." Cynne turned to go to the wagon.

"No, it is too late," he rasped, "and besides, some of my wounds are below the sternum." He chuckled weakly.

"But if I can get you back to Sandor—"

"Child, there is no Sandor anymore."

"But that can't be true!"

"Child," Beortrich repeated, breathing heavily, "can't you feel it? It's gone. The race of the Lady is now few and about to be fewer."

"No, it can't be!"

"Why?" He coughed. "Because our people are too powerful? All power passes. It's as inevitable as the sun rising tomorrow. It's not right or wrong, just the way of the world. Seraphina is full of forgotten races that once considered themselves as we do. The Hadrada used to live on these plains in their tens of thousands. Where are they now? Where are the Gaels? Where are the Visigottes? Almost overnight all these once mighty people were Forgotten, ancient lands changed hands, and we, the Serendips, in our pride and arrogance, not only began the war, but took our share with Gildas and Acraphea. I don't know why we have been attacked, or why today, but the seeds were sowed a long time ago."

Beortrich coughed again and this time flecks of blood appeared at his lips. Cynne was crying and Offa felt his cheeks burning and a pain greater than the pain of his arm.

His breath laboured, face ashen, Beortrich pinned them both with his twinkling blue eyes. "In my entire life I have never crossed the threshold during the feast of Enninmyra. To do so is shameful, like fondling yourself in public. It's odd to want to do it and worse by far to be caught in the act." He managed a weak chuckle. "Your fathers did not know we went to the Fair. They would never have agreed. I took you without their knowledge or permission because I was driven to do so by the Lady." Beortrich wheezed and hacked and his eyes closed again. He was trying to hang on, to summon a last ounce of energy. "Don't try to go back. They will be hunting us down all over the east. Do as our people did when they first came to this land. Go south, to the heart of the ancient forest of Muir. I know that is where the remnants of our kind will gather. Go as Thegns or better yet, as commonfolk. Rub dirt in your golden hair, bury yourselves in anonymity and rags." He spoke so quietly that he was barely audible.

"I don't understand," Cynne said, tears streaming down her face, "why Muir?"

"It's where our people came from and possibly, if the ancient way is still open, our only way to escape. And if not, well, the forest is dense, and even the Acrapheans will find it difficult to hunt you there."

And with that, his hand still clutching the crystal pommel of his sword, Beortrich passed out of this world and into the next. Cynne reached out and took Offa's hand and they turned back to the wagon. Tears ran freely down both of their cheeks. On the horizon, in a simoom of dust, they could see the armies of Acraphea returning from Sandor.

And then, suddenly, everything shifted, and there were clouds. There were clouds passing before her eyes. Where was she? Lying on the ground, staring at a familiar sky. Who was she? Not the boy. Not any longer. He was gone, replaced with feelings of . . . of what? Cold, salty tears ran down her face, damp grass beneath the flat of her back and a vast emptiness where another's soul used to be.

"Penny? Penny! What is it? What is it?" Someone was calling her name, someone familiar. "Penny, please! Talk to me!"

Charlemagne shook her gently while Siam tried to lick away the tears.

"Charlie," she said weakly, sitting up.

"Oh, Penny, when I saw you lying there I thought . . . I can't lose anyone else. Crazy, I know . . ." She paused. "Don't cry, Penny."

"I m-must have fainted," Penny stuttered and then remembered the crystal. It was still there, clasped in her palm. Slowly she opened her fingers and revealed an opaque, cloudy-grey ball. The light had gone—burned out. At the same time, she noticed her watch: barely five minutes had passed since she had sat down on the bench. A shiver ran down her spine.

Charlemagne looked at the ball and then back at her. "Fainted?"

"I-I went for a walk with Cairo. We were supposed to have a picnic, but—" Penny's words caught in her throat as she thought of Eryn. He had given this to her. Why? Did he know what it contained, what it would do to her? Again she broke into sobs, but this time managed to choke them back. She had to pull herself together, had to think.

"We met that boy from the wake and . . . Charlie, I know you think I have an over-active imagination, but I think she's in danger somehow. There's something strange about that boy. He . . ."

How could she explain? *He gave me a crystal, called it a family heirloom, that showed me another life from another world?* Charlemagne hadn't believed her when she said someone was in her room the night before, she would hardly believe this.

"What?" Charlemagne said.

"He's living rough and he must be at least nineteen."

"Well—" Charlemagne began, but a high-pitched scream filled the air.

"What was that?" Charlemagne said.

"It came from the house!"

"Cairo!"

Nine

Crakes

THE MORNING DAWNED clear and chilly with a crispness that hinted at a premature end to the summer and, Crakes hoped, to their time in this world. He was in good spirits, and despite his doubts, filled with a renewed sense of purpose. Hamquist, too, seemed less dour than usual, invigorated by the prospect of hunting this girl, this Cairo Agonistes.

"Summon the Wandering Mist," Hamquist ordered, and Crakes set about conjuring it from the ground. But despite his efforts, the Mist failed to manifest.

"Again!" Hamquist said, and again Crakes attempted to bring it forth.

Nothing.

"By the gods," Crakes said, beginning to panic.

What if it had escaped? What if it had died? He knew nothing about the sentient vapour's lifespan. In desperation, he made a huge sweeping gesture with his good arm, and finally the Wandering Mist rose in a swathe of silver steam.

"It should be called the Bloody Temperamental Mist, if you ask me," Crakes muttered in relief.

"Or the Fickle Drizzle," added Hamquist, not bothering to keep his voice down.

The jibes were a mistake. The Mist thinned out and threatened to disperse altogether. Crakes had to coax and flatter it for another twenty minutes before it finally thickened into a fog and curled seductively around them. When it cleared, Crakes found himself jammed between two evergreens, a branch pressing into his backside.

"Thanks a lot," he muttered and the moody brume melted away.

He reminded himself that despite the Wandering Mist's petulance, he should treat it better. It had brought them to the land of the solar sun, and when the time came, they would need it to take them home, and he didn't mean back to the semi-detached house. It was supposed to be their servant, bestowed to them in bondage as part of the unnatural bargain with the Erinyes. But he didn't trust it. The Mist had been held in captivity by the witches for years and who knew how twisted it had become.

Pulling himself loose, Crakes saw they were at the edge of a garden rich with purple hues. In front of them was a field, behind them a large white house. The surroundings made him uneasy. He could sense where they were, whose house this was.

Hamquist sniffed the air. "The quarry's on the move," he said.

"Do we go after her?"

"No, she'll come to us." He glanced towards the forest.

"How long?"

Hamquist sniffed again. "A chiliad of strides."

Crakes frowned. "About ten minutes then."

"Aye."

They moved back under the cover of the evergreens, the trees serving as a natural barrier between two separate properties. Soon Crakes saw a glint of red coming away from the great forest and towards the house. It was Cairo Agonistes. She was a graceful specimen with her flowing auburn hair and willowy walk. He cursed as he saw she had a companion: another girl, short and dark with the same know-it-all expression as Mia, the same wrinkly nose. But unlike Mia, she had a tiny dragon-nail birthmark on her cheek.

Interesting, he thought. Turning to Hamquist he whispered, "She's not alone."

"It makes no difference."

"But what if—"

We take her head! Hamquist snapped with a mental command.

Crakes sighed. He suddenly lacked the appetite for this. One more head felt like one too many. He didn't want to hurt this girl.

He shook himself. What was he thinking? Hamquist would take *his* head if he suspected disloyalty, even in thought. His destiny was to serve Hamquist, just as Hamquist's destiny was to serve the divine. Crakes could not defy him in this. It was against his nature.

Taking a deep breath, Crakes edged away from the trees. In that moment, the smaller girl looked up and a rush of sound, like the beating of dark wings, filled his ears.

The red one, the black one, or both?

The red one?

The black one?

Or both?

The realisation cut through him like a seax. *Both* were coming towards them. The red one would not be the last; they would be sent after the black one next, he just knew it. The one who looked like Mia. He pivoted back under cover of the evergreens. The dark-haired girl hesitated. To her eyes, he would have been a blur, no more. She wouldn't even have been sure of what she saw—a shape perhaps, a flickering. She said something to the red one and shook her head. They walked on.

"What are you doing?"

Crakes couldn't speak.

"Take her!" Hamquist roared.

Crakes' body jerked forward, compelled by Hamquist's command, but he managed to hold himself in check, just.

"No," he replied, voice shaking.

"No?" Hamquist asked in a flat tone.

"We can't."

"Why?"

Because there is something not right here, something rotten at the heart of the divine instruction, though we follow it anyway. And because the dark one carries the mark of the dragon, and because she reminds me of Mia.

"W-we're too out in the open," Crakes stammered. "I sense at least one watching from the house, but there could be more. Then there's the other girl and . . . and the dogs."

"What of them?" Hamquist snarled. "Bestow the milky black dream on them all if you have to. I'll do the rest."

Visualising the scene about to unfold, Crakes shook his head. The one who looked like Mia would be wounded or worse if Hamquist lost control. Suddenly an explosion of pain ripped through his head and forced him to the ground. It was Hamquist's consciousness hacking into his mind like an ice pick.

What are you hiding?

Crakes knew it was futile to resist, and, in a matter of moments, Hamquist understood everything: his thoughts about the girl, his doubts about their orders, and the rebellion that brewed in his mind.

Hamquist glowered, death in his eyes, his face consumed by fury. Crakes shuddered with apprehension. He had seen that expression once before. It was the day he lost his arm. Crakes had to say something to distract him.

"Look at the way the red one walks," he said quickly. "The girl has grace, yes, but she's tense and angular. There is a subtle drag to her feet. Her body's pulling her one way, but her mind is already dragging her back to the forest."

"So?"

"She will come back this way, and soon, and then we can take her without the collateral damage."

Hamquist said nothing but tightened his fist around the shaft of the sword. Was Hamquist going to attack her alone? It was against their code, but then so much had changed since coming to the land of the solar sun. Interminable seconds passed and the girls came closer.

Crakes held his breath.

Hamquist's eye twitched feverishly and then, just as the girls were upon them, he gave the slightest of nods and ghosted behind the trees. Crakes followed. They let their cloaks fall over them, leaving body and face in shadow. The girls walked past on the other side, oblivious.

"She won't be long," whispered Crakes, "I promise."

Hamquist said nothing.

"In the woods we can . . ." His voice trailed away under Hamquist's stare.

"You defied me," he said slowly. "To defy me is a dishonour."

Crakes tensed and his neck suddenly felt large and flabby. *Fight or flight*, he thought. Not that either would make a difference; if Hamquist chose, he could end Crakes' existence in an instant.

He suddenly felt a rush of air and a rock whistled past his head, missing by inches.

"Who are they? What are they? *Why* are they?" a voice screeched from behind them.

Spinning around, Crakes saw a man not a hundred feet away. He had crept up on them while they were distracted. Inwardly, he thanked the gods; anything to divert Hamquist. One of the man's hands was balled around a second stone, the other outstretched and pointing. His face was red with anger and when he spoke, he shook.

"I don't know this one, and I don't know this one," he said, pointing aggressively at them both, sweeping his finger back and forth. "So I say again, who are they? What are they? *Why* are they?"

The sputter of words could have almost been a form of high speech, but poorly taught or long forgotten. The man wore a yellow cravat around his neck—the ancient mark of Serendip service—and then it dawned on Crakes. He was a Ward! Watching the Lady's house, guarding it from any who may trespass there. They should back away; they had no business with him.

"Well?" the Ward screeched at them.

Hamquist crossed his gigantic arms.

"Grave trespass! Grave consequences, I say!" the man cried, his eyes popping from their oyster-like sockets.

They needed to step away. Crakes waited for Hamquist's instruction, wondering how they would extricate themselves. They knew who the Ward was protecting, who he worked for. Anything but an honourable retreat would be disastrous.

"Well!" the Ward screeched again, his eyes practically popping out of his head.

"I'll eat them jellies if he carries on," Hamquist said quietly, winking. Crakes forced a smile.

"Oh! You smile, yes? Tough ones, yes? I've seen bigger than you gag on their . . . their toughness, while their flesh is flayed strip over strip. You see me and think, he's only one, and a slight one, and we're two and he knows not what we are. But mark! That you are here is enough for me. Two friends do *my* bidding. So it is you who are outnumbered, it is you! Gary will reave you, Mildred will grieve you, yes, yes she will!"

Hamquist stared at the man and then broke out laughing.

The man threw the second rock at him. This time it landed at least two feet short.

"A . . . a girl's throw!" Hamquist roared, holding his sides.

The man's face purpled and Crakes felt himself flush, for some reason embarrassed for them both. They were supposed to be above this sort of thing.

"G-Gary! G-Gary!" the man rasped, barely managing to spit out the name in his fury.

The back door of the house flew off its hinges and Gary came hurtling out. He was at least three hundred pounds and foaming unnaturally at the mouth. In the same instant, the man pulled back his jacket and there was a flash of silver. Excitement surged through Crakes' veins. He knew what the Ward held from one of Mia's lessons, but he had never seen such a weapon before.

"Say hello to Mildred!" the man screamed and released a round of molten lead.

Hamquist grunted and drew out his blade. He casually blocked the missile and it fell with a dull *plink!* to the ground. The man cursed and shot at Crakes instead—three bullets straight at his chest. Crakes shimmied, trying to look as relaxed as Hamquist, but Mildred was quick and one of her missiles almost bit off part of his shoulder.

Better make this fast, he thought. Crakes rushed forward and snapped out his left fist, connecting easily. He was tempted to follow through with an uppercut, but resisted. It was unnecessary. The man fell to the ground, unconscious, Mildred limp in his hand. At the same instant, Hamquist's sword flashed and the Ward's head rolled.

Gary smashed into Crakes, almost knocking him off balance. Wrestling with the dog's huge jaws, Crakes reflected sadly that *all* animals hated him. They always had, from the wildest to the tamest. Even horses bit him, even fish! He pushed the teeth away but the mastiff whipped its thick neck around and lunged at Crakes' groin. Tensing just in time, his adductor muscles absorbed the brunt of the blow. Crakes wasn't hurt, his muscles were like iron, but it was close. Some parts of him were less like iron than others.

The instinct of the creature was to drag, shake and hold on, so Crakes kicked up with the back of his heel into the dog's huge underbelly. Shifting weight, his fist smashed downwards, connecting with the muzzle. Stunned, the dog loosened its jaws and Crakes pivoted away.

The mastiff shook its head and then came again. It was as big as a courser, ferocious as a jackal, and Crakes was beginning to think that perhaps the Ward had conjured its speed. No dog moved that fast naturally. This time it lunged for his stump and Crakes watched as the huge maw ripped at the metal thimble. He sighed, took a step to the right, and hoisted it from the ground by the scruff of its neck.

I'll give it one last chance, he thought.

"Go!" he said, holding the creature's gaze in his own. "You cannot win." Dazed, the mastiff shook it's massive head as if considering its next move. *Please,* thought Crakes.

Gary snarled and bared his teeth, but then slowly backed away before turning and fleeing towards the woods.

Crakes turned back to the Ward, the pale body cooling beneath his feet. A deep sense of unease coloured his thoughts. In the past, watching Hamquist take lives elicited a sense of relief, something that Mia claimed was not a real emotion, but rather a lack of emotion. This time, however, staring down at the poor, forked creature, he felt something else.

Regret?

The Ward's single-mindedness and personification of weapons suggested that years in this world had driven him mad. Struggling with his thoughts, he turned to Hamquist for reassurance.

"We had no choice," he said hopefully.

"No choice at all." Hamquist slid the two-handed sword through his fingers to slough off the blood. He flicked his wrist and the gore splattered to the ground, leaving both hand and blade completely clean.

He's like a non-stick pan, Crakes thought irritably.

Hamquist inspected the edge before replacing the sword in his belt, leaving it to hang naked and blue against his pristine woollen stockings. Crakes sighed. His own leather breeches were ripped to shreds. He had gone all the way to a place called Camden to find a pair with a mustard-yellow stripe, and now they were ruined.

"This is bad, isn't it?"

Hamquist nodded. "Aye."

"They won't be pleased."

"Nay."

Hamquist could be so monosyllabic when discussing something uncomfortable. Sighing, Crakes bent down to pick up the head. How soft the hair felt. The pinched lips were frozen in a rictus scream and the accusing eyes stared out at him.

Was I an evil person? they seemed to ask. *Did I deserve . . . this?*

"A pretty little fish," Hamquist said, rather unhelpfully.

"What do we do now?"

Hamquist shrugged. Crakes gestured down the garden. Another shrug.

Crakes scratched his chin with his stump, and then, for want of any better ideas, swung the head in a circle, and threw it as hard as he could. Arching high in the air, it twirled and sprayed blood before landing with a thud in the adjoining field.

"There," he said, pleased with himself, "the stench will attract a nibbler and that will be that."

Hamquist said nothing but pointed to the ground, to the headless corpse already beginning to attract flies.

Ah yes, Crakes thought, *the problem of the rest, the bigger piece.*

"I'm not throwing that thing," he said hurriedly, suspecting that this was somehow becoming his responsibility.

After taking a life in Divine Judgment, a huge conflagration would rise, consume the body, and release the spirit. No mess, no fuss. However, when battle degenerated into farce, when a mere man had the audacity to challenge demigods, it was all they could do to keep their dignity. There would be no soul-purging fire for this Ward. Crakes would be unable to conjure one even if he tried.

"Agh," snarled Hamquist suddenly, "forget this for a game of soldiers."

He raised a hand and the ground opened up before him; twelve feet of solid earth displaced in an instant. He gave the body one sharp kick and it plunged down into the cavity. He then flicked his wrist and the earth fell back into place, burying the body in a deep, inescapable tomb.

Crakes stared in stunned silence.

"What are you looking at?" Hamquist crossed his arms.

"You've never done that before."

"Never needed to."

"What is it for?" Crakes asked. All talents had a purpose.

"Don't ask."

"Tell me."

"No," Hamquist said and turned towards the woods.

"All right." Crakes shrugged, not willing to push it. "I'll meet you there."

"What?"

"I need to replace these." Crakes gestured at his leather breeches. They hung in strips, torn away completely at the groin. He would have to find something in the Ward's house, unless he wanted to continue the hunt naked.

Hamquist raised an eyebrow. "I'll see you there, then . . . tiny."

Crakes forced a smile at what he assumed was a joke, still shaken by the earlier confrontation. Was his defiance forgotten? Or would Hamquist's fury rise again?

In the sky, the dark clouds that had been mustering finally snuffed out the sun. The commonfolk believed that rain out of season was a sign of a god's displeasure—the drops of water, divine spittle. Perhaps it was. He cursed under his breath. Watching Hamquist stride towards the forest, he thought again about Cairo Agonistes. And her sister, the one who looked like

Mia. The first drops of rain ran down his cheek and dripped from his chin and Crakes wondered how long it would be until they could finally go home.

Ten

AIRO! CAIRO!" PENNY called through the house. No reply.

"You definitely saw her come in?" Charlemagne said.

Penny thought back. The last thing she saw before her . . . vision was Cairo stalking into the house, still upset about Eryn. "Didn't you see her?"

Charlemagne bit her fingernail. "I was in the library. I just happened to look out the window and see you on the ground. I didn't see Cairo. I didn't hear her either, though I was . . ." She trailed off.

"Was what?"

"Nothing."

They both jumped as a long, low moan reverberated through the house. The hairs on Penny's arm stood on end.

"Just the wind," Charlemagne said.

"Why doesn't she answer?"

They split up and searched downstairs, going into each of the rooms in turn, calling for Cairo. As they looked, it seemed to Penny that the house assumed a menacing aspect, all shadowy corners and Gothic angles.

"Does it look like the house just became darker to you?"

Penny asked, meeting Charlemagne in the living room.

"It's the light outside. The sun's gone in and it's started to rain."

"I don't mean that, I mean . . ."

How could she articulate that, at times, she was afraid in this house? That it seemed to have a personality of its own, and that right now, that personality was hostile?

As they walked down the narrow vaulted passageway towards the staircase, she couldn't bring herself to look at the photographs. Sometimes she could swear they moved, but it was like the dark patch in the corner of her eye which, when faced head-on, suddenly disappeared.

The second floor also yielded no results, but this time they did not split up, instinctively staying close to each other as they looked in and out of the unfamiliar rooms. The house *was* menacing, and Penny knew Charlemagne felt it too. It took on a deathly stillness as they looked into the dark, unused bedrooms, with their layers of dust and heavily draped windows. Penny had been in all these rooms before, but now it seemed as though the walls pressed in, the rooms themselves no longer innocent and interesting, but sinister.

It was silly that she felt this way, silly that they were this frightened, but that scream had been real. They'd both heard it, and it had come from inside the house. When Penny opened the door of their grandparents' bedroom, Charlemagne put a hand on her arm.

"We can't," she said with authority.

"Why?"

"It would be an invasion of her privacy."

"But Cairo . . ."

"She won't have gone in there. Why would she?"

Why would she have gone in any of these rooms? Why would she not answer when they called her?

"Let's at least try the third floor first," Charlemagne said, heading towards the winding elm staircase. Reluctantly, not wanting to argue, Penny followed.

There were only two rooms at the top of the house, separated by a short corridor: the locked, forbidden room and opposite that, a small sewing room which Penny had explored a couple of days earlier. Its only contents were an antique, foot-powered sewing machine and a stool. Everything was covered in dust and the room carried a distinct air of neglect. It was a shame, because the views from the windows were beautiful and she could just imagine an old nanny sitting there many years ago, darning socks while she looked out over the evergreens and flowerbeds. She couldn't imagine Ogg this way, though; Ogg just didn't seem the needlework type. Charlemagne was about to go in, but Penny stopped her.

"I don't think she's in there," she said, her heart in her throat.

"How do you know?"

She pointed to the other door. "Listen."

A muffled voice could be heard coming from the forbidden room. The two sisters stared at each other and then, leaning forward, put their ears to the door. It sounded to Penny like someone was calling out, but she couldn't be sure of the words. Penny strained further forward and a floorboard creaked loudly underneath her shifting weight. They both jumped.

"Penny!" rasped Charlemagne, her hand over her heart.

"Sorry!" Again Penny experienced the irrational fear that, somehow, the house itself didn't want them up here.

Charlemagne knocked on the door. "H-hello?"

Silence.

"It's probably locked, but we may as well check," Charlemagne said, slowly turning the handle. The thick wooden door creaked open an inch, groaning on its rusty hinges as it did so.

"Careful!" Penny said.

Charlemagne pushed open the door.

Nobody.

Penny let out a deep sigh, partly from relief, partly in disbelief that the room was empty. There were some sparse furnishings—a table and two chairs in the centre, and at the far wall a heavy drape or wall hanging, but no Cairo, no anyone.

"The voices definitely came from in here," Penny said.

"Maybe a radio or TV?"

"Where?"

"I don't know. Somewhere."

Glancing upwards, Penny said, "Charlie, the roof!"

Dangling from the ceiling were at least twenty skeletal hands, each with an orb clasped at the end of its long, twisted fingers. The way they hung, it was as though the hands had pushed through the ceiling, the fingers ready to let go and grasp something else at any moment. Penny noticed the crystallised spheres were identical to the one Eryn gave her. They hung on slightly different levels, creating a dim net of light, each with its own faint glow.

"I thought the ceiling was supposed to have collapsed? Ogg said—"

"Maybe the damage is structural," Charlemagne said, cutting her off. "Something we can't see."

Because that's likely, Penny thought but did not say. She had noticed that lately, whenever she mentioned Ogg's name, Charlemagne became tense, bristling at anything that might be perceived as a criticism. She changed the subject. "The furniture in here is so strange, isn't it?" She traced her fingers over the table. It was clay, or some similar substance. The word *catlinite* came to her. In the centre of the room was a kind of table-top fresco, a lady's face cast against a background of flames.

Penny shivered. "The Golden Lady of the Serendips," she whispered.

Charlemagne started. "W-what?"

"The image on this table."

Charlemagne gripped her arm. "How do you know?"

Then, breathlessly, Penny explained about Eryn's crystal, about how she had lived another life for a few hours, and during that life she'd seen an image almost identical to this. To her astonishment, Charlemagne not only believed her, but added details of her own.

"Y-you've been there too?" Penny said.

"Yes, during the wake. I lived the life of another, an entire existence condensed to a few minutes."

"How is it possible?"

Charlemagne didn't answer but stared, mesmerised by the image of the Golden Lady, withdrawing into herself. So Penny hadn't imagined it. Charlemagne's growing other-worldliness, her withdrawal from her sisters. Somehow it was linked to whatever happened at the funeral. Penny shook her sister's arm in an attempt to rouse her.

Slowly, Charlemagne's eyes cleared and she spoke as if nothing had happened, continuing the conversation as if she hadn't just fazed out. "Oh, Penny . . . I thought I must have been going mad," she said, and wrapped her arms around her sister, holding her tight.

And what if we both are? Penny thought. What if they were experiencing post-traumatic stress over their mother's disappearance? The fantasy, stimulated by this strange house, had resulted in an improbably similar experience, like a collective hysteria. Except that Penny couldn't deny the physical reality of the crystal, nor Eryn, nor even the image that stared up at them. Deep down she knew, with as much conviction as she had ever known anything, that what she experienced as Offa had really happened. She realised something else, too—that before she *became* Offa, the night sky was familiar because she had *seen* it before, in her dreams of the witches on the cliff, looking out over a blue-black sea.

"If Eryn gave me the crystal, then somehow he must be linked to all this," Penny said. "And there's something about him, something other-worldly, and for some reason he's using

Cairo. I'm worried about her. Since Mom disappeared . . . she's become reckless."

Charlemagne didn't reply, lost in thoughts of her own. She was staring at the image on the table.

"Charlie, what about Cairo?"

"Huh? Oh . . . yes, I'll talk to her," she replied. "When we find her."

A shiver iced its way down Penny's spine as the same muffled cry they'd heard from outside the room came again, more desperate this time.

"It came from over there!" Charlemagne gasped.

"The wall hanging?"

"B-behind!"

They edged over to it. On closer inspection, they saw that the huge swath of fabric was like a stage curtain. There was a thick, arched cornice above and a pull-cord with a frayed golden tassel on the side. The curtain itself was embroidered with golden figures and symbols woven on an expanse of dark purple. More emblems from this *other world.*

On one side was an angular city, its architecture Gothic, towers standing sentry at the gates. Outside the city, an army amassed, pressing in on both sides. There were strange creatures petrifying crowds, knights dismounted by old men and knights striking down peasants—the little bloody dramas of the war within a war.

In the centre was an elaborate golden face, shrouded in flames, unsmiling. And then, to the far side, one detail that turned Penny's blood cold: a man sitting on the ground next to a wagon, three arrows in his thigh, knights slain on either side, and a girl and a boy bent over him.

"Charlie," she said quietly, facing her sister. But there was no reply. Charlemagne was again lost in thought, her fingers outstretched, caressing the burning city.

"*He-e-e-lp me-e-e!*"

Penny started. The muffled cry had again come from behind

the curtain, and suddenly, incongruously, Penny thought of the old black-and-white horror movies she used to watch with her sisters on rainy Sundays. This was the part where the audience screamed, *Don't look behind there! Do anything but that! Please don't look behind there!* Penny imagined the curtain being pulled back to reveal some twisted horror, or perhaps a fresco of the roof caving in, just before the roof caved in, a fate befitting unwelcome guests who failed to heed the warning.

"Pull it with me," Charlemagne said.

Reluctantly, Penny stepped forward and grasped the frayed rope. Cold dread clawed at her stomach. Charlemagne nodded. Penny sucked in her breath and pulled.

The scream was out of her mouth before she could even process the image. Suspended from the ceiling, arms outstretched, was Cairo, her eyes a piercing, inhuman green, her hair ablaze in a crown of flames. Behind her, and through her, burned a thousand lights, as though she was lying on a blanket of stars, a diaphanous constellation in the night sky. She smiled in welcome, but the expression that should have soothed, chilled Penny to the bone. It was not Cairo's smile, but a leer. The vision reached out its arm, straining to touch Penny, but in the instant before it did so, disappeared.

"Why did you scream?" Charlemagne said, her hand on her chest.

"You didn't see?"

"See what?"

"It was . . ." Penny hesitated. It was Cairo, but not Cairo. She was beautiful but somehow corrupted. "I thought I saw . . . I m-must have imagined it," she said, fighting down her panic.

"Well, you nearly gave me a heart attack."

Penny buried the image in the back of her mind. She would pull it out later, inspect it when there was time to think, when she was alone. Her trepidation about Cairo came flooding back. Where was she?

Behind the tapestry was a large alcove with a four-poster

bed flanked by two side-tables and a single easy chair. To the left was another door, slightly ajar, leading to a bathroom. It was like a self-enclosed apartment within the house—either that, or a jail cell. In the ceiling were the same globular fixtures, each giving off a very dim glow, but not enough to properly light the space. On one of the tables was a jug of amber liquid and a glass, next to that a flickering candle.

"It's burned halfway down. Someone *is* here, or has been very recently," Penny said.

Just like the main room, there were no windows, but three charcoal portraits adorned the walls. One of them was very familiar.

"It's Dad," Charlemagne said, her eyes drawn to the same picture. "But as a boy. I've never seen a picture of him as a boy."

"Me neither," Penny said, realising for the first time that all of their family albums began *after* her parents' marriage, when they were already in their twenties. There was something else about the portrait, too, something that jogged her memory but which she couldn't quite place.

"A handsome little thing, wasn't he?" a voice said from behind them.

Penny spun around, fearing for a moment that Ogg had caught them in the forbidden room. But standing in the doorway was a tall woman, very old, very thin, wearing a long, pale dress. Judging by her face, she must have been over eighty, despite her straight posture. She was grinning mischievously, her arms outstretched, palms upwards in a gesture that seemed to say, "Who? Me?" Her wrists looked as brittle as twigs but at the same time, Penny could tell by the way the fabric hung from her body that there was something else there too. A hardness, *the old steel.* Her eyes were at once penetrating, amused, and slightly off-kilter.

"Don't look so worried. I won't eat you," she said. "Not yet, anyway."

"Who are you?" asked Charlemagne.

"I should be asking you that, shouldn't I? You're in *my* room, after all. But then, I already know who you are, so we'll let it pass. You can call me Aunt Cynthia." She drifted towards them.

The old lady took Penny's hand, clasping it between her two. The grip was very firm, the skin papery and dry. A large, round diamond flashed on her index finger, its opulence in contrast to her plain dress.

"Why are you locked up in—?" Penny began.

"Shh!" their Aunt replied, cutting her off. "They may be out, but you never know who else might be listening. The house has ears . . ." Releasing Penny's hand, she swept out of the alcove, leaving behind an aroma of lavender and mothballs. Craning her neck into the corridor, she looked both ways and then quietly closed the door, locking it from the inside.

"That's better," she said. "Now, take a seat and let me look at you." She gestured to the bed. Penny hesitated. Cairo had been just there, hanging suspended over the bed like a Christmas tree decoration, wrapped in a blanket of stars. Taking a deep breath, Penny sat down.

"That's it. Make yourselves comfortable. My apologies there aren't more chairs. I'm not used to social calls, as you can probably tell. It's difficult when you don't see many people. You get into peculiar habits. So you will tell me if I begin to wander, won't you? Sometimes I think my faculties are intact, other times they seem to leak like feathers from an old mattress."

Their aunt poured herself a large glass of the amber liquid and sat in the wicker chair. "Ah, the joys of manderlay wine. Won't you both have some?" She gestured to the jug. Both sisters shook their heads. "No? How peculiar. It's the one thing that helps me focus. Very little manderlay left now, or so Gaff likes to tell me when he brings a bottle up, which is less often than I'd like. Tell me, why have you come to see me?"

"We thought we heard our sister scream. We thought it came from up here," Charlemagne said.

"I believe it did."

"You heard it too?" Penny said.

Their aunt huddled forward in her chair and lowered her voice to a confidential whisper. "It was me."

"You?" Penny said.

Still whispering, her eyes rolling slightly, she said, "I saw my death waiting for me."

Penny glanced at Charlemagne, who looked relieved. The scream hadn't come from Cairo but from their aunt, who seemed a little delusional. They had worried for no reason.

Aunt Cynthia rambled on. "This morning Gaff brought my breakfast, same as always, but afterwards he left my door unlocked, the first time in . . . in years. I was rather anxious at first. You get used to the security, you know. You might not be able to get out, but at the same time others can't get in."

"Others?" Penny asked.

A shadow crossed their aunt's face. "The Manciple," she whispered and took another sip of wine, although this time it was more of a gulp.

Penny thought back. Where had she heard that name before? And then it came to her. The man at the wake, the one with deathly cold eyes, as though all the emotion had been sucked out long ago, the one who took Charlemagne away.

"But I listened at the door and when I was sure there was nobody about, I crept out and into the sewing room, just to look out of the window, just to see the sky, and that is when I saw them. The Kalasians, standing in the trees like long, white tombstones. I had no doubt my time was up, that the Manciple had somehow summoned them across worlds."

"What are . . . Kalasians?" Charlemagne asked.

Aunt Cynthia hesitated, as though choosing her words carefully. "They foreshadow one's death, except . . . well, I'm still alive, so they were not here for me after all. Which of course raises the question, if not me, who?" She tilted her glass, rotating it in small concentric circles, airing the wine. Her brow furrowed. "I heard you come crashing into the house, but until I saw who you were, and saw the way you looked at my tapestry, I stayed hidden."

The sewing room, thought Penny, *she was in there the whole time. But then whose were the voices we heard?*

"Why are you locked in here in the first place?" Charlemagne asked.

Instead of answering, their aunt finished the wine and set the empty glass on the side table. She stood up and studied the picture of their father. Penny glanced at Charlemagne, who shrugged in return.

"Offa, my boy, what can I say?" she muttered.

"Our father's name is Alfred," Charlemagne said matter-of-factly.

Turning, their aunt chuckled softly and the wrinkles grinned with her. "Of course it is."

Penny felt as though her heart had fallen through the floor. *Offa.* She called him Offa.

"I don't understand," said Charlemagne.

"No, but the little one does. I see that."

For perhaps the first time in her life, Penny couldn't think of what to say. In fact, she could hardly breathe. If she opened her mouth at all, she would probably giggle hysterically. Of course it was him. That was the reason why the picture looked so familiar. Not just because it was an adolescent version of her father, but because she had seen him before, as he was back then.

"Are you all right?" Charlemagne whispered, a confused expression on her face.

"Offa," Penny replied under her breath. "That's who I became when I went . . . there."

Aunt Cynthia poured herself another glass of wine. "They want to know why I am locked in here," she said, still addressing the portrait. "That is a long and painful story." She put out a bony finger and traced it along Offa's face, and to the edge of the frame, then down a spidery crack in the wall. She traced it almost to the level of the bed until she reached a small hole, no larger than a pebble-sized chip in the plaster. She put her finger in, held it there for a minute, then slowly pulled it out.

"Once they start with the questions it's like trying to plug a hole in a dam, Offa. I can't stop it. One leads to another, and besides, it has already begun. They are being sucked in."

Again she hesitated, as if weighing how to proceed. She turned to the girls, her expression at once sad and animated. "Our people, your father and mother, are refugees here."

"From another country?" Charlemagne asked.

"From another world. Your parents . . . never wanted to you to know. And after what they went through, who can blame them? But it's too late now. The light of the old world burns in your veins. I could see that by the way you stared at my tapestry. You hardly believe, you hardly yet understand who you are, but you are beginning to see." She paused and put two fingers to her head, the bones almost visible through her pale, translucent skin. "You want to know why I am imprisoned here? The answer to that question lies buried in the past." She took another draught of wine and sat back in the chair, a faraway look in her eyes. Penny was afraid she had clammed up, when, as if in a trance, the old lady began to speak again:

"We were in a great forest. Our people, the Serendips, had fled from the armies of Acraphea to make a last stand in Muir. It was said the race of the Lady emerged from that same forest many centuries ago. It made sense that we would die there too.

"I remember that I was boiling water for stew, though we had precious little to put in it. Supplies were low but foraging was suicidal. Every time we went out, half our number would return, the rest picked off by Fyrd scouts. We knew the end was near.

"As the water boiled, I sensed a presence beside me. It was our *Lady*."

"The Lady!" Charlemagne said.

"Our god walks among us in times of great need. The Lady was the spiritual made corporeal, her essence manifested in the body of a high Serendip."

Aunt Cynthia's eyes clouded over, and when she next spoke, the voice was not her own.

"*Stay your hand and look upon the water. Imagine each bubble is a universe, the land, the sea, every star in the night sky, encased in one delicate blister. The bubble's journey upwards is the universe's passage through time until, millions of years later, it breaks on the surface and is no more.*

"*Look upon the water.*

"*Sometimes two bubbles touch, travelling together for a few moments, or for an eternity, two worlds so close that in certain places you can almost see from one to the other, where the skin is so thin one could almost reach across.*

"*Add your ingredients now.*"

Their aunt's hands began to move, pantomiming the crumbling of her ingredients, dropping them into the pot. She began to stir the imaginary mixture, her eyes still far away.

"I remember I was distracted. From across the camp I could hear Offa, your father, thrashing in his prison, and then the sound of sticks, and then nothing. I remember the tears on my cheeks. For although I rarely showed it, I loved that boy."

She suddenly started, the stirring motion frozen.

"*Can you smell the sea?*' the Lady said.

"'Yes,' I said, conscious of its half-illusory tang.

"*A millennia ago we took that salty, blue-black path to escape a different war. Now our fate is that of the ancients and a new journey waits across the worlds. They do not share our air, our people, or even our sun. But in this moment, this world, this bubble, this Earth is so close to Seraphina, that if we can only reach out, we may fuel our dying embers in its heat.*

"*Will you go?*'

"'Yes,' I heard a voice reply, and it took a moment to realise the voice was mine. Red lips brushed my ear. Golden hair fell over my face. The Lady whispered the refrain:

"*Hafram Deagalis, Hafram Deagalis . . .* '

"The words moved along my veins like a gentle effervescence. I hardly felt it when a blade pierced my neck, spilling my blood into the pot. Strength left my body and an agony of darkness consumed me. My spirit passed from one world to the next, dragging a reluctant body behind.

"I woke in another forest, but under an alien sky, and there I waited for the others." Her hands shook violently, and she gave out a loud, mournful groan.

Charlemagne squeezed Penny's knee. *Yes*, Penny thought, *I recognise it too.* The ancient wood moaning on the wind was their aunt, trapped up here, remembering the past.

"And they found you? When they came?" Penny asked.

Aunt Cynthia's eyes cleared as she seemed to return from the past, her expression now one of almost infinite sadness. "They found me, eventually, but not as I was. You must understand that just because the bubbles of two worlds touch, it doesn't mean they are always travelling at the same speed. Time may move faster or slower here, than there. Time is never certain, and the passage of the spirit is not like catching a . . . a train." She reached for that word *train*. It sounded foreign on her tongue. "The Lady waited before sending the rest of us, needing to be sure. Sure there was no other way, and sure she could bring all of the faithful with her. I was the advance guard—a test, if you like. A single week passed in the forest of Muir, while for me, I waited almost half a century." She coughed back what might have been a sob.

"When I left our people, I was not much more than a girl. I lost my father in the massacre, but I still had Offa, and I still had my . . . my betrothed. When I saw him again, I was almost seventy and he was still twenty-three."

Penny recognised her then. It was a single look—tired but resolute, old but with fire still burning behind the eyes. "C-Cynneforth," she said.

"Call me Cynne, my child."

"It's your photograph downstairs, isn't it?"

Cynne rubbed her chin, her hand speckled brown with age. "Those pictures . . . Old Gaff took a liking to those spirit-takers when he first arrived, snapping at anything—cars, tea-shops, joggers, hedgehogs." She took a long draught of wine. "Eventually he turned the lens inward, chronicling our people in their new land. The archer? At a feast someone suggested playing the dance of arrows, to remind everyone of home. The boy in the photo went first. The string snapped and almost sliced his hand in two. Rumours spread like wildfire after that. *The gift has gone, the gift has gone.* Why the fools even bothered, I don't know. What is there to shoot around here anyway? Hedgehogs?" She choked a laugh into her glass. "Sorry," she said. "Spend enough time talking to yourself and you make your own jokes."

"And you? When was yours taken?" Charlemagne asked.

Cynne's brow dissolved into a mass of furrows. "I never really forgave Gaff for that one. I suppose he wouldn't have it up if he knew how much it hurt me. When the Lady sent me here, I went through a very bad time, not understanding the world around me. I lived rough. People thought I was crazy, and they were probably right. It was, of course, Offa who came looking for me. Trawling through nearby towns, he heard about an old tramp who, if you gave her enough whisky, would rave about another world, about a war, about a Lady. When he found me I was living in a cardboard box, lost and alone for almost fifty years, disoriented, a shell of who I once was. Gaff was with him, and the first thing he did was snap, snap, snap with that spirit-taker for his damn chronicle."

Cynne looked longingly at the decanter on the table, but this time she did not refill her glass. She sighed and stood up. "And so we come to the point," she said.

"*Where have you been?*" Cynne shouted, fixing Penny with a malevolent stare.

"I . . ." Penny began, shocked at the sudden outburst.

"*What have you said?*" Cynne spat. "*Who have you spoken to? Quickly now. Did anyone believe you? What? No answer. I'll start again. Where have you been! Still no answer. Something to help you remember!*" Her hand snapped out towards Penny's face, but missed it by an inch.

It was only then Penny understood. Cynne was not speaking to her, but remembering what had happened after their father found her all those years ago. Cynne turned away from them, for the first time looking her age, the shoulders rounded, her body shrunken. Gingerly, she lowered herself back into the wicker chair.

"The inquisition went on and on. The Manciple said I had placed the community in jeopardy, that someone might take this mad old woman seriously and come looking for them. He didn't care that I had been abandoned all these years." There was a slight catch in her voice. "It didn't matter that a lifetime ago, he was . . . going to be my husband."

"The Manciple?" Penny gasped.

"He was good once, before his mother, father, brother, sisters and friends were slaughtered in Sandor. He thought I, too, had perished on that fateful night, but when I saw him in Muir, I realised that it was he who had died. Died on the inside. He had no love left, consumed by hatred of those who had done this to him. He became the Lady's most faithful servant, the rod of Her power, our mortal leader. He couldn't stand the sight of me. It suited him to put me away."

"But that must have been over twenty years ago!" Penny said.

"Almost twenty-five," she replied.

After a slight hesitation, Cynne refilled her glass and took another long draught of wine before proceeding. "In one way what he said was true, all those years of wandering alone un-balanced my mind, but that was not why he imprisoned me."

"What do you mean?"

"Half a century in isolation was a long time to cultivate a hatred of my own, of what the Serendips had done to other races, making refugees of them all—a hatred of our greed, of our culture, of the teachings of the Golden Lady."

"But you said yourself, the Lady saved our people!" Charlemagne cut in.

Penny noticed the use of the word *our* and the angry tone of her sister's voice. Cynne, too, seemed to pick up on it and she studied her, as if seeing Charlemagne for the first time. Slowly she took another sip of wine, her hand trembling slightly. "What are gods?" she said finally. "Beliefs that have come to life because of those who believe. And just like every other living thing, they fight and claw to stay alive. You must understand, this journey, it was always about her survival. She knew that if they stayed in that forest, they would perish. And without their faith, she would die with them."

Charlemagne grew very red. "But because of Her, the Serendips live on here!"

"Live? You see a transplanted people in a world of distraction. The Lady, she cannot hang on. The old faith is dying out, and her with it. How can a people from one world live in another without becoming part of it? No true Serendip is born here. They're all pure . . . ground? Or is it pure brown?"

"Earth?" offered Penny.

"Yes, of course," she said impatiently. "Your world is here because of the solar sun, yet it is named after the cold, dark dirt you bury yourselves in. The Serendips have been here quarter of a century, and with each passing year, there are fewer who believe that the past was even real. They pretend, of course, like at the wake, drinking what's left of the manderlay wine to let the old world in, except these days they wouldn't even do that if not for the Manciple's threats." Again a shadow passed over Cynne's face before she spoke again. "The young ones stand around laughing, not believing, thinking the whole thing is some reference to when their parents were burnt-out hippies.

And who knows, maybe they are right. When Offa first found me, I know I couldn't say for sure. So think of those born here, without the Seraph sun etched into their skin. Who in their right mind would believe?"

"So what will happen to the Lady?" Charlemagne asked urgently.

At first their aunt didn't reply, and instead stared into her wine and chinked a fingernail slowly on the glass. "For years she's been a shadow of herself," she finally whispered, "weak, starved of belief, starved of true followers, sustained only by the devotion of the Manciple. And then suddenly, she begins to rise again."

"Why?" Penny said.

"The Manciple has found a way to commune with the old world, to tap into its power, though what dark forces he has marshalled to do so, I dread to think. The Lady rises again, manifested in Oggram Tali, your grandmother. And now her servants, the Kalasians, walk abroad once more. Then there is you, the three sisters with the light of our lost world burning within you, children born on Earth and yet . . . of the Seraph sun, able to see it, feel it, perhaps in time, even return to it. In the last few weeks, the wall between our worlds has become thinner than it has ever been."

"We came because of our mother," Penny said.

"Of course you did, of course you did. I wonder . . ." She trailed off.

"What?" Penny said, experiencing a sudden sense of unease. She glanced across at Charlemagne, but her sister seemed not to be listening, and was staring into space again.

"Nothing," Cynne said, her eyes now also fixed on Charlemagne.

"We have to go," Charlemagne said. "She is coming."

Ogg and Gaffer are back? Penny thought. *They can't be.* The dogs always barked like crazy when anyone pulled into the drive, but it was silent downstairs.

Charlemagne stood up to leave, but with a speed that belied her age, Cynne whipped out a bony hand and pulled her back.

"Don't mention you've seen me, nor that you came up here," she said.

"I . . . I won't deceive her."

"No, of course not, but don't *offer* the information if you're not asked."

"I have to tell her."

"Why?" asked Penny.

"Because she would want me to."

Cynne shook her head. "No. She'll be angry with you for breaking her rules, for coming to the one room you were forbidden to enter." She leaned towards the girls and whispered, "She might even send you home."

Charlemagne said nothing, but her face grew a shade paler; without another word, she headed downstairs. As if on cue, Penny heard Siam then Cowper barking, followed by a manic scramble to the front door. Somehow Charlemagne had known.

"What's happening to her?" Penny said.

"The Lady has her, is working on her mind, encouraging her belief in a thousand ways and drawing new strength from that belief. The Lady's attention is dangerous. I hope I have taught you that much. How long has she been acting like this?"

"Since we arrived here, or at least after the wake."

Cynne rubbed her chin. "Of course. It makes sense now. The Manciple staged it for her."

"So there wasn't really a funeral?"

"Oh no, the poor boy at the wake was dead—a motorcycle accident—and yes, he was one of us, but the Manciple used the opportunity to unhinge Charlemagne's mind, give her a glimpse into the world of her ancestors, and let the Golden Lady in."

"But then why is it . . . wasting her?"

"Wasting? Not wasting, just robbing her of her identity, her choice. That is what faith is. Eventually she will be drained of her volition, her strength of mind, and even her sanity. With the Manciple at the Lady's side, drawing her on and out, I fear for your sister. He believes the Lady will be powerful once more. And he will make sure of it, no matter what the cost. If he has brought the Kalasians here, then his power is already greater than I imagined."

"What can I do for Charlemagne?"

"She is not entirely in the Lady's thrall yet, just as Ogg is not entirely the Lady. Try pinching your sister when she seems particularly peculiar. But your father must come and take you away from here. You must get hold of him or else Charlemagne will be lost."

"But why Charlemagne? I mean," Penny said, "why not me or Cairo? You said the light burned in all of us."

"It does! Because of who you are, because of your storied ancestry."

"I don't understand."

An expression of immense sympathy passed over Cynne's face. "Oh my poor girl, your mother really told you nothing, did she?"

Downstairs, Penny heard Gaffer talking to the dogs. Something about the heavy.

"There's no time to explain now, and you can't be caught here. It might be all the justification he needs."

"Who? I don't understand."

"The Manciple wants me dead."

"What?!"

"He knows that belief can be manipulated, whereas knowledge is dangerous. He's afraid of our meeting, afraid that I would tell you more than you could ever guess. That in talking to you, I would understand what your father could not have anticipated—that by sending you here, he has sent you into danger. And that I would tell you the truth, because despite the risk, I would not let any harm come to Offa's children.

When you speak to your father, you must tell him everything. He must come and take you away, no matter what else he is going through. He must! Come to me this evening and bring me your other sister. It is important that I see her."

"I will if I can prise her away from Eryn."

Cynne's eyes widened. "Who? Tell me about him. Quickly."

Penny could hear Gaffer calling for her downstairs. Rapidly, she described her meeting with Eryn.

"And he gave you a crystal, you say? Like one of those?" Cynne pointed to the ceiling and the dull round globes, each omitting a small light.

"Yes," she said, recognizing them now as the same.

"Those are crystals of Acraphea, one of the few substances that travel across worlds. The crystals contain the imprint of a spirit, the last memories of the dying. Warriors wore them on their swords or armour so that their kinsfolk would know that they died with pride and perhaps how, at the end, they were thinking of them. In our world they speak to us and reveal their secrets, but here, they are silent."

"We heard voices in this room, before you came in."

"Silent in this earthy place, and yet, for you, the lost lights of our world, they speak again."

Penny thought back to her vision. "Beortrich's pommel!" she said. "It was an Acraphean crystal!"

"Beortrich," Cynne said, and her eyes grew misty.

"Penny!" Gaffer's voice boomed from the top of the stairs, followed by Ogg's angry echo. "Where is she?"

"Listen," Cynne said and grasped Penny's hands, "I'm not certain, but this man your sister is with, it could be bad, very bad if what I fear is true. She could be in grave danger. How old is she?"

"Fifteen."

"Not of age, not quite yet. That's good."

"What is it?"

"No time to explain. Come to me tonight after they've

gone to bed. I'll find a way to keep the door open. Until then, whatever you do, keep Cairo away from him. Now go! Quickly!"

Penny rushed to the door but Gaffer was already there. She tensed.

"Ah . . . there you are, Penny," he said. "Hiding in the *sewing room* were you? Whatever for?" He spoke loudly and nodded to Cynne before gently closing her door.

Penny remembered how strange Gaffer had been that morning, asking them if he could do anything for them. Anything like *leave the door unlocked to the room you keep asking me about?* Had he planned for this?

Gaffer smiled at her. "I just wanted to ask, would the fiddle like anchovies and toast with her afternoon tea?"

Eleven

Cairo

CAIRO SAT ON the bench outside the front door watching the breeze play with the overhanging wisteria. It nudged the purple tails back and forth, back and forth, as if in time to some long lost hymn.

Crack!

A gunshot rang out from behind the house.

Crackety-Crack! Crack!

Three more shots reverberated across the sky.

It must be deer season, thought Cairo, *or possibly the troll from next-door shooting bottles to let off steam.* She could picture him doing that, belly flat to the ground, his puffy face brightening every time the glass exploded. Yes, almost certainly her poor troll. As the echo died away, Cairo put a finger in her ear half-anticipating another volley. None came. Instead the air acquired an unnatural stillness and the day darkened. A few moments later the first cold, grey tears dropped from the sky and bounced off her naked legs. Cairo didn't mind. She liked the rain and this was her favourite spot, in front of the house, commanding views of poplars, willows and the water, reminding her of that other pond—and Eryn.

Why don't you go back? asked a voice inside her. *He didn't want you to leave. It was Penny. You know that.*

Poor Penny. Cairo loved her sister dearly, but why did she have to pry into everything? Couldn't she see that Eryn didn't like questions? He was a very private person.

All that intelligence and yet she just can't tell when to keep her nose out.

They had walked home from the forest in near silence before Cairo stormed off, leaving her sister in the garden, not wanting to talk about Eryn, not wanting her emotions to spill over. After going inside, she paused in the kitchen, intending to rap on the window and mouth a "sorry" through the frosted pane. But Penny was distracted, fishing in her pocket for something. She pulled out Eryn's crystal and stared at it lovingly, caressing the edges. She then held it up to the light and smiled as a prism of colours appeared on her arm. Cairo felt a pang of jealousy and tore herself away, ashamed of her feelings, sick of her obsession. She wanted all of Eryn, all his gifts, the good and the bad, all the gaudy trinkets, and his heart.

Then go back. Don't wait. Go back to him.

She smiled. Sometimes Cairo thought Song loved Eryn more than she did.

Song, the voice in her head, was named for the way she lulled and trilled and seduced. A part of her since childhood, Song was like a persistent imaginary friend, except that she was real. When Cairo spoke, Song's voice gave lustre to her words and potency to her emotions. Song was her confidant and companion, her conscience and her demon.

Go to him.

But if she went back to him now, he might not welcome her. He said to come tomorrow. She stared into the pond and let the rain soak into her skin.

Thinking of Eryn, she could hardly believe it had only been a week since she met him on that drizzly walk before the wake. Even then Song urged her on, her voice excited in a way she had never heard before. Cairo remembered standing in the living room, drinking Ogg's strange tea, and as she stared out of the window, Song began her prattle, telling her to go to the forest. Eryn drew Cairo towards him, and Song pushed all the way.

Among the dark, shadowy oaks she found him, lying on the ground, no more than a scrap of rags, existing as willow and wisp, his first words so strange, yet so intimate.

"Finally, you have come." His voice was thin, his cheek pale and diaphanous.

"Yes," she replied, hardly knowing what she meant.

"I've dwelt in hedges, woods, and copses, sleeping on sodden earth, chilled, barely surviving, not existing, waiting, always waiting for you. Do you know who I am, child?"

"No."

"Then let's just say . . . I am in need of your help." He smiled, and the emotion that rushed through her was more powerful than anything she had ever felt. She had heard of love at first sight, but this feeling went well beyond love. She had found Eryn, and he wanted her, and the overwhelming hurt and loneliness that had cast a shadow over her since her mother's disappearance began to fade.

Yes, of course, somewhere, deep in the recesses of her mind, another voice told her to be careful, that what was happening to her could not be trusted, that this man may not be safe, but that voice was drowned out in a wave of exhilaration and excitement.

In the short time she spent with him, he seemed to revive. He'd wanted her to come back that same evening, and she said of course, she would find a way to avoid her grandparents, to miss the wake, but Eryn said no, she must go, that he would find her there, and he had. How much improved he was since then—healthy, vibrant, that terrible bone-chilling cough almost gone.

Because of you, Song said.

Because of us.

Every morning Cairo brought him food, which he devoured ravenously, and every day he was better than before, and looked at her with more affection. They would talk for hours, until late into the afternoon. She recalled their conversations now, remembering every word, every expression, drinking deeply from her precious pool of memories. She was tantalised by his looks, his wicked smile, the snatched kisses, the promise of something more. And if he wanted to do more than kiss, would she? Her stomach filled with butterflies, but at the same time the thought electrified her. She had never felt anything like this for a boy before.

The blast of a horn startled her. It was her grandparents, turning into the drive without bothering to signal; the horn, as well as a stream of invectives, had come from the car behind. As they drove towards the house, Cairo saw that they were arguing, Gaffer with his head bobbing, Ogg shouting and red-faced. Surely they weren't arguing over Gaffer's driving? Her grandfather never signalled when he drove, but seemed instead to trust his luck. It had never bothered Ogg before. Cairo stood up and pushed her now dripping hair away from her eyes and for the first time was conscious of her soaking clothes sticking uncomfortably to her skin.

Seeing her, Ogg said something sharply to Gaffer and they composed themselves.

Gaffer wound down the window, despite the rain. "Hello, fiddler!" he said with forced jocularity. He hopped out with five bags of groceries in each arm, banging the door shut with his bottom. Ogg hurried through the front door, carrying nothing but her umbrella.

Mustn't get the 'do wet, thought Cairo.

"Do you want a hand?" she said.

"A hand?" said Gaffer looking rather startled.

"With the groceries."

"Oh, Grr-ha-ha! For a moment I thought—" He stared at

his fingers. "Oh, never mind. Yes please then, dear. Just bring what you can from the boot. I'll come back for the rest."

"Don't worry, I've got them," Cairo said. The remaining bags seemed to consist almost entirely of anchovies, rice pudding, and something called Jammie Dodgers. Cairo rushed into the foyer, trying to keep it all dry.

"Do you know where your sisters are?" Ogg said, appearing again, her voice a few tones higher than usual.

"I think they're inside somewhere. I don't know, I've been out here for a while."

"Hello, Siam, I've got your heavy!" said Gaffer as the dogs almost bowled him over. "You too, Cowper, don't worry. Don't jump up now, don't jump up!"

"Where exactly in the house?" Ogg said, her eyes narrowing.

"I don't know."

Ogg made a sign to Gaffer who half-muttered, half-laughed, "I'm sure it's nothing," and disappeared down the corridor with the bags.

"Anything the matter?" Cairo said.

Ogg glared after her husband then said, "No . . . of course not. I . . . just like to know where you all are." She forced a smile but it came out badly, like toothpaste through a split in the tube. Cairo wondered what her grandmother would say if she knew about Eryn—although "The Ogg" seemed only to care about Charlemagne. At times, it was like she and Penny didn't exist, which was just fine with Cario.

"I was thinking of going for a walk," she said brightly.

"After you've dried off and had some tea, perhaps?" Ogg said with what seemed like a forced smile. "You know, I admire your stamina, always out and about walking. Very good for you, all that fresh air. I wish I could join you but the knees aren't quite what they used to be."

"Really?" Cairo said. Ogg looked more formidable, more brilliant than ever, if a little flustered at that exact moment. The truth was, Cairo was a little afraid of her grandmother. It was the touch of Cruella De Vil that did it, the set of the jaw, the glare in the eyes.

"Now where has that useless man got to?" she said, then, "Ah, Charlemagne!"

Charlie came rushing down the stairs, beaming.

"Ogg!" she cried, pushing past Cairo and embracing their grandmother.

"Hi, Sis, pleased to see you too," Cairo muttered and opened the door to the kitchen. Gaffer had left his bags on the table, so she put hers next to them. Perhaps there was something she could appropriate for Eryn.

Outside she could still hear Ogg carrying on about where Penny was. Why did she care all of a sudden? Shrugging, Cairo began to put away the groceries. May as well be helpful. Apart from the anchovies, rice pudding and Dodgers, there was beetroot, Spam, Marmite, artichoke hearts, more anchovies, frozen fish, frozen pears, frozen spring rolls, lard, baked beans, naan bread, ten bottles of wine and a wide variety of Pop Tarts. Her grandparents were almost certainly the oddest people she had ever met. Gaffer bumbled through the door as she was laying the last of the groceries on the counter.

"Did you happen to unpack a sheep's brain?" he said urgently.

"No."

"Must have left it somewhere. The butchers? No. Ogg's hair salon? Maybe." He scratched his chin. "Ooooh, biscuits!" he said, spying the Jammie Dodgers and rubbing his hands together. "Quick," he whispered, "but don't tell the old lady. It's almost tea time."

Cairo opened the packet and handed him four of the cookies. The kitchen door opened and Gaffer promptly shoved them in his mouth. It was only Penny, but the damage was done. He blinked at them, his cheeks stuffed to capacity, unable to speak.

"Cairo," Penny said, glancing uncertainly towards their

grandfather. "Where were you? We've been looking for you for the last hour."

We? Charlemagne had barely noticed her. Penny's cheeks were flushed, as though she had taken a very hot bath, and her normally self-assured voice was peculiarly stilted.

"Well, here I am." Cairo smiled.

By the time they had finished putting away the groceries, and Gaffer had fielded an angry call from the hairdressers about the missing brain, it was time for the afternoon tea. Ogg ushered them all into the living room.

"A cup of my special brew is just what we all need," said Ogg, "and I've got some nice éclairs too, fresh from Marks and Sparks. You all stay here and make yourselves comfortable."

Ogg was calm again, but there was still some unspecified tension that pervaded the air; even the house seemed agitated, all angles and points. Both Penny and Charlemagne sat on the edge of their seats. Gaffer kept looking at his hands until finally he got up and left the room.

"You know, sometimes I think the main difference between England and home is the endless cups of tea," Cairo said, still smiling. She half expected a clever quip from Penny, perhaps concerning tea's origins, or the real difference between England and America, but both her sisters remained stonily silent.

Shrugging, Cairo walked over to the window. The rain still poured down, drumming on the window pane, bouncing six inches off the patio. She stared at the ancient trees in the distance. How was Eryn coping with the rain? Would he be missing her? She tapped gently on the glass.

"You're not going back out again, are you?" Charlemagne said quietly.

So that explained it. The silence and stares. Penny had told Charlemagne about Eryn.

"I *had* to say something," said Penny, anticipating her train of thought.

"I see."

Charlemagne sat up straight, and put on an air of superiority. "I know you think everything's fine but he's older than you and—"

"Did he give you a crystal too?" Penny interrupted.

"What?"

"Something that took you . . . somewhere?"

"No," she snapped.

What was Penny trying to prove? That Eryn favoured her sister with a gift and not her?

"Or have you had any dreams about faraway places, or about mom?"

Cairo said nothing. Her dreams were her own. And why did Penny have to bring up their mother? The truth was she *did* have nightmares, tortured images of her mother trapped and out of reach in a strange place, but she certainly wasn't going to talk to Penny about it. Just because her baby sister liked to analyse her dreams in public didn't mean everyone else did too.

Cairo crossed her arms and felt her bottom lip jut. "No, I haven't been given a crystal and no, no dreams other than how *annoying* my sisters can be."

"We're just worried about you," Charlemagne said gently. "It might not be safe, being alone with Eryn—"

"Do you think I'm stupid?" she snapped, not allowing her sister to finish.

"I know he's spending an awful lot of time with a fifteen-year-old girl, and he must be, what? Twenty? That's not even legal," Charlemagne said.

"You're in danger!" Penny shrieked.

"Lay off, Pen, do you hear how crazy you sound? You don't know anything about him! He was only acting strangely today because he was tired, and you kept going on in that way you have, all those questions . . ."

"Questions?" Penny said. "I didn't . . ." She took a deep breath. "It's not that. He is not what he seems."

Cairo laughed. She couldn't help herself. Her

thirteen-year-old sister giving advice, as if Cairo didn't know all about Eryn. As if it made any difference. She would not let them make her angry, she would not! Penny was being Nancy Drew, too clever for her own good, prying into everything, overplaying her part. Quite frankly, it was embarrassing.

"Well, thank you for the concern," she said lightly, "but I think it's time to be off." She walked towards the door.

"What is wrong with you, Cairo? Since when do you know everything about everything?" Penny snapped.

Ha! I'm the smart-aleck. Right.

"It's throwing it down out there," Charlemagne said, "you'll be soaked to the skin."

Cairo smiled. "I'll dry out in his tent then!"

Penny grasped her arm. "There are things here you don't understand."

"I'm beginning to see that," Cairo said through gritted teeth.

"I'm telling you not to go." Charlemagne said.

"You're *telling* me?"

"Yes."

"*It's a good thing you're not my mother then!*"

Song's words were out of Cairo's mouth before she could stop them. Penny and Charlemagne pulled away as though they'd touched something very hot, their expressions a mixture of shock and hurt, the one blending into the other.

"Tea, anyone?" said Ogg heartily, coming through the door carrying a tray stacked high with éclairs.

Cairo burnt her tongue drinking the tea so quickly, but at least she was outside. She squelched down the garden path, aware of her sisters watching from the window. The rain soaked her to the skin again, but she didn't care. Anger and anxiety steamed from every pore and kept her warm. Her hair fell wet across her face and she took deep breaths.

Why had Song betrayed her? When their mother

disappeared and the world became suddenly dark and cold, Song was there to share the pain, to whisper softly in the night, to grieve with her. She was her closest friend.

But that was not all, was it?

After their mother disappeared, Song had grown, looming larger than she had for years in Cairo's mind, her presence more distinct, more insistent, more than her childhood imaginary friend. And since arriving here, Song could apparently talk for herself, using Cairo as the vessel for hurtful, hateful words.

Or so you want to believe, Song said.

No! She wasn't like that. She wouldn't have said that to Charlemagne.

But you did.

"It was you!" Cairo retorted aloud.

There is no 'you', only us.

Cairo rubbed her temples, trying to shake the voice away.

After Ogg came in with the éclairs, they had drunk their tea in an uncomfortable silence, Cairo bolting hers, wanting to flee from her sisters' hurt expressions. Ogg's presence ensured there would be no more discussion about Eryn and so, excusing herself ostensibly for the bathroom, she escaped.

As she hurried through the garden she vaguely wondered where the troll was with his, "Who goes there?" questions. It was the first time he hadn't showed. Maybe he didn't come out in the rain. For some reason his failure to appear made her slightly uncomfortable. She crossed into the fields and through to the forest.

Picking her way through the thick, dark trees, she came into the smoky clearing. Eryn sat under a length of orange tarpaulin tied maybe twelve feet above the ground. It spanned across the makeshift wooden table, four huge stumps with a natural pit in the middle. A spitted dear hung over the cavity, a fire roaring beneath. Eryn peeled off a strip and tossed it casually to Titus, his huge, grey, Irish wolfhound.

"Good boy," he murmured.

Cairo smiled. He looked better again, better even than this morning. There was lustre to the auburn hair, his skin was flawless, and his eyes, bathing in their sea of green, seemed preternaturally clear and bright.

"I said not to come until tomorrow," he said shortly.

"I know, but . . ."

"It is tomorrow that you turn sixteen?"

"What?" she said, startled, and then realised he was right. With everything else going on, and since coming to England, she had lost all sense of time.

"Yes, it's my birthday tomorrow. How did you know?"

"You mentioned it . . . once, after I told you I thought you were a little young for me."

Had she said that? She didn't remember, and she tried so hard to remember all of their talks. She stood uncomfortably for a moment, wondering if Eryn was going to send her a way, but he sat on in silence, staring into the fire.

"I-I came because I thought you might be hungry," she said.

"For once, Titus has paid his way." He gestured to the deer.

"I brought wine."

Eryn turned to her, a grin breaking across his face. "Wine? Ah, well in that case, I never say no to wine. Come and sit with me."

Sitting at the table, she unpacked the knapsack. One bottle of cabernet—a screw-top, one tartan picnic cloth, plastic plates, forks, and just for good measure, anchovies and olives. If Eryn didn't eat them, Titus would. That dog ate anything; one day he'd devoured a jar of red pickles and licked the inside clean. Typical boy.

Pouring them both a glass of wine, Cairo reflected that it had probably been wrong to take the bottle without asking. Then again, her grandparents wouldn't mind. Ogg had said, "Help yourselves to anything."

Eryn sniffed his glass and frowned slightly.

"Is it not good?"

"Oh no . . . no, it's lovely, thank you. I hoped it might be one of the old manderlay bottles they had at the wake . . ." Looking up at her, he added, "But your company would make any liquid sweet."

The words sent a shiver of excitement down her spine. He edged closer to her. Their bodies actually touched on the narrow stump.

Eryn finished the glass in two mouthfuls and then reached for his battered case of rolled cigarettes. He tapped one out and held it to the fire, seemingly impervious to the stray flames that licked his hand. He took a long drag and then turned to her. "Cairo, my Cairo, sweet as the woodland flower, welcome as the pine in winter, what am I going to do with you now?"

Cairo's cheeks burned. Was he going to kiss her?

"Do with me?"

"I told you to come *tomorrow*. It's not safe to ignore my wishes, not safe." He put the cigarette in his mouth and then flicked open his silver clasp knife. "You could catch me off guard, in a different, less benevolent sort of mood," he said, inspecting the blade. "I could do something I might regret." He peeled off another strip of venison and threw it to Titus.

Cairo felt her heart pound in her chest. Tentatively she reached across and touched the back of his hand.

He turned to her, taking her hand in his, clenching it. "Today, there is something very dangerous in the air, something unsavoury . . ."

"I-I don't understand."

"Ghosts of the past," he said, eyes wild. "The servants walk abroad, the Will and the Way. Why are they here? And how did they come? Once, the Kalasians did my bidding but that time has gone . . . long gone . . . but it will come again, it will, it must! It is our destiny."

Cairo didn't ask what he meant. Eryn often trailed off into cryptic stories to explain his fears or the hurt that clawed at him from the past. She was used to it now. At least he was holding her. Eventually the rambling subsided, his agitation cleared, and they sat at the table to their makeshift dinner.

Eryn poured himself another glass of wine and then, despite the earlier protestations, ate the anchovies and the olives and a quarter of the spitted venison. Cairo ate too, hungry after having no appetite for most of the day. She bit into a chunk of the meat. The skin crackled and juices ran down her chin and onto her plate.

Whatever would Penny say? She giggled to herself. She was like a caveman.

Eryn insisted Cairo sat at different angles until her t-shirt and shorts were completely dry. She put her tennis shoes on two sticks next to the fire like marshmallows, but not close enough to go gooey.

When they were both full, Eryn slid the remainder of the deer from the spit, gave it to Titus, and whispered gently to him to be off. Obediently the dog took the meat in his mouth and headed for the trees. Cairo rolled up the blanket and put the glasses and the empty bottle back in her knapsack. She sat back down next to Eryn while he tapped out another cigarette and puffed on it slowly, staring into the flames, lost in thought.

They often sat for hours like that, sometimes talking, sometimes not. There was a chill in the air and the damp seemed to close in on them. The rain drummed on the tarpaulin, setting in for the night. It was getting late.

"Well, what shall we do now?" Cairo said. She had an hour, longer if she dared. It would still be light at nine-thirty and she could be back by ten if she ran all the way.

Or, you could just stay out, Song said.

Eryn said nothing but continued to stare at the fire.

"Eryn?" she said softly.

His expression had become suddenly dark and brooding, and his mouth twitched as though trying to hold something in. That he was changeable, even erratic, was apparent from the first time she met him, but he was usually better for being with her.

"What if the Kalasians were coming for me after all? The timing is too much of a coincidence. Dawn then, it has to be dawn. Tomorrow night might be too late." He exhaled a stream of smoke and threw the cigarette into the flames. "Would you do something for me?"

"I-I would do anything for you," Cairo replied, the heat flushing through her.

"Anything? Well, what I have to ask you is perhaps a little less desperate than *anything*. Come and lie down with me."

Goosebumps pricked all over her, as though she was charged with electricity. He smiled, gently took her by the hand and led her towards the tent. His shelter wasn't much more than tarpaulin over sticks with a groundsheet, but secured on all sides with heavy rocks and lined with several old deer pelts and other skins, it was dry and warm.

She thought she knew what was coming. Was she ready? To calm herself, she focused on the smooth red glow of the fire's embers. All she could hear was the patter of the rain and his breathing. She lay back, shivering, and for the first time she could remember, she felt cold.

Think of that face, those eyes, that soul.

He loves you. And he needs you. That is clear.

Cairo shuddered. Was Song pushing her into this? *No*, she said to herself, *don't use that*. She wanted this. Eryn sat by the flap, his back facing outwards. In the triangle above his head, Cairo could just make out a silvery slip of the summer moon, fighting with the clouds as the sun had earlier in the day.

"Put your head on my lap. Good. Close your eyes. That's right. Don't flinch when I do this next thing. It won't hurt, but it might feel strange."

Cairo pressed her lids together. Because the tent was so dim, she had the sensation of looking into a void. Her other senses seemed to heighten. She could smell Eryn, the musk of honey and pine, and then something touched her cheek—his hands gently massaging her temples.

"Keep your eyes closed. To open them half way through would be, well . . . problematic."

Cairo heard a match strike and a curious aroma filled the tent. Breathing in, she became aware of a strange, rhythmic language.

Jala kala falin nyar, jala shalona falin gra . . .

Behind her eyelids the darkness began to shift.

She saw nomads crossing miles of rock and ice that faded into desert, and then changed again to become a land rich with summer's bloom.

Memories filled Cairo's mind; not hers, but those of a mother thinking about her dead children, lost on this ten-year journey, this trail of tears. A girl clung to the woman's hand. She was a gift from God and had many names. Some called her the Favour of the Incubus or the Gilded Cuckoo. To others she was the Song of Aquinas. The woman simply called her Lila. The child of another, the girl shamed her husband's memory it was true, but he was dead, and Lila was her comfort now.

"Where are the yurts, Mama?" the girl asked, her brow wrinkled with concern.

"No more yurts, my darling. Today we begin a city."

"Where, Mama?"

"Watch."

Two old men led a calf in front of the vast crowd. Attracted by the lush grass, it made for the marshy riverside, but the Elders held the tether. With a plangent "moo" it strained forward until, giving up, decided to graze on firmer ground. A cheer erupted.

Lila's eyes widened. "A . . . a cow marks the spot?"

"Yes."

Lila paused for a moment, thinking. "May I unpack my sack now?"

"Not yet, my love."

"Why do you look so sad, Mama?"

The woman did not answer but ruffled Lila's hair.

A score of men wheeled a huge slab of granite to where the calf had grazed. It was the keystone of their first city in this new land; when it was laid, the two Elders addressed the crowd, speaking in unison so their papery voices carried through the air:

"Praise to our Lord Ferin Aquinas for
Delivering us to this fertile land,
Which we do name Gildas in his honour.
Remember those lost on this hard passage,
For their sacrifice we begin anew."

"You *are* crying, Mama!" said Lila.

"Just the wind, my darling."

Lila reached up and with the sleeve of her smock gently wiped away her mother's tears. Behind them, the haunting melody of panpipes broke out, followed by the twangling of a lyre and the beat of a goblet drum. If the Gildas could remember how to feast, they would feast tonight.

The edges blurred and centuries passed, spreading out like the leaves of an oriental fan. Cairo could see everything, feel everything, the passage of time, the heartbeat of a people thriving, pullulating. One settlement became a town, and one town became many, until time itself began to slow and Cairo found herself face-to-face with a beautiful auburn-haired girl.

She was hopping back and forth across a cat's cradle tied to some kitchen chairs. The cook griped that the ropes were a death trap and messed up the scullery, but the girl simply laughed and hopped even faster.

There was something breathtakingly familiar about her small, lively figure. Skipping towards Cairo, she reached out. Their skin brushed and Cairo gasped as the girl's thoughts and memories flooded her mind. It was like being submerged in a pool of freezing water; the jaw-rattling cold fused with her body. Cairo heard the child's voice echo in her head, or perhaps it was the other way round, because when she opened her eyes they belonged to the girl.

I see what she sees.

"What did you say?" said the girl, head cocked, foot suspended mid-hop.

Who are you?

The girl laughed. "How funny!" she trilled and stabbed her foot through the ropes before flicking it out again. "I am you and you are me."

The cook looked up, saucepan in hand, puzzled by the girl's chatter.

Tell me your name.

"Cairo Song," she said proudly, "but everyone calls me Song." The girl giggled as her imaginary friend pretended to faint. Song knew she was still there, though. Song's voice was part of her.

"Run along now," Cook said, patience lost. "I have to get supper ready."

Carefully, Song unhooked the ropes from the chairs and wound them around her arm. When she was older, Song wanted to win the Dance of Tines, and so she practiced every day using a broom handle for her *kon* until Cook got fed up and told her to play somewhere else. For once, Song didn't mind; she had to finish early anyway. Mormor was expecting her. Hanging the ropes on a peg behind the door, she went upstairs.

Song loved her great-grandmother. The Cantor at the *Fari* said Song resembled her, but that couldn't be true. Nobody was old enough to remember what Mormor looked like when she was a girl. Perhaps he was using what Mormor called "oily words," shaped not for the hard grain of truth but for soft, easy, palaver.

Puffing and blowing, Song climbed the many steps to the grand blue room at the top of the villa. She knocked gently and pushed open the door. Mormor was hunched in her chair, looking out over the stony canopy of the city. Her face was screwed up, as though in pain, but seeing Song, she brightened.

"My little charm," she said softly.

"Mama says I'm to keep you company because you're too sick and too old to leave the room, but I came because I wanted to."

"That's good," Mormor said, adding, "you're getting old yourself. How many name days are you now?"

"Seven and three moons."

"And three moons! You're growing up."

Song stood a little taller.

Whenever her great grandmother's name was mentioned at the *Fari,* Song flushed with pride. Everyone knew Veribas Song was the first woman to sit on the Council of Elders. She had represented the whole of Gildas at the great Settlement of Sigon.

"Tell me about when you were my age, Mormor."

"Your age?" Mormor said and winced slightly.

"*Please?*"

"Hold my hand and I'll tell you."

Song used listen to the stories while sitting on Mormor's knee, but these days she made do with a cushion by her side. Her great-grandmother was supposed to stay in bed, but insisted on sitting on the old Council chair. Song couldn't understand why when she sat in it herself; the finely wrought carvings worried her back, and the hard, angled seat was terribly uncomfortable. Seeing her squirm, Mormor smiled and said, "One never rests easy on a seat of power." Song had no idea what that meant, but nodded wisely anyway. Mormor took her hand and gave it a little squeeze.

"Though it was many years ago, I remember being your age. I was seven when the Elders took me from my home to study at the great *Fari* in Acqui. I had only been to the city once, and that was to see the lanterns during the Dance of Tines. Everyone said it was an honour, but I missed my family."

"But why you, Mormor?"

"They said I had the gift of the Gildas of old."

"What's that?"

"It's difficult to explain exactly. I suppose you could say I was charming. With a smile, a miserly baker would part with his barn cakes for nothing, or with a laugh, a mourning widow would smile again. Somehow, I always knew what to say and how to say it. There was talk about the Aquinas bloodline."

"The Spirit of the Incubus!"

Mormor flushed slightly. "Yes, descended from Lord Aquinas himself. I have his voice, I have his charm, but not, thankfully, his appetites. I'm a little surprised you know about—"

"Cook told me. When the Gildas first came to this land, Lord Aquinas made a baby from the tears of his people and gave it to a grieving mother who had lost her child. And that baby girl, Lila, was our ancestor from over five hundred years ago."

"Made from tears? No, not quite."

"Then what?"

"You're too young yet." Mormor coughed into her handkerchief. "Anyway, at the *Fari* I was unhappy. The Elders tried to take care of me, but they were stuffy old men absorbed by their politics. What could they know about a little girl? I cried myself to sleep most nights and grew up quickly." She put the handkerchief in her sleeve.

"Just a few short weeks after I arrived, the first raids from the Hadrad Mountains began. Outlying farms were pillaged, Foxrall was sacked, and the ruined townsfolk sent a delegation to the Council. I remember one man in particular, dreadfully worn, white and thin, his hair in lumps as though torn half out."

Mormor's expression changed then, became red and angry, like the carbuncle on Cook's nose. "Who are these barbarians that take our livestock and enslave our people? And who are you to let it happen?" she roared.

Song shrunk back. Mormor told stories in character. It was very dramatic, but sort of frightening as well. Song felt like she was sitting next to the lumpy-haired man. Her great grand-mother's expression became more dignified. Another character was about to speak. Perhaps an Elder.

"The Hadrada worship only destruction and pale shadows conjured by their Wiccan gods. Have faith in our Lord Aquinas, practice your *kon* staff, attend the *Fari*, and we shall prevail."

Her face changed again. The carbuncle was back, but sadder this time.

"But how will that make up for the sheep I've lost, and the three daughters taken by the savage men?"

Song could imagine the lumpy-haired man, desperate, grieving, a hot tear in his eye.

The serious face replied, "Look to the currency you have left. A broad-hipped wife will have more babies, your verdant pastures will bloom again, and the bloodline of your lost daughters will temper a wild and savage people—and perhaps one day make them our friends."

"Friends?" Song asked, puzzled. "But I thought the Hadrada were banished to become Forgotten?"

"Remember, child, this was before the great war of Sigon, a simpler time when there were more possibilities about which way the world would turn."

"Tell me about the other races, Mormor," said Song. "The ones that became Forgotten."

Her great grandmother said nothing but closed her eyes and sighed.

Song waited.

Mormor didn't stir.

Song was about to nudge her, fearing her grandmother had dozed off—or worse—when Mormor's eyes flicked open and she asked, "Do you know who the Chamberlin is?"

"An Elder on the Council?"

"Not just an Elder, but *the* Elder, the first of our people. When I was twelve name days old, he summoned me to his quarters. I trembled all the way up the hundred steps to the crow's nest. The room was thin and high, like the shape of the tower itself, like the shape of the Chamberlin himself. Crammed into the walls were books, scrolls, and every artefact of learning, stacked all the way to the ceiling. There was a ladder to reach the upper volumes and when I came in, he was leaning back on his chair, his feet resting on the rungs.

"'Ah, Veribas,' he said. 'I have a question for you.'

"As he spoke, his slippered feet walked a couple of rungs up the ladder causing him to lean almost horizontal in his chair. The thinning grey hair that was usually so neatly combed over his scalp flopped from his bald head. His dressing gown billowed lazily to the floor."

"He was in his pyjamas!" exclaimed Song.

Mormor nodded.

"'A question . . .' the Chamberlin repeated, pushing himself back into an upright position. His gangly arm pulled a scroll down from the shelf. Slowly he unfurled it on the table, weighting the corners with four small pebbles.

"'This one never wants to stay open,' he muttered. 'Now, look on it, Veribas, what do you see?'

"'A map.'

"He bobbed his pointed nose at me. 'Of course it's a map. My pet fish would know it was a map. But what do you *see?*'

"I saw Gildas lying beneath the northerly territories of the Serendips, the Visigottes and Acrapheans, and twenty other races scattered across the land, some in settlements, some nomadic. Inscribed next to each were symbols depicting the size and nature of the people. There was the stone-hewing glyph for the Visigottes, a mannequin for the Viscara and next to the Acrapheans, a simple eye.

"'Well . . . ?' the Chamberlin said.

"'I see a land rich in its diversity, the fruit of the Seraph Sun . . .'

"'Pah!' said the Chamberlin, stubbing his finger on the parchment, his nail white with the pressure. 'You sound like a rustic preaching at the *Fari*. I see a land fast becoming crowded, of resources being squeezed. These Hadrada raids are just the beginning. There are other races on the move; the Viscara poach in our forests and other races press in at our borders. The first great war of Seraphina is coming and this'—he stubbed his finger again—'this, Veribas, is a battle map, stolen from our friends the Serendips, who as we speak, are readying for war.'

"'War?'

"'They eye the northern territories, and why not? They have the men, they have the resources, and they have a powerful god who will help them in battle. Mark my words, they have their heart set on Khare.'

"He let the words sink in and then fixed me with a cold, granite eye. 'And when war comes, my young Veribas, we will turn to you for guidance.'

"'Me?'

"'The Serendips are not the only people with a powerful god. You have the blood of Aquinas in your veins, and with it the Voice. All sides will trust you, all sides will treat with you, and through your treating, we will be left unscathed, only to be drawn in at the end when we are sure of the outcome.'

"And he was right. The war of Sigon raged for ten years, and only in the last three did Gildas finally commit to the cause, sure of the outcome, knowing that the east and west would be divided by the great House of Serendip, who began the war, and the great House of Acraphea who ended it. For just three legions of men, supplied at a crucial time, the Gildas were granted the Great Lakes of the south. We were the only race to end the war with more people than we began it. "

Song's great-grandmother sat silent then, her eyes fixed downwards as though still staring at the map, the land of Seraphina as it was, before the war of Sigon ripped it apart.

"Mormor?" Song said softly, gently squeezing her great-grandmother's hand.

"Bedtime now," Mormor whispered, a tear glistening in her eye.

*

Song hid behind the velvet curtain and cried silently into her smock. Her great grandmother's house was teeming with relatives and she hated them all.

"We need to hurry!" said a voice from the corridor. It was her uncle, the bearded horror with a red face. He wasn't even a blood relative, but what Mormor called an *outlaw*. "They'll strip the rings from her fingers if we're not there, or worse, let the old bat be buried in them."

"Oh, don't! You'll make me laugh," warbled Aunt Mingus.

"I'm serious, you pigfish!"

Song heard a fumble and then an irritated "get off!" followed by the sound of kissing. She felt nauseated. All through lunch, Aunt Mingus had sucked oranges like a weasel might suck a brain. She wasn't easily denied.

"I could kill for another glass of wine," Aunt Mingus said when they came unstuck. Song could tell by the way she said "glash" that she probably didn't need one.

"We have to go!" said the uncle through clenched teeth.

Yes, hurry! thought Song.

"Can't you see I'm upshet!" slurred Mingus.

But he must have dragged her away because a moment later Song heard footsteps clatter down the corridor. Opening the folds of the curtain, she crept out after them.

Song was barred from Mormor's room by her harridan aunts, but standing just outside, she could watch through a crack in the door.

"A toast to our Lord Aquinas!" said the Cantor, holding up a goblet.

The family knelt around the bed, faces grave but

unconvincing. Aunt Mingus was crying, but that was the wine.

The Cantor pushed the goblet between Mormor's lips and lifted her head so she could drink.

"You're choking her," sobbed Song quietly.

Her great-grandmother's half-closed eyes seemed to flick towards the door and then with a faint movement of the hand, she motioned the Cantor towards her. He bent down, head level with her mouth. "Send them out," she rasped.

"All?"

"All but the little girl standing outside. Bring her to me."

"But the last rites—"

"Do it."

The family murmured protests, but while Mormor breathed, her word was law. Filing out, they shot livid stares at Song, all except her mother who winked encouragingly, but then tottered back and forth and stumbled over a non-existent step.

The Cantor led Song to the bed and left them alone. Song saw flecks of spittle and blood in the corner of Mormor's mouth, and the lines on her face were deep and tinged with yellow. This, then, was what death looked like.

"I trust only you," Mormor whispered. "Your great-grandfather died before you were born, and I know what my daughters are. My fault, I suppose. I should have paid more attention to their upbringing, but . . ." She tapered off, fighting for breath. "I have given my life to Ferin Aquinas and the great race of Gildas, and yet I foresee the downfall of all my work. False friends in black encircle our lands, and the dark wings of war beat on the horizon. The Gildas were the victors of Sigon, but the cost was too great . . . too great. Some wars that are won in arms are lost in the greater, hidden conflict of the soul." She broke off again, eyes watering, unable to breathe.

"Mormor," Song said, her lip quivering.

"Don't cry, my charm," Mormor whispered, extending a skeletal hand and resting it on Song's head. "You are the last of the House of Song; a god's blood runs in your veins and the essence of his spirit is in you even now. Inchoate your Voice may be, but you have the gift, and once you come of age that gift will grow, whether you will it or not."

Song thought of her imaginary friend, the voice that dwelt deep inside her. Could it be that it was not her imagination at all but . . . him?

"But h-how can you know?" Song asked.

"Because, since you were born, his voice has faded from me. Oh, he's still here," she said, gently tapping her heart, "but he prefers the young to the sick, to the weak. Aquinas only thrives when the vessel is strong."

"But I don't understand . . ."

"Hush, my charm. No questions. I am dying and you must hear what I have to say so *you* can be prepared for what must come, in a way that I was not." Her pale lips tried to smile. "Long ago, our god walked abroad as a man, feasted with us, lay with us, and we in our innocence venerated him. But in time, he lost interest in the Gildas, and in truth, we in him. Through the incubus he found another way to live, a lazier way."

"But he is the god of the Gildas!" Song said, alarmed.

"Oh, we pay homage to him, and the *Faris* are the centre of our worship and learning. It's easier for the Elders to rule that way, to honour the trappings of ceremony, without actually having the faith. And there is value in the Aquinas culture, in our learning, in the way of the *kon* and the creed of self-reliance. It has kept our people strong." Again, she fought for breath before continuing. "As long as his bloodline survives, passing down through the female line of our House, he too will thrive. When I die, his spirit will live on in you, and when you die, your children will carry the . . . the burden."

"But what if I have no child?"

"That is the dangerous time for him. Unless he can find another mortal to lie with, he will fade from this world. She must be a willing partner, someone he cannot use his powers to charm into acquiescence, someone who bears his child in the full knowledge that she condemns her offspring to live in bondage to him, until she and her descendants die out."

"I don't understand," said Song, tears coming to her eyes.

Mormor's voice was low now, her breath, deathly shallow, but still she held on. "When you come of age, his spirit will come to you as the incubus. He will become one with your voice, your mind and . . . your body. From that moment onwards, a part of him will always live in you. The gift of Aquinas is powerful. You will charm everyone without even trying, people will fall over themselves to do your bidding, but . . . there will always be a part of you that is not yours." She gasped, and her body shuddered with pain.

"You will always be aware of his presence, drawing from your soul and your spirit. While you live, he cannot die, thriving on whatever plane he chooses, a god with no duty to his people, no duty to anything but his . . . whims."

Song could hardly hear Mormor now. Her face was like a stiffening mask. "Th-they say I did great things for Gildas at the war of Sigon with all those bloody bargains I struck . . . but understand this, my child: since my sixteenth name day, I have never truly been free . . ."

And with those words, Song's great-grandmother slumped back on her pillow and into the sleep that lasts forever.

*

It was the perfect afternoon, soft and sweet with the odours of spring. Fresh gorse flashed from the hedgerows and violets peeped from the banks. Young lambs gambolled over greening pasture and lyrebirds trilled in the silver sky.

Song walked through the fields, absently swishing at the hogweed, a trail of dead flowers in her wake, her mind distracted by the rumours that had reached Gildas, and were now spreading like the plague.

Dread war has come to the Serendips and
The land of Enninmyra is no more!
Have a care, fair folk of Aquinas, lest
Ravening Acraphea marches south.

Surveying the sun-dappled lake and tranquil plains, she wondered whether it could be true. Surely she would feel something if Seraphina was burning.

A team of Madras farmers ploughed in the adjacent field, their rippling muscles working with the oxen as one. Perhaps they had heard something. Leaning over the low-lying hedge she called to the nearest, "Hail Madras! What news of Acraphea?"

"I know not," replied the man without breaking his stride, "but our master says we must finish planting before the new moon, for the barley may not have long to grow."

"War?"

The Madras shrugged and carried on.

Song shivered. She would go and see Jaquin. He would know. She watched the men for a little longer, fascinated by their huge sweeping movements. The Madras never tired of their work, despite its physical nature, despite the monotony. Turning towards town, the old *Fari* rhyme came unbidden to her mind.

Madras for the fields, Calliope for the sea,
Sylvans for the forest and in fair Gildas we,
As chronicled in Sigon, have bannermen three.

The doggerel failed their proud subjects. They were so much more—artists, craftsmen, and warriors. That is why her great-grandmother secured those races as vassals after the great war of Sigon. The Serendips had the Thegns and myriad minor races; the Acrapheans had the Fyrd and Viscara; the Gildas had the Madras, the Calliope, and the Sylvans. The rest were banished as Forgotten.

The memory of Mormor brought a pang. She was dead eight years but Song still missed her. Her own parents had died the same year from what Cook called "the curse of the sipping sauce." And on the day of her mother's interment, Aunt Mingus moved into the great city house and Song was sent to live with her cousins near Lore, never to see the dreaming spires of Acqui again.

Walking through the huge gates, she smiled at the pretty town. Trees and potted plants lined the streets and all of the buildings were yurts, except the *Fari* where Song taught. The townspeople of Lore upheld the ancient traditions. On their fourteenth name day, every child was banished from the town with only a *kon* staff and a net. The skinny bodies that returned thirty nights later were adults, granted a lien for five acres. Most returned starving after three or four nights to be children for another two years.

The other provinces of Gildas looked down on Lore as backward, its people simple, but Song loved it. Everyone knew everyone else, and it had none of the pomp of Acqui.

As she made her way through the square, small children just let out from the *Fari* raced after her, swishing rushes and trilling, "Miss Song, Miss Song, Miss Song." She stopped and handed them each a sugared plum and they hurrahed with delight.

"What did you learn today, little ones?"

"About the ancient Dance of Tines!" they cried in unison.

"Show me," she said, laughing.

The children stood in various stiff poses and looked terribly earnest, hopping from one leg to the next. One ambitious child tried a kick and jump, but landed on his back. Jaquin's youngest brother pulled him up and brushed him down. No harm done.

"That's very good! Very good!" said Song.

"Next week the Master says we will use real tine ropes tied across the square!" said a raggedy girl called Quilly.

"And a *kon* too?" Song asked, smiling.

"No, no," said the boy who'd fallen, "we're to practice with rushes first and then the *kon*. Soon we'll be like you!"

"You'll be much better than me!" Song beamed and the children squealed and gambolled after her before dispersing into their homes for supper.

"Where are you going?" asked Quilly, her brother in tow, nose dribbling.

"I have to go and see Jaquin."

"Ah," Quilly said, nodding wisely, "is he your *special* friend?"

Song flushed. "I . . . I . . . no."

"He is! He is! You have a special friend! You have a special friend!"

Her little brother took his thumb out of his mouth and joined in. "Speckled prend! Speckled prend!" he shouted at the top of his voice.

Reddening further, Song kissed them both and hurried down Jaquin's street. Although just fifteen, he already owned a yurt whereas Song still lived with her cousins. Having survived the wilderness, he was considered a man.

"Anyone home?" she called, ducking through the entranceway.

The spicy scent of *kon* oil filled the air and the plush red carpets that usually covered the floor sat carefully stacked in the corner. On the table was a long staff held in place by two clamps. Jaquin was leaning over, his tongue poking out of the side of his mouth in concentration, a shock of auburn hair wet over his forehead. His militia uniform lay on the ground and he was naked from the waist up. He was planing some parts of the shaft, sanding others. Hanging over the fire was a brass incense holder. The finest *kons* had three applications of oil, rubbed in until every drop was absorbed. He was in for a long day.

"Song!" he said, looking up from the bench and beaming.

"A new *kon* staff?"

"Mine's not fit for the Dance of Tines, let alone fighting."

"It's true, then," she said, a lump in her throat.

"What?"

"That war is coming."

Jaquin paused his sanding. "I know only that two nights ago a party of Serendips were spotted on the outskirts of the Stony Marsh. Close behind were Fyrd and Viscara hounds, tracking them as though they were a steaming herd of mannequins."

Song plumped down on a floor pillow. "The Fyrd here?" she said. "That is against the treaty."

"They weren't out in the open. They kept to the cover of trees, crossing back across the border whenever they saw us. It hampered their efforts. The Serendips found sanctuary at a Madras farm and then fled in the night for Muir."

Song breathed a sigh of relief. "So they escaped."

Jaquin shook his head. "A scout saw smoke coming from an abandoned barn some way north of Jaylen. Inside the remains of seven bodies. Two were children."

"No!"

"An envoy has been sent to Acraphea, but as yet there has been no reply."

"Perhaps they mean to send none!"

"Lore has raised the militia, and so you see me oiling my *kon* when I should be tending my fields."

"But what good will militia be against an army?"

"There won't be an army. If the whispers are true and red war has come to the Serendips, then Acraphea can't possibly have the arms to worry about us." He held up the oak staff. "Fit for Lord Ferin Aquinas himself."

"Don't say that!" Song said. She didn't like Jaquin to be so flippant. Song remembered her great-grandmother's strange words from all those years ago, although she wasn't sure she believed them anymore, if she ever had. She still had her Voice, her old companion and friend, but it had faded. She liked Jaquin better. He flipped onto the chair, balanced on the rim and then with one sweeping movement swept the feet of his imaginary foe. He was as agile as a cat.

Jumping down next to her he said, "And now I have a question for you."

"Yes?"

"Are you really my speckled prend?"

*

Two months passed. The rumours, so vital at first, became withered and cracked with age. There was no army. Sightings of rag-tag bands of Serendips fleeing through Gildas took on a mythical quality. The part-time militia returned to their work. Harvest was coming. There was no time for imaginary wars.

"I don't like it," said Song as they sat in the tavern.

Jaquin sighed. He had been in the field all day and his first mug of ale sat before him. He took a long draught. "What can we do?" he replied, wiping his mouth.

"They have destroyed a people and taken their lands. We should do something. The Council should do something. Instead the Elders grant them audience."

"Wait until you hear what they have to say."

The Acrapheans had sent emissaries to every town in Gildas in the name of friendship. Their holy men were to address Lore today, an *apologie* for the war, delivered from a platform erected outside the *Fari*.

"I don't want to go." She sounded unconvincing even to herself. She would go. No Acraphean had been in Lore for over half a century.

Jaquin shrugged and drained his glass.

"Time for one more then?" he said.

She bit her lip. "If we hurry."

*

They were late and the square was thronging with people.

"We're not going to be able to see anything," Song said.

"I can fix that." Buoyed by the ale, Jaquin took her hand and, with a little unfair play, pushed all the way to the front. "Official militia business, excuse me, make way for the militia!"

Song ducked and weaved but couldn't escape the glowering faces or children squealing, "Miss Song! Miss Song!" as she jostled past their parents.

"Jaquin!" she rasped when he finally let her go.

"You said you wanted to see."

"Yes, but . . ."

They were barely ten feet from the dais. Others had been waiting hours. She sighed and took his arm. Partners in crime. Jaquin smiled.

"Tell me what these Sextons believe in again? The Lady?"

"Jaquin!"

"I can't remember."

"Serendips worship the Golden Lady. The Manciple is her servant. The Acrapheans believe in the prophecy of the Sext, the six that will come again. Their dark Sextons are the seers who sit on the Star Chamber, the Council of Acraphea."

"Well I think all these gods are for the weak-minded. They always seem to be *about to come*. When was the last time anyone saw our Ferin Aquinas? Five hundred years ago?"

"Jaquin!"

"I can't believe in what I can't see."

Song suddenly felt very hot and was relieved when one of Lore's Elders finally addressed the crowd. He said a few words of introduction and applause broke out all around them.

Flanked by four Seneschals, the Acraphean Sexton walked onto the dais. His black-cassocked figure was imposing and silence settled over the crowd.

The Sexton. His eyes gleamed, his tonsure gleamed, his teeth gleamed. He was like a perfectly polished weapon. Holding his arms out in the pose of a preacher, the folds of his cassock hung down like great black wings. He paused for a moment longer, and then his voice rang out in parley:

> *"Good people of Gildas, a corruption*
> *Has grown to the west of our peaceful land.*
> *House Serendip, vassals of the tarnished*
> *Lady, did hatch a plot so bloody red*
> *And foul that all must fall before its scourge.*
> *Sext of the Achromat;"*

Here the Seneschals bowed and repeated, "Sext of the Achromat."

> *"Sext of the Achromat; Godly, Mighty.*
> *Lord Acraphea, Lady Acraphis,*
> *Fair daughters; Aphretes, Tor, Kallis and*
> *Malacrae who will, one day, come again*
> *To restore the lands of the Seraph sun*
> *To grace, sweet order, and tranquillity,*
> *Have in their wisdom, bestowed a vision*
> *On our Order, lest the vile Serendip*
> *Vanquish Acraphean, Gildas and all."*

The Sexton put out his palms in the traditional blessing of the Acrapheans.

"Was that it?" asked Song in disbelief.

"I think so, the official speech anyway. They are staying on for the *friendship* part. Talking things over with the Elders."

"But that was just some high speech palaver," Song said

loudly. "It told us nothing!"

Jaquin smiled and put a finger to his lips. Song ignored him.

"Sext of the Achromat! As if the Gildas want anything to do with that charnel house of superstitious prophecy."

"They're just trying to be . . . diplomatic."

Song folded her arms and felt her blood rise. "What if the next time the vision is of 'vile' Gildas?"

"Song . . ." Jaquin sounded strained as he looked over his shoulder.

The crowd began to drift away, apparently satisfied.

Watching the Sexton exchange pleasantries with Lore's elders, Song felt the blood beat in her head. She thought of the children, both those smiling around her and the poor, charred bodies found outside the Spinney. Suddenly, she found herself shouting.

"Sexton! Hear me!"

All faces turned to her and the crowd sucked back into place.

"What are you doing?" said Jaquin between his teeth.

What was she doing?

What needs to be done, replied a voice inside her head, one she had not heard for a long time.

"Address Sexton Gravales by his full title or not at all," said one of the Seneschals coldly.

"Aye, cenobite, we're in Lore, not Acraphea." She squared her shoulders. "Sexton, why do you talk to us of visions? We have no belief in your house gods. We came to hear why our friends and allies were slaughtered and why you took their lands."

The Seneschal tried to speak again, but the Sexton held up his hand.

"Child," he said, fixing Song with a stare, "I speak only the truth." His smile was like a gash across his face.

"Tell us then, *in truth*, why."

"That has already been pronounced."

"Yes, but of what were the Serendips found guilty?"

"Divine foresight requires no justification," the Sexton said, addressing the crowd rather than Song. "But, for the doubters,"—he returned his gaze to her—"we have Serendips who will testify to their planned treachery."

"I'm sure they will," sneered Song under her breath, "after a long date with the frowning cat." She turned on her heel and the crowd parted for her, like paddlers from a scorpion fish. She walked until she was outside Lore and into the Stony Marsh, stopping only to pick up her *kon*.

*

"The Sexton was asking about you," Jaquin said.

"Oh?" Song tore a strip of meat from the spitted venison. With just a *kon* and quick feet, she had taken the deer that afternoon, dragging the carcass all the way back to Lore. Her muscles burned but she felt better.

"He wanted to know about your family, where you are from, and whether you hold any office."

"Maybe he likes me."

Jaquin said nothing.

"Don't look so worried!"

"Acrapheans are not to be taken lightly. There are things here we don't understand."

Song shucked a bone from her mouth. "They've nailed that speech to the *Fari*. I saw it when I came back. What does that tell you?"

Jaquin said nothing.

"They say it's the same in every town in Gildas. A single crystal scroll, words burnished in gold, worth more than half the yurts in Lore."

"Then perhaps someone will steal it," Jaquin said, finding his grin.

At that moment she loved her brave man more than she could ever say, but no, she could not let him. It would be suicide. "There's too many eyes and it's bolted on. You'd have to take off the whole door."

"I was only joking. I'm militia!"

"Oh, o-of course, I was joking too," Song said, looking down and wiping her hands on her soiled tunic.

*

"I'm thinking of staging a demonstration," Song said, sitting on the end of Jaquin's bed, her knees pulled tight to her chest.

"Huh?" grunted Jaquin. It was still hours before dawn.

"The *apologie* was ages ago and there are more Acrapheans here now than then. They have to leave, Jaquin. It will soon be winter."

"Careful my love, the Friends won't like it."

"The Friends can sit on their *kon* staves for all I care. Who do they think they are anyway?"

The Friends of Acraphea had mysteriously sprung up all over Gildas, volunteers to help the visitors with local customs and show them around. There were whispers of other favours too, and silver crescents changing hands.

Jaquin sat up and rubbed the sleep from his eyes. "Good morning to you too," he said sleepily and lent towards her. She gave him a brief peck on the cheek.

"I just don't understand it. Why are we letting this happen?"

"This ill wind will pass. They all do. All you need to do is stay out of trouble," Jaquin replied.

Song said nothing.

"And darling?"

"What?"

"Happy name day."

She had forgotten. She was fifteen years old.

*

Song's hands were bound with hemp and her wrists ached. Curiously, she welcomed the pain. It was a reminder that she wasn't dreaming. Each throb was like the beat of a small drum, a people marching into bondage. For their sake, she would be strong.

The hearing room was hot and stuffy. Despite the efforts of the Elders to downplay her trial, half of Lore had turned out to watch and the gallery was packed. The Sexton was there, as were the Seneschals, standing around like beatific llamas.

Unconsciously her eyes strained for Jaquin but she knew he wasn't there. The militia had been sent on a border patrol of Muir with the Fyrd. He wouldn't be back for another week. They had arrested her the day he left, taking her while she taught her class at the *Fari*. She would never forget Quilly's tear-smudged face.

Despite the heat of the room, Song shivered, almost as though she could feel the snow thick on the ground outside; winter had come early this year.

"Cairo Song, you stand accused . . ."

Conscious of all the eyes on her, Song stared at her feet. Then she felt the throb in her wrists. It was like a stab of shame. Her great-grandmother had been on the Council of Acqui when she was Song's age, not a cowering little girl.

" . . . having contravened the law . . ."

Song looked up, clenched her fists and swallowed. "And whose laws are those?" she said, interrupting the Elder. Her voice was loud and true, startling her audience—startling her.

"You do not have the right to address the bench yet," said the Elder, fixing her with a reluctant eye.

"But I do, my Lord, for I know of no *Gildas* law I have offended."

There was an intake of breath from the gallery and the old man coloured. Would he have her gagged? Song had seen it done for less: a cloth pushed deep into the mouth of a noisy penitent until it was time to plead. But hers was a minor offence and the worst they could do was warn her. The show was for the Sexton.

The old man shifted on the dais. Picking up a sheaf of papers he appeared to study them. He cleared his throat. "Very well," he said, reading. "Let me enlighten you. Lore, seventh province of Gildas, upholds an Edict of Friendship, which requires—"

"Edict?"

"You may not speak yet!"

"But Edicts are Acraphean law. They are not recognised in Gildas."

There was a murmur from the gallery.

"The accused is a tutor at the *Fari*, and knows the Edict states that all who hold office must swear the Friendship Oath—"

"I can't do that, my Lord," Song said.

The old man looked down at his papers and sighed again. The hearing was getting away from him. His gown had come slightly loose from his shoulder. His red nose, coloured over the years with manderlay wine, seemed to throb.

At the back of the room someone coughed.

A chair scraped and a Seneschal from the petitioner's bench approached the dais and passed the Elder a paper. The old man's eyes crinkled as he studied it.

He began again. "You have not only refused to take the Oath, but you have preached against the Edict to a room of *children*, souring minds entrusted to your care."

There was a groan from the gallery. On the petitioner's bench, Quilly's father folded his arms. Song had forever been a friend to his children, but the poor man craved silver crescents more than her friendship.

Her mouth felt suddenly dry. "If a tutor at the *Fari* cannot be trusted to teach what she feels to be the truth—"

"The accused holds a privileged office which has been abused. The High Cantor himself has mandated that—"

"I follow only the teachings of Ferin Aquinas."

"The Cantor has mandated that teaching of the Sext is consistent with—"

"An Acraphean Sexton pulls his strings, you know that."

A shocked hush swept across the room. If Song was already on thin ice, she just felt it crack. The Elder motioned to an orderly. The gag. There was no turning back, not now.

"What do *you* believe, my Elder of Lore?" she dared.

"That is enough, Song!"

"Ah! He uses my name," Song said, looking around the room. "As though he remembers the face of my great-grandmother who first gave him preferment; as though he remembers dancing the Tines with my grandfather as a boy; as though he remembers my father, and his promise to protect me when I was left all alone in this world."

The old man's hands shook and he dropped the papers on the table.

"But the accused is not alone," a voice whipped out from the bench. It was one of the Seneschal llamas, turned feral.

"No indeed," said Sexton Gravales, standing up, his black robes rippling before him. "The accused *cavorts* with another, yet no true union do they share."

Song regarded him for a moment and then laughed. She couldn't help herself. She was fifteen, a woman grown by their law, and could "cavort" with whomever she wished. Her trilling arpeggio lit up the room and the gallery laughed with her.

"Enough!" said the Elder. "The accused will recite the Oath or be stripped of public office."

"No! We want justice for inciting children against our people!" demanded the Sexton, still standing.

"It is not your place—" the Elder said quietly.

"We *will* have justice!" replied the Sexton.

The Elder said nothing more and the room became thick with silence.

"And for . . . preaching against the Edict, I pronounce six lashes of the smiling cat."

Song shuddered. *Lashes!* She felt her lip quiver, but managed to hold it steady.

"Do you have anything to plead?" the Elder said.

"Nothing. Though you tie my hands and whip my back, it is not I who is restrained and beaten."

The orderlies led her away.

*

"You can't do this!" Jaquin implored. "The Sexton will have you flayed, strip over strip."

"Which is exactly why I have to do something," Song replied.

Jaquin looked so worried that she laughed, and then winced with pain as the skin over her missing ear cracked. She had preached outside the *Fari*, telling the people of Lore to have a care because their spirit, their culture, their very beliefs were being eaten by wolves in cassocks. Her voice was compelling and crowds began to gather in ever-growing numbers. For this, the Sexton demanded a tongue. The Elder gave him an ear.

The cut bled when she laughed or smiled, which she still did despite everything. Jaquin said she was more beautiful than ever, with her long auburn hair covering the hole. Nevertheless, she felt the lack. Dismissed from the *Fari*, and a pariah in the town, the children ran away from her now when she produced sugared plums.

"Let me get a cloth," said Jaquin, seeing the blood well.

"I've got it," she said and pulled out the rag she kept in her pocket.

Standing up, hand on ear, she walked to the door of the yurt. She could see the permanent shroud of smoke that hung over the camp where Jaylen Spinney used to be. The camp was one of half a dozen staging posts built across Gildas to supply the Acraphean forces in preparation for the final assault on Muir. The generals knew they would lose ten for every Serendip once inside the forest, but they had plenty of soldiers. It was uncertain what threat the Serendips now posed, reduced as they were to a thousand men, maybe less. But the House of Acraphea only dealt in absolutes.

"It can't be done," said Jaquin. Song said nothing. "This man, the commander, is not like the Sexton."

"I know," Song replied.

"I don't think you do."

"Tell me."

"His eyes are black as coals, and haunted. He drinks all night but come the dawn he is possessed with an unnatural fire. Nothing escapes him."

"You sound as though you admire him!"

Jaquin did not reply.

"He's a killer, like all the other Acrapheans," said Song.

"No, not like the others. At the age of five he was found outside Castagna's walls, and picked up by some beer seller to work in the kitchens. They thought he was Forgotten, his parents killed in some skirmish on the western roads. For Aquinas sake, *he* thought he was Forgotten, and for years he lived with the Hadrada and other barbarians on the plains, habituated to their customs, their rituals, their bloody ways."

"I don't understand," Song said, "I thought he was an Acraphean."

"That's just it, he is!" Jaquin said, his eyes widening. "All the time he was the youngest son of the most powerful family in Acraphea. The boy didn't even know his true name."

"What?"

"It was *planned* all those years ago. His father foresaw that this boy would find a way to unite the Forgotten. The Treaty of Sigon divided lands, resources and bannermen so equally, that no race could overpower the other. They did not count on the Forgotten. They said Castagna could never be taken, but this boy knew how, and with his army of barbarians, he overwhelmed the city."

"So the camp is full of Forgotten?"

"Some but not many. After the war, he disbanded the forces. They returned to the plains and their families, replete with enough food for two winters, and enough iron to protect themselves for years to come. They are now his own personal vassals, something the Council of Acraphea hadn't foreseen. They will come when he calls, and die ten times ten on his word. They call him the King."

Song felt her face harden.

"Come here and lie down," Jaquin said.

Song pulled herself away from the door and stretched out beneath him. He took out a small bottle of oil and gently rubbed it into her back, their daily ritual.

"You said he was haunted," Song said.

"There was a woman, a high Serendip, whom he loved more dearly than life. She was slain during the battle of Castagna and since that day he has never been at peace, their child—born a Serendip but every inch his Acraphean blood—a reminder of how much he has lost."

This, then, was the adversary against whom she would risk all.

"Please," Jaquin said softly, "you have been lucky so far and you still have many friends, but do this thing—"

"I have to do something."

"This is not our battle. Your attempt will be suicide and . . ." He hesitated. "I need you."

His words sunk in, comforting her, warming her like the

oil, smoothing over the scars left by the smiling cat. Her back had healed but the lines of knotted skin would always be with her. The Elder had shown restraint that day. The Sexton wanted the frowning cat, with iron rather than leather tails. She would have never walked again.

"Well?" Jaquin said. He had stopped rubbing and his hands had become tense.

Reluctantly, Song turned slowly and met his eyes. "I have no choice," she said.

Jaquin stood up, his face flushed. He walked to the door of the yurt and looked out. "I have to get back on duty," he said, and disappeared into the early evening air.

*

Leaving Lore was easy. The gates were not watched until nightfall and the sun was only just setting. It was spring again. Song had hardly noticed. She wore a dull navy cloak with a hood to cover her head. Her legs shook as she walked.

Her heart sank as she approached the camp. Four watch-towers, balistraria and only one narrow entrance. The palisades were thirty-foot trunks, and at their base was a deep, dry moat. There was no chink in its armour, no crack through which she could climb or wriggle.

Song cursed under her breath. How had the Elders let this happen? First the Friendship envoys, then the "conversions," and now the army itself outside their gates.

She retreated to where Jaylen Spinney used to be, reduced to a few trees and stumps, and waited for the cover of darkness, her breath misting on the night air.

There were a few people about: camp itinerants, supplies going back and forth, an occasional party of Fyrd, cooks, blacksmiths and fletchers, out to stretch their legs or just to stare at something not encased in four wooden walls. All returned through the main gate.

Song sat underneath an elm, one of the few that had escaped the axe. It was dark now and she was hidden by night's long shadow. In the distance she could hear the hubbub of the camp. Those returning along the path now spoke in hushed tones, as if the darkness itself appealed for silence.

Ignoring the appeal, one voice rang out, deep as a milk vat, rich as honey: "Ha! Well met, my friend, well met!"

"Chandra," Song whispered. It was the Madras butcher. One moment he was addressing a trader, the next he was sharing a bawdy joke with some soldiers, white teeth shining out of his gorgeous dark face, his ancient nag trotting slowly on.

Song walked alongside, staying beneath the eaves. His progress was so slow that eventually everyone overtook him, and when they had, Song stepped out from the shadows.

"Chandra!" she said, beaming at him.

"Song, my girl," he said, "what are you doing here?" He was as genial as ever, but Song detected a change in his manner.

"Taking a stroll. You?"

"Delivering my wares. I am the camp's carnifex, you know."

"Yes, I heard. Good fortune indeed." She stared at his large crystal ring and tried to smile. She had ever known Chandra to be a good man. He owned the farm across from her cousins.

"No," Chandra said suddenly and pulled the nag to a standstill.

"What?"

"Whatever you are about to ask. The answer is no."

Chandra, though a Madras, had more charm than most Gildas and far more common sense. He was an important citizen of Lore and stood high in the esteem of his people. Even when he rebuked, his words were gently spoken.

"Wait!" Song held the horse's bridle and stroked its nose. Chandra sighed. "Still the same mare. Smoky, isn't it?"

"Yes. My weakness," he replied. "She is over thirty now and

no longer so smoky, but the dear girl is as reluctant to part with me as I am with her."

They stood in silence, the horse with ears pricked forward, grunting softly under Song's touch.

"She likes you," he said and then let out another sigh. "I have eleven children."

"I haven't said anything!"

"No, but I've known you since before you could say 'Chandra' when you came for those long summers with your cousins. You used to call me Cha-cha. Do you remember that? I suppose not. It means 'poo' in our Madras tongue. But as you were the prettiest, happiest little girl, I did not mind. You still are a pretty one. Still the favourite of my lads. And why? Because of your smile, because of the fire in your eyes and the sweetness of your breath, and because of the life that burns within you. And tonight, my child, your fire is out, dead as the meat I carry. Something is wrong. You are in need of help, and based on what I've been hearing lately, that means trouble. And so I say again, I have eleven children."

Song closed her eyes. "I have to get into the camp."

Chandra slapped his palm to his forehead. "Oh by the Lord Ferin Aquinas himself! What can you possibly want in the camp?" He thrust his arm out. "No, no, don't tell me! I want no part of this. No part."

Song said nothing but continued to hold the horse's bridle.

Remember, the blood of Aquinas runs in you, a voice inside her said. *Remember the past.*

Song thought of happier times: playing with Chandra's children by the hearth; cutting blocks of ice from lake Laverne in winter, a young Smoky dragging their day's work on a sleigh and then packing the ice tight with sawdust in the cold-cavern with the promise of hot, dipping apples afterwards; Chandra's laugh echoing through the night.

He met her eyes. "You know you are the one Gildas I would do anything for, and yet I can do nothing. I am truly sorry."

Song cast her mind back: the annual Dance of Tines with the entire province gathered around the Town Square. She had trembled with excitement. Only children of eleven years could compete and it was her turn. Win, and she would represent Lore in Acqui. It had been her dream for as long as she could remember.

The Dance began and Song moved in perfect rhythm across the low-hanging cat's cradle covering the Town Square, avoiding the pots of thick, sticky oil in every fourth or fifth diamond-shaped hole.

In, out, in, out.

She criss-crossed back and forth using her *kon* for balance, her toes synchronised with the music. Even the slightest brush of hemp and the competitor was out. There were twelve dances in all and the last dance finished on a never-ending drum roll. But the games usually ended well before then; the winner declared when there was only one left standing.

The eleventh Dance had been particularly difficult. Twice her foot had entered a thurible and twice she whipped it out at the last moment, avoiding the oil with its deadly drag. The crowd oohed and ahhed.

Going into the final Dance, the fabled "Song of Seraphina" three contestants remained: Song, Jaquin, and Mali, Chandra's eldest son. There was a sign from the Elder and the fiddle and drum struck up again.

Jaquin was tiring and Song smiled to herself. Panting, his foot disappeared down a thurible hole and came back sodden, heavy with oil. The crowd gasped. He managed a few more steps but his balance was off, and he struck the tines. With a rapidly congealing foot, he hobbled away from the square.

Close, but no cheroot.

The music ran on.

Mali dripped with sweat. Twice she saw him brush the hair from his eyes, almost losing his balance as he did so. Madras had come from the hinterlands and even other towns to cheer him on, will him to victory. But it would do no good. They had practiced together for years and Song knew she had the beating of him. He would make it to the beginning of the drumroll but then he was hers. She flew across the tines.

From the corner of her eye, Song could see Chandra, shaking with nervous energy, his usually genial face serious as stone. Called "clubfeet" by the Gildas, no Madras had ever gone to the finals, or even to the last Dance. But now there were only two: Gildas and Madras, Song and Mali, their feet drumming, *kon* staffs spinning, the outcome poised.

Back and forth Song's feet moved, truer than an arrow is straight. Mali was at her side, almost matching her tip for tip, but becoming slower, less agile as the song built to the beginning of the drumroll.

And then suddenly she made a mistake, snatched at a hole and fell out of sequence. Her toe almost touched a tine. The next hole had a thurible and, out of rhythm, she was unable to whip out her foot before it was doused in the syrupy oil. Planting her *kon*, she managed three more steps with her unsoiled shoe but finally had to go down on her right. Her foot slipped out from underneath her and she fell onto the tines.

The crowd gasped. There was a stunned silence, and then the Madras erupted. Mali was crowned champion of Lore. He did not win in Acqui—the competition was too fierce—but his people stood taller from that day onwards, no longer the "clubfeet."

Only one person was wise enough to know she threw the Dance that day, and that gentle man stood in front of her.

"Agh!" cried Chandra, banging his head against the frame of the wagon. "Though they may take my head, get in the back and don't make a sound."

"Will they look?"

"They never have, probably because nobody in their right mind would try to get into the camp. You can climb out when we get to the kitchens. There's so much hustle and bustle while we unload that as long as you keep your head down, nobody will notice."

Song stepped lightly onto the stoop while Chandra muttered about being too soft. The back of the wagon was insulated, the air sealed inside by two layers of canvas flaps at the front and back. It was unnaturally cold. Precious winter ice lay piled in blocks on a wooden platform, making a false ceiling. It was dark, but Song's eyes quickly adjusted.

A pheasant hung from a pike; whole pigs, their mouths stuffed with apples lay beside horizontal venison and calves, eyes glassy, but almost human. Song shuddered. The smell of so much raw flesh almost made her gag. Holding her nose, she stood behind one of the meat hooks and tried to stop her stomach turning over. The wagon bumped along.

A few minutes later they were at the gate.

"Hail, Madras!"

"Hail!"

"Your business?"

"Filling hardy bellies with succulent meats," Chandra replied, laughing richly.

Song heard the faint ruffle of papers. "Aye . . . carnifex. You're late."

"The horse is not what she once was."

"Send it to the knackers' yard then."

Chandra said nothing.

"Drive on, Madras, and next time don't be late lest we find another meat man."

"Yes, sir," Chandra said.

The wagon began to move.

"Stay your horse," a new voice said. Song heard Chandra shuffle nervously in his seat. "The King would have a word."

The King!

Song heard the chinking of steel as two or three men approached the wagon.

"Tell me, what are your wares, carnifex?" The voice was

deep and genial, but it seemed to Song to carry an edge.

"C-commander Astroka sent a billet . . ." Chandra began.

"I didn't ask *why* you are here. What are your wares?"

"Three pigs, two calves, sweet meats and a half dozen venison."

"That all?" the voice said quietly.

"Yes," said Chandra, his voice suddenly hollow and airy, like a reed blowing on a riverbank.

"May I take a look?"

"B-be my guest," Chandra said, the words almost sticking in his throat.

There were more chinks as the King walked to the back of the wagon.

Song pressed herself behind the hanging calf. Then, holding onto the meat hook, she lifted her feet and bent her body so that it was a perfect silhouette against the cadaver. The back flaps opened and a face peered in. Song held her breath and then felt the calf move, gently pushed out of the way with a drawn sword. The King's eyes locked on hers.

Jaquin called him haunted, but it was more than that. His faced burned with a dangerous vitality, like a blade too keen for its scabbard. He held her stare, unblinking, before finally pulling his sword away and letting the calf fall back into place.

"Ah-ha, Madras," he said slowly, stepping away from the wagon, "I knew you were hiding *something*."

"I-I can explain," said Chandra.

"A pheasant," the King said, aspirating the word. "You've brought me a pheasant. I could *smell* it. We'll enjoy that rare bird on my table tonight. Drive on, carnifex, drive on. Best not to keep the good cook waiting."

The wagon rolled on.

Song lowered her feet to the ground, trembling.

The King ruled with an iron hand. He was known for his ruthlessness and discipline. And yet he let her go. What did it mean? There was no time to dwell as Chandra's face appeared through the flap at the front.

"We're at the kitchens," he rasped, "get out! For Aquinas' sake, get out!"

Song had never seen such a brown face become so ashen.

"I'm sorry, Chandra."

"Did he see you?"

"Yes."

"Then I must look to my family," he said quietly.

Song said nothing but put out a trembling hand and held his shoulder. She could feel his anguish. She wanted to say that perhaps it would be all right, but she would not palaver to a man like Chandra.

Outside the wagon she heard the discordant chimes of the kitchen: pots, pans, knives, spills and curses. "Let's be having your wares, carnifex!" one of the camp cooks shouted.

"Good bye, my friend," Song whispered, "I won't forget this." Chandra nodded.

As the back of the wagon was ripped open by eager scullions, Song climbed out through the front. It was easy to pass unnoticed by the kitchens; everyone was too busy to worry about a small cloaked figure.

Song kept to the shadows, creeping along the rows of huts. It was late now. Oil lamps had been lit and throughout the camp fires burned in old, tempered kegs.

Jaquin was right. This was suicide. The camp was a maze and she had no plan. Once inside, she imagined it would be easy to find her way, perhaps by winnowing directions from an unsuspecting camp hand. The reality was dark-haired, dark-browed soldiers at every turn, stolid as stone, and dedicated to their King. And *he* knew she was here.

"Where are you going?" demanded a man suddenly stepping out of the shadows, not three feet away from her.

Song's heart skipped a beat. She was caught! Or was she? He was looking over her shoulder to a Fyrd standing behind her.

Song just needed to keep walking and look as though she knew where she was going.

"Two Pails," the second man said. "I'm relieving the guard."

"The guard? I don't know why we bother. It's not as though they could break out."

"We bother because of the King's orders, brother."

"Of course, sir," said the man.

Relieving the guard! That was it! All she had to do was follow them. Song slowed her pace. The man would overtake her and then she would slip in behind him. Turning, she stole a quick glance backwards. The men had stopped talking and were staring at her. She snapped her eyes forwards again but didn't have time to react as a third figure stepped around the corner and pushed a black hood over her head. The flat of a sword rapped across the back of her calves and her feet went from under her. As she hit the ground there was a dull thud, and she later remembered thinking it must have been her head because everything became very black.

Twelve

ONG WOKE TO a pounding head and desert thirst. A lump throbbed behind her earless hole and, sitting up, she grimaced with pain.

Day 1

She was in a dark and musty room. There was a bed consisting of straw on a crude wooden shelf. She lay next to it, prostrate on the stone floor. To her right stood an iron pail filled with liquid, and above that, a tankard on a hook. Though her tongue was a snake in sawdust, she would not trust the contents of the tankard, whatever they were. Adjacent was a second, larger tin pail placed beneath a brick-shaped indent in the wall; the indent was stuffed with dock leaves. Crude comforts indeed. The walls and door were the thick wood of the Spinney, the peculiar aroma of Jaylen pine unmistakable.

Song stood up, a blanket of stars passing before her eyes, and she tottered backwards almost into the waste pail. As she held onto the wall for balance, the peephole pushed back and an eye appeared. There was a rattle of keys and the door opened.

A tall man entered. His skin was pale, his handsome face framed by straight black hair. He wore a plain tunic and breeches and carried a small three-legged stool that he placed on the ground opposite the bed.

"So, how is our pheasant this fine morning?" he said, smiling. "My name is Commander Astroka." The man pulled out a tinderbox, struck the flint, and lit a torch on the wall. He motioned Song to the bed, and then sat on the stool. He rested his hands on his knees.

"Cairo Song, what are we to do with you?" She said nothing. "The King said you wanted something in here, in the cells of Two Pails, and now . . . here you are." The man reached over to the iron bucket, unhooked the tankard, and ladled out some water. "May I?" He did not wait for a reply, but took a long draught. "Ahh," he said and wiped his mouth. He hung the tankard back in place. "You'll forgive me if I don't test your other bucket," he said, smiling, and resumed his position on the stool.

"Do you have any idea what the punishment is for breaking into an Acraphean camp?"

Song still said nothing.

"No? The King is *very* particular about security. That's why we have sentries. They watch for cloaked figures who study the camp and do nothing in particular, except try to look as though they are doing *nothing in particular*." He stared at her, unblinking. "During war—and believe me, we are at war—the sentence for breaking into our camp is death." He paused again and then smiled. "But I hear you humiliated our dear Sexton, and for that the King applauds you, though his irreverence gains him no friends."

The commander stood up.

"It's curious, the Gildas have taken to the Sext like fish to the Blue-Black Sea. So many conversions, so many *Faris* now temples of the Sext. A few silver crescents here, some crystal there, and everyone is a *true* believer." Commander Astroka held up four fingers on one hand, and two on the other, steepling them together in the same way she had seen the

Sexton do. It was the sign of the prophecy, the two feeding the four that will come again. "The Sext of the Achromat," he said in a sing-song voice, "and not one blow struck. Now that's what I call a victory."

Song bit her lip and the taste of iron filled her mouth.

"Where was I? Oh yes . . . entering the camp." He leaned towards her. "*I* said we should hang this Cairo Song by the wrists until her hands were like a bowl of overripe grapes, ready for plucking. But the good King thought not. No, instead he has decided that you will rest here for . . . how old are you?"

"I have seen almost sixteen name days," she said.

"Yes, sixteen days, to be taught a little humility. Next time we shall not be so lenient."

"And then what?" Song said. It was difficult to speak; her mouth was so dry.

"Oh, then we will let this poor pheasant go, back to that pretty boy you . . . what was it? *Cavort* with in town. But you need to watch yourself from now on. *We* certainly will be."

In the torchlight she could make out every part of his face, every line of battle etched there. His eyes were black, humorous, but unforgiving. She did not want to extend their conversation but she had to ask something.

"What happened to Chandra?"

"The Madras carnifex? He has been dealt with."

"W-what does that mean?"

Commander Astroka put a hand over his heart, and then, in the Acraphean gesture of death, squeezed the air in front of it. "Now, now. Don't look like that. He was no child and knew the rules. You may be a fool, and reckless to boot, but he accepted our silver for his wares."

Song began to cry. She tried to hold it in, but the sobs came out, uncontrollable, her shoulders shuddering. Commander Astroka pulled her chin up, gently but firmly, his black eyes staring into hers. "There is no action without reaction. Remember that."

The man then smiled again, withdrew his hand and picked up his stool. "One last thing," he said. "While you are in here, do not speak. Any noise at all and your tongue will be forfeit. A second time and it will be your head. Please heed my words. I would not have you damaged further, Cairo Song." He snuffed out the torch with his gloved hand. "Food will be left by a scullion and the pails refreshed twice a day. When he comes, do nothing but sit on your bed and stare at the wall. The rest of the time is yours, and remember: silence."

Day 2

Song cried for twelve straight hours and still it did not seem enough. She cried until her throat was raw and her knuckles were bloody from being scraped across the wall.

Chandra!

Exhausted, she slept and when she awoke she cried again, until there were no more tears left to shed.

Day 3

Song paced back and forth. She hopped on the bed, then onto tiptoes, then back onto the floor. She did this two or three times. She hopped and walked for perhaps three hours. She had to keep moving; if she didn't her mind would wander back down that path of unbearable sorrow.

What would she say to the family?

Did they know already?

Another hour passed.

She began to think of Chandra again.

Lying down, she scratched three lines on the wall with a loose piece of stone. She pressed as hard as she could and hurt her fingers in the process. The pain felt good. Three lines and she had the beginnings of a haystack, the passing of time.

An hour later, she caught herself laughing. But it was the

hysterical, dangerous laugh of irony. To think she had come to rescue the children and had succeeded in orphaning a family.

Later she prayed to Lord Aquinas.

She had a lot to ask.

Day 4

If Song pressed her ear against the wall and listened carefully, she could hear talking. She heard it the first time while using the tin pail, but the best place to listen was lying on her bed.

"You're not the usual scullion," said a boy's voice.

"He's sick," came the reply.

"But you're a girl," said the boy, puzzled.

"Apparently," replied the girl, a touch of humour in her voice.

There was a pause.

"You're an Acraphean, aren't you? I thought only Fyrd were scullions? You must be very low born."

"And I thought *you* weren't supposed to speak to anyone," said the girl.

Song heard the chinking of pails.

"Don't go," said the boy.

There was silence, but no movement.

"Forgive me. It's . . . being locked up all day. We've been here . . . well, a while, and until today I've seen no one but the scullion and spoken to nobody."

"Well, now you've spoken to me," the girl said and then added in a hushed tone, "You've been here two moons."

"Oh," he said quietly. "What about my . . . ?"

"She is a couple of cells down. And yes, she is all right."

"How did you know what I was going to say?"

"I just . . . did."

"Have you spoken to her?"

"No."

There was another silence.

"Why are you talking to me?" the boy said.

"I . . . I can't tell you."

"Who are you, then?" The boy sounded suddenly on guard.

"A friend," she said softly.

"Gildas *friends* betrayed us."

"I'm no Gildas."

"No, you're worse. The Acrapheans destroyed my people."

"I have to go," the girl said.

This time there was no reply. The pails chinked again. Song heard the cell door creak open and then close.

Song expected to see the girl when her own pails were changed, but instead the scullion boy came, same as always, flushing deep red as he entered.

Day 5

The next day there was a new voice behind the wall.

"Don't even look at her if she comes again!"

The new voice was harsh. Song imagined the speaker hard, whip-thin, and edgy.

"I think she means us well," said the boy quietly.

"Well?" the new girl said incredulously. "Why do you think they have put us together?"

"I don't know, but I'm sure it was to do with her."

"After all we've been through, you're still such an innocent."

"She's one of us!"

"Are you blind? Have you seen her? She's the King's own daughter come to spy on us! Weeks of solitary confinement, not a word, and now here we are sharing our breakfast. Either they think they might learn something, or this is our last supper."

"No!"

"In this war there are no prisoners. What do you think they are going to do when they assault Muir? Leave us here?"

"That won't be for some time yet. The bulk of the army have yet to cross the Plains."

"How do you know?"

"She told me."

"Pah! They don't even need the *bulk of the army*. There's only a few hundred left."

"We don't know that! Maybe thousands escaped to Muir."

There was the scrape of somebody getting up and the sound of pacing.

She had to make contact. With her heartbeat thumping in her ears, her hand trembling, she knocked on the wall of her cell.

Rap-rap, rap-rap, rap-rap.

Immediately there was silence. She didn't dare knock again.

Day 6

At first, Song thought the boy and the other prisoner were sharing a cell, but they weren't. Their meetings were a concession—two to three hours a day at breakfast. The girl thought it was some sort of trap. The boy wanted to believe it was because of his pail-bearer. Song stretched along the bed, her scarred ear flat on the wall. Lying there for hours she would get up stiff and cold.

Day 7

"Don't listen to her! Don't look at her! Don't trust her!"

No matter where the conversation began, it always came to this.

"But I do!" the boy said in a tone so sincere it almost brought tears to Song's eyes.

"She's *his* daughter. The man who destroyed Castagna, the man who slew our companions in cold blood, a man who they say will do anything to achieve his ends. He knows no mercy."

"He's had mercy on us."

"Has he? Has he really? Or does he think we know

something? That's why he sends that doe-eyed daughter to befriend you and catch you off guard. It's working like a charm. She's probably listening now."

"She wouldn't."

The girl snorted with derision.

There was a lengthy pause and then the boy said quietly, "What if everyone had judged you by *your* father?"

They spoke no more that day.

Song walked for five hours, back and forth, forcing herself to keep moving. Four steps and turn, four steps and turn, until her feet were red with blisters. She walked and thought, and thought and prayed.

Day 8

"She said her father can't stand her," said the boy.

"Of course she would."

"He won't look at her, won't even let his men talk to her. He knows she comes down here, but he is beyond caring what she does."

"More lies. They're listening to us, trying to catch us out, trying to find something they can twist so they can claim our death wasn't murder. *She* will give them what they need."

"No!" the boy said, raising his voice. "She is trying to help us. I see something in her. I see it! She is—"

"*I see this, I see that.* Are you an Acraphean now?"

The girl called for the guard and was escorted back to her cell.

Day 9

It was not yet dawn when Song heard the other girl's voice.

" . . . there," she said softly.

Still groggy with sleep, Song pressed her ear to the wall.

For a long time, there was no other sound and Song began

to think she had imagined it, the girl's voice the entrails of a restless dream.

"But my cousin . . ." said the boy.

" . . . thinks I am the enemy. Perhaps she is right. I've seen so many dead now I hardly know myself. What does your heart tell you?" the pail-bearer asked.

"Sometimes I think my heart has turned to stone."

There was a pause, but Song thought she heard something; the softest touch of lip on lip.

"Yes," he said.

"Then it's decided."

Day 10

Another day, another line etched on the wall.

There were two haystacks now, each with four vertical strands and one tied across the middle to make a sheaf.

Song took a draught of water. Her mouth was dry with disuse.

The scullion refreshed her pails and brought in the meagre food. She stared at the wall. Unexpectedly, there was a second knock and he came in again, this time wheeling a clay tub full of steaming water with a lip that contained a fresh bar of lye soap. On a stool he placed a hard, itchy towel and a fresh tunic, blushing all the while.

The bath was a pleasant diversion; boredom and sorrow too often ate into her mind. Each day she continued to walk and hop and pray but only the voices kept the despair at bay. Without them, she would be undone.

Song already knew about her neighbours, how they came to be in captivity. The two Serendip fugitives were betrayed by Gildas Friends when they tried to cross Lake Laverne in a boat full of holes.

As soon as she had heard the story, Song knew she had to help them. If asked, she would not have been able to say why exactly, but something drove her on. They were important, she felt it in her bones. They could not be allowed to die. She had broken into the camp to rescue them, but now she was herself a prisoner.

She prayed to Ferin Aquinas to save them. She could do nothing else.

Oh please, Lord, take my life and let them live.

The fate of all Gildas lies with their breath.

Today the voices in the adjacent cell were silent.

Quietly, Song began to panic.

Day 11

There were raised voices outside the cell.

"What are you doing spending so much time down here?" It was commander Astroka.

"What I am asked," replied the girl tersely.

"The King will hear of this."

"It is by Father's command that I am here."

"He has not told me."

"He does not tell you everything. Some missions are . . . too delicate for your crude hands."

There was a pause. "I will ask him."

"Do that."

The sound of boots clattered down the corridor.

Day 12

Silence. All day, all night. Nothing.

Where had they gone?

Did the Serendips still breathe?

By the time the scullion came into her room, she was mad with anguish. When the small, smudgy boy put down the plate of bread and cheese, she faced him and said, "What has happened?" She tried to make her voice warm and rich, but it came out scratchy with disuse. Mormor said she had the gift to charm those around her, but if so, it never showed.

The dark-haired boy dropped the plate and stared at her wide-eyed.

Song smiled.

"D-Don't speak!" he rasped in a frantic voice.

"Tell me! Are they still alive?"

The boy nodded and hurried out.

Day 13

Her cell was still pitch black when Song heard their hushed voices. If she hadn't been awake, she wouldn't have heard them at all.

"I trusted you!" the boy said weakly.

"I-I didn't know," she said. The girl was crying. "Oh . . . oh, your poor mouth, your poor face. I . . . I will bathe your wounds."

Song heard the pail chink against the wall.

"I bought something to eat as well, to restore your strength."

There was no reply.

"Please. You've had nothing for three days. You have to eat even if it hurts. Here, I'll mush it up."

There was no reply.

"*Please.*"

Now came the sound of a utensil on the plate, and then after some time, the plate being put on the ground.

"Thank you," said the girl.

"We don't know anything." His voice trembled.

No reply.

"What are you doing?" he asked.

"Holding you."

Perhaps an hour later, the door of the cell quietly opened and the girl slipped out.

Morning came and went, then Song heard the cell door

creak again. There was the dull thump of what sounded like a body falling to the floor. The boy gave an exclamation of despair.

"They're killing us . . ." whispered the boy's cousin, "strip by strip."

"Don't say that."

"Just look at yourself," said the girl, "covered in your *scullion's* favour, the red and black hand of kindness. Your eye, your mouth belies how much the King's daughter has helped us."

There was a pause and then the sound of sobbing.

"I want to fight. I want to hold on, but I don't know how much more I can take," said the girl, her words punctuated by tears.

"B-but you were always the strong one."

"And you the one who didn't know his strength."

Another pause.

"We're not dead yet," said the boy.

"No . . . no."

A faint rustling sound.

"Eat this," the boy said, "it has a sprinkle of *filo* seeds."

"*Filo!* Where did you get it?"

No reply.

"Oh . . . my poor, poor boy. She'll be the death of you. It won't be the torture, or the lack of food, or the days and months living in this cell. It will one black arrow shot straight through your heart."

The boy said nothing.

"*Filo,*" the girl repeated. "Perhaps they mean to beat us again later. All those senseless questions. *Who sent the Gildas girl to rescue you? Who do you know in Lore? Who sent the Gildas girl to rescue you? Why did she break into the camp?* Over and over."

On the other side of the wall, Song let out a silent scream. She had made everything worse, not better.

"The King's daughter won't let us die," said the boy.

"Even if that were true, the King won't let us live."

Day 14

"I have something to say," said the boy.

"Go on," said his cousin.

"They've set the date."

There was a pause, an intake of breath, and silence again.

"Good," she said finally, "and may the Lady protect us."

"You don't want to know when?"

"What difference does it make?"

The boy laughed. "I can't believe you don't want to know!"

The girl laughed back then, which made the boy laugh even harder. For minutes they were in uncontrollable fits. They tried several times to speak, but each time collapsed again.

"T-tell me then," the girl finally managed.

"No!" said the boy, the cue for more hysterics. When they had finally calmed down, the boy said, "On the morning of the next moon."

"Well, that's helpful seeing as there is no window in my cell."

"Two weeks."

"That long?"

"There will be many watching. The cuts and bruises need to mend."

"Just in time for the crystal blade."

"They are not beheading us."

"What then?"

"Hanging."

A pause.

"The death of the traitor," the girl said. "She told you all this?"

"There was a piece of paper in my rations, delivered by the old scullion. I haven't seen the King's daughter for two days. They are watching her."

"I thought she could do what she wanted?"

"Commander Astroka is in charge of the prisoners."

"That's her story."

Another pause.

"You know, some days I wake up feeling quite optimistic," said the boy, "as though something may happen yet."

"That's because you're in love."

There was a sudden, high-pitched giggle, different from the laughter before. "No I'm not," he said.

Day 15

It was perhaps an hour or two past midnight and Song lay awake.

Next door, the cell door brushed open and then closed.

There were whispers, too soft to make out, and then a raised voice.

"But you can't!" said the boy, "I won't let you."

"Quiet!"

"You can't!" the boy repeated.

"We have no choice," said the girl.

"*You* do!"

"No," she said quietly, "not anymore."

The door opened and closed.

When she had gone, Song could hear the boy tossing and turning, unable to sleep.

Day 16

The wooden panel slicked back, eyes appeared then disappeared, and Commander Astroka walked into the cell.

"Ah, there you are, Cairo Song. I trust your stay has been a pleasant one," he said.

Song blinked at the ground, silent.

"That's very good, but don't worry, I'm not trying to catch

you out. Well . . . sixteen days and fifteen nights. Tonight is your last night. And in the morning, as soon as dawn breaks, your door will be unlocked and you may go. Do not tarry. Do not talk to anyone. Take the path on the right and it will lead you out of the front gates. And remember, we will be watching you."

That day, when her scullion came in, Song put her arms around him and kissed him on the cheek. The boy flushed even more heavily than usual, and then left, carrying his two pails a little unsteadily.

Tomorrow she would see Jaquin, and part of her—the selfish part—was elated. To be in his arms, to be welcomed by that smile! Another part of her loathed herself for feeling this way. Chandra would never see his family again. His life was taken for nothing, cut off because of her. And those poor doomed children. She had felt so strongly that their lives were somehow her destiny, that she would be the one to rescue them. How laughable that seemed now. She had succeeded only in bringing suspicion on them and provoking a vicious beating.

She flexed her muscles. The daily exercise had helped keep her relatively lithe. Calluses had formed on her heels and mid-foot. Her neck was sore from all the hours spent pressed against the wall, but her mind was clear from still more hours of meditation.

That night she slept in fits, haunted by nightmares. Chandra's severed head floated in front of her, shouting. She strained but could not hear his words. And behind stood his family, their eyes frantic, their mouths sewn shut. His head burst into flames, and when the smoke cleared, she saw the Serendips, hanging, their bodies white, swaying back and forth before a crowd, the King and his daughter laughing with their companions.

She woke soaked in perspiration and stared into the darkness.

" . . . do not talk like that, I beg you," said the King's

daughter. Song pressed her ear-hole to the wall.

"I speak of what I must. Soon my life will end and I will have no opportunity to say what I truly feel," the boy replied.

"Do not talk of death. It imagines us cold, unmoving lumps so removed from what we feel."

"Then let me talk of love."

"No. Love makes us fools in this time of war, and fools are sure to lose their hearts and minds . . . and heads."

"For my part, I would have it no other way. Your eyes have been the light that shines in this dank cell, your presence, my hope . . . and my despair," the boy replied.

"Despair?"

"I can live with being condemned, but not with condemning you."

There was a pause. "There is no me without you," the girl said quietly.

"Go then, until we try to cheat death itself."

There was the sound of skin on skin, lip on lip, a lingering embrace and then, nothing.

Song didn't go back to sleep. For the first time she was embarrassed for eavesdropping on this personal, secret language.

As soon as it was light, she heard the door of her cell unlock. She stepped outside and walked through the camp. She looked at no one. On the way to Lore she saw Pyro, the carnifex from the south side of town, his dirty caravan making its way towards the camp, pulled by two gleaming stallions.

*

"No!" shouted Jaquin, smashing his tankard on the ground before storming out to work. Song threw up her arms. She wanted to cry, but checked herself. It was childish and there had been enough tears.

In Lore, all had turned against her. While locked in Two

Pails, the Friends had earned their crystal by spreading rumours and blaming her for Chandra's untimely death. She couldn't find work or even a friendly face.

On the first day back she had steeled herself and gone to Chandra's house. Her stomach felt like a basket of eels, but she had to go, to share her deep sorrow and deeper regret. His widow chased her from the door as his sons stared sullenly from the window.

She had laughed bitterly then, admiring the foresight of the Acrapheans. To take her life would have made her a martyr. Taking Chandra's ensured the whole of Lore would revile her, and by extension, anyone who resisted Acraphea. The sixteen days of her imprisonment was exactly the right length to allow the anger to foment in town, but not long enough for it to cool.

Song had wanted to make a stand for her people and for the Serendips. Instead, Sexton Gravales and the Friends were more powerful than ever. Jaquin was almost dismissed from the militia. Only a single vote allowed him to stay, and he was demoted to the lowest rank of foot soldier. He had been next in line for captain. Jaquin, forever kind-hearted, did not say a word of this, but she knew; plenty of others were willing to share the news.

Song was tempted to run away, to begin again in another town, but the Acrapheans were all over Gildas. And besides, she could not go, not while the Serendips still breathed. She strained for news of them. Every day the new moon edged closer. Every night she missed their voices.

She cleaned up the broken pieces of the tankard. The hot tea soaked into the rug.

I bought him that rug, she thought sadly. It was a gift for Jaquin on his seventeenth name day. It cost more than a month's pay. Song had never been so excited to give anyone anything, the blue and gold thread in the pattern of two lyrebirds, one speckled, one plain. The pile had felt so soft but so sturdy beneath their feet. Jaquin laughed when he saw it, and when he laughed he lit up the world. It seemed an eternity ago now.

Song made herself a cup of tea, sat at the table and looked out of the window. It was strange somehow, but the faces that passed by were not so much different than before the Acrapheans came. And yet how much had changed! Many townsfolk had prospered, and it showed in their clothes and bearing. The influx of people, the camp's construction, the conversion of the *Fari* to a lavish temple, a row of stone houses for the Sexton and other dignitaries had all been good for trade. But didn't the Gildas see the cost? Tomorrow was the new moon and blood would be spilt in Lore.

She saw Jaquin striding back towards the yurt and her stomach turned over. He sometimes came back for lunch, but that was still hours away. He was flushed and out of breath, his *kon* rigid in his hand. She could read his expression like parchment. *He's been dismissed.* The Sexton had somehow forced another vote. They would be cast out together.

"Oh, Jaquin, I am so sorry," she said as he burst through the door.

"Sorry?" he said. "I just ran all the way back to tell you. Your Serendips have gone! Escaped!"

"Tell me!"

He could not stay long, but before he went back to work he told her the story and then held her in his arms, the bitterness of the past week forgotten.

Once left alone, Song began to plan. They had escaped during the night; nobody knew how. Song was certain that they would try to get to Muir, but against Viscara hounds and Fyrd they would never make it. Unless . . . if Song could make contact with them, lead them through the tricky terrain, give them supplies and somehow throw off the hounds, they might have a chance. She would leave under cover of darkness.

Only one thing troubled her: how would she tell Jaquin?

*

"They know where they are," said Jaquin when he returned.

"The scouts found them already?" Song's stomach turned over.

"No."

"How, then?"

"The King has a hunch."

Song cursed. "Where?"

"The Stony Marsh. They'll send in a party just before light to catch them off-guard."

"How many?"

"Twelve."

"Against unarmed children?"

"They're taking no chances. The King is mad with rage. They say he'll hang the guards."

Song shivered.

"There's something else," he said slowly.

"What?"

"I'm to go with them. They are taking four of us as guides."

"No," she whispered.

"Yes." Song said nothing. Jaquin held her by the shoulders and stared into her eyes. "I will be hunting you," he said.

"You . . . guessed."

"I know you, my love. I don't pretend to understand but—" Jaquin's lips shook with emotion. "No, it's good actually. I can help to keep them off your track, maybe find a way to slow them down."

"Oh, Jaquin!"

"It's all right," he said.

"But they'll know! They'll—" She couldn't finish.

"I'll be fine, but . . . whatever happens, they won't let you live." His eyes welled and he wiped a hand across his face.

"Now listen to me," he said quietly, "they've laid traps around the marsh."

"Traps?"

"On every path. I don't know what they are, but our captain says there is no chance of anyone making it through."

The Stony Marsh was huge, but there were only a limited number of paths in or out.

"I have to try," said Song.

"I know."

They kissed.

"This may be our last," said Jaquin.

"I love you more than my own life."

"And I you."

*

That night Song packed as many supplies as she could carry and raided Jaquin's hunting stores for a tinderbox and other things she might need. She packed blankets and materials for making a shelter, but then discarded them. They were too heavy and there wouldn't be time to make camp. She thanked Lord Aquinas it was almost summer.

What they would do if they actually got in sight of the forest, she didn't know. Jaquin said the perimeter was garrisoned by Fyrd, but by how many men, he couldn't say. She focused instead on the Stony Marsh. If they were there, she would get them out or die trying. It was a four-hour trek on foot, but Song was fleet, the moon bright, and she would make it in three.

Doing her best to hide her supplies under her cloak, she put her fingers to her lips, then touched Jaquin's pillow. She then picked up her *kon* and disappeared into the night.

As she walked through the town gate, the night watchman pulled her back.

"Where are you going?"

Song's heart sank. The sentry was a Friend. If she was to be delayed . . .

"Nobody may leave Lore after dark unless on camp business."

"Since when?"

"Since it was decreed by the Sexton. Things have changed since you were away."

The man's name was Niall, a recent convert to the Sext. He was in the militia and often held the gate. Song had known him most of her life. They were at the *Fari* together as children but she had not spoken to him in years, except in his official capacity as gatekeeper.

Song took a deep breath. "Well, it's only me," she said.

"State your name and purpose," he replied stonily.

Song sighed. Why was he being like this? Niall had never been the brightest, always quick to follow and easily led, but at one time they were friends. She changed her grip on the staff. If she knocked him out with the *kon*, how long would it be before he was discovered? Not long. She dismissed the thought and smiled.

"Oh, Niall," she said in a honeyed voice. "If you must know, I have terrible . . . cramps. The type that come with the moon." Song made herself flush deeply and saw with satisfaction that Niall looked uncomfortable. "The only relief is a brisk stroll."

"Outside the city gates?"

"Well, you know . . ." She put a hand to her eyes to wipe away a conjured tear. "In town I only see unfriendly faces, and . . . and I just had a row with Jaquin and I don't want to see him. He wants me to convert, but I . . . I can't. I told him sitting in the temple doesn't make me a member of the Sext any more than standing in a field makes you a cow."

She smiled tentatively.

Niall frowned. "You may not leave."

It didn't work. The Gift of Aquinas. Wasn't she supposed to have charm?

You're flirting, not charming.

It was the Voice. Perhaps she could use the it!

"Niall, please let me go," she said loudly.

Niall pushed his *kon* towards her. "Last chance. Go home now or I will arrest you."

Not like that. Reach inside.

Concentrating, Song reached inside herself and focused on the words she found there. "*Please Niall,*" she said. "*You know me. We were friends. Please, let me go.*"

She hardly recognised herself as she spoke. There was a resonance to her words she had never heard before, so powerful, so alluring and yet so . . . tiring. She put her arm on Niall to steady herself.

He looked at her curiously, then rubbed his head.

"Go," he said quickly. "Before I change my mind. Be back before midnight. The gate is locked at midnight and I'm going out with the hu—" He checked himself. "And I won't be here."

"Thank you."

She made good time trekking north away from the town. Her keen eyes saw no-one, which meant either they were not watching the road or they were very good at staying hidden. She hoped it was the former.

As the sky turned from orange to a salt-sprinkled blue-black night, Song thought she could smell the sea, as though the darkness brought out its tang from beyond the Forest of Muir. The moon shone brightly and she smiled, remembering a boy in her class who told her that the Seraph moon was more important than the sun because it provided light at night, whereas the sun only shone in the day, when the light wasn't needed.

Insects buzzed and whirred with their silver song and a never-ending hunger for skin and blood. The blowflies were the biggest irritant, but even their wicked bites didn't knock her off her stride. In the past few months Song had learned to tolerate pain.

She ran through the outcrops of forest and brush, through the smallholdings where the trees had been cleared for Calliope farmlands, then on to the border of the wetlands. Here she began to slow. The marshy terrain was treacherous, breaking into pockets of continuous water three or four feet deep. There were well-worn pathways criss-crossing the wetlands. The area was often tapped for irrigation, but in the middle there was a giant causeway of rocks, scrub and caves that created a dry island in the otherwise sodden terrain.

The Stony Marsh almost looked man-made, but it was too vast and had been a feature of the terrain since the Gildas first came to these lands. Song was taught that they were formed by volcanic eruption, but when she actually saw the Marsh, she couldn't help thinking there was something else at work, a wiser power. The rocks looked sculpted, so smoothly were they hewn, and hidden caves stood like witnesses of some ancient civilization.

As Song trekked along the path, she kept away from the trees. Though this meant occasionally stepping into the water, sometimes up to a foot high, it was safer. The trees of this part of the marsh had snakes in them; the black death serpents hung in tight nests and spiralled down onto their prey. One drop, one bite, one death. They were so sensitive to light and temperature, they existed across just one degree of latitude, but on that latitude they were as plentiful as they were deadly.

The water was at its highest just before the Stony Marsh, and the trails narrowed and became increasingly uneven, limiting her movements. This was where the traps would be. Song wondered what form they would take. Nets triggered by the brush of a tine? Holes harbouring poisonous arachnids? She imagined both would appeal to the Acrapheans.

She looked for silver threads and disturbances in the earth, but saw nothing. Suddenly she became conscious of a strange flapping noise above her head; strange because egrets and other birds tended to be near the ground. Looking up she saw a large piece of parchment tied between two cypress, and next to it another, and then another.

In the still night air they made an eerie susurrus. She stared at them for a moment, trying to see what they were supposed to do or how the trap worked. It made no sense. Craning upwards she moved cautiously forward. Her toe snagged on a mannequin hair, very fine but too strong to snap outright with her weight. In the same instant an arrow, released from a tree to her left, buried deep into her shoulder. She stumbled, looking at it with incredulity. The blood came thick and fast.

How could she have been so stupid?

She felt something spread through her arm—the cloudy progression of poison.

Darkness.

"Why are we wasting our time with *her*?"

Song could hear words but she could not see. And even the words sounded strange. As though her head was immersed in a bowl of soup.

Soup.

She could smell soup!

"We can't just leave her to die," said a second voice.

"She won't *die*. Not before they find her, anyway. Look at the blueness in her veins. It's the poison of Arran. It clouds the head and paralyses the muscles, but it takes a long time to kill."

"But her arm?"

"It's patched up well enough now. Gila flesh, though the Lady knows we need it for ourselves."

"It would have been wrong to let her bleed to death."

"*Thank you,* because I need an Acraphean's view on ethics. We're running for our lives, from *your* father, and now we've spent half the night trying to save one of the scouts they sent to find us."

"She took an arrow!"

"I didn't say she was *smart*."

"We couldn't just leave her," a boy's voice said.

"Yes, yes, she's already said that! I don't know why you bother expressing an opinion anymore—it's always the same as hers. Just remember the odds of us living shorten every moment we waste with this scout."

Song could feel her fingers. Her head was slowly coming out of the soup.

"I'm not a scout," she managed.

She felt all three faces turned to her.

"Oh, great. She speaks. Offa, do me a favour and hold her while I slit her throat. That way she can't call out to her friends."

"Don't," said the boy. "Not even in jest. There's been too much blood."

Song felt a hand behind her neck, helping her sit up. Her head pounded as though she had drunk a keg of manderlay black. Her shoulder ached with bone-splitting pain. The shades of grey became distinct objects around her.

She was in a shallow cave somewhere in the Stony Marsh. There was a small fire, positioned so that the smoke rose up against the rock before dispersing at the mouth. Hanging over it was a pan of thin soup. Her backpack was on the ground. Her *kon* staff was gone. Facing her was a woman of about twenty, her face incredibly thin and pale with fading contusions. Next to her was a flaxen-haired boy, younger by a few years. He sat hand-in-hand with a dark-eyed girl whose hair was black like a raven's wing. The King's daughter.

She looked the same as in Song's nightmare, the same face, the same smile. How was that possible? Song had never seen her before. Somewhere deep inside she felt strangely comforted, but had no idea why.

"How are you feeling?" the dark girl asked kindly. "I'm Saffron."

"Fine," Song replied automatically, and then a wave of pain broke from her shoulder and nausea washed over her.

The older girl was packing away a needle, thread, strips of canvas dressing and a soft lump of pink meat—gila flesh. "We need to go," she said sharply.

"I know, Cynne. We will," said Saffron. Turning back to Song she said, "We've left you some soup. It's not much but it might help you feel better."

Offa kicked dirt over the fire and they began to move out.

Song was desperate to tell them she knew who they were, had been with them in Two Pails, and was here to take them to Muir or die trying. But her head was swimming and her strength was gone. "I . . . I came here to help," was all she could manage.

The older girl spun around. "I saw you sneaking towards us. Tell us another, Gildas trickster!"

With an immense effort she concentrated on her words. "I-I came to find you, to guide you to Muir."

"Guide?" said Offa.

"Don't listen to her! She's a scout!"

"But the arrow," said Saffron.

Cynne stood, hands on hips, eyes blazing. "Even if she's not lying, she can't walk and we've wasted the night on her. Any more help like that and we'll be caught before morning."

"I brought food," Song said, "as much as I could carry. It's yours. Please." She gestured towards the backpack.

"Careful," said Cynne.

The boy sighed and looked at Song. She nodded and he began to rummage. "*Filo* water," he said in surprise pulling out the bottle. He sorted the food into three neat piles and was almost finished when, upon opening a black jar, he began to gag. Cynne drew a knife.

"What is it?" she said, eyes on Song.

"I-I don't know," he coughed, holding up a small fold of tissue. A stench filled the air.

"Stink fish," Song managed. "Several moons in the ripening. For the hounds."

Cynne sheathed the dagger, smiling. "Put it back in the jar, quickly!"

Offa, holding his nose, replaced the lid and put the jar in his pocket. He then picked up the three small piles and distributed them among their packs.

"Do you really know the way from here to Muir?" asked Saffron, arching her eyebrows.

"She can't come," said Cynne. "She'll slow us down. That's why trackers use Arran. It's a disabling poison, making the whole party an easier quarry."

"You'll never make it without knowing where you're going," Song said, forcing out the words. "They've laid traps."

"Whereas with you, we'll skip through the night. We'll take our chances," said Cynne, pulling on her pack. The other two did the same.

The night, thought Song. There was something about the night she had to remember.

"What time is it?" she asked suddenly.

"About an hour before dawn, why?"

"But it was not yet midnight when I reached the Marsh."

"You've been out for a while."

"What is it?" asked Saffron.

"They are coming for you! A pre-dawn raid!"

The three fugitives stared at each other and just for a moment looked like the children they were.

"It's too late," said Saffron. "They'll have seen the smoke."

"How far?" asked Offa.

"Ten minutes, no more," Saffron replied.

How could she know that? thought Song.

Her head was finally beginning to clear, the adrenalin overpowering the poison.

"Is this it, then?" asked Offa, looking at Saffron. She took his hand.

"No," said Song. "You can escape. Head west. They will not suspect the west way. The paths are concealed and difficult to find. I'll take you." Ignoring the pain, she pulled herself up.

"You can hardly walk," Cynne said.

"Give her the *filo* water," Saffron said.

"You need it," Song replied.

"Drink it or we leave you," Saffron said.

The boy pulled out the bottle in which the blue liquid was contained, unstopped the cork, and handed it to Song. She took a gulp. The oily, sickly sweet liquid burned her throat and flames of energy ripped through her. The effect was as immediate as it would be fleeting. The liquid press of the rare *filo* seed gave even the most broken body a rush of vitality. It was rumoured a dead man could run for an hour driven by its flames. For that reason it was one of the most prized substances in the whole of Seraphina. A whole bottle was worth a fortune. Mormor had left it to Song in her will, with a note that read simply, "You'll know when."

As she drank, Cynne stepped towards her and whispered something in her ear. Song tensed and then nodded.

"Are you sure?" said Cynne.

"Yes."

Cynne regarded her for a moment. "Then your gods be with you," she said.

The howl of hounds suddenly broke from the south side of the Marsh.

"Let's go," said Cynne.

Burning with *filo,* Song ran to the edge of the Marsh and quickly found the hidden west way, sprinting where the ground was firm, slowing where the trail narrowed and the rocks stuck out like the gnarly shinbeaters they were. The path was even more uneven than she remembered, and although her vision was good and the *filo* augmented her senses, it was still difficult to see in the pre-dawn light; the moon's power faded, the sun not yet over the horizon.

"Wait!" she said suddenly, raising her hand.

Silver threads glistened in front of her, dissecting the path like a low-lying cobweb.

"What is it?" said Cynne coming up behind her.

"Traps."

Their path was blocked, but there was no way around it. To the left and right, the water was deep and boggy and would suck them in and slow them down. To their rear were the hounds.

"I'll create a path," Song said.

"How?"

Song said nothing but readied herself. Legs astride, she rolled the left shoulder and then, with gritted teeth straightened her arms and focused. Running down the narrow causeway, she tripped the first silver streak of mannequin hair, pivoting as she did so. The arrow missed her by an inch. Her planted left foot then disappeared down a borehole and for a split second she felt a sharpened spike cutting through her moccasin. But she was ready and snapped it upwards, at the same time tumbling over onto her hands and triggering the next hair. There was a *whirr* as another shaft was released, but she was already flipping skyward. This time she landed on her left arm; it should have given way, but the *filo* sustained her and she sprang up again just as a waist-high hair was tripped. An arrow flew at her from behind, biting the air, hungry for flesh. But Song was quicker, pivoting left and right, in and out of boreholes, tumbling through threads, tripping each in turn. Skipping to the left, she hit the final hair, but weary, she vaulted a moment too late. She tensed and time seemed to slow as she waited for the shaft, but it never came. The last trap was a dud.

The other three picked their way in behind her, stepping through the spent tines, avoiding the deadly holes.

"How did you do that?" Offa said.

"Luck," she said, looking at the limp arrow, hanging from the last tree.

"Thank the Lady," Offa replied.

"Thank Aquinas," Song said.

"We have to go," Cynne said.

As they continued marching west towards Muir, Offa took the rear and began spreading small pieces of stink fish. One piece he threw onto a raised causeway between two rivulets, another into a boggy clearing, a third down a rabbit hole.

Song couldn't help smiling to herself. His face was green, and his mouth looked like he was chewing on a lemon rind, but he would do anything rather than complain, not with Saffron there.

Song experienced an overwhelming sense of déjà vu; Offa's determined face, Saffron's concern, she was sure she had seen them before. But that was impossible. She shook her head. It must be the poison.

They made good time across the marshes and soon the wetlands thinned out. A dust of light pigmented the trees, the brush and the intermittent rock formations. Song could make out the hemlocks, blood oaks and silver maples, and the false spinneys that peppered the landscape in the last few miles to Muir. They had been running for hours now. Her muscles protested and her shoulder seared with pain. The *filo* was wearing off.

Song began to fantasise about drinking more *filo* water, but even if that were possible, it would do no good. The entrails of the first would nullify the second, and it took a day and a night to leave the system.

Despite the chill of the early morning air, sweat ran into her eyes. She was burning up. She dropped back a step and then another.

"Wait!" shouted Saffron from ahead.

Cynne paused. "What?"

Saffron gestured to Song.

Song shook her head violently. "No! Go on!" she shouted waving them forward, but to her dismay they came back to where she was leaning against a tree.

"How far behind do you think they are?" Cynne asked, breathing heavily.

Saffron closed her eyes. "Hard to tell exactly. The hounds have slowed them down, dragging them left and right, but I think they've got our scent again." She paused for a moment and looked at Song. "There's something else, too. One of them keeps leading them north, a longer way round."

Song thought of Jaquin but said nothing.

Cynne made an impatient noise. "Well, are they gaining or falling behind?"

"They are much further away than when we first left the camp, but every time they find our trail, they gain fast."

"And they will move faster now they are out of the wetlands and beyond the stink fish," Cynne added, passing around a water skin.

Song leant back on the trunk. She felt so tired, so hot. She could sleep right here. The *filo* had run its course, and soon the nausea would come back, the numbness in the limbs, the pain . . .

"Song!"

"Yes?" She tried to rouse herself, suddenly aware she had faded out.

"How much further?"

Song looked around her, then panicked. Where were they? She had been this way many times before, but couldn't recognise anything. If she had strayed, they could be miles out of their way. They would never make it to Muir. She began to hyperventilate. Everything was copses and shadows. The path was gone!

"I . . . I . . ."

"Take your time," Saffron said gently.

"It's the poison, its disorienting her," said Cynne.

"And the shoulder's bleeding again," said Offa.

"I'm fine," Song said, forcing herself to smile, turning up the corners of her mouth, making her eyes bright, not giving in to the crushing fatigue that was coursing through her body. If they lost confidence in her now . . . She felt them respond to the smile. The gift of the Gildas, it flowed through her. Breathing steadily she began to get her bearings. The angle of the sun had thrown her off.

"We're close," she said. "A league, no more, west."

Saffron suddenly looked back the way they came, a strange expression on her face.

"What is it?" said Cynne.

"They're gaining fast. Whoever led them off course before has been . . . silenced."

Jaquin!

"Song?" Nothing escaped Saffron's dark eyes.

"It's n-nothing." Song pushed away thoughts of Jaquin, together with the pain and the poison. She would not let her three companions down, no matter what. There would be time enough to grieve, if it came to that.

"This way," she said, and they trekked on.

Somehow Song kept going. Her head swam, her shoulder burned, but she stayed focused. One foot in front of the other, almost matching the others, tip for tip. They were very close now. Her vision was beginning to blur, but she could see the huge blood oaks of Muir peeping above the lower-lying brush.

The forest was garrisoned, but its western perimeter was twenty leagues and there would be gaps in the cordon. She prayed they would be lucky.

"I hear the hounds!" shouted Offa from the rear.

"Come on!" grunted Cynne between gritted teeth.

They half-ran, half-stumbled forward towards the trees. Cynne pulled the bow from her shoulders. Saffron did the same. Could they even use them? Neither looked like warriors. Song wished for her *kon*, if only to stand with them.

In pursuit were the giant hounds, released by their masters, baying for blood. But the Forest was in front of them. If they could only keep going they would make it to Muir, and once in Muir, take refuge with their people.

Beyond pain, almost transcendent, Song watched herself dodge in and out of the trees almost as though her body wasn't full of *arran*, as though her arm wasn't almost falling off. And then Song saw something that turned her veins to ice: standing against the trees were two Fyrd knights, waiting for them. She hesitated. They were caught like hares in snares!

"Keep going!" shouted Saffron.

Cynne also stopped at the sight of the two knights, but Offa sprinted ahead, oblivious to the danger, following only Saffron's command. *No!* thought Song. *They'll cut him down! Surrender! Surrender!*

Unsheathing a sword that looked too heavy for the frame that wielded it, Offa swung at the knight, somehow connecting. The knight collapsed to his knees. Inexplicably, the second knight didn't move at all.

"Get away from there!" Saffron screamed.

Automatically, Offa sprang back, and as he did so, three thin black shapes thumped to the ground, landing where he had stood only a second earlier. And then Song understood.

The black death serpent.

The knights had kept watch under a nested tree. Only their armour held them upright. They should have checked the branches, or their position. A few hundred feet further south and the serpent would be as mythical as a gilded unicorn. The dark snakes slithered out from under the plate, the armour nothing but an empty shirt hiding the decomposing bodies within.

"Here they come!" said Cynne suddenly, and Song spun around.

Three hounds broke into the clearing, teeth bared and running in formation. Song had never seen this strange race before. She gasped at the sight. They were men, but more like animals than people, living only for the chase. Their naked bodies were hunched over and covered in mud, their huge noses angled towards the ground, their small angry eyes hugging the uppermost limit of their sockets. No wonder the Acrapheans called them hounds.

"Now!" cried Cynne.

Saffron, Cynne and Offa released their shafts. Their awkwardness confirmed they were not marksmen, but two of the arrows drilled home, their flight changing in mid-air. Only Saffron's was wayward. The first found a throat, the second a midriff. Both hounds collapsed to the ground, yelping.

The third hound bore down on Song, a sleek, compact mass of dirty brown muscle. His broad chest smashed into her and she thudded to the ground, winded. The hound rolled away only to spring again, his neck straining towards her throat. She could smell his breath and see the saliva dripping from his viciously sharpened teeth. Scrambling up, she avoided his jaws by a mere inch.

There was another dull *thwang!* and then the Viscara hound barrelled forward again, almost as though it was unaware of the shaft that now protruded from its skull. But then the legs buckled, and he fell to the ground. As though in a final moment of long forgotten instinct, the arms went out to break the fall. And there he lay, eyes glazed over, tongue lolling. His legs twitched in a nervous paroxysm, but he was already dead.

Cynne pulled Song to her feet. "Are you all right?"

"I'm fine," she said staring at the fallen man, her breath unsteady, her ribcage cracked. Tears welled in her eyes. She was in danger of going into shock.

"We have no time to mourn our enemy. If we're going to shake off the Fyrd, we have to go now," Cynne said.

"Can you carry on?" asked Saffron, but Song was already back up and staggering forward into the forest. They only needed to go a little way. Without hounds, the Fyrd would find it almost impossible to track them in the thick vastness of Muir. Then, if they could only make it to the camp, they would be safe.

Song counted her steps, *one-two, one-two, one-two-three-four* . . . She managed half a mile before collapsing. This time she didn't try to get up. What she had set out to do, she had done. They could go on without her. She crawled a few feet and vomited, and then dragged her limp body to the stump of a tree. Leaning against the thick bark, she closed her eyes and let the darkness overtake her . . .

But then Saffron was shaking her.

"Go away," Song said weakly.

"What do you think?" Saffron looked up at Cynne.

"She's my patient. You go on, I'll tend to her and then follow. When you get to the camp, bring help. Otherwise I'll be right behind."

"No," said Saffron firmly. "If we get split up we'll never find each other. We'll all stay."

"Cripple one and they'll all be caught," Cynne muttered, pulling off her backpack.

"Please go!" Song moaned.

"We may be beyond them now," Offa said, patting Song's shoulder. She winced with pain. "Oh!" he said, realising too late what he had done.

"You have to go on," she tried again.

"Just let me do my work," Cynne replied, her expression fixed. The canvas bandage was soaked in blood, and Song's arm was purple with the bruising and poison. Cynne pulled away a small part of the dressing and let out an involuntarily groan as she did so. The stitches had come open and the hole in Song's shoulder was weeping profusely.

Cynne sniffed the wound. "It's not infected yet, but unless I clean it out, lay with gila and stitch again, it will be. That would mean losing your arm, if you're lucky, if not, your life. And you've gone as far as you'll go today. The poison, the loss of blood, and this mad journey have all taken its toll. It's time to pay back what the *filo* took."

"But the Fyrd," whispered Song.

Cynne turned to Saffron, who closed her large brown eyes. They waited for a moment and then she shook her head. "I don't know."

"That settles it then," said Cynne, "we'll rest here. Offa, don't step in the vomit. That's it. Kick over it with dirt."

They passed around some water and then Cynne got to work in earnest. She picked up a small branch, stripped the bark away and put it in Song's mouth. The bandage had clotted to the wound despite the gila flesh, and Song bit down as Cynne removed the last of the dressing.

She swam in and out of consciousness and when she next came to, the arm was dressed and a wet cloth cooled her forehead. Saffron was missing part of her shirt.

"Looks good," said Offa.

"I try," said Cynne.

"Shall we eat then?" Offa's stomach growled. "I'm starving."

Cynne nodded and smiled at her cousin.

"Here they are!" a gruff voice suddenly shouted and a Fyrd scout tore into the clearing. In a single fluid movement, the skeggox was off his shoulders and hanging over Cynne. Two more men appeared: a Fyrd knight in light plate and Niall. Song sucked in her breath.

"Remember our orders," said the knight.

"One's a Gildas," replied the scout.

"Makes no difference."

"What about the King's daughter?"

"She comes with me," said the knight.

Offa went for his sword.

"Oh no you don't," said the knight and knocked him to the ground with the flat of his axe. Stepping behind Saffron, he began to bind her wrists. She yelped in pain. Offa lunged with a fist, but was tripped and sent sprawling. The scout kicked him in the chest and he rolled on the ground, winded.

"Anyone moves another inch," said the scout, "and this one loses her head." He gestured to Cynne who was still crouching next to Song. "So," he continued, "I wondered how you found the paths so easily. It appears you had help after all. Cairo Song, no less." He knelt down and whispered in her ear. "I promise you, Jaquin will be well rewarded for the pretty part he played."

Song ignored him and instead closed her eyes in concentration, digging deep into herself.

"*Niall*," she said, her voice dripping with resonance, "*help us.*"

Niall's eye flickered but his expression remained fixed.

The scout turned on her quick as a flash. "Speak your oily words again and I'll smash your mouth in."

"Niall," said the knight, "track back and alert the others. Commander Astroka will want to see them before their execution. They have led us a merry dance."

Song focused all her dying energy on this one last thing.

"*Niall, hear me! You are Gildas, the proud race of Ferin Aquinas. Fight, Niall, and let these innocents live. Fight them . . .*"

And then darkness crashed down as the scout hit her with the haft of his axe.

*

It was dark when Song awoke, the night closed in around her like a cold blanket.

"The children . . ." she murmured.

"Ah," said a soft voice, "she wakes."

"Jaquin?" She could not see.

"Song."

Was she in the life beyond? No, her head, shoulder and entire body was in too much pain.

"The children?"

"Safe, or at least gone to their people, although I worry about the King's daughter. Many Serendips were slaughtered by her father's Forgotten army."

"She has a gift," Song said.

"She'll need it."

"What happened?"

"You need to rest."

Song could just about make out Jaquin's face. Her head was in his lap. He looked tired and very sad.

"Tell me," she said, "please."

He sighed. "Niall slew the scout as the coward was striking you, a single, tremendous blow with the *kon*. The knight tried to slay him, but the Serendip boy drew his sword, gutting the knight from the side. Together they overpowered him. He was one of the King's best men."

"The boy has luck. What then?"

"Niall was gravely wounded but limped back to the hunting party, spreading a lie about how they were ambushed by Serendips. I was charged with looking after him. In his dying breath, he told me where you were. He saved your life as surely as your heart beats now."

Song closed her eyes, stricken with grief for the boy she used to know.

"What about you?" she asked.

"An old trick. I left to relieve myself and never came back. They'll think I've fled. A court-martial already waited for me in Lore, now it will be the Two Pails."

"We don't have to go back."

Jaquin said nothing.

"We can live on the plains like the Forgotten. Perhaps others will join us, others who mourn the way of the *Fari*. They shall come to us and we shall start a new life, free, the second coming of the Tribe of Aquinas." Song was aware that her words were feverish, overexcited, but the dream sounded so good.

"You must rest," Jaquin said softly. "The Serendip hale said you could lose your arm, and then where would I be with an earless, armless, speckled prend?"

She closed her eyes, suddenly weary. She felt droplets on her forehead. Jaquin was crying.

She pulled herself back to consciousness. "What sadness have you not told me?"

There was a pause.

"Nothing. Just that you are hurt and it pains me."

"Jaquin."

"My love," he said quietly, and another tear hit her cheek.

"Tell me."

He wiped a hand across his face. "You already know."

And she did.

The poison of *Arran* had to be leeched from the body to prevent it from getting into the liver. It was a simple but time-consuming procedure, and it had to be carried out within a few hours of *Arran* entering the system. Song would recover, and the effects of the poison had already worn off, but her life would be a short one. The residue of *Arran* would slowly corrode her liver until it stopped functioning altogether.

Cynne had whispered the prognosis to her in the Stony Marsh before they set out. She wanted Song to know, in case it changed her mind, in case she wanted to stay, to be discovered and healed. Then, when Song was unconscious, and with the diligence of a hale, Cynne had told Jaquin, her next of kin.

"We all have to die some time, my love," she said quietly.

"But a year! Two at best!"

"Then let's try to enjoy them."

More droplets hit her face and trickled down her cheek.

Poor Jaquin.

"Don't leave me," he said.

"Never."

She nestled her head on his lap. Her last conscious thought was that it was raining. She could hear the drops drumming on the deer hide tent. The aroma of the night and the oaky damp of Muir descended.

*

Song watched the day break over the great Plains of Corocupina. The veldt opened out and the darkness fell back like a retreating wave on a vast, unbroken sea. There was no sound in the air or cloud in the unveiling sky, only the moon creeping off, as if afraid to wake the sleeping morning.

She sipped her tea tiredly, thinking, as she often did, of her three fugitives. More than a month had passed and she had heard nothing. Song's shoulder had healed, leaving a pallid, white scar to go with those on her back and head. She sighed, feeling somehow nostalgic for old wounds. She knew her days of adventure were ending; the ache in her liver said so.

Song never returned home to Lore and Jaquin had done so only twice. The first time he crept into town like a thief in the night, taking from their yurt only what they could trade for food with itinerant merchants. The second time was last night, and he had still not returned.

Song's stomach squirmed with nerves. Jaquin was wanted by the militia, and to be caught in Lore would mean imprisonment—or worse.

Was it worth the risk?

The assault on Muir had begun, and they wanted to hear the tidings, to hear what had happened to their friends. And so Song did her best to disguise him. He had grown a beard and she dyed it grey. She made him wear a cloak with a deep hood that partially obscured his face. But it was still Jaquin underneath and only a fool would not know him. If he were captured . . . she shook away the thought.

She looked out of the window and over the sprawling settlement. In contrast to the lush environs of Lore, the landscape had a bleak beauty and it appealed to Song's sensibility in a way she never thought it could. The land was unforgiving but here, at the border of the Great Plains of Corocupina and Gildas, a rough sort of living could be eked out between gorse and scrubland. More importantly, it was remote enough to avoid attention of the Acraphean empire, at least for now.

Officially, Gildas still existed. Unofficially, it was a colony of Acraphea and the culture of the Sext had spread throughout the land. Starved of followers, some said Ferin Aquinas, the old god of Gildas, walked abroad, a paltry shadow, lamenting the fall of his people.

More migrants arrived from Gildas each week, and their settlement was growing; over a hundred yurts now. The latest rumour was that a large train of wagons was coming all the way from Foxrall and the far eastern towns. In a meeting of the settlers, Jaquin jested that they would soon need a name for their growing community. Someone suggested *New Gildas*.

"Not Gildas," Jaquin said, "this place will beat with one heart. Gildas, Sylvan, Calliope, Madras and all who come in peace. Coerellian, we shall call it, the Steel-hearted One."

They cheered, for his words and for the first time the people feasted. Someone struck a goblet drum and the air filled with the twangling of lyres. That night, Song was reconciled with Chandra's sons, but not his wife; Chameli's pain ran too deep and Song had to accept that it always would.

She took another sip of the tea.

Their hut was simple, a single room with a wooden bed, a fireplace, a table, two chairs and a window. They had not wanted to build a yurt; too many memories, now soured. In the afternoons she taught the children on a makeshift square. There was no *Fari* anymore.

A pain passed through her mid-section, making her nauseous. In another life, it might have been the sickness of the morning, her belly rounding with Jaquin's child. But she would never be a mother, could not, after *Arran* bit her veins.

She thought of Mormor. If what she had said was true, Song had been passed over by the spirit of Ferin Aquinas, because her sixteenth name day had come and gone and only Jaquin came to her bed. Perhaps that was a blessing, although she never really believed that his spirit would enslave her, or that her Voice would become his.

She vaguely wondered if the line of Aquinas was at an end. Somehow, it didn't seem important anymore. Even so, she couldn't help thinking that whatever it was her great-grand-mother had expected Song to do, she had failed. The false friends wrapped in black had come, and Gildas was no more.

She heard noises outside, the sound of Coerellian waking from its slumber. Plumes of smoke rose from the yurts, and men in faded smocks came out to stretch, exchange greetings and share a pipe.

Where was Jaquin?

She stood up and began to pace back and forth, tracing the same steps she had so often made as a guest of Two Pails. The rhythm of her movement gave her solace and slowly she began to relax. She walked for hours.

At about ten o'clock she heard a thump; someone fell against the door.

The latch clicked.

She held her breath.

A dishevelled figure tottered in.

"Jaquin!" she cried.

"Who were you expecting?" he said, grinning, and added, "I've been up all night!"

"Where were you?" she snapped, suddenly furious.

"Lore," he said and the foolish grin stretched from ear to ear.

"I know that! But why are you so late?"

"Because of this!" Pulling off his cloak hood, he whipped out what looked like curls of mannequin fur and placed it on his head. The wig was so bushy it covered his eyes and ears and fell in untidy tresses down the side of each cheek. With his dyed beard, he was a perfect double for an ageing Calliope.

"What a disguise!" he roared, and then began hobbling around using his *kon* as a walking stick. It was a comical sight and Song, giddy with relief, began to laugh.

"S-so what happened?" she managed to stutter.

"I went to the tavern and found Mali. It was packed and nobody seemed to notice me. One or two of the Friends gave me a hard stare, but there was too much in the air . . . and, come to think of it, too much hair!" He laughed, pulling on one of his locks.

"I don't understand."

"The tavern was alive with tidings from Muir. Picture it, my love," he said, spreading his hands wide as if to denote some sort of wobbly canvass, "the whole town gathered to watch a hundred Viscara hounds blazing a trail into the forest, followed by a legion of the Acraphean army. After a four-day trek, the Viscara found the camp and the soldiers could have taken it there and then, but with the thoroughness of Acraphea they first razed the trees and drew their lines, and then . . . poof!"

"Poof?" said Song puzzled.

"Nothing. The Serendips have disappeared."

"What? All of them!"

"All but a crazed old man jabbering about how he had been left behind. With the entire army looking on, the Acraphean commander demanded to know where the Serendips went. The old man just put out his hands and said . . . *poof!*"

"He didn't!"

"The commander slew the old man where he stood and burned the camp to ash."

"No!"

"It gets better. Back in Lore, the Sexton didn't look kindly upon the death of the only witness, and so the commander sits in Two Pails waiting on His Holiness's pleasure. I'll wager he'll be waiting until his chin is as silver as mine!"

"But where have the Serendips gone?"

"Nobody knows. No doubt there will be a pronouncement from the Sexton on what *really happened*." Jaquin paused to stroke his beard in an exaggerated fashion. "But for now, rumour's fire burns quicker than they can put it out."

"And what about the King?"

"That is the absolute best bit! He's disappeared as surely as the Serendips." Jaquin put out his hands. "Double poof!" He laughed at his own joke and then continued. "His entire camp left two days before the legion arrived. Some say he has finally been driven mad with grief for his dead lover, others that he is a broken man haunted by his daughter's betrayal, and others still say he foresaw the empire's failure at Muir and has returned to the Forgotten on the Plains."

"Jaquin?"

"What, my love?"

"Your nose doesn't *have* to touch mine when you talk. I can hear you perfectly well."

"Sorry," he said and tottered slightly. "Perhaps I better get to bed."

"Perhaps you best."

Jaquin planted a sloppy kiss on her lips and Song could taste the sour ale and, yes, a hint of jellied pie. He then took two steps and collapsed onto the bed. Soon he was snoring.

Song leant back in her chair, sipped her tea and thought. They were gone then, all three, into the night, perhaps across the great Blue-Black Sea, perhaps into dust. A tear fell from her eye and she didn't know why. She should be happy. These were the best tidings she could have possibly imagined, and yet she was sad. She never had a chance to say goodbye.

*

Song was sick today. Splinters of pain wracked her ribcage. Putting a hand to her chest, she pressed lightly. Even the slightest touch made her wince. She knew the bone-crunching ache would pass as the morning wore on, but for the moment her ribs felt as though they were broken. Except, of course, it wasn't her ribs at all, but the ravages of *Arran*. She would have to get used to it. As the liver deteriorated, the pain would spread to her back and finally to her entire torso. Suffering would become her constant companion.

Nearly a year had passed since the poisonous shaft had shortened her life.

Would she be able to endure it?

She had to, for Jaquin's sake.

She told herself she would manage. But despite her resolve, fear and doubt rose in her mind like locusts on the wing.

What would happen when she died? Her life had been so fleeting. Would there be life after this life?

Outside, a voice interrupted her meditations—one of Chandra's sons giving directions to the hut. His tone was almost hostile.

A stranger, she thought.

Song heard a soft "thank you" and a moment later there was a knock on the door. A small brown figure entered, not waiting to be asked. Her clothes were in rags, little more than a patched-up sackcloth wound in loose layers. A cowl obscured her face. No wonder Mali tarried outside the window.

The stranger leant against the closed door, apparently catching her breath.

"May I help you?" Song asked. The figure said nothing but slowly pulled back her hood. "Saffron!" Song rushed to embrace her, ignoring the pain in her chest.

"My friend."

"I don't believe it!"

Song hadn't recognised Saffron's outline in the doorway and, holding her, she realised why. Saffron was changed; her face was painfully thin and she was no more than skin and bones beneath the rags. Heat emanated from her touch and she was running a dangerous fever.

"Sit down and rest yourself," Song said, suddenly uneasy. Pulling a chair from the table, she gently eased Saffron onto it. Her friend was as light as a lyrebird's feather.

Saffron murmured a breathless *thank you.*

For a moment neither of them spoke.

There was a muffled snort from the corner of the room and Saffron's eyes flicked to where Jaquin was snoring and muttering.

"A long night," Song said hurriedly. "He finds it difficult to sleep now."

"Oh."

Those large brown eyes miss nothing, thought Song. A single glance and Saffron understood all: that her Jaquin needed the bottle to sleep; that watching Song fade away was not good for his health; that, possibly, after she was gone he might get better.

"Well," said Song lightly, "how about some tea?"

Saffron nodded. Song placed a pot of water on the wood burner and lingered over it, giving herself time to think. What had happened? Why hadn't Saffron gone with the other Serendips?

Saffron would never willingly leave Offa. Something was very wrong; the girl's eyes told her that. They burned with the same haunting intensity she had once seen in the King's, that face *like a blade too keen for its scabbard.* Resisting the urge to interrogate her, Song waited for the water to boil and then poured the tea, wishing she had *filo* water instead.

"Thank you," Saffron stared at the steaming patina.

"You need something to eat," Song said. "I've got some stew." Saffron did not reply. "I'll take that as a yes." Song dished up a helping of last night's supper, still warm from sitting on the wood burner. She served it with a fresh hunk of bread spread thick with butter.

Saffron remained silent, but looked into the distance with febrile eyes.

"Saffron?"

"Oh . . ." she said, coming out of her reverie, "thank you, but I couldn't eat."

"You have to."

"I couldn't . . ." She stopped, and then with a sudden, desperate quietness added, "He's gone, Song. They've all gone."

"I don't understand."

A tear rolled down Saffron's cheek. "They didn't let me in. After everything we went through, they beat me away like a stray dog. Offa tried to tell them, but even his own mother wouldn't listen. To them, I was the King's daughter. My half-Serendip blood counted for nothing." She shook her head. "Poor Offa. He went all that way to find his people and they locked him away, the same as the Acrapheans had. One night he knocked himself senseless banging on that wooden cage, trying to escape, trying to come to me. And now he's gone and I feel as though I shall go mad."

Looking at that fevered face, Song could believe it. "What about Cynne?"

"I only saw her once. She brought me food, told me she would help, but she never came back and I knew she was already gone, a week before the others."

"But where? Where did they all go?"

"They just . . . disappeared." Saffron's eyes burned dangerously. She had been so self-assured, so confident on the journey to Muir, but now she was unhinged.

"They must have gone somewhere. Perhaps across the Sea?"

Saffron shook her head. "There was an old man left behind raving about an ancient path, the god's way, to another world . . . *Hafram Deagalis*, he called it. I thought it was a story, everyone did, invented like most of the chronicles, but it's true. Their Golden Lady has taken them beyond this world and I . . . I cannot follow."

Song knew then that Saffron was losing her mind. This poor girl, half Serendip but Acraphean in features and blood, was tearing herself apart.

"The old man? I thought he was . . . killed," Song began.

"He was. I found him *before* the soldiers."

So, she had stayed on the edge of the camp the entire time, watching, waiting, starving. And they beat her off with sticks.

"Please, Saffron . . . you have to eat something. You have a fever and I fear that if you don't take care of yourself, you could die."

"Part of me already has," she said and absently clawed at her hair. Then, as if suddenly aware of Song's gaze, she pulled her fingers away and inadvertently knocked her tea from the table. "Oh, I'm sorry . . . sorry, sorry."

"It's nothing," Song murmured. "I'll pour you some more."

Head in hands, Saffron rocked back and forth. Song put her arm around her shoulders.

"It's all right," she said. "Stay with us."

"I can't."

"Why?"

"Because I have to find a way to follow him."

"But you said they had left this world!" Song replied, fearing those reckless eyes.

"There is one who might know."

"Who?"

"The Lady of Carabrienne, the old soothsayer of Castagna. She predicted this red war before anyone believed her."

"Of Castagna? She survived the attack on the city? How?"

"I don't know and it doesn't matter. They say *she* knows the way."

"A soothsayer? But surely, Saffron, they're all fakes and charlatans, telling old women what their bunions mean, or foolish girls about the tall, handsome strangers about to come into their lives. How can she know?"

"I don't think she is a soothsayer now," Saffron said, adding quietly, "if she ever was."

"I don't understand." An ice-cold trickle of unease ran

through Song's veins.

"She is a necromancer now."

Song sucked in her breath. "A necromancer? But surely they are not real?"

"She wouldn't be the first of the old legends to step from the scrolls."

"But in the scrolls they are undead! Witches who have delved so deeply into the spirit world that they have become consumed by it, forever hungering for new souls to sustain their endless appetite. It is a child's story."

Saffron did not reply.

Song felt nauseated, but for once it wasn't her liver. "S-surely, if such a creature existed you would not seek it out."

Saffron's eyes grew preternaturally bright. "A necromancer knows how the spirit can move from one world to the next, one physical state to the next."

"But she will demand things you cannot possibly give." *She will take your soul.*

"I will give her what is required."

"No matter what the cost?"

"No matter."

There was nothing Song could say, not to those eyes. Saffron was beyond reasoning, beyond everything. She was like a wraith; touch her and she would collapse like a stack of empty clothes.

"Saffron . . ."

"I have to go, but last time we didn't have the chance to say goodbye . . ." Saffron's voice trailed off. A shadow passed across her face and Song felt a surge of sorrow. They would not see each other again and both knew it.

"I . . . I wanted to say goodbye, too," Song said in a cracked voice.

They embraced and Saffron pulled Song close, whispering into her earless ear, "I never had the chance to say thank you . . . for everything." Saffron gave one last squeeze and released her. Then, picking up her small pack, she pushed back her hair, pulled over the cowl, and without turning around, disappeared into the morning.

Later that day, when a bleary-eyed Jaquin asked, "Why are you so sad?" Song could not bring herself to tell him. If it hadn't been for the tea stain on the floor, she might have believed that the morning had been a dream or, if it had been real, that Saffron was already a spirit.

*

It was almost two years since *Arran* bit her arm and Song could no longer move. On bad days—and they were all bad now—she couldn't stop repeating the word over and over in her head.

Arran, Arran, Arran . . .

It was as though she had convinced herself that if she said it a thousand times, she would somehow ease the pain. She could no longer feel her muscles and knew how she must look, despite Jaquin's protestations. He called her his fair one, even now.

Every breath was an effort.

Every sensation a pain.

She was rotting from the inside out.

Inside out.

That was another refrain. When a thousand *Arran's* had eased nothing, she would move onto a thousand *inside outs*. Song never told anyone about these little insanities, these mantras that got her from one hour to the next. They were for her alone. For Jaquin she smiled, and did not cry out, and did not cry.

"It's not so bad," she'd say, while her mind secretly raced.

Inside out, inside out, I'm rotting, inside out.

This evening she had sent him to fetch a bottle of manderlay from the traders, now permanently camped in Coerellian. A bottle of wine and a pheasant, a supper fit for the kings of old. He would be an hour choosing and fussing and talking, and she loved him for that. In fact, she relied on it.

Was she a coward? Was it selfish to die alone?

She told herself that it was for both their sakes. She could not bear to see his face when she said goodbye, and it would be too painful for him. She knew how much he loved her. But deep down she harboured another reason, a truer reason. It was because of her great-grandmother, and because of that last abiding vision Song had never been able to shake: the husk of the body at the moment her Mormor's spirit departed, the death-rattle and the *aghhh!* escaping her windpipe, as though somehow her very spirit was in pain and reluctant to pass on. Some days it was all Song could remember of that proud lady, and she would not risk leaving Jaquin with such a treacherous memory.

The spirit passing on.

She thought of Saffron and said a silent prayer to Ferin Aquinas to keep her friend safe, to help her on her way. Her shoulder quivered and there was a final stab of pain. She died with a smile on her lips, and without fear. At last, Jaquin would be free.

*

Her eyes snapped open and a man removed his hands from her face.

"W-who are you?" she said.

"It is natural to be disoriented," he said, "but the feeling will pass."

Something was very wrong. Pain no longer rent every inch of her body and the bone-aching weariness had vanished. Unconsciously she put a hand to her ear, feeling it, folding its fleshiness in her fingers. A wave of vertigo crashed over her.

"Where's Jaquin?" she said unsteadily.

The man smiled. She didn't trust his eyes and yet, she felt an overwhelming urge to *like* him.

"Cairo," he said gently and with that one word, *Cairo,* memories of another life came flooding back.

He stepped towards her. She backed away.

"H-how long have I been gone?" she said, her voice higher than she remembered.

"Not long, a couple of hours."

"But that's impossible!"

"The past exists outside of time. Going in, coming out, can take time, yes, but the past itself is fixed."

"What have you done to me?"

"No more than tell you who you really are, and where your people came from, and the tragedy that befell them and their god." Eryn put out his arms to her, his eyes piercing her very soul. "Can you guess what is expected of you?"

"Don't!" she cried, suddenly agitated. "Tell me who you are!"

He smiled a wolfish grin and his body glowed in the tent's dusky light. "Do you really have to ask that question? I have shown . . ." Outside, a bone-chilling howl filled the air. The smile vanished. "Titus!" He pulled on his cloak. "Wait here!" he said and, flinging back the flaps of the tent, stepped into the night.

Cairo sat on the furs and pulled her knees up to her chest.

What had happened to her?

She had just lived a whole other life. The images were fading, relinquishing their physical grasp, but that made them no less real. She had *been* Song, had seen the world through her eyes, had thought her thoughts.

But why? What did Eryn expect of her?

What Song could not give.

What has made him weak.

What has brought him close to death, and across worlds, and to you.

Her inner Voice. But it was different now. It had changed since they came to England, since she found Eryn. A chill of realisation struck her. It was not her voice at all, not anymore, and it was beginning to exert an influence she didn't entirely welcome. This Song seemed to speak *for* her rather than speaking with her. What was it Mormor had said?

"When you come of age, his spirit will come to you, become one with your voice, your mind, your heart."

She bit her lip. Is that what she wanted? And there was something else, too. Why had he singled her out? Cairo did not have his blood in her veins, so how could his spirit *unite* with her?

You said you would do anything for him.

And as Song spoke those words, an overwhelming sense of need washed over Cairo, drowning out any doubts, any anxiety. Only he was important.

Yes, when it came to it, she *would* do anything.

Suddenly there was a blood-curdling snarl, followed by a dull thud and then . . . nothing. The outline of a hand appeared on the roof of the tent and before she could react, the canvas was ripped from the ground and flung to the side. It blew away like tumbleweed.

Bearing down on her was a sleek, powerful man. He had long silver hair and bible-black eyes. He wore thick boots from another time and shorts that didn't fit over his tree trunk legs. His torso was naked but for a jigsaw of scars. He was missing a forearm and an ugly dull cap covered the stump. There was no cruelty in his expression, only sadness. She stared into his endless eyes.

"Cairo Agonistes," he said.

Thirteen

Crakes

AMQUIST SNIFFED THE air and then skipped back like a startled gazelle. It was a peculiar movement for a god.

"What is it?" Crakes asked.

"Nothing."

"Then why . . . ?"

"I *said* it's nothing." Hamquist pointed to the tent in the far corner. "She's in there."

"Oh . . . right then."

Crakes pulled his cloak around him and stepped into the clearing with a confidence he did not feel. It had taken them hours to find her. The clearing was hidden by a hundred conjured deceptions, despite the fire burning at its centre. And there was definitely something strange about the air, something old, something he couldn't quite place. Hamquist knew, but wasn't telling, and Crakes didn't dare push it. Hamquist was still furious about what had happened this morning, about Crakes' *betrayal*.

Three steps in, Crakes heard a snarl and then an enormous wolfhound broke from the trees. Charging with huge loping strides, it seemed intent on ripping his head off. Forced to defend himself, Crakes raised an arm. The jaws thrust towards his neck. He jabbed. There was a snap and the wolfhound slumped to the ground.

Why did they always have to have dogs? He liked dogs.

The poor animal had only followed its protective instincts and now it was dead. He prodded it gently with his toe, wondering whose it was. Not hers, that was for sure. Stepping over the body he was conscious of a chafing sensation. The Ward's wardrobe had not been extensive, and the pale yellow shorts were the only thing that had stretched over his thighs. Even then it was a squeeze.

He put his hand on the roof of the tent and, striving to make an impression, ripped it from the ground, exposing the girl to the elements like a winkle without its shell.

"Cairo Agonistes," he said.

She didn't flinch, but held his gaze as though she had seen worse than him, as though death were somehow old hat. For she knew he was Death. The wisdom shone from her eyes like emeralds. Crakes hesitated. She was so young and there was something familiar about her.

The realisation cut him like a seax.

She was *her* daughter, the lady with green eyes. Those same pools of green stared up at him now. He took a step backwards, guilt gnawing at him like a plague.

I can still feel the lady with green eyes.
Alive, but tormented by Erinyes.
In great pain she reaches out to me and
Pulls me in, an entire world away.

From the edge of the clearing came a sniff. Hamquist was watching. The sniff was a reminder. *Hurry*, it said.

"We have come," Crakes said, a little unsteadily.

"I see that," the girl replied and smiled, unsettling him further. He could see she was beautiful, even in the firelight. He felt a crushing pain in his heart.

Did they really have to kill her?

As if in answer to his silent question, Hamquist's cold blade pressed against the nape of his neck. "Why the pause?" he growled.

"I . . . No reason."

"Good," Hamquist said and pressed a little harder—not quite enough to draw blood, but enough to make a point. The herald poked along by the heralded.

"Any last words?" Crakes asked hurriedly.

The girl considered for a moment and then cast her eyes towards his mid-section. "Nice shorts," she said and smiled again.

Take the wench! Hamquist roared, the thought coming as quick and deadly as mercury.

"Wench?" The girl arched her eyebrows.

Crakes stopped dead.

She had heard Hamquist's thoughts.

That was impossible unless . . . He turned to Hamquist. "How can she . . . ?"

"Take her now or I'll skewer you both," Hamquist snarled.

Crakes didn't move.

Do it!

Crakes raised his fist, but as he did so, an explosion of light knocked him off his feet, smashing him into one tree trunk and then another, felling five great oaks before finally coming to a rest, two thousand years growth gone in an instant. Staring up at the moonlit sky, he felt every bone ache, every joint out of kilter.

What *was* that? Had Hamquist turned on him?

Gingerly, he pulled himself up onto his elbows and stared across the clearing. The scene read like an ancient scroll, unfurling before his eyes. He saw immediately who had hit him, and who this girl was about to be, and why they wanted her dead. He felt a new kind of pity for her.

"You!" Hamquist said, levelling his sword at the stranger.

"Kalasians!" Aquinas hissed back, squaring his shoulders.

"Eryn!" Cairo cried, her eyes bleeding worry, her composure gone.

"Run!" Aquinas stood his ground.

"No!"

"*I said go!*"

The girl skipped up and flew into the forest. Crakes had never seen a mortal run so fast and with so much grace. Aquinas, or "Eryn" as she called him, had used the Voice. She had no choice but to obey.

Letting her go, Hamquist turned to Aquinas, sending another mental command to Crakes as he did so:

Aquinas first, then the girl.

Hamquist and Aquinas circled each other like a pair of scorpions, each waiting for the other to make the first move. Suddenly, Hamquist slashed left but the fallen god shimmied away with impossible speed. Though he had no sword, Aquinas had godly talents. Hamquist swung at his head. Aquinas parried with a fist and then cupped his palms. A ball of blue energy ripped from his hands, knocking Hamquist backwards.

So that's what hit me, thought Crakes.

"A pretty little firework," Hamquist growled and shot a glance at Crakes.

To me now, he said with a mental command, *and we'll take him together.*

Wearily Crakes pulled himself up. He had no appetite for this clash of titans. Win and they would still lose. He wanted the girl to live and be free, but that was impossible, no matter what the outcome.

To me! Hamquist roared.

Should he pretend he was hurt? No, that was pointless. Hamquist would know. He always knew. Reluctantly Crakes strolled over, rolling his shoulder to loosen up.

Hamquist slashed again and this time Aquinas pivoted a moment too late. A rent opened in his chest. Hamquist nodded and Crakes smashed his stump into the crook of Aquinas's back. The old god staggered, arms clutching his chest, but he did not fall. Theirs was a brutal business.

"*Stop!*"

The shout rang out from the edge of the clearing. It was Cairo Agonistes. Hamquist hesitated, and as he did so, Aquinas snapped upright and delivered a frightening uppercut. Hamquist toppled backwards, the ground reverberating with his fall. In the same instant, Aquinas shot out another burst of energy which sent Crakes sprawling.

"Cretins!" he brayed triumphantly, his stomach glowing, the wound beginning to heal itself. "This is too easy!"

Cocky, thought Crakes, *and careless*. Hamquist's tree-trunk arm rose from the ground and grabbed Aquinas's leg. Shrieking, he tried to pull away, but it was too late. Hamquist had a tight grip and a tug of war ensued, the two gods wrestling over the limb. With an almighty wrench, Hamquist wrestled Aquinas to the ground and then rolled on top of him, knees digging into the half-healed chest. Aquinas cried out in agony. Hamquist smashed his forehead into his nose, and then his mouth, Aquinas muttering and spitting all the while through broken teeth and blood.

Turning towards Crakes, Hamquist snarled, "Get the girl."

Crakes raised his stump towards his mouth as if to bite an invisible knuckle, fretting. Should he? Shouldn't he? Could he resist Hamquist's command again? But then the dilemma solved itself as the girl ran past him, leapt into the air, and landed on Hamquist's back.

What was she doing?!

"No! No! Get away!" Aquinas cried, real fear in his voice for the first time.

Ignoring him, the feather of a girl tried to pull Hamquist away from her lord. Hamquist, whose real mass was reckoned in tons.

"Get off him!" she screamed.

Hamquist squirmed as though a nest of fire ants swarmed

all over him. He wasn't used to mortal contact and her touch pained him. He lived only through vicarious sensation, a life felt through the thrumming of a blade. Panicking, Hamquist flailed wildly, trying to reach around to the small of his back. He got to his knees but still could not claw her off. Aquinas's expression changed, his eye-popping fear turning to a grin. Another moment and he would wriggle free.

"Yes! Yes! That's it! Go on!" Aquinas cried.

In agony, Hamquist tilted sideways and the girl slipped between the two seething giants. Fearing she would be crushed, Crakes whipped in his hand and pulled her out, tee-shirt bunched in his fist, a puppy held by its scruff. The two gods then careened towards him and he had to dive backwards to avoid the wave of bodies. Too late he noticed the tree behind him; too late he felt the girl collide with the trunk; too late she slumped to the ground, unconscious.

And in that instant, everything changed.

Hamquist's head snapped around, his eyes burning crimson. "At last," he snarled and threw Aquinas to the side like some old rag doll. He swept up the sword and closed in on the girl's unconscious form. The blade sliced downwards, a death blow.

It pranged backwards, an inch from her neck.

The sound rang through the forest like a dirge while Hamquist stared in disbelief at the crude iron stump that blocked his way.

They were supposed to be as immutable as the elements, but Crakes was not. This world had changed him. Mia had changed him and there was no going back.

For this act, he was condemned to die. Hamquist would destroy him, summon a new herald and walk the world with a different shadow.

Death burning in his eyes, Hamquist turned to face him. Crakes expected the blade to take his head, but instead the ground swallowed him up and he plunged downwards. In the shady recesses of his mind, he recalled something about the tomb of Onan where recalcitrant gods were consigned to death, to be incinerated by the ethereal flame, their ashes entombed in the depths.

So, that was the talent that Hamquist had improvised for the Ward, but this time the hole was left uncovered. An open trench to be filled with fire, vanquishing all within. Crakes peered out over the edge, frozen by Hamquist's will.

"Stay here," Hamquist said, avoiding the intimacy of a mental command, "and after Aquinas I will come back for you. Two gods will die today."

Aquinas was on his knees, trying desperately to revive the girl, his strength all but gone. This was why Aquinas had wanted her to run away. While she lived, they could not hurt him, not really, not while his blood ran in another, even if it was only a young girl. They could knock him down, beat him until he was little more than a broken spirit, but he would return. Now Aquinas, too, was doomed, his wounds too deep to heal.

In another age, they would have done this god's bidding, maintained his justice, but he had lost the faith of his people, and had no power to command.

Hamquist slashed at the girl's neck. Aquinas parried weakly. Hamquist reversed the blade, angling it back the other way. Aquinas scrambled to parry again, but this time he was too slow and the block was partial. The blade slipped downwards, slicing across the girl's stomach.

"No!" Aquinas cried.

Cairo's eyes flickered, the blood already welling at her chest. Hamquist roared in frustration. The cut would serve, but it was against the etiquette. She would fade out of the world slowly, conscious of her passing. That was not their way.

The old god of the Gildas screeched, flying at Hamquist like something possessed, dealing blow after blow despite his wounds. The two gods fought on, and in the confusion the girl opened her eyes and spoke to Crakes.

"Please," she said weakly, "help him."

"I can't," he replied.

"But he's killing him."

"I . . . I can't." He was trapped there by Hamquist's command.

She closed her eyes. Either she was gathering herself for another appeal, or she had passed out.

"*Come to me!*" She used the Voice. "*Come.*"

Crakes found himself climbing out of the grave towards her. The girl's eyes opened and behind them lay a pain greater than her wound.

"Save him, please," she said, her strength all but gone, the Voice gone.

"I'll try," he said. "Not for him, but for you."

Aquinas moaned on the ground, bleeding and broken. Hamquist, sword raised, was about to deal the death blow when Crakes smashed into him from behind. The next moment they were wrestling, *mano a mano*, so close, so graceful, it was like a dance. Back and forth, cheek to cheek, two ancient friends having one last waltz.

The sword fell between them and three hands grappled for the shaft.

Hamquist was bigger, stronger, faster than Crakes. He always had been. He was Death itself while Crakes was merely his herald. Hamquist overpowered him easily, holding Crakes with one arm, heaving the sword upwards with the other. He raised the blade high in the air. One slash would do it. Crakes prepared himself for oblivion.

But then Hamquist lost his footing, slipping on the wet ground. It was only for an instant, but in that split second he released his grip on the sword. They locked eyes. Crakes secured his hand on the shaft and thrust the blade deep into Hamquist's sternum.

It was a chance in a million.

Hamquist had never slipped like that before, not once.

And his eyes had never implored like that before, not once.

The strange thing was, Hamquist could have stopped the battle in an instant, paralysing Crakes with a single command; how could Crakes have surprised him in the first place, when Hamquist could read his mind? Crakes remembered an old Acraphean saying: *There is no trap so dangerous as the one you set for yourself.*

Hamquist stumbled backwards, both hands on the shaft. With an immense cry he pulled the blade from his stomach and dark ichor poured forth. His crimson eyes turned stygian black in the endless stare of the ended.

Thank you, my old stump . . .

The words flickered across his mind like a prayer and for the second time in a millennium, tears welled in his eyes. They rolled down his cheeks, joining with the rain and the wind and the eternal sadness that burned in his heart.

An eerie silence filled the air, then half the clearing exploded into flame as the ethereal fire raged, consuming Hamquist's body until ash fell like snow from the sky.

"Hamquist," Crakes said quietly, but he was gone.

"Help me!" gasped Aquinas.

"*Hamquist!*" Crakes screamed.

"Help me . . ."

In a daze, Crakes turned. Aquinas was bent over the girl, his hands like small animals, trying to push the blood back in. But it was too late. She had a few minutes at best. Anyone could see that. It had all been for nothing.

"You must help me," Aquinas gasped.

"She is beyond help," Crakes murmured, and put his hand on the old god's arm.

"But she can't die!"

"I'm sorry."

"Why couldn't you leave us alone?" he shouted, eyes wild with grief.

"You mean," Crakes said, "leave her to you."

The girl carried the god's blood in him, but Aquinas wanted more than that, he wanted her spirit, and would take it once he had lain with her as the incubus, and every worthy child of hers, securing his future for as long as the female line of Cairo Agonistes survived.

Flakes of grey formed in patches on Aquinas's skin. As she died, so his own end was upon him.

"No, no, *no!*"

"You can still save her."

"What do you mean?" For a moment hope flickered across the god's eyes.

"*Hafram Deagalis.*"

Aquinas's face fell. Save *her*, not him.

"When she crosses the worlds as a spirit, her heart will stop, and I will die," he said desperately.

"Nothing can prevent that now. Whether she crosses or not, her heart will soon stop."

Aquinas pulled away from her, struck by the inevitability, withdrawing into himself. He didn't care about the girl now that she was beyond saving, and had no use for him.

"She is of *your* blood," Crakes insisted. "A vestige of you may live on if you can move her across worlds." He doubted if this was true; Aquinas's power came from the spirit, not the blood, but he knew only a selfish appeal would move this fallen god.

Aquinas's eye twitched and then, with an effort, he picked up the girl and carried her to the huge oak stumps that lay in the middle of the clearing. He placed her flat, snaking her body around the diamond-shaped cavity in the centre. He murmured a few words and flames licked upwards. Incanting, he dropped a few seeds into the fire and the stench of incense filled the air. He pulled out a silver clasp knife, ran the tip along his fingers, and squeezed the ichor into the thurible.

"Hurry," Crakes said. He didn't need to do all this, surely? The girl was barely breathing.

Slowly, Aquinas removed his cloak, folded it in two and smoothed it flat on the table. In the flame-light, Crakes could see the crust of grey that now coated his skin. He was beginning to harden. Entranced by his own body, Aquinas ran a finger along the skin. Grey dust covered its tip.

"Hurry!" Crakes implored again. "You don't look so good."

"Cairo?" Aquinas said.

But the girl was unconscious. Crakes could feel her. She was deep inside herself, aware her life was over. She despaired that she would never say goodbye to her sisters and her father, and she was in agony over leaving this god with whom her time had been so short. Her despair was a palpable, a heart-wrenching sorrow. Aquinas had twisted her mind and soul. Then, Crakes sensed a change, the beginnings of relief—that sense of wellbeing that comes so unexpectedly to the dying. Half her spirit was already there, in the great, endless sea where mortal concerns no longer ache or even signify, where everything was washed away, and everything was at peace.

Should they just let her go?

Aquinas peeled away her t-shirt and spoke the incantations. He then traced the clasp knife across her stomach. Her red lips began to murmur in protest as if in the throes of a bad dream.

"Hush," he said and then thrust the blade into her heart.

Her eyes snapped open, bulging, a last moment of pain.

"Eryn," she whispered soundlessly.

"Not Eryn, my child, but Ferin Aquinas. You know that. I am your Lord and . . . your father."

Cairo's eyelids fluttered, then opened for a final time.

Crakes hoped that in that last flicker of consciousness she saw Aquinas as he once was, the most beautiful and charming of all Seraphina's deities, and not the dull, flaking gargoyle that stood before her, the god who had lived for too long and had taken his faithful for granted, until they, in turn, abandoned him.

Aquinas was greying rapidly now. Crakes put out an arm and

rested it on his shoulder. The first crack in his skin appeared, and then the next, like a hardboiled egg smashed with a spoon. Aquinas tried to smile, or so Crakes liked to think, before his face shattered across his jaw and his body crumbled.

The ethereal fire raged through the clearing again and Aquinas turned to ash. The girl burned with him. They made a pretty pyre. And then, almost too suddenly, they were gone, and it was very quiet, and for the first time in his long existence, Crakes was all alone.

Fourteen

Charlemagne

CAIRO WAS MISSING. As if by some unspoken agreement, Penny and Charlemagne converged in the kitchen, the room that their family dramas always seemed to begin, if not end.

"I can't believe she's not back yet," Penny said.

"She's just trying to make a point. She'll be back," Charlemagne replied, hoping she was right.

"She's going to miss Ogg's curfew." Penny flipped open her cell phone to examine the screen before shutting it again with a snap. It was the fifth time in as many minutes. Charlemagne stood up and walked over to the window.

"At least it's still light," she said, but her words sounded hollow even to her own ears. The dusk was thick and soupy and it would be dark in another few minutes.

"She's in trouble, I can feel it."

"Penny, please don't start."

"We shouldn't have let her go!"

"We didn't have much choice," Charlemagne said, thinking back to the scene in the living room, and Cairo's words, *you're not my mother!* How could her sister be so callous?

"Yes, we did," Penny said quietly.

An awkward silence fell between them. After Cairo stormed out, Penny had wanted to rush out after her, but Ogg, overhearing the whole thing, said they should let her go, let her walk off whatever it was that had got into her. Charlemagne agreed, of course. There was no point trying to talk to Cairo when she was in that mood. She wouldn't listen.

Penny flipped open the cell phone again, and again snapped it shut. "I don't think Cairo knows what she's doing."

Charlemagne fought back an urge to say she thought Cairo knew *exactly* what she was doing. Instead she said, "We tried to find her."

When Cairo didn't come back for dinner, Penny began to fret and insisted they go after her. Charlemagne would have preferred to wait for the spoilt brat to return like Ogg suggested, but Penny was inconsolable.

So they went in search of her, walking around the spinney for hours looking for the clearing, even though it was obvious Penny didn't know where she was going. Eryn's camp was always "just around the corner," but they couldn't find it. Charlemagne nearly snapped when Penny said it had somehow "been hidden" from them.

It was after eight o'clock when, soaked to the skin and miserable, they finally came home. Charlemagne wanted to see her grandmother, but when they returned, the house was eerily quiet. No Ogg, no Gaffer, not even the dogs bounding up to them as they walked through the door. Charlemagne checked the garage and, with a sinking feeling, saw they had gone out.

Inwardly she cursed her sisters. *Cairo, doing god knows what with lord knows who. And Penny, who's always imagining things about this person and that person, and is now obsessing over what our clearly confused Aunt said about Eryn. As if Penny needs any encouragement.*

Of course what had happened to them was strange. The wake, and then Cynne's room, but in another way she knew that if they just trusted Ogg, everything would be all right. In the kitchen, when they could be alone, her grandmother whispered that she would soon explain everything, Charlemagne just had to have faith.

She had to admit though, now it was almost dark, another part of her was getting worried. Cairo had become particularly reckless lately. Charlemagne's stomach became queasy and her mouth tasted like she had been sucking batteries—what Granny Hickory used to call "a queer feeling."

"Perhaps if we'd told Cairo about Cynne she might have listened to us," Penny said fretting.

"Of course she wouldn't."

"Why are you whispering?"

"Because *you* are! It's like you're afraid of waking the dead or something."

"Charlie! Don't say that!"

Charlemagne's stomach churned uncomfortably. "Look," she said hurriedly, "if Eryn wanted to hurt her, he's had plenty of opportunity before now."

"Perhaps he was working up to it. Cynne told me Cairo was in grave danger."

"You said she didn't know for sure."

"I think she didn't want to scare me, but she knew."

"She seemed rather confused to me."

"Confused? How?"

Oh, let me count the ways, she thought, but Charlemagne said nothing and they sat in silence. The clock on the wall clicked past ten. Penny flipped open the cell phone again, and snapped it shut. Charlemagne had to bite her lip. It was so annoying. She wanted to yell at her to stop.

"I wish Dad would phone," Penny said. "Why doesn't he call back? I have to speak to him."

"He did call," Charlemagne said. "This morning before we were up. Ogg said so. He's fine, everything's fine."

"This morning? So, about two a.m. his time? And he didn't want to speak with us despite my messages?"

"He didn't want to wake us up!"

Penny looked like she was about to protest when they heard the front door bang open. Charlemagne's heart jumped. Was it her grandmother?

"Cairo?" Penny said hopefully.

Charlemagne flushed with confusion. Their sister was missing. Her first thought should have been for her. Even so, she felt a rush of elation when she heard the dogs run down the corridor, followed by the muffled voices of her grandparents.

"Ah, there you are, dears," Ogg said, sweeping into the room.

Charlemagne smiled broadly, and a sense of wellbeing washed over her.

"Where have you been?" Penny asked.

Ogg frowned and Charlemagne cringed. It was none of Penny's business. Pulling out a set of keys, Ogg said, "We went out, and now we're back."

She locked the back door. Charlemagne was about to say something about Cairo, but Ogg glared at her and the words dried in her throat. She was not permitted to speak.

"Gaffer and I are going to bed, dears, but I'll just make a quick cuppa to take up," she said brightly. She put on the kettle and hummed a tune while she waited for the water to boil. Charlemagne and Penny sat in awkward silence, watching the steam.

Ogg poured two cups of tea, one creamy with lots of sugar, and one black. She then whisked out, taking with her the half-eaten packet of Jammie Dodgers. With a dexterous foot, she pulled the door closed behind her.

"It's like a prehensile tail," Penny muttered.

"What?" Charlemagne snapped.

"N-nothing," Penny said, then added tentatively, "but you see what she's done, don't you."

"Upset everyone, as usual."

Penny looked puzzled and then blinked. "Not Cairo, Ogg!"

"Cairo broke the rules. She knew she had to be back before dark." Charlemagne crossed her arms.

Penny reddened. "The rules? Charlie, she might be in trouble! But instead of being concerned, Ogg locked her out!"

"Then why didn't you say something?" Charlemagne felt herself growing angry. "It doesn't always have to be me!"

"I . . . I tried, but I *couldn't*. The words wouldn't come. It was Ogg's eyes. She was smiling, but she seemed to look through me as though I was nothing. And I know it sounds crazy but I couldn't say anything, because how can *nothing* speak?" She paused. "It was like when that phantom came into our room."

"So Ogg's the phantom now?"

"No, I said it was *like* that."

"I see!" Charlemagne said through clenched teeth. "Well, we can let her in through the window."

"You mean you haven't noticed? All the downstairs windows have locks on their fittings. You need a key."

"Noticed?" Charlemagne's irritation was boiling over now. "Why would anyone notice window fittings?"

"She wants to keep her out."

Charlemagne wanted to scream. She didn't like Penny making insinuations about Ogg, trying to make out their grandmother wasn't on *their side*. "You're ridiculous," she spat, a red haze rising in front of her eyes.

Why was she letting Penny get to her? Wasn't she always speaking out of turn?

Her sister had a habit of taking an already tense situation, processing it through an over-active imagination, and making it even worse. Take their, mother for example: it wasn't enough that she had left them and possibly committed suicide. In Penny's imagination she had been kidnapped, and even now was being horribly tortured by witches. While they were looking for Cairo, Penny even speculated that her mother had been taken to that other world, and that, impossibly, their father had found a way to follow her and that's why he never called.

Neither Penny nor Cairo seemed to get it. Charlemagne couldn't explain her experience at the wake, or even much of what their crazy Aunt had said, but she knew their mother was gone. Ogg was their family now. Ogg loved them. Ogg would look after them. And if they didn't see that? Then maybe they should leave.

She noticed Penny was staring at her with wide, pained eyes and her face had become very pale. She looked as though she was about to cry. Inwardly Charlemagne cursed herself. What was she thinking, yelling at her little sister at a time like this? Charlemagne put a hand on Penny's shoulder.

"Look, I'm sorry. I'm just worried. Perhaps I should go and speak to Ogg. She doesn't even know Cairo's not home."

"Of course she knows."

Charlemagne felt another spike of irritation, but said nothing.

Outside, the English summer sunshine finally gave way to a black, moonless night for seven or so brief hours. If Cairo was trying to make a point, to punish them for prying into her affairs, she had succeeded. Cairo the Petulant, they should call her. Cairo the Selfish, Cairo the—

"Do you know what I'm thinking?"

How could I possibly? Charlemagne thought. But instead she said, "What?"

"I think it's high time for some ice-cream."

Charlemagne breathed a sigh of relief. "Good call," she said, her anger, the red haze that throbbed in her temples like a migraine, began to clear.

Why had she had been so hostile a moment before? Why was she becoming so quick to anger? She loved her sisters. One might be in trouble and the other needed her support.

Penny pulled the rocky road from the freezer and two bowls from the cupboard. Charlemagne put on coffee, filling the kettle, preparing the French press. It struck Charlemagne that they had done this so often in the last twelve months it was almost becoming routine.

First it was Granny Hickory. On the night she died, the three sisters and their mother had crowded around the table, talking late into the night about how they would miss her and the times they'd shared. They munched their way through a whole packet of Oreos and half a tub of vanilla bean.

Then it was their mother. The first night she didn't come home, they were glued to the phone, glued to the local radio, and checking in with their father every five minutes as he drove the streets looking for her. For weeks afterwards, Charlemagne and Penny continued the ritual, sitting up into the small hours night after night.

Charlemagne poured the coffee. Penny scooped each of them two dollops of ice-cream. As unpleasant as the circumstances were, she knew this would forever be a bond between them. Even when they were younger, when Charlemagne was Penny's age and Penny was just nine, it was the two of them against the world.

Cairo, on the other hand, was indestructible. Or so it had always seemed. Now, however, Charlemagne's father's last words came to her again: *Take care of your sisters, especially Cairo . . . she needs the most looking after.* It was an age ago, and yet it was only a week.

As they ate, Penny's conversation again turned to the other world, telling Charlemagne in more detail everything she had seen in Eryn's crystal, about their father, Offa, about Cynne, about the genocidal war they had somehow become involved in, and the perpetrators, the Acrapheans, a dark race with the gift of foresight.

"And I've been thinking, why did Eryn show me that? Of all things, why that? Of our father, of Cynne and the war with Acraphea?"

"I don't know. Maybe it was just coincidence."

Penny shook her head. "I believe he had a reason, that he was trying, in his twisted way, to tell me something. I need to understand, Charlie," she said. "What exactly happened to you when the Manciple put you into a trance?"

And Charlemagne found herself talking, going over it again. She spoke of her life in Castagna, of Loki, of Saffron. She spoke of the Lady, who heroically protected her people until the fateful day the city was destroyed. And all the time, she thought of Ogg. Would she approve of her telling Penny?

When they were finished, the whole tub of ice cream was gone and it was almost ten-thirty.

"You know, I've been thinking about Granny and Grandpa Hickory," Penny said, scraping her spoon around an empty bowl, picking up the last, melted scraps.

"Oh?" Charlemagne poured them both a fresh cup of coffee.

"I don't think they were our grandparents at all."

"Who were they then?"

Penny tapped her finger on the table. "Granny Hickory once told me that Mom rented a room from them when Mom and Dad arrived in America."

"I remember it, just about. We stayed in the back of their old house, the one that looked out over Lake Warren."

"But why would Mom rent from her parents?"

"Because they were adults and expected to pay their way."

"I know, but . . . it just doesn't feel right. *I* think Granny and Grandpa were an old childless couple who happened to have a room for rent. Mom got to know them and adopted them. You know how she had a thing for the lonely, for the waifs and the strays. And I think maybe she needed them too," Penny continued, "for her, for us."

"What do you mean?"

"Mom could pretend she had another past, and we'd grow up with grandparents and without any awkward questions."

"Well it obviously didn't work on you, did it?"

Penny smiled wryly. "It's taken a long time to figure out.

I always knew Granny Hickory was hiding something. They didn't even look like us, did they? And of course there were no photos. They had plenty of themselves, but none of Mom as a baby or a young girl."

"Maybe we just never saw them."

"Or maybe they weren't our grandparents at all."

Charlemagne shook her head and blew on the steaming coffee. The surface curdled like a sarcoma. As she watched it, an immense weariness took hold of her, her body weighed down with too many cares. She wanted to close her eyes and curl up on the floor.

Penny took a sip of her drink, and then rested her chin on her knuckles, her brow furrowing into the face she would one day grow into. *Thirteen going on thirty*, Charlemagne thought. It wasn't fair. Most teenage sisters sitting up at this time of night would be talking about boys, not keeping vigil, waiting for bad news.

This *was* Cairo's fault. How could she stay out like this, with everything else that had happened? It was so thoughtless, worrying them, worrying Ogg, because it was clear their grandmother was worried. Ogg *seemed* unconcerned, but now Charlemagne could . . . well, she could *feel* her grandmother's growing agitation.

This time, when Cairo finally showed up, Charlemagne would hold nothing back. She would tell her sister exactly what she thought. Cairo had to hear it from someone. The whole world thought her sister walked on water. Cairo would smile and say she was very sorry, and Charlemagne would want to believe her, want to forgive her, but she wouldn't, not this time.

The kitchen door banged open, making them both jump. Charlemagne expected to see Cairo, beaming, having just found some chink in the house's armour, some window open to the elements. But it was Ogg, followed by Gaffer, and behind them, the dogs barking excitedly.

"You see," Ogg said, turning to Gaffer, "she's not here!"

There was an edge to her voice and the composure from earlier had gone.

Of course it has, Charlemagne thought. Their grandmother *was* deeply concerned about Cairo, always had been, despite what Penny said.

"If that girl has . . ." Ogg choked on the words, hardly able to speak through her rage.

"Not back yet then?" Gaffer smiled uncomfortably.

"No," Penny said.

"Oh." He stared down at his hands.

"Is that all you have to say?" Ogg said through clenched teeth.

"Well, I—" he began, but stopped. "I'm no good at this . . ."

"You're no good at anything!" she barked. "The Manciple said we could not trust that girl and now she . . ." Ogg trailed off, her words lingering uncomfortably.

What was she going to say?

For a moment, nobody spoke.

"Perhaps I should go out with the dogs," Gaffer offered feebly.

"You'll stay right here," Ogg snapped.

"But she's only fifteen," Penny said.

Ogg stopped short as though slapped in the face. She looked like she was going to explode, but then she smiled, or at least the corners of her mouth turned up at the edges. Deep down Charlemagne could feel Ogg's anger, and it made her angry in turn.

It was too much. First Cairo, now Penny. Did they not understand? The Lady could not be contradicted. Her rules, her words, were *law*.

However, when Ogg spoke again, her voice was composed. "Look, my dears, I know you're worried and that's perfectly natural. We all are. But I'm sure Cairo's fine. She's smitten with that boy. I'm no fool. But he's harmless enough. I know his parents very well. They live just a few houses down the road, very respectable people. It's just a bit upsetting. You're in my care, after all. I wanted to teach her a lesson, make her have to ring the doorbell, make her understand she can't stay out all night, but as you can see, it's getting beyond a joke."

Charlemagne felt a wave of relief wash over her. Everything *was* going to be all right, and it wasn't her responsibility after all. Ogg understood the essence of the matter and knew what to do. Cairo wasn't in danger, she was just being her usual inconsiderate self. It would be all right.

"But he's not living in a house down the road, he's living in the forest," Penny interrupted.

Her sister's voice grated in Charlemagne's ears like fingernails on sandpaper.

"Oh," Ogg said. "He told you that, did he? Yes, yes I see that. It does make him sound more mysterious, doesn't it? I don't blame him. Living at home at his age? It's pathetic. But really, you girls shouldn't be so gullible."

"*I* didn't go to see him," Charlemagne said quickly, not wanting to be associated with the source of Ogg's displeasure.

Penny's eyes narrowed. "But I did, and I've seen where he lives in the forest."

Two blotches of red appeared on Ogg's cheeks but she continued as though Penny hadn't said anything at all. "Living rough. Ha!" She forced a laugh. "He doesn't know the meaning of the word. He's a layabout, always has been. I've never met anyone more idle. I wouldn't put up with it. But then, I'm not his mother."

Yes, Cairo is being Cairo, wasting time with this . . . layabout.

Charlemagne was desperate to add, "It wouldn't be the first time," although that wasn't actually true. Did that matter? The words would please Ogg. That was the important thing. But before she could say anything, Penny was at it again.

"You're lying."

Charlemagne tensed. What was Penny saying? What was she doing? Sacrilege!

A deathly stillness settled on the room. Ogg shook, her face and neck turning scarlet. Charlemagne felt herself cower.

Penny held Ogg's gaze, but had become frighteningly pale.

Ogg seemed to grow and, impossibly, the walls of the kitchen seemed to close in around her, making her appear even larger. "Who are you to call *me* a liar!" she exploded.

"Love, love," Gaffer said softly, putting his arm around her shoulder.

"Get off me you . . . you *soft man!*" She wrenched away from him. "Can't you see I'm being insulted!"

Her hand alighted on a wine bottle and she hurled it across the room. It shattered on the opposite wall, covering everything in glass, a red stain spreading across the paint. And then they were all on their feet while the dogs ran around barking madly.

"We're all worried, dear," Gaffer said, trying to placate her, but it was too late for that. Her face had become distorted, as though battling something deep inside her. She thrashed around, as though trying to control it, until whatever it was inside her, won out. "Love," Gaffer moaned.

"I will cast you out," she said to Penny, her voice suddenly ice-cold and emotionless. "You, with your mother's face and cunning ways are not worthy to be in my presence. Neither you nor your bastard sister." Her words hung in the air, as though infecting the very atoms all around them.

Charlemagne froze.

"Oggram!" Gaffer gasped.

"Which sister?" Penny said.

Ignoring her completely, Ogg turned to Charlemagne. "Have you never felt it?" she said in that same ice-cold voice. "Ever? Don't you see it? You are not like them. You belong to *our* House." Ogg's flaming eyes pinned her to the spot, forcing her to see something in their golden glow. Yes, Charlemagne could see it. She was pure, blood of the Serendip, and now that she had found the Lady, nothing else mattered.

"Ogg!" Gaffer interjected again.

"Yes, that's right, you understand me," the Lady said.

"Oggram, I must insist," Gaffer said putting his arms out to her, crossing Charlemagne's field of vision.

Charlemagne blinked.

"Get away from me!" Ogg roared, but suddenly she seemed to have diminished. The glow was gone and her words no longer echoed in that unearthly way. "The Manciple shall hear of this."

She snatched her purse from the sideboard and stormed out of the house. Siam and Cowper chased after her, and a few seconds later the car screeched out of the drive.

Penny reached across and deliberately pinched Charlemagne hard on the leg.

"Ow!" Charlemagne said. "What was that for?"

Her words died in her throat as she saw Penny's face, ashen and trembling, of the pool of wine still spreading slowly on the floor, and Gaffer, staring at his fingers, appendages he couldn't stop fiddling with.

Charlemagne's head seemed to empty out in an abrupt, radical shift of her inner bearings, as if the world around her had lost its reality. She felt like a shadow, as though asleep, but with her eyes open.

What had just happened? And why did the kitchen suddenly feel freezing cold, as though the chill of Ogg's words had infected the very house itself?

"Gaffer," Penny said, her voice shaking, "what did Ogg mean?"

Gaffer pulled out a chair from under the kitchen table and sat down. He buried his face in his hands. "It's . . . it's complicated," he said through stubby fingers.

"Complicated?" Penny said. "She's crazy!"

Charlemagne felt her anger rise again, but this time fought it down.

"Remember whose house you're in," Gaffer said, but without conviction. "Something . . . set her off just now." Gaffer raised his face and tears were streaming down his cheeks. "I . . . I need a drink."

In a daze, Charlemagne opened a cabinet and felt around for something strong. She picked out a bottle of brown liquid. It looked about right: British Navy Rum. She poured half a glass, and then decided to fill it to the brim. Gaffer took it gratefully and polished it off in a single gulp.

"Thank you, love," he said, wiping the back of his wrist across his beard, "that's better." He rubbed his eyes. "I'm sorry about that. Ogg is not herself. She's been through so much and . . . well, now the other is breaking through."

"But what did she mean about Cairo? Is this what you and our father fell out over all those years ago?" Penny asked.

"I . . . I can't tell you." He sniffed.

"You can and you have to!"

"I can't. She . . . she *won't let me.*"

"I don't understand," Penny said.

Gaffer looked on the verge of tears again. Penny held his hands. "Please, Gaffer, you have to try, no matter how difficult it is. You have to help us understand."

"It . . . it doesn't work like that, my fiddle. I would tell you if I could but *She* won't . . . let . . . m . . ." His face contorted and he couldn't get out the words, his mouth working over as though chewing a stringy piece of meat.

"Give him some more rum, quickly!" Penny said.

Charlemagne poured and again Gaffer gratefully accepted the glass. He drank it down and belched loudly. "Excuse me," he said softly.

"What *can* you tell us?" Penny said. "Like, what do you mean, something set her off?"

"She s-saw something as we drove home, in the distance, el-eldritch blue lights, and then, just now, an explosion coming from th-the f-forest . . ."

"The forest!" Charlemagne said in alarm, "But Cairo was—"

"I know!" Gaffer moaned.

"But why did it set her off?" Penny cut in.

Gaffer shook his head. "She d-doesn't tell me, n-never tells me."

"But you have an idea!"

"E-earlier this evening we saw . . . we saw the Manciple. She insisted on me going too. She didn't trust me here alone . . . with you. Didn't trust m-me!" Gaffer's eyes bulged with the effort of speaking, but he clenched his fists and carried on. "I-I couldn't really hear what they said, but he was w-worried . . . ugh!" His mouth began the strange chewing movement again. The unsavoury piece of gristle was back.

"Give him more rum!" said Penny.

"But—"

"I think it helps."

Gaffer nodded in strangled agreement. Charlemagne hurriedly poured another glass. Down it went.

"Why were they worried?" Penny asked as soon as he had swallowed. This was becoming an interrogation. They were torturing him with rum.

"The Manciple was expecting to hear from someone. He didn't turn up. He's not the type of person who *doesn't turn up*, but she didn't think too much of it, not then. I heard her say, 'it takes time,' but then she saw the explosion and she suspects some deep, impossible betrayal. With the Manciple's help, she can reach the Kalasians. Always. They are her servants, in a sense, but sh-she can't reach them now . . . ugh!" Again his mouth contorted.

"Gaffer, please! *What* about the Kalasians?"

Gaffer tried to speak, eyes wide as pumpkins. He reached for the rum glass, but it was empty. Charlemagne filled it again and Gaffer took it in one draught. The bottle was finished. Gaffer clenched his fists as though working up the energy to force the words from his reluctant mouth.

"Sh-she never liked your mother. The hatred goes back a long way and runs deep. For the sins of her father, your mother was an outcast in society. There are some *blood truths* you cannot forget, and when the r-red fiddle came along, that was it . . . your grandmother called her things your father could not forgive." He choked. "And the next morning, you were gone. Your grandmother might have forgiven her, did so in time, but the Lady, never. Th-the Manciple has been drawing her out for weeks, burnishing the god, burying my wife. It was he who somehow brought the Kalasians here, consorting with dark forces. And now he sends them out to do heaven knows what—"

"Kalasians? Is that who Cynne is afraid of?"

"C-Cynne . . ." he groaned, and made a sound like he was crying. Charlemagne couldn't tell if he was drunk or whether the words had been strangled back again. By this stage, she thought he was probably just drunk. He said something but it came out as a muffled sob.

"What was that?"

Gaffer looked at Penny with bloodshot eyes. "You h-have to understand how much we lost, w-what genocide does to a people, h-how much she has lost, all of us have lost. Everything she does, she does for *us*, but the test of our faith is sometimes too much, the path too hard."

"What happened to Cynne?" Penny implored.

Gaffer buried his head in his hands, his shoulders shaking with sobs. "She knew you and Charlemagne saw her, just as I knew Cynne would tell you what I . . . I was too much of a coward to tell you myself. The Manciple, he . . . he . . ." Gaffer's mouth seemed to dry up again, and he smacked his lips like a newly caught fish, all the moisture gone.

"I don't understand," Penny said desperately, but Gaffer was losing his coherence.

"My poor Ogg, what has the Manciple done to you?" His face twisted horribly. "She wakes in the night, haunted by her own voice . . . *The red one, the black one, or both?* Cairo, and you, Penny, are in d-danger . . ." Gaffer gave them a final startled stare and crashed onto the table.

"What's wrong with him?"

Charlemagne lifted his head, concerned that he might have swallowed his tongue. But he was just unconscious. She shook him, but it was like trying to wake a lump of lead. He lolled back and forth and began to snore. Penny sat down next to him and lifted each eyelid in turn, but it did no good.

"Maybe we shouldn't have given him so much rum," said Charlemagne.

"It wasn't the rum."

"But he drank it so quickly."

"It seemed to help." She looked down at him. "And now we'll never know what he meant."

"Meant? He was drunk, Penny. I couldn't make sense of anything he said. I'm sure we're not in danger. How could we be? Don't you see? We are under the Lady's—I mean, Ogg's protection. She didn't mean what she said about casting you out. When Cairo comes back I know, I just know, she will explain everything."

Penny regarded her steadily. "Gaffer's words made sense, we just don't know enough to understand them."

"He was drunk. It was all nonsense," Charlemagne repeated, convincing herself if not her sister.

Penny said nothing, but began to trace lines on her palm, using her finger like a pencil, a look of intense concentration in her eyes.

"Penny?"

"Ogg called Cairo a . . . well, you know what she called her. She can't be our sister, or at least not fully. Mother must have been . . . unfaithful. Father forgave her but Ogg never did. It wasn't just infidelity, it was something else, a deeper betrayal."

"Cairo's our sister. Ogg was just a little emotional, which is not surprising after you were so rude to her."

Penny shook her head. "Think about it. Cairo has red hair. There's no red in our genes. And just look at her. I mean, no offence, but neither of us has her face or . . . shape."

"Who does?"

"Well, exactly, but then there's me . . ."

"You look like Dad!"

"Oh I *know* they're my parents, but my blood is all Mom's, like in a mixed-race marriage where the child adopts all the genetic features of a single parent. My colouring, my . . . I don't know . . . my blood. Don't you see? I'm dark, and so is Mom. We're not like you. And Gaffer said himself, our mother was an outcast. To the Lady, we're the enemy. That's why she hates me, and Cairo. We're not part of her 'House.' That's why Gaffer and Cynne were afraid."

"That's absurd. Remember whose house you're in!"

Penny regarded her steadily. "That's what Gaffer said, right before he was gagged." Charlemagne began to reply, her anger rising, but her sister put out her hand. "Charlie, listen, please. Ogg's concern over Cairo was an act. An act for you and possibly even for Gaffer. She doesn't care about Cairo. She locked her out, was happy to leave her to Eryn, until she saw that explosion in the forest. Then something happened, something she didn't expect, something that went against her plan. It changes things somehow, that's why she flew into a rage."

"Th-that's crazy!" stuttered Charlemagne.

"We have to speak to Cynne. We've waited too long already. She'll be able to tell us more, about these Kalasians, and about what Gaffer said," said Penny. "We'll break down the door if necessary."

A thousand thoughts flashed through Charlemagne's head. All of them about Ogg. Their grandmother was trying to help them, if only Penny could see it. Sometimes, for all her insight, she was so blind. Didn't she realise how good Ogg had been to them? Penny should be grateful to her. Instead, she made their grandmother the subject of her dark fantasies. She was about to tell her exactly what she thought when Penny's face suddenly blanched and her birthmark pulsed like blood spilt on a carpet of fresh snow.

"What is it?"

Penny looked winded, like she was going to collapse.

"What is it?"

"It's Cairo," Penny said, staring blankly, "she's dead."

Charlemagne's heart stopped and the air rushed from her as though winded. "Y-you can't know that!"

"Oh Charlie, she's dead, she's dead, she's dead!"

Fifteen

Penny

ENNY RAN UP the stairs towards Cynne's room. She was shaking, and felt like she needed the bathroom without actually needing to go.

"But how can you know Cairo is . . . is dead?" Charlemagne said from behind her.

"I just do!"

One moment Cairo was there, on the borders of Penny's consciousness, the next she was gone, leaving a Cairo-shaped hole in the universe. Penny could feel the absence as acutely as she had felt her sister's presence.

"Well, I can't see how," Charlemagne replied breathlessly as they reached the top of the staircase.

"It's difficult to explain."

Penny tried Cynne's room, but it was still locked. She banged on the door. "Cynne! Cynne! It's us! Cynne!"

No reply.

"What do we do now?" Charlemagne asked.

Penny took a deep breath and kicked out, smashing the ball of her foot straight into the door handle. The brass fitting wobbled and then fell to the ground. Charlemagne stared at her.

"Taekwondo," Penny said and pushed open the door. Immediately she could sense something was very wrong. There was a draft and the air felt too cold and too . . . fresh. Charlemagne reached for the light switch, but nothing happened. As her eyes adjusted, Penny began to see why. More than half of the ceiling was gone, leaving a huge yawning gap in the roof. The moon shone through, its pale, round face couched in a blanket of stars. She shuddered, remembering her unearthly vision of her sister from earlier in the day, hanging against a similar backdrop—the Cairo who wasn't Cairo, smiling and leering, godlike and demonic.

As she looked around the room, her heart dropped. The alcove was destroyed, the bed was gone, the tapestry was gone and, most importantly, their Aunt was gone. Everything smashed to pieces, rubble and plaster everywhere.

"And only today she was sitting just there . . ." Charlemagne said weakly, gesturing to where the alcove used to be.

"I think I'm going to be sick," Penny replied.

"Who could have done this?"

"Who do you think? It must have been during all those hours while we were out looking for Cairo," Penny said, and then without thinking added, "It was Ogg."

"How dare you say that!" Charlemagne snarled, an angry shadow passing over her face.

Penny cursed silently. *That was careless.* "Sorry, I'm not being clear," Penny said hurriedly, and then laughed. "I just meant Ogg said the roof was caving in, that it was dangerous. Maybe today was the day they finally got around to doing something about it, and the builders came by with a wrecking ball. Gaffer just forgot to mention it."

"Yes. That must be it! The room was condemned!" Charlemagne replied, her face clearing slightly. The voice was hers, but the tone was wrong, somehow flat and almost canned, like someone talking without really thinking about their words, as though they came from somewhere else.

Charlemagne couldn't possibly believe what she was saying. If the room was condemned, where was Cynne? And why hadn't they taken out her furniture first? A force like a whirlwind had swept through, destroying everything in its path. In the half-light Penny could make out chunks of table, a shattered bedpost, and fragments of the pictures that used to hang on the wall. She knelt down and picked up a small piece of dusty fabric. She felt a lump in her throat. It was the tapestry, the magnificent artwork of purple and gold, reduced to a few shreds.

Was Cynne herself buried in the gloom, under a half foot of rubble?

Penny shuddered.

She turned her attention back to Charlemagne. Slowly the shadow passed from her sister's eyes, and her face became her own. She knew in her own way, her sister was fighting it. Wanting to stay with her, but sinking under the their grandmother's influence.

"Perhaps Cynne left us a message," she said tentatively. Gaffer said he had warned her.

"In this mess?"

"She would have left us something if she could, I'm sure of it. When I saw her today she had something she needed to tell me, tell us, just before Gaffer and Ogg came home."

"I think we should just get out of here," Charlemagne replied and began to make her way back towards the door.

Penny wracked her brain. If it were her, and she knew she only had moments before everything was destroyed, what would she do? What would still be standing?

"The wall," she muttered.

"The wall?" Charlemagne turned.

"It's the only thing left," Penny said, already clambering over the rubble to the shattered and dark enclave where the pictures used to hang. She passed her hands over their outlines. "There are so many cracks now," she said, feeling rather than seeing them. She traced her finger along each in turn. "*It's like trying to plug a hole in a dam, Offa.*"

"What?"

"Just something Cynne said," Penny replied, remembering her Aunt as she traced her own finger along one particular crack. "And here's the hole!"

"Well?" Charlemagne said, shivering in the cool night air.

"There's something inside!" Penny cried, "but I can't reach it. My fingers are too short! Charlie, come here."

Charlemagne sighed and gingerly began to step over the rubble as though afraid of twisting her ankle. Penny reached out and took her hand and then guided it down to the pebble-shaped hole in the wall.

"I can feel something," Charlemagne said. "It's right at the back, hang on." She pushed a second finger into the cavity and then, using them like pincers, eased the object out.

"What is it?"

"Can we please get out of here first?"

Penny nodded, and they picked their way back across the carnage. They headed downstairs, Penny glancing behind them repeatedly to make sure the corridor was empty before slipping into their bedroom.

"What was that all about?"

"Just a precaution," Penny said, choosing her words carefully.

Charlemagne raised her eyebrows but said nothing. Together, they sat on the end of the bed and Charlemagne slowly opened her palm. She had a small round object, like a pebble, folded in a piece of paper. Penny gently unwrapped it. Inside was Cynne's diamond ring.

Penny's heart sank. Their great-aunt had left an heirloom, and likely a very valuable one, but Penny had been hoping for something else, something that would have helped them. "Why would she have left us this?"

"I don't know."

"What's wrong?"

Charlemagne's face had become very pale. "Her ring. I-I don't think she can be coming back."

"No," Penny said, but she'd known that from the moment they walked into the bedroom. *It wasn't a wrecking ball, Charlie, at least, not the type that's attached to a crane.*

"Wait, aren't those letters?" Charlemagne said.

"Where?"

"On the paper."

Penny snatched the wrapper from the floor. The handwriting was tiny, but yes, Cynne had left them a note: a single word written in minute, elegant cursive. Even when she held the paper up to the light it was difficult to read, but she could just about make out the word. She had no idea what it meant.

"Well?"

"It makes no sense," said Penny. "It just says *Saffron*."

Charlemagne sucked in her breath. "Saffron!"

"Yes."

"That was the name of . . . of my daughter."

"Yes! The girl you were telling me about. The girl from your . . . your sketches."

Charlemagne nodded. "But why would Cynne write that?"

Penny turned her attention back to the ring. "Of course!" She pulled the crystal out of its setting.

"What are you doing?"

"It's not a diamond at all," Penny said, angling it towards the light bulb.

"I don't understand."

"You will. Look!" Penny gestured to the prism of colours on the carpet.

"What?"

"Wait."

"But nothing's happening," Charlemagne said.

Penny turned to reassure her, but her sister was gone, and she was walking across a dusty, sun-baked land.

Sixteen

NE MOMENT PENNY was sitting on the bed, the next a merciless sun beat on her back and a ravening thirst hung in her throat, pricking her tonsils like a cactus. She squinted. She stood on a vast, arid plain and except for occasional outcrops of spiny plants and low-lying brush, all she could see was sand. In the far distance were mountains, shimmering blue in the heat, their peaks obscured by cloud.

Where was Charlemagne? She thought she would be here too, that they would somehow experience this together. But she could not see her, and just as importantly, could not feel her.

There was a flicker of movement on the horizon and a small brown figure came into view, walking over the dunes and across the sand. Rags obscured her face and she was wrapped in thin swathes of fabric, almost like a mummy. Long black hair, dishevelled and dusty, hung down her back and her steps were laboured.

Instinctively Penny knew she had to make contact. She called out, but could hear nothing, almost as though she were in a vacuum. As the figure came closer, she was struck by an overwhelming sense of familiarity. In slow motion, she watched herself put out a hand to touch the stranger. There was a flash of light and the girl disappeared. Incessant chattering, like a swarm of cicadas, filled Penny's mind.

When she looked up, she now faced the sun. Blinded by its glare, she raised a hand to her eyes and saw that her arm was swathed in bandages. She looked down at her dusty, sandalled feet. They were square, almost like small bricks, almost like . . . A jolt of recognition passed through her.

The other's consciousness took over her then, the rush of noise building like an oncoming wave until it was all she could hear, all she could feel. And in that last moment, before her voice washed away, she opened her eyes and smiled.

Mother.

*

Saffron reached around to her back, feeling for the waterskin that had run out some miles back. Unstopping the cork, she hoped for any last drop that might be hugging the bladder. Her brown hand squeezed. One drop, two, three. And that was it. She replaced the cork. In another hour she would repeat the action as she had done so twice before, remembering only now. It was the onset of disorientation brought on by endless walking, the relentless sun, the thirst, and the soft pat-pat of her feet.

Was it three days since she last ate?

She rubbed her cracked lips and tasted blood. A precious drop fell from her mouth to the ground, a single spot on a parched, endless land. She could not go much farther. She wanted to lie down, and the sand looked so inviting, like a vast yellow blanket. But then, like a breath of wind on dying embers, she thought of Offa. She stumbled on, driven by an overpowering emotion, greater even than the exhaustion that dragged her down.

A flicker of movement caught her attention. On the

horizon she could see tents, white and billowing, a parade of ghosts haunting the eastern plains. They weren't real. As she approached they would turn into flat pools of water, and then to sand and dust. It was a common mirage.

There was more movement. The imaginary tents spawned three imaginary horsemen, white headdresses flowing to their rumps. Spears out, they charged towards her. Saffron vaguely wondered why they were so aggressive. Mirages were usually a one trick act—appear then disappear, forever disappointing.

"What do you seek?" the rider demanded, startling her with his material presence. The sun burned behind him and she couldn't see his face, only a dark silhouetted outline. But for all that, she knew what he was: Forgotten, terror of the plains.

"What do you seek?" he repeated and pushed the spear against her throat.

Saffron wasn't afraid. "Carabrienne," she replied, her voice hoarse and scratchy.

"The Conjurer of Spirits?"

She nodded.

"Why?"

"My . . . my message is for her alone."

The silhouette considered for a moment. "Then perhaps, you are the one she has been waiting for."

He made a sign and the young woman to his left lowered her spear and vaulted from her horse. She unbuckled a small waterskin and pressed it to Saffron's lips. "Drink," she said. Saffron hesitated. "Go on."

She drank deep. The liquid was rich, thick, and unbearably sour. Saffron pulled away fearing poison, but the girl held her hair and tipped up the skin, forcing her to drink and letting go only when it was all gone. Saffron fell back, bent double and choking. The other two riders laughed.

"Beware the kindness of the Forgotten," the girl said, thumping her on the back.

"What have you . . . ?"

"Wait."

Saffron's coughing subsided and then she felt it, the liquid coursing through her veins, easing her aches and pains. Vitality returned to her limbs, her muscles relaxed, and a cooling sensation washed through her.

"There," the girl said, smiling. "Not so bad, is it?" Saffron nodded. Her thirst was gone and she felt stronger than she had in days. "It will make your skull ache later, but you'll have energy for the journey."

"What is it?"

"That would be telling," the girl said and vaulted onto the horse. "Come, you will ride with me." Reaching down, and with a strength that belied her size, she pulled Saffron up into the saddle behind her.

"What's your name?" Saffron asked.

"Athene."

"Pretty name," Saffron said, not giving her own.

"A shield maiden's name. It means *the one who protects,*" Athene said, taking the reins. "Hold me tight around the waist. You'll fall otherwise." Athene kicked the mare and they galloped east towards the shimmering mountains. As they rode, the landscape changed. The scrub became sparse, the shade miserly and the ground riven with steep escarpments and dried out pools. Saffron couldn't remember seeing anywhere so bleak.

"Where are we?" she asked.

"The Veridian Plain. Almost nothing lives here."

The captain made a sign and they slowed to a trot and then stopped altogether, pulling up the horses near a small patch of mulga. The mares steamed with sweat and their tongues lolled. The mountains were still a league away. Saffron wondered how the poor beasts would make it, exhausted by the heat and the pace. All three riders dismounted, leaving Saffron in the saddle. Each began to crawl, scraping the sandy ground with their hands.

What were they doing?

"Here," said Athene, tapping on something wooden with her boot. She hunched down and swept her hand across the sand, brushing it to one side. The others helped her, and slowly they uncovered a circular trap door. As they removed it, Saffron could see a large chain running deep into the ground. It was a well.

The men drank first, ladling out huge scoops of water from the bucket attached to the chain. When they were sated, Athene dunked the bucket back in and handed it to Saffron. The water was so cold it made her teeth and head ache. She grimaced with the pain. Athene laughed, filled the bucket again, and then drank without so much as a wince. When all had taken their turn, they filled their skins and watered the horses.

"At one time it was death for a stranger to see a well," Athene said, replacing the wooden cap and kicking over the sand.

"And now?"

Athene looked grave for a moment and then said quietly, "We take them to see the spirit conjurer."

"Athene!" the captain said.

"Besides," she said more lightly, "how could any stranger find it again?"

"And you, how do you find it?"

"If you live on the Plains for long enough, you begin to feel them breathe. I know where there are underground caverns rich with fish and where there are patches of brush full of hares. And I know where death lies, where the shadowcats roam, and where spirits walk abroad at night."

"Athene," said the captain again, "enough talk. Let's eat."

It was late afternoon by the time they finally mounted the horses and continued their journey. Nodding against Athene's back, Saffron began to drift off, lulled by the rhythm of the hooves, and strangely comforted by the musk of sun, equine and savage.

"Go on," Athene said over her shoulder. "I'll make sure you don't fall."

"Thank you," she murmured, already half-asleep.

When she awoke, they were approaching the mouth of a great cave near the foot of the Hadrad Mountains.

"We're here," whispered Athene and Saffron rubbed the sand from her eyes.

A swarthy, shaven-haired stable-hand appeared from one of the many lithic outcrops and nodded. A hundred pendants hung from his neck, crude wooden sigils to keep errant spirits and wisps at bay. Saffron touched the single ornament she wore around her neck, a small but valuable Acraphean crystal, a gift from her dead mother on her seventh birthday. She had always worn it for luck. Today, she would need it.

They dismounted and the boy, after exchanging a cursory greeting with the captain, took the horses away. The wards rattled as he walked. The entrance to the cave was narrow and dimly lit and from its mouth came a thin, constant stream of smoke. Above the entranceway hung a Wiccan's rune, the crude outline of a man pierced with a thousand shafts. Saffron felt the tiny hairs on her arms stand on end. In Castagna, the old Lady of Carabrienne told young lovers' fortunes for a single silver piece, and for a copper she would touch a baby's head for luck. No one had believed her prediction of oncoming battle, but her warning rang in everybody's ears as Castagna went up in flames.

"Come," Athene said and led her by the hand through the narrow cleft. The air was thick with incense and she found it difficult not to choke. Torches lit the way, and on the walls Saffron could make out crude images of death flickering in a hundred shades of red: death in battle; death in illness; death by torture; death upon the fangs of wild beasts; death during childbirth.

They continued on through a wide limestone arch and into a huge cavern. Crystalline formations hung from the ceiling emitting a pale yellow light. In the centre was a raised causeway, two pillars at one end, a dais, and marble throne at the other.

The air was clearer but still soupy with wisps of burning incense from censers along the cave wall. The wall itself was adorned with strange maps, pictograms, and ancient symbols.

Exotic furs and skins covered the ground. There were mannequins and bearskins and though it seemed impossible, shadowcats. A single cat could drag down a thirty-hand warhorse, crushing the bones of beast and rider in a single bite. Hunting them was suicidal. Only the Viscara would even try. Along the walls were shelves, five stacks high. There were jars and bottles containing all manner of creatures preserved in oil of *seetha*. There were old leather tomes crammed together and bookends made of bones. Chryselephantine pots stood in clusters, each filled with some type of seed, bonemeal or herb. To the left of the dais was a statue of a great head distorted in a horrific grimace, a heresy of the Golden Lady of Castagna. To the right was a sculpture of the mythical Acraphean Sext, the family of six that will come again.

There was only one thing Saffron recognised from Castagna: Carabrienne's old scrying sphere mounted on a thin column on the causeway. It had fascinated her as a child, with its strange, swirling smoke.

"Wait here," the captain said, and the two men disappeared down a passageway.

Athene gave Saffron's arm a slight squeeze.

"The City was burning, every last Serendip put to the sword, and yet she found her way over a hundred leagues here, with all of this." She swept her arm around the room. "How is that possible?"

"She has power, drawn from another world."

"But not back then. Someone must have helped her." Saffron stepped cautiously down the causeway towards the glowing crystal ball. As a girl she had peered at it through the window of Carabrienne's caravan, giggling with her friends, never daring to take a step inside. Even then, Carabrienne had an aura of strange and frightening power. She remembered the older children saying that her den was always rich with powerful incense. Was that to hide another stench? Drawn to the crystal again she put a hand up to the glass and touched its exterior.

"Don't touch anything!" said Athene, putting her hand on Saffron's shoulder. "You don't know what these instruments are capable of."

"Sorry," Saffron said and withdrew her hand, her palm tingling. "It's just that . . . it reminds me of home."

"Home?" Athene asked, and then whispered, "I hope you know what you're doing. In this place, death lies everywhere."

Saffron said nothing but continued to stare at the sphere. For the first time she noticed that the patterns of the smoke inside were not random but almost like a creature, prodding and probing, looking for a way out.

"Beautiful, isn't it?" a voice rasped, startling Saffron. An old woman in red velvet appeared from the passageway. She was followed by the two other Forgotten, a couple of steps behind. She stood about four feet tall, but was almost doubled over with the burden of years. Grey hair hung in ringlets to her waist. She looked so frail, as though a puff of air could blow her over. She leaned heavily on a gnarled staff, her bony hands twisted around it. "Beautiful, but terrible too." Her voice was not much more than a whisper and yet it filled the entire cave.

"How so?" Saffron managed to reply.

At first the crone didn't answer, but tapped her way along the causeway towards where Saffron was standing. It was difficult to believe she was *evil*. Saffron's inclination was to take the old lady's arm and assist her, but a deeper instinct held her back. Necromancers walked in the shadows of the dead, tortured spirits and wielded dark and terrible forces.

"That crystal contains the Mist of Oromis," she hissed, "also known as the Maddening Mist. It is one of the four sentient vapours, and one of the most powerful. Only the Wandering Mist has more scope for mischief. But a single breath of this brume and reason is stripped from the mind quicker than a night kite from her bodice."

"But if it's so dangerous, why do you keep it?" asked Saffron with horror.

If it had escaped in Castagna . . .

"Why? Because it pleases me to see it *squirm,*" Carabrienne replied between clenched teeth. As she hobbled past and climbed up onto the great stone chair, Saffron became conscious of a pungent odour—the sickly-sweet smell of decay.

The crone's eyes were a cloudy grey, like a fish left out in the sun, all cataracts. Her face was crinkled, her mouth rotten with blisters, and her head shrivelled in its large velvet ruff. But despite the sores, she was as Saffron remembered her from the dockside. Somehow she had expected a more dramatic change, a physical manifestation of a soul corrupted by spirits.

As the crone stared at her, Saffron glimpsed a movement, a thin black line underneath the skin, writhing, pushing upwards. A centipede crawled out of her eye socket and writhed across the bridge of her nose. As its last leg emerged, the eyeball, still held by a single stalk, sucked back into place. Her face twitched and an arachnid with violin markings on its back crawled from her hair and down onto her left cheek. Blowflies congregated at her lips, feeding on the sores. Saffron choked, fearing she was going to gag. The necromancer laughed, a toothless, black, mirthless laugh. The inside of her mouth was full of legs, wings, mandibles. Tiny white dots moved along the surface. Eggs. Suddenly the crone banged her staff on the ground and the swarm of insects disappeared, scuttling back into the hidden crevices of her body.

"Leave us," she hissed. Bowing, the Forgotten retreated from the vault, Athene giving a small wink of encouragement before finally turning and following the others.

"Now, child, what do you seek from me?"

Saffron was shaken. She had prepared herself for almost anything and was prepared to die for her cause, but parleying with a reeking corpse? She steeled herself, and though she could hardly trust her voice, she somehow managed to repeat the words long rehearsed in her head.

"The Serendips have passed from this world into another."

"Not all of them."

"No."

"You, for instance."

"Me," she said, and a cold dread washed over her. Necromancers were powerful, but how had she known Saffron was half Serendip? Could she know her from Castagna? No, impossible. To the old lady she would have been just one of hundreds of children who milled outside her den, never actually going in. There was something important here, something that eluded her. If only she could think clearly. But she was too frightened.

"Go on," the old woman said.

"There is one who went with them against his will, a boy."

"Of course. I expected as much. There is always a boy at the root of it."

"I have to be with him."

"So they *all* say . . ."

Despite herself, Saffron reddened and looked at the ground. Carabrienne was making fun of her and Saffron felt self-conscious under the scrutiny of those cold, cataract-ridden eyes. She wondered whether her story was so very different from those of the blushing maids at the dockside. The price would be different.

"He is gone, never to return," Saffron said, almost in a whisper.

"And so you come to me, though you know it is foolish and that, in my lair, a thousand spirits crave your soul."

"I heard tell that—"

"*You heard tell, you heard tell!*" the crone screeched in falsetto. Carabrienne shook her head slightly, then continued more evenly. "You heard tell that I had knowledge beyond this world, that I could somehow show you the way." Saffron nodded. "And in return you would give *me* something." The necromancer rubbed her chin. "Something like . . . your *soul*. Not straight away, of course. That would be pointlessss." Her sibilant intonation was that of a python. "But let's say I give you a score of years to enjoy your *boy*, and then you would be mine."

Twenty years, thought Saffron. *It would be enough.* She nodded again.

"But how could you know to trust me?" the crone continued. "I could take your spirit *now*. No need to wait." She suddenly added, once again in the falsetto, "*Yes! Yes! Take her now! Let's eat her! Eat her!*"

"But there is honour," said Saffron, trying to keep her voice from shaking, "even in Wiccans."

"*So sure of her course,*" the old woman continued to screech, her pallid eyes blackening. "*Yes, yes have her, we must. Eat her, we must!*"

"No!" the crone hissed back at herself. "Remember the pledge!"

"*No!*" she screeched in her second voice. "*No pledge. Have her now! And when he comes, eat him too!*"

He? Saffron thought.

Carabrienne began to shake violently until finally she rasped, "Enough!" and banged the staff on the ground. "I am your mistress!"

An ominous silence filled the cavern and slowly her eyes became pale again. Seemingly back in control, she turned to Saffron and smiled. It was the most ghastly grimace Saffron had ever seen.

"His own mother beat you away like a stray dog and yet you wish to give up your soul for this *boy*. Why? I can understand *love*, I've seen the havoc it wreaks more times than you can imagine. But there is something more here, *Saffron*. Something you are not telling me."

Saffron experienced a taste like copper coins. The crone knew who she was, knew what had happened to her.

"Oh yess," Carabrienne continued, as if hearing Saffron's thoughts, "I know all about you and your dead mother and your father, not that feeble cuckold Drakefield, but the *King* as he is now . . ."

Saffron's heart skipped a beat.

The crone leered at her again. " . . . And what a King. The Forgotten rally to his banner and half of Acraphea do his bidding. None are more powerful in the mortal world. He is a King indeed." She paused, and then said slowly, "I have been *waiting* for you."

"W-waiting?" For a moment Saffron did not understand. "Then you will help me?"

"*Yes! Yes! Help her! Then have her!*" A wisp of black escaped from Carabrienne's eyes. "No!" she hissed to herself and then, adding more evenly to Saffron, "No. Your *boy* has gone from this world. I cannot help you."

Saffron's head swam and she felt like she was going to faint. She had been so sure that the necromancer would show her the way. She had travelled a hundred leagues on the strength of that promise. The crone was lying. She *had* to be lying.

"Foolish child," Carabrienne said, standing up from the stone chair. "It was *I* who sent the rumour across the land to bring you here, I who began those seductive whispers in the night. *There is one who knows about moving between worlds and the passage of spirits . . .*"

Saffron felt her blood turn to ice. "I don't understand."

"They never do when they are blinded by love," the crone hissed disdainfully. "Your father is a powerful man. There are many in his debt."

Saffron saw it then, the escape from Castagna, a safe passage across a hundred leagues of barbarian land, the Forgotten who brought her here. The crone called her foolish, and she was right. How could she have been so short-sighted?

Carabrienne stared at Saffron as though she wanted to eat her, her eyes oscillating between a smoky black and the cataract grey.

Under her cloak, Saffron felt for her blade. She was not going back to her father, dead or alive. "Where is the King?" she asked, surreptitiously unsheathing her weapon.

"Close enough," said the crone and turned away from Saffron to stare at one of the large maps adorning the cave walls. Saffron took another step towards the dais. "Three days' ride," Carabrienne muttered. "The Forgotten will go."

Saffron pulled out the blade. It glinted before her. It was now or never. There was a flash of red as the crone spun around at astonishing speed and caught Saffron's wrist like a viper with a mouse.

"Let go!" Saffron said trying to pull away.

"Drop the blade." Carabrienne bent Saffron's wrist back so far that she could feel her joints separate. In excruciating pain, she dropped the knife. "Better," the crone hissed.

Saffron could smell her fetid odour, and something with legs fell from her nostril onto her leg. Saffron flicked it off, shivering in disgust. The creature scuttled into a corner.

"Be careful, my pretty," Carabrienne whispered, "I would not want you damaged in any way. And I have only so much patience."

The old woman was trembling. She banged her staff twice on the ground and before the echo died, the Forgotten appeared from the smoke-filled antechamber.

"The King is camped in the Crystalline Pass," she hissed. "You must go to him and tell him I have his raven."

"The horses need to rest," Athene replied. "They are too tired for such a journey."

"Then whip them to within an inch of their lives, kick them until their sides are raw and bleeding. The beasts will not fail, my boy has seen to that."

The Forgotten bowed and turned to leave.

"Carden," Carabrienne hissed, calling back the captain. He approached the steps. "I don't like the look in your shield maiden's eye."

"My lady?"

"When you return, you will give her to me."

His eyes widened, but he quickly recovered. "Y-yes, my lady." His steps echoed away down the antechamber.

"And now for you," Carabrienne said, hobbling down the causeway. She picked up a catlinite pestle from one of the shelves. Thrusting her hand deep into one of the urns, she pulled out some red seed.

"I am going to give you something to drink. Something that will dull your spirit."

Saffron noticed that the crone's voice was pitched a little higher than before. Dropping the seed into the pestle, she turned to a second urn and this time brought out what looked like a dried green herb. Was it bloodgrass?

"The boy will take you to his cave, about half a league from here. It will be easier for us both that way. I won't be able to . . . feel you."

Her hand pulled out a fistful of dried berries from a third urn. Over a table she crushed the contents into powder. The flies buzzed around Carabrienne's mouth as she worked.

"You'll sleep like the dead, but more than that, you will heal. Flesh will return to your bones, lustre to your eyes, and by the time your father graces our humble halls, you will wake."

She poured the powder onto a piece of wax parchment and then made a small sachet by folding the paper.

"Boy," she whispered, and instantaneously the shaven-haired boy appeared from the antechamber, a breathless apparition. "The Forgotten?"

"Gone, my lady."

"The horses?"

"Oil of Carrick mixed into the seed. They will stay the course."

"Good. Bring me tea."

"Tea, my lady?"

"For the girl."

"Oh . . ." For a moment he hesitated, as though he was going to speak further, but then he nodded and ducked back into the antechamber. The request had confused him. The necromancer fed on her guests, she did not entertain them.

Saffron felt a pang of sorrow. *Athene*. She decided that whatever else, she would not let Carabrienne have her.

"I wonder at your gifts," Saffron said. The crone didn't reply but cocked her head slightly, as if trying to smell the direction of the conversation. "So powerful that you can control spirits from another world," she continued. "Some would say as powerful as a god."

The crone laughed. It sounded like a groan of pain. "What crude palaver," she hissed. "Do you take me for a fool?"

"No, but . . ." Saffron paused. "You do know, don't you?"

"*Eat her!*" Carabrienne suddenly screeched in that other, strangled spirit voice. "*Raven hair, raven eyes, raven ways. She pries at us! She pries! Eat her now! Give her to us!*"

"No!" Carabrienne hissed back, her eyes black and smoky.

"*Then tell her! Tell her! Make her squirm. The knowing but not having will hurt her and we shall feel it. Tell her! Tell her! Tell her!*" The words echoed around the cave. The crone swayed, gripping the table, her pale knuckles whitening further. "If you find a god, you find a way," she rasped in a breathless whisper.

"Yes, but how do you find a god?" Saffron's pulse quickened.

"How indeed?" Carabrienne feigned self-control, but still clutched the table as though in danger of being swept away. "W-why would a god want to be found? A god parleying with mortals is like mortals conversing with the *kine*. Cattle provide sustenance, but make very strange playfellows."

"Then it is impossible," Saffron said quietly.

"It is . . ." Carabrienne began, but then shuddered violently. Her eyes burned and a dark mist began to rise from her mouth.

"*Not impossible!*" she screeched. "*One walks abroad even now, wandering the plains, hunted by Furies, and soon to be no more, no more . . . But you! You can't have him!*"

"Why?"

The spirit voice screeched with laughter. "*He is dying on the Plains. His pigs have deserted him and eat their swill from another's trough. His bloodline is all but finished. And when he is gone, the way of the Hafram Deagalis is closed to you! So squirm, half-breed daughter of the King! Squirm and we shall feed! We shall feed!*"

Carabrienne shook uncontrollably. "No, no!" she hissed. Her head snapped back, arms splayed out to her sides, and a screaming black shadow climbed out of her mouth.

"*Now we shall eat you!*" the spirit screeched with glee. Black wisps of air took shape before Saffron's eyes, long, bent legs, carapace and fangs. A reanimated arachnid.

Something smashed behind her. The boy had returned with the mug of tea, now in pieces on the ground. Eyes wide, he turned and ran, his wards rattling around his neck. Saffron instinctively knew they wouldn't save him, not this time. Almost fully formed, the creature continued to scream in anticipation of the feast.

For the first time since entering the cave, Saffron knew exactly what she had to do. She edged back along the causeway.

The creature reared its black head and a thousand eyes stared out at her. Behind the spirit hung the husk of Carabrienne, suspended upright like meat on a hook. From the old crone's mouth, a long, rotting umbilical stretched, connecting the host to the spirit. Carabrienne was still conscious, but hissing in pain as her undead entrails stretched across the floor.

From what she had read in the chronicles, Saffron knew the spirit and host were symbiotes; one could not exist without the other, and while one lived the other could not die, creating a never-ending paradox. It was both their greatest strength and their greatest weakness.

With a click of its mandibles, the arachnid scuttled towards her, and before Saffron could move, it was upon her, its barbed proboscis extended towards her neck.

She had one chance.

Saffron took a deep breath, then spun and kicked out at the column behind her. She felt her toes break, but that was of little consequence. The column shifted slightly on its plinth and the crystal of Oromis slipped. It tumbled onto the stone cave floor, shattering into a thousand pieces.

Immediately the Mist snaked out in all directions. Quicker than adders, the white vapour poured into Carabrienne's mouth, nose and eyes. The crone convulsed as the mist tore through her, infecting her with insanity. For a moment, the arachnid's proboscis twitched, an inch from Saffron's neck and then with a violent *crack!* it crunched in on itself. There was a low moan as the broken, black creature fed on its own limbs in its madness.

Then another cry. The boy. He had been too slow and the mist had caught him. Still holding her breath, Saffron concentrated on the antechamber. If she could she make it out of the cave and into the open air, it was possible she would have a chance. She began to run but her broken toes slowed her down. The blood pounded in her ears and spots appeared like splashes of ink in front of her eyes. She was only at the limestone arch. She had to breathe or she would pass out.

"Gahh!"

She gasped for air, and the Mist took her, coursing along her arteries and up into her brain. Reality blurred at the edges. The walls of the cave became soft, like a sea sponge, enveloping her.

There's no need to run, no need to resist.

No!

Saffron concentrated, focusing past the brain fever that gripped her. She wouldn't let the nefarious vapour rip away her sanity. She would see beyond the illusion, see what was really there. Wasn't that the gift of the Acrapheans, after all?

The walls were still solid underneath her hand, and she could feel her way out of the antechamber towards the mouth of the cave. She would make it, she would be fine.

Then she heard something. It sounded like, "N-n-n-nh!"

Or was that just the noise red makes?

Or the sound a hole makes?

Oh no, I have gone insane.

Bam! Bam! Bam! Two gigantic mutes jumped on her back. Staring behind her shoulder, she saw a man in red. His tunic was red, his sandals were red, his skin an impossible red. The reddle man. He stomped up and down like an infuriated child, his face sphinctery with rage.

"No! No! No! No!" His interminable negative rolled into endlessness.

Next to him stood a man in blue. His stockings were blue, his boots blue, his complexion an impossible blue, even the whites of his eyes were blue. His fists were clenched and blue spittle flew from his mouth.

"Yes! Yes! Yes! Yes!" he shouted.

Their cries filled her ears and she thought, *How can they even speak when they are mutes?*

And how can two giants fit on her back? Stomping on the exact same spot.

Oh. That's how. She had lost her mind.

"No! No! No! No!"

"Yes! Yes! Yes! Yes!"

As she watched, one of her eyeballs left its socket and glued itself onto the red man, the other to the blue. Still shouting, the mutes stepped apart, and her eyes extended on their stalks, stretching further and further from her face.

Please! Not that, anything but that. Not my eyes!

The stalks became thinner and thinner until . . . *Snap!* Her eyeballs snapped off and chased after the mutes, all legs and mandibles.

Oh dear . . . in the madness she had pulled out her eyes! Her own eyes!

"No! No! No! No!"

"Yes! Yes! Yes! Yes!"

The mutes were no longer there, but their voices rolled into infinity.

Perhaps her eyes would crawl back?

Frantically, she patted on the ground. There was nothing but the cold, hard, spongy, soft, cave floor and some words, lying to next to her.

"I am here," they said.

Where did the words come from? Could she trust them?

As if in reply to her thoughts, a hand took hold of hers. It was warm and comforting.

Mother? she said. *Is that you?*

What was she thinking?

Her mother, Lady Charlemagne Drakefield, was dead. Long dead. Hadn't Saffron herself watched her die at the hands of her father's men?

Do not trust her.

What was that? A second voice? This one was smooth and seductive.

"But the hand is so real," she protested. So real whereas everything else was so . . .

If it's real, how can the skin be that hot?

She realised then that the hand was burning her. She tried to pull it away.

And that's not skin you're touching.

No! Those were scales! To her horror, talons and claws closed around her. She was in the creature's grip. She could feel its eyes on her. It was something old, something long gone from this world, like necromancers and arachnid wisps.

"Do not listen to Oromis," the creature said.

And then suddenly she was moving and she could smell smoke and hear a boy blubbering. A rational thought struck her: the creature had taken her out of the antechamber, away from Oromis. Next, cold air hit her face and she heard crickets, clattering like weapons in the night. She was flying now, held tightly in the creature's talons until, set down gently, she felt the sand beneath her feet, and a hot breath on her face that growled, "You are free."

*

When Saffron awoke, she was a league or so outside the cave. She had sunk into the sand a few inches and the silica grains scratching her skin felt like a miracle.

Opening her eyes, the silence, sun, and sand was like a mirage itself. Relieved, she propped herself up on her elbows and the sting of her broken toes shot up her leg. It didn't matter. At least she could see. Her vision of self-inflicted blindness was just another illusion of the Maddening Mist. In contrast, the burn marks on her hand and around her stomach were real. She was covered in blisters, and her skin peeled off in swathes.

Saffron shuddered. It was a small price to pay. The vapour would have trapped her for eternity if something had not pulled her out. But what was it? Who was it? She did not have time to think now. She had to find the one Carabrienne spoke of, or die trying. She made her way, rubber-legged and shivering, back towards the Veridian Plain.

*

Two days passed and the sun beat down with unerring brutality, a yellow eye in the sky that watched her, and burned her. Gritty white flakes of salt coated her skin and infection festered in her wounds. She could go no further. She took four more steps and thudded face-down into the hot sand.

I could lie here and grow old, she thought.

She must have lost consciousness because when she opened her eyes it was dark and she was shivering. She could no longer feel her limbs. A desert rat sniffed at her stomach, working up to take a bite. Saffron could sense it, patiently waiting for the right moment.

No, not yet, it thought, *but soon*. She was still breathing. It would perhaps give her an hour more, maybe less. There was no point risking anything. The meal was not going anywhere. Still, it would need to get in a few bites before morning, before its unwelcome fellows descended to tear flesh and suck marrow. So it stayed within reach, waiting. Admiring the creature's resolve, Saffron wished the rat luck. But then, unexpectedly, it skittered away. Something had startled it.

She opened her left eye, and in the narrow slit of vision could make out a dirty sandal.

"Offa," she croaked and reached out her hand.

She was delusional, of course, it couldn't be him. But thinking of Offa cleared her mind and she realised who stood before her. "You," she croaked, but her blistered lips did not move and the word only existed in her head. That did not matter. He could hear her. "I need your help," she said.

He laughed, hollow as bones.

"*Hafram Deagalis,*" she said.

The laughter dried to dust.

She waited.

He said nothing.

If he didn't act soon, it would be too late. She was fading.

Then slowly, very slowly, he got down on all fours. She could see his cracked teeth and smell his fetid breath.

"There is a price," he hissed.

"Anything."

"It will turn your pretty brown eyes greener than viridian jade."

"Anything," she repeated.

He lent even closer and whispered in her ear. The proposition made Saffron shudder with revulsion. He would find her in the next world. Lie with her. She would bear his child and when that child came of age, the incubus would lie with her, and all her female progeny. Ferin Aquinas would give Saffron passage, and in return Saffron would give him a new bloodline from which his spirit would forever draw sustenance. She thought of this poor unborn child, a daughter of a god and a Gildas. Would Offa understand?

"Well," he said, "decide. You are fading fast."

She thought of Offa, alone in a world beyond this one, and in her failing breath murmured, "Yes."

Incanting he pulled out a clasp knife and thrust it deep into her neck. He would follow her to this new world and then one day claim his reward. Her last conscious memory was of his mirthless, hollow laugh.

What have I done?

Seventeen

DOWN, DOWN, DOWN. She was drowning. She couldn't breathe and all around her was a cold, wet darkness that seemed to stretch on forever. Had she fallen into the Blue-Black Sea? Which way was the surface? Remembering that bubbles always rose, she blew some precious air from her tightly pursed lips. Nothing happened. Panicking, she kicked out and prayed it was in the right direction. The darkness began to close in and her head pounded. Desperate, she kicked again, and still she had no idea which way she was moving.

Oh Offa, was it all for nothing?

But then suddenly the current took her, pushing her upwards in a rapid, lung-bursting, gut-wrenching ascent.

"Gahh!" she spluttered, breaking the surface.

A wave of vertigo washed over her as she realised that the strange black sea had disappeared and she was lying on a faded green carpet. She steadied herself, gulping for air.

A girl was beside her, eyes closed.

Charlemagne.

The thoughts and memories came flooding back then. Half of her mind was still Saffron, but that consciousness was receding and in a few more moments, Penny was herself again.

There was a moan and Charlemagne's eyes suddenly

snapped open. She, too, was hyperventilating, fighting for air.

"It's all right," Penny said, putting an arm around her, "we're back."

Charlemagne said nothing, but stared at Penny as though she was a stranger.

"Charlie, it's me."

Slowly her sister's eyes cleared. Penny held out her palm. The crystal had turned grey, its story told, the power spent.

"You were there too," Charlemagne said, gingerly standing up.

"Yes," Penny replied.

"I didn't see you, but I knew you were there."

"How?" Penny said.

"Because you pulled Saffron out . . . out of the Maddening Mist. How is that possible? If what we saw has already happened, then how could you pull her out?"

Penny paused, considering what she would say, what path she would take. "I don't know what you're talking about," she replied, keeping her voice absolutely flat.

"But it was you!"

Penny shook her head.

Charlemagne looked as though she was going to argue the point, but then changed her mind and said, "That was our mother, wasn't it?"

"Yes."

"Which means before, in the wake, I lived the life of our . . . grandmother. That's what the Manciple showed me."

"Weird."

"Weird? My head feels like it's going to explode," Charlemagne said.

"At least now you know where your name came from."

"I wonder why mother changed her name to Athene?"

"Perhaps she didn't want to be found."

"By who? That awful man?"

Penny shook her head. "I don't think it was that. She made

a deal with . . . a god. I don't see how anyone could break that. That's why Ogg called Cairo a—" She could hardly bring herself to say the word. " . . . A bastard. A god, not Dad, was Cairo's father."

"I guess it explains the legs."

"Did you think there was something familiar about him?"

Charlemagne shrugged. "I couldn't see him very well. I mean . . . *Saffron* couldn't really see. I could feel his presence, but that's all. He seemed a bit of a mess . . . for a god. Why do you ask?"

"A bit of a mess," Penny repeated, and knew exactly who that god was, as unlikely as it seemed. Eryn, the rootless creature of the woods. He had murdered Cairo, or something worse, but there was nothing she could do about that now. Cairo was gone from this life. Penny felt it. She knew it. Now all that mattered was Charlemagne. She would not let another god consume her. But what should she do?

Staring at the crystal, she said, "We just lived through our mother's last day in that other world."

"As I said, my head feels like it's going to explode."

"She gave up everything to follow him . . . to follow Offa, our father."

"I never knew she loved him so much," Charlemagne said.

"It was more than love."

"What do you mean?"

"I'm not sure. She loved him more than anything, but . . . it just felt like there was something else as well, driving her on."

"What?"

Penny tried to reach back into her mind, back to how it felt, being their mother. There was something there but it eluded her. "I don't know," she said.

"Why didn't they just tell us?"

"Would you have believed them if they did?"

"Well *I'm* glad we've come here," Charlemagne said.

Of course you are, Penny thought, *you are in the grip of the Lady*.

Downstairs they heard Siam barking.

"Ogg's back," said Charlemagne with a beatific smile. Suddenly she looked so relaxed, so relieved, as though all her confusion and agitation had been washed away by that one thought.

"We need to go," replied Penny carefully.

"Go? Why?" Charlemagne demanded, an edge to her voice.

Yes, the shadow was back, that slightly deranged look around her sister's eyes. The Lady's hold on Charlemagne was deep and seemingly growing by the hour.

They heard voices outside. There was more than one person. Penny rushed to the window that looked out onto the drive, but the people, whoever they were, had already disappeared into the house. An overwhelming sense of foreboding came to her.

Charlemagne regarded Penny with suspicion, looking like anything but her sister. As though, as Cairo had suggested flippantly, she *had* been replaced by a body snatcher. Cairo. Penny refused to lose both of her sisters, and in that moment she made a decision

"Charlie, listen to me, we're in danger, I can feel it. We can't let ourselves be found here."

"I agree," said a voice from behind them.

They spun around. A huge figure, well over six foot, stood in the doorway, his eyes like boreholes in snow. He was wearing a tattered cloak, and a white flaky powder covered his skin.

"You!" said Penny. "I saw you earlier, in the trees."

"I was hunting your sister," he said, miming a chopping motion with his arm. Penny noticed that it was cut off a few inches below the elbow, and on the stump was a crude, metal thimble.

"Where is she?" said Charlemagne.

"Gone."

"You killed her!" Penny cried.

"No."

No, he hadn't, but she was still dead.

Charlemagne began to speak, but he put out his massive left hand. "No time for words," he said. "I came here to . . . to help you."

"Help?" asked Penny.

"They are coming for you."

"Who?"

"The one who ordered Hamquist . . ." His voice trailed off and he put a hand to his eyes.

"Yes?" Penny said.

"Brrr!" he said and shook himself. "The one who gave the order to kill your sister."

"Kill?" cried Charlemagne. "He said *kill!*"

"But he said he didn't do it," Penny said, turning back to the giant. "You said you came to help us. How?"

"By escaping," he replied simply.

"Escape where?" Penny asked.

"You already know," he replied, looking at her with those endless eyes.

And deep down, she did. But how could they possibly travel across worlds? He didn't look like a god, someone who could perform the *Hafram Deagalis.*

"Wh-what's he talking about?" stuttered Charlemagne.

"He wants us to leave with him."

"Leave? With him? Is he insane? Where could *he* take us?"

"To the other world."

"But he tried to kill Cairo!"

"Are you a god?" asked Penny.

The man bowed his head slightly. "Demigod," he muttered.

"Is that enough. I mean, will it work?"

He glowered and replied, "Decide now. Her emissary is almost here. If he commands me, I will not be able to resist.

We have been in thrall to him, and to her. I am Kalasian and bound to their law."

"What are they planning to do with us?" Penny said.

"I can't know for sure."

"Guess."

"I do not *guess*."

"But I need to know," Penny said.

He sighed. The room seemed to shake with his breath. "You will be killed. You are the black one. Your sister Cairo was the red one. Maybe it will be made to look like an accident. Maybe not. Bereft of family, your Serendip sister, all alone in this world, will be bound more tightly than ever to her god, seeking solace, welcoming the inevitable bondage in her sorrow. She will become a gilded fly in amber, and the Lady, more powerful than she has been in years, will perhaps become powerful enough to begin a cult here in this world. Or powerful enough to return." He wrinkled his nose awkwardly. "Or at least that's my guess."

Charlemagne leaned towards Penny, shaking. "He's mad," she whispered. "On three we'll scream and run for the door. One, two—"

"I *can* hear you," the man said. "I came here to . . . try to atone. I won't force you to come, but don't throw your lives away. Out there"—he gestured to the hallway—"lies only death for you, one way or another."

His words were fantastic and she had no reason to trust him, but his voice was so disarming, so sincere, that Penny knew he told the truth. She could hear the other voices coming from downstairs, unfamiliar and harsh. A lump formed in her throat.

"Decide quickly. I will prepare the way," the man said.

With a glance at Charlemagne, he turned the key in the door, locking them in. Then, picking up the vanity, he rammed it underneath the door handle. Next, he toppled the bed onto the vanity in a makeshift barricade before finally dropping to his knees near the centre of the room.

"What's he doing?" Charlemagne rasped.

The man waved his arm in a sort of circle while his tattered cloak flapped around him.

"I told you!" Charlemagne went on. "He's *crazy*. We have to get out of here while he's distracted!"

"I think we should trust him," Penny said quietly.

"Trust him? He was *hunting* our sister! Come on!"

The man now had his ear pressed to the floor while his good hand caressed the faded carpet. "Please," he implored, "do this one thing and I swear I'll set you free, free to wander for eternity, free to . . ." He pulled a face. "Haze, drizzle and fog." He looked up at the girls with an apologetic expression. "It's a fickle thing," he said by way of explanation. He turned back to the carpet. "No, no, the rude one is . . . gone." His voice cracked on the word *gone*. "It's only me now, and . . . some passengers. Come, I promise, this will be the last voyage . . . home."

"Penny!" growled Charlemagne through her teeth.

"Look," Penny replied.

A vague wisp of steam began to rise from the floor.

Behind them, the door handle turned, and then was jiggled rapidly up and down.

"Come on! Come on!" said the man to the steam.

"They're in here!" shouted a voice from outside.

"Careful!" said another. "The Kalasian is dangerous, even on his own."

"Let me through!" said a third. "He is mine!"

This last voice Penny recognised. The Manciple, cold and cruel as death.

In the centre of the room, the Kalasian gesticulated wildly in an elaborate semaphore, and the fine vapour thickened into a fog and began to curl around his legs.

"Wait! Not yet!" he cried to the whiteness.

"Girls, girls! This is your grandmother. Open the door," Ogg shouted from outside.

"Ogg!" called Charlemagne, beaming and running to the barricade.

"It's a trap," said Penny.

Charlemagne nodded frantically, misunderstanding. "We're trapped!" she yelled.

"Last chance," the Kalasian said. "Are you coming?" He held out his left hand.

Charlemagne began to tug at the bed, trying to get it away from the door.

"Girls, listen to me. That man is dangerous! He's wanted by the police. They're out here with me! Don't go near him. Don't move. We'll get you out!"

"You see?" Charlemagne said turning to Penny, a sort of twisted triumph burning in her eyes. "We're coming!" she yelled. "Penny, help me get the bed!" Not waiting, she rammed it with her shoulder, and this time it came down with a crash. She then pushed the vanity away from the door, infused with a frantic energy.

Penny took the man's hand, but immediately strained away from him, as though he was holding it by force. He regarded her curiously, but said nothing.

"Help!" Penny yelled.

Charlemagne turned back from the vanity. "No!"

"Charlemagne? Are you all right?" called Ogg.

"He has Penny! Help us!"

Outside, the third voice said, "Stand aside, I'll break it down."

Charlemagne stepped back.

"Our mother?" Penny whispered to the man, while looking like she was straining every fibre to escape his grip.

"She lives," he replied, "there."

Her hand tightened around his.

What she was about to do would colour her relationship with her sister forever. It was even possible that Charlemagne would hate Penny for the rest of her days. It would be difficult, to be despised by the one person she loved and respected more than any other in the world, but she also knew that she had no choice. She had to save her.

"Charlie!" she screamed. "Help me! Help me! He's dragging me in!"

Charlemagne rushed at the man as heedlessly as she had rushed at the bed. She attempted to push away his bulk while trying to get a grip on her sister, placing herself in between them.

Oh Charlie, Penny thought, *you were always the brave one.*

Charlemagne grabbed Penny's free hand. Penny gripped it tight.

"Thank you," she whispered and nodded to the man.

The mist whipped around them both. Charlemagne's eyes widened with horror.

In the same instant the door exploded off its hinges, and in the doorway stood the man from the wedding, the Manciple. He looked a foot taller than Penny remembered, and was distorted somehow. Standing next to him, shimmering in a golden light, was Ogg.

Charlemagne screamed as if in terrible pain.

But it was too late.

They were gone.

Epilogue

I N A SMALL community, at the end of an isolated cul-de-sac, was a street called Canary Row. A misleading name, because there were no canaries, whereas all the other streets represented local birds. There was Merganser Way, Grebe Close, Shearwater Lane, Killdeer Place and Anhinga Corner. But Canary Row stood by itself on a back road off Killdeer, an interloper, forever looking in. The houses had the same stucco exterior, the same two-car garage and the same rather modest patch of lawn in front, but even their uniformity could not hide the fact that the street was a last-minute afterthought, hastily named and tarred, like a curving question mark at the end of an otherwise neat development.

It was late September and Mrs Connelly sat on her porch, sipping her morning coffee and reflecting that Canary Row had gone to Hell. She chastised herself for using that word, even if it was only in her head, but it was true.

She blamed the Agonistes' at number five. It was all their fault.

First, the mother had gone missing in the spring. They had never found the body but everyone knew it was suicide. Apart from anything else, it was inconsiderate, the type of misfortune that hurt property values. Not that Mrs Connelly had been at all surprised when it happened. It was the way that woman had of mooning about at night when she thought nobody was watching, and that look in her eyes, as though waiting for the other shoe to drop.

She had invited the mother around for a cup of coffee when they first moved in, just to try and make her feel welcome, and find out what sort of people they were. Mrs Connelly knew they were English, although the mother was supposed to be American, but beyond that, nothing. They exchanged some pleasantries, but when she asked about where they were from, the pale-faced woman clammed right up.

After that, Mrs Agonistes had been polite enough, in a manner of speaking, but she was so withdrawn it was almost offensive. Mrs Connelly always said, "How do you do, Mrs Agonistes?" and she would receive the reply, "Fine thank you, and yourself?" and that was it; no gossip, no conversation, nothing to get your teeth into. The father, of course, talked to no one. He was even more tight-lipped than his wife. Mrs Connelly didn't even know what he did for a living. It was all very irregular.

And then, one day, the rest of the family simply up and left, just like that. A taxi came for the girls one evening at the beginning of the summer and the father left early the next morning. The girls had apparently gone to their grandparents in England. She had discovered this from a boy who was idling around their yard, looking stricken. He was searching for the red-haired one, that Cairo. He was at least five years older than her.

The whole street, hell, the whole town missed her pretty face, but Mrs Connelly wasn't taken in. She knew trouble when she saw it, and that girl was trouble. If Mrs Connelly had a penny for every time a boy called on that house while they were living there, well, let's just say her mortgage would be a lot smaller than it was. She could spot the boyfriends a mile off, milling along the street, trying to look casual but nervous as a ferret inside. Yes indeed, trouble with a capital T.

And then there was the youngest with that queer way she had of looking at you. Or looking *through* you, more like it, as though she was always prying, always judging. Who did she think she was? Mrs Connelly couldn't stand her.

Only the eldest, Charlemagne, wasn't completely objectionable. But even she had a ridiculous name. Charlemagne, Cairo, Pendragon, and Athene, the mother. They were like a travelling circus.

When summer ended and the new school semester was about to begin, the general consensus at her bridge club was that the family would return. Not the mother, of course, but the girls and their father. Mrs Davies who worked in the school administration office swore to it.

"The younger two haven't been taken out of school. By law their father would have to notify us."

Mrs Connelly had been the lone dissenting voice. "I tell you, they are not coming back and good riddance."

"Don't say that. The children are nice girls, really," Mrs Davies had replied, always trying to come across as some sort of goody-goody.

"Nice or not, we've seen the last of them."

Then, sipping a highball, she told them all about it.

For a start, the garden had gone to seed. Didn't she have to stare at the sprawling mess every day? They had a man who trimmed the hedge, mowed the lawn and cleared out the worst of the weeds, but by the middle of July, he had stopped coming. The account was no doubt overdue. She had thought about going over with secateurs herself, just to trim away the worst of the laurel, but she didn't in the end. Well, as a rule, she didn't like to interfere in other people's business. Instead she sat on the porch, watched the hedge spill untidily onto the street and waited.

Soon after that, some people came from the bank, turning up every week or so to knock on number five's door. Seeing her on the porch, they strolled over and began to ask questions.

How long had they been gone?

All summer.

Had she seen the father?

No, not since July.

Did she know any of their friends, or better yet, relatives?

As far as she knew, they didn't have any. At least she'd never seen any.

Was she expecting them back?

Why ask her? She was only their neighbour. She didn't monitor their every move. On the contrary, she liked to keep to herself.

"Well, here's our number," they said. "Please let us know if anyone comes by. You've been very helpful."

They didn't actually say they were from the bank, just that they were trying to get in touch. But of course they were, two young lads wearing suits, already a bit puffy around the middle, definitely from the local branch. She had received a titter from the ladies at this witty observation, all except Mrs Turner, whose husband was a teller in town. *Well*, Mrs Connelly thought, *he could do with losing a few pounds too.*

And then the sign went up. It was a disgrace. They had never had a foreclosure before. What was next? Repo men, picking up that nice new suite they had in the living room?

Secretly she thought that if they did, she would have a quick word before they took it away. From her porch, Mrs Connelly could see into number five's front window when she craned her neck and the light was right. She had admired the suite many times. She had just the space for it if the price was reasonable.

In August, a contracting firm cleared out the garden and put a lick of paint on the front of the house. It looked tidier, but Mrs Connelly had to call the number on the side of the contractor's van to complain. The men had left half a dozen cigarette butts just lying in the street. The woman on the phone said she'd have a word, but Mrs Connelly knew she wouldn't because she could hear a nail file going back and forth as they spoke, as if she didn't give a sweet damn.

The book club ladies began to come around to her view. Only that Mrs Davies, with her "inside information" maintained her conviction that the Agonistes children would return. But it was Mrs Connelly who had been proven right. School began and there was still no sign of the family. And now it was almost October.

Mrs Connelly put down her cup, her coffee finished. She was tempted to have a Danish, too, but that was a slippery slope. She'd eaten one already, and she liked to keep her figure. Standing up, she stretched her legs and was about to go indoors when she noticed a person walking down the street. It was someone she didn't recognise. She sat down again and picked up her mug as though there was still something left in it. No harm in watching what they were up to. After all, somebody had to keep an eye on the neighbourhood.

As she came towards the house, Mrs Connelly saw it was a child. Now that wasn't right at all. It was Tuesday. The girl should be at school. Perhaps she should report it. "I'm afraid you have a truancy problem, Mrs Davies." Yes, that would take her down a peg or two.

The girl stopped outside the Agonistes' house. She stared at it for a little while, looked quickly over her shoulder, and then opened the gate.

Mrs Connelly wondered if she should say something. No, perhaps it was better to wait. She was creepy, this girl, like one of those "Gothic" types. She had spiky black hair, skin-tight black jeans and a face as pale as alabaster. She could almost smell the petunia oil from the porch. If the girl actually tried to get into the house, Mrs Connelly would call the police. She lifted the cordless phone from its cradle.

The girl suddenly turned away from the door and stared right at her. Startled, Mrs Connelly dropped the phone. It clattered to the wooden decking and the battery fell out.

Smiling, the girl walked back up the driveway, through the gate and towards her house. Mrs Connelly scrabbled around for the battery. Her hands shook as she pressed it into the phone. Twice more it slipped out, but there! It was in, just as the girl was in front of her. Her finger hovered over the number nine.

"C-can I help you?" said Mrs Connolly, trying to regain her composure.

"Maybe."

The girl was the spit of the youngest daughter. Not her, but very like. She had that same unnerving stare. This one wore glasses, but the raven eyes shone through regardless.

"Do you know the people who lived here?" she asked, affecting a casual air.

"No, dear, not as such."

"I see you keep an eye on them."

Mrs Connelly said nothing.

"They haven't been here for a while, have they?"

"I-I'm not sure I should be telling you. Are they friends of yours?"

The girl considered for a moment. "Relatives," she said.

"Oh," Mrs Connelly replied.

That figured. This girl had that same unusual accent and she was weird enough to be one of them, all spiky hair and black bangles.

"They've gone all summer then?" the girl continued.

"Yes," said Mrs Connelly, liking the girl's manner even less.

"And the father?"

"Yes."

The girl was unnerving her now. She had a disturbing way of wrinkling her nose when she asked a question. And why didn't she know the answers herself? If she *were* family, that is.

"Has anybody else come by here?" she said.

Do you mean like the three men from the bank? Or the nine love-struck weirdo boys who came on two consecutive nights on the thirteenth and fourteenth of September? Or do you mean weird

Gothic girls, like yourself, in which case, my dear, you are the only one so far. Aloud she said, "I really can't recall. I'm too busy to—"

"Two men, for example," the girl cut in. "You'd remember them. They are very tall, and one has only one arm and the other carries a sword."

The girl was clearly out of her mind. Wait until the bridge club heard about this one.

"No. Nobody like that."

The girl said nothing more but continued to stare at her. She showed no sign of going. Mrs Connelly began to feel very uncomfortable.

"Do you want to leave a message with me, just in case the family comes back?" Mrs Connelly said, needing to fill the silence.

The girl did not reply.

"If you left a name, I could—"

"My name is not important."

Mrs Connolly really didn't like the look in the child's eyes. She hadn't blinked the whole time, but seemed to look right into her, as though seeing her very thoughts. It was the queerest feeling. Again, her finger hovered over the phone. *If she doesn't go in a minute . . .*

"Thank you. You've been helpful," the girl said suddenly, and turned away to walk down the street.

Mrs Connelly watched her all the way. Just in case. The girl didn't look back.

There was a bang and Mrs Connelly jumped in her seat, again dropping the phone. It was just the wind, slamming the door on its jamb. *Damn arthritis*, she thought. Her grip was going. Her gaze returned to the street, but the girl was gone.

How was that possible?

Even if she had sprinted the length of the road, she couldn't have made it around the corner yet. Mrs Connelly suddenly felt quite queer. She didn't like these kinds of shocks. Standing up, she walked down the steps of her veranda and into the road. No, the girl had disappeared into thin air. Either that or Mrs Connelly had somehow passed out for a moment without realising it. She decided that she would keep that part of the story to herself. She didn't want anyone to think she was going *off.*

As she walked up the steps, she couldn't help but notice number eight was letting their herb garden go. The borage was all over the place. She must remember to drop a polite hint.

*

A world away, three witches sniffed the air.

"They are here!"

"All of them?"

"All!"

"Why can I not feel them?"

"The dragon mark eludes you."

Their thick, brightly coloured cloaks billowed in the wind and their faces shone with an awful vitality. The Erinyes were ever the fairest in looks, sound and shape. Joining hands, they formed a triangle within a circle, the sign of the three.

"We must bite them!"

"Smite them!"

"Turn them to wights!"

Hanging above them in a wooden cage, a willowy, emaciated woman swung back and forth. She was whiter than death and her skin was full of weeping holes.

"Shall we . . . poke her?" said the first with a crafty wink.

"Yes! Poke her," said the second, smiling.

"No," said the third, looking into her crystal. "It is too soon, we will wear her *too* thin." Her eyes flicked back to her sisters. "Let them settle, and *then* we'll poke her again."

"Yes! Draw them to us!"

"Drive them mad!"

"And then they will be ours!"

Their laughter ran deep into the cold, starless night.

Acknowledgements

Thank you, Christine, for all your support and patience.

Thank you to the first readers who inspired me to keep writing: James Roger, Jos Hearn, Lauren Houghton and Andrew Nevins.

Thank you to Jamie Hamilton for all of your helpful insights, encouragement and suggestions.

Thank you to the team at Tenebris Books, particularly Zoë Harris and Sammy Smith, without whom this novel would not be possible.

About the Author

Jude developed a love of fantasy from a relatively early age after realising an innate talent for making stuff up could result in something other than detention. A somnambulist, insomniac, lover of letters, Jude writes late into the night, most nights, tumbling down the rabbit hole to dream of other lives. Jude currently lives in Pennsylvania with an over-enthusiastic family and absurdly entitled dog.

Also from Tenebris Books

Willow, Weep No More

Fairy tales once held an important place in the lives of people of every age and social rank. Handed down from generation to generation like precious heirlooms, these stories told of the struggles between good and evil, rich and poor, and often culminated in an allusion to how we reap what we sow. They served both as social commentary and morality lessons, seasoned with magic spells, mythical creatures, and enchanted objects. However, their enduring appeal is perhaps not only in the fantastical journeys on which they take us, but in the fact that they allow even the lowliest of us to believe there is reason to hope and dream.

Willow, Weep No More is a collection of traditionally inspired tales that capture the magic and charm of the fairytale realm, whilst seeking to explore the depths of human wisdom, beauty and strength.

Available in hardback and e-book formats.

Published November 2013

Dollywagglers by Frances Kay

After the plague, most of us are dead, and some of the survivors aren't behaving very well. But we can still have a laugh, can't we? Letting go is for softies. I'm alone – delightfully and comfortably alone. I don't do crying . . .

That's the wonky philosophy of Billie, a dollywaggler on a far from sentimental journey. The Eppie – a worldwide flu pandemic – has left London with nothing but a few beastly survivors with appallingly unwholesome habits. Watch out for Rodney; he is particularly nasty. Oh, and don't try to escape the madness by fleeing to the country – things may be even worse out there. Besides, a greater intelligence is planning to identify and control the living remnants nationwide, as order begins to be restored. It's time to find out who the real dollywagglers are.

Available in paperback and e-book formats.

Published April 2014

www.tenebrisbooks.com

CPSIA information can be obtained at www.ICGtesting.com
Printed in the USA
LVOW11s1537270916

506409LV00003B/660/P